a good girl's guide to murder

Also by Holly Jackson

A Good Girl's Guide to Murder series

A Good Girl's Guide to Murder

Good Girl, Bad Blood

As Good as Dead

Kill Joy (a Good Girl's Guide to Murder novella)

Five Survive

The Reappearance of Rachel Price

Not Quite Dead Yet

a good girl's guide to murder

HOLLY JACKSON

delacorte press

To Mum and Dad,

this first one is for you.

Delacorte Press
An imprint of Random House Children's Books
A division of Penguin Random House LLC
1745 Broadway, New York, NY 10019
penguinrandomhouse.com
GetUnderlined.com

Library of Congress Cataloging-in-Publication Data is available upon request.
ISBN 978-1-9848-9636-0 (trade) — ISBN 978-1-9848-9637-7 (lib. bdg.) —
ISBN 978-1-9848-9639-1 (pbk.) — ISBN 979-8-217-11677-5 (deluxe edition)

Originally published in paperback and in slightly different form by Electric Monkey, an imprint of Egmont UK Limited, London, in 2019. Subsequently published in hardcover in the United States by Delacorte Press, an imprint of Random House Children's Books, a division of Penguin Random House LLC, New York, in 2020.

Artwork for Holly Jackson Files: paper clip by Sergii Moscaliuk/stock.adobe.com; transparent tape by Simon/stock.adobe.com; wooden background by LIGHTFIELD STUDIOS/stock.adobe.com; binder clip by gearstd/stock.adobe.com; old open file, folded lined paper, and old closed file folder by macondos/stock.adobe.com; paper texture by Артём Ковязин/stock.adobe.com; Polaroid photo frame by genioatrapado/stock.adobe.com; ripped paper by Lumos sp/stock.adobe.com; spool of red yarn by Olga Zarytska/stock.adobe.com; spiral notebook by vovan/stock.adobe.com; coffee cup circle by AminaDesign/stock.adobe.com; grunge metal texture by anammarques/stock.adobe.com; empty file folder by Willee Cole/stock.adobe.com; vintage paper by MMphotos/stock.adobe.com; drawn circle by svetolk/stock.adobe.com; and paper by Sociologas/stock.adobe.com

Manufactured in Italy
10 9 8 7 6 5 4 3 2 1
2025 Deluxe Edition

The authorized representative in the EU for product safety and compliance is Penguin Random House Ireland, Morrison Chambers, 32 Nassau Street, Dublin D02 YH68, Ireland, https://eu-contact.penguin.ie.

Dear Reader,

Here we are. It's been five years since *A Good Girl's Guide to Murder* first hit shelves. In February 2020, I pinned all my hopes and dreams on this little book, praying that it wouldn't just disappear without leaving any mark. I spent sleepless nights crossing my fingers that at least a few people would buy it. Well, more than a few people did.

It feels surreal to be writing a letter like this, for a deluxe edition of my first book, which is now—unbelievably—a worldwide bestseller. This book changed my life, and so did you. It didn't happen overnight. It was a slow build, with readers taking a chance on me, recommending *A Good Girl's Guide to Murder* to their friends and family or to strangers on social media. And I'm so incredibly grateful that you did—that I got to complete Pip's story with a full trilogy and that I got to bring Pip and Ravi to life in a TV show adaptation.

These are all incredible milestones I never dreamed I'd reach. But I did reach them, because you took that chance on me. I will never forget it.

Thank you,

Holly Jackson xox

part one

SENIOR CAPSTONE PROJECT PROPOSAL 2019/2020

Student number: 4169
Student's full name: Pippa Fitz-Amobi

PART A: TO BE COMPLETED BY STUDENT

The courses of study or area(s) of interest to which the topic relates:

English, Journalism, Investigative Journalism, Criminal Law

Working title of Senior Capstone Project:

"Research into the 2014 Missing Persons Investigation of Andie Bell in Fairview, CT"

Present the topic to be researched in the form of a statement/question/hypothesis.

A report on how print, televised, and social media have become key players in police investigations, using Andie Bell as a case study, and the implications of how the press presented Sal Singh and his alleged guilt.

My initial resources will be:

Interview with missing persons expert, interview with a local journalist who reported on the case, newspaper articles, interviews with members of the community. Textbooks and articles on police procedure, psychology, and the role of media.

SUPERVISOR'S COMMENTS:

Pippa, this is an incredibly sensitive topic, as it concerns a terrible crime that happened in our own town. Your project has been accepted only on the condition that <u>no ethical lines are crossed</u>. Please find a more focused angle for your report as you work through your research, and there is to be NO CONTACT made with either of the families involved in this case. This will be considered an ethical violation, and your project will be disqualified.

STUDENT DECLARATION:

I certify that I have read and understood the regulations as set out in the notice to students.

Signature:

PIPPA FITZ-AMOBI

Date: 7/18/19

one

Pip knew where they lived.

Everyone in Fairview knew where they lived.

Their home was like the town's own haunted house; people's footsteps quickened as they walked by, and their words strangled and died in their throats. Shrieking children would gather on their walk home from school, daring one another to run up and touch the front gate.

But it wasn't haunted by ghosts, just three sad people trying to live their lives as before. A house not haunted by flickering lights or spectral falling chairs, but by dark spray-painted letters of "Scum Family" and stone-shattered windows.

Pip had always wondered why they didn't move. Not that they had to; they hadn't done anything wrong. But she didn't know how they lived like that. How the Singhs found the strength to stay here. Here, in Fairview, under the weight of so many widened eyes, of the comments whispered just loud enough to be heard, of neighborly small talk never stretching into real talk anymore.

It was a particular cruelty that their house was so close to Fairview High School, where both Andie Bell and Sal Singh had gone, where Pip would return for her senior year in a few weeks when the late-summer sun dipped into September.

Pip stopped and rested her hand on the front gate, instantly braver than half the town's kids. Her eyes traced the path to the front door. It was possible that this was a very bad idea; she had considered that.

Pausing for just a second, Pip held her breath, then pushed the creaking gate and crossed the yard. She stopped at the door and knocked three times. Her reflection stared back at her: the long dark hair sun-bleached a lighter brown at the tips, the pale white skin despite a week just spent in the Caribbean, the sharp muddy-green eyes braced for impact.

The door opened with the clatter of a falling chain and clicking locks.

"H-hello?" he said, holding the door half open, with his hand folded over the side. Pip blinked to break her stare, but she couldn't help it. He looked so much like Sal: the Sal she knew from all those television reports and newspaper pictures. The Sal now fading from her memory. Ravi had his brother's messy black side-swept hair, thick arched eyebrows, and oaken-hued skin.

"Hello?" he said again.

"Um . . ." Pip faltered. He'd grown even taller since she last saw him. She'd never been this close before, but now that she was, she saw he had a dimple in his chin, just like hers. "Um, sorry, hi." She did an awkward half wave that she immediately regretted.

"Hi?"

"Hi, Ravi," she said. "I . . . You don't know me. . . . I'm Pippa Fitz-Amobi. I was a few years below you at school before you left."

"OK . . ."

"I was just wondering if I could borrow a second of your time? Well, not *only* a second, we're already way past that. . . . Maybe like a few sequential seconds, if you can spare them?"

Oh god, this was what happened when she was nervous: words spewed out, unchecked and overexplained, until someone stopped her.

Ravi looked confused.

"Sorry," Pip said, recovering. "I mean, I'm doing my senior capstone project at school and—"

"What's a capstone project?"

"It's kind of like a senior thesis you work on independently, alongside normal classes. You can pick any topic you want, and I was wondering if you'd be willing to be interviewed for mine."

"What's it about?" His dark eyebrows hugged closer to his eyes.

"Um . . . it's about what happened five years ago."

Ravi exhaled loudly, his lip curling with what looked like anger.

"Why?" he said.

"Because I don't think your brother did it—and I'm going to try to prove it."

PIPPA FITZ-AMOBI
7/30/19
CAPSTONE PROJECT LOG—ENTRY 1

Our capstone project logs are supposed to be for recording any obstacles we face in our research; our progress; and the aims of our final reports. Mine will have to be a little different: I'm going to record all my research here, both relevant and irrelevant, because I don't really know what my final report will be yet or what will end up being important. I will just have to wait and see where I'm at after all my investigating and what essay I can bring together.

I'm hoping it will *not* be the topic I proposed to Mrs. Morgan. I'm hoping it will be the truth. What really happened to Andie Bell on April 18, 2014? And if—as my instincts tell me—Salil "Sal" Singh is not guilty, then who killed her?

I don't think I'll actually solve the case and figure out who murdered Andie. I'm not deluded. But I'm hoping my findings might lead to reasonable doubt about Sal's guilt, and suggest that the police were mistaken in closing the case without digging further.

The first stage in this project is to research what happened to Andrea Bell—known to everyone as Andie—and the circumstances surrounding her disappearance.

From the first national online news outlet to report on the event:

> *Andrea Bell, seventeen, was reported missing from her home in Fairview, Connecticut, last Friday.*
>
> *She left home in her car—a white Honda Civic—with her cell phone, but did not take any clothes with her. Police say her disappearance is "completely out of character."*

Police began searching the woodland near the family home this past weekend.

Andrea, known as Andie, is described as white, five feet six inches tall, with long blond hair and blue eyes. It is thought that she was wearing dark jeans and a blue cropped sweater on the night she went missing.[1]

Other sources had more details as to when Andie was last seen alive, and the time frame in which she is believed to have been abducted.

Andie Bell was "last seen alive by her younger sister, Becca, around 10:30 p.m. on April 18, 2014."[2]

This was corroborated by the police in a press conference on Tuesday, April 22: "Footage taken from a security camera outside the bank on Fairview's Main Street confirms that Andie's car was seen driving away from her home at about 10:40 p.m."[3]

According to her parents, Jason and Dawn Bell, Andie was "supposed to pick (them) up from a dinner party at 12:45 a.m." When Andie didn't show up or answer any of their phone calls, they started reaching out to her friends to see if anyone knew of her whereabouts. Jason Bell "called the police to report his daughter missing at 3:00 a.m. Saturday morning."[4]

So whatever happened to Andie Bell that night happened between 10:40 p.m. and 12:45 a.m.

Here seems like a good place to type up the transcript from my interview with Angela Johnson.

---

1 www.ustn.com/news/2014/04/21/local-teen-missing, 4/21/14

2 www.fairfieldctnews.com/fairview/crime-4839, 4/24/14

3 www.ustn.com/news/2014/04/22/missing-schoolgirl-698834, 4/22/14

4 Forbes, Stanley, 2014, "The Real Story of Andie Bell's Killer," *Fairview Mail*, 4/29/14, pp. 1–4.

TRANSCRIPT OF INTERVIEW WITH ANGELA JOHNSON FROM THE MISSING PERSONS BUREAU

ANGELA: Hello.

PIP: Hi, is this Angela Johnson?

ANGELA: Speaking, yep. Is this Pippa?

PIP: Yes, thanks so much for replying to my email. Do you mind if I record this interview for my project?

ANGELA: Yeah, that's fine. I'm sorry, I've only got about ten minutes. So what do you want to know about missing persons?

PIP: Well, I was wondering if you could talk me through what happens when someone is reported missing? What's the process and the first steps taken by the police?

ANGELA: When someone is reported missing, the police will try to get as much detail as possible so they can identify the potential risk to the missing person, and an appropriate police response can be made. They'll ask for name, age, description, the clothes they were last seen wearing, the circumstances of their disappearance, if going missing is out of character for this person, details of any vehicle involved. Using this information, the police will determine whether this is an at-risk missing persons case.

PIP: And what circumstances would make it an at-risk case?

ANGELA: If they are vulnerable because of their age or a disability, or if the behavior is out of character, which indicates they could have been exposed to harm.

PIP: Um, so, if the missing person is seventeen years old and it is deemed out of character for her to go missing, would that be considered an at-risk case?

ANGELA: Absolutely, when a minor is involved.

PIP: So how would the police respond?

ANGELA: Well, there would be immediate deployment of police officers to the location the person is missing from. The officers will get further information about the missing person, such as details of their friends or partners; any health conditions; financial information, in case they try to withdraw money. Police will also need recent photographs and might take DNA samples, in case they're needed in subsequent forensic examinations. And, with consent of the homeowners, the location would be searched thoroughly to see if the missing person is concealed or hiding there and to establish whether there are any further evidential leads.

PIP: So immediately the police are looking for any clues or suggestions that the missing person has been the victim of a crime?

ANGELA: Absolutely. If the circumstances of the disappearance are suspicious, officers are instructed to document evidence early on, as though they were investigating a murder. Of course, only a very small percentage of missing persons cases turn into homicide cases.

PIP: And what happens if nothing significant turns up after the initial home search?

ANGELA: They'll expand the search to the immediate area. They'll question friends, neighbors, anyone who might have relevant information. If it is a teenager who's missing, we can't assume the reporting parent knows all of their child's friends and acquaintances. Peers are good points of contact to establish other important leads—you know, any secret boyfriends, that sort of thing. And a press strategy is usually discussed because appeals for information in the media can be very useful in these situations.

PIP: So if it's a seventeen-year-old girl who's gone missing, the police would contact her friends and boyfriend early on?

ANGELA: Yes, of course. Inquiries will be made, because if the missing person has run away, they are likely to be hiding out with someone close to them.

PIP: And at what point in a missing persons case do police assume they are looking for a body?

ANGELA: Well, timewise, it's not— Oh, Pippa, I have to go. Sorry, I've been called into my meeting.

PIP: Oh, OK, thanks so much for taking the time to talk to me.

ANGELA: And if you have more questions, just shoot me an email and I'll get to it when I can.

PIP: Will do, thanks again.

I found these statistics:

80% of missing people are found in the first twenty-four hours. 97% are found in the first week, and 99% of cases are resolved in the first year.

That leaves just 1%. 1% of people who disappear are never found. And just 0.25% of all missing persons cases have a fatal outcome.[5] So where does this leave Andie Bell? Floating incessantly somewhere between 1% and 0.25%.

Even though Andie has never been found and her body never recovered, most people accept that she is dead. And why is that?

Sal Singh is why.

5 www.missingpersonstats.com

two

Pip's hands hovered over the keyboard as she strained to listen to the commotion downstairs. A crash, heavy footsteps, skidding claws, and unrestrained boyish giggles.

"Josh! Why is the dog wearing my shirt!" Pip's dad shouted, the sound floating upstairs.

Pip snort-laughed as she clicked to save her capstone project log and closed her laptop. It was never quiet once her dad returned from work.

Downstairs, Pip found Josh running from room to room—kitchen to hallway to living room—on repeat. Cackling as he went.

Close behind was Barney, the golden retriever, wearing her dad's loudest shirt, the blindingly green patterned one he'd bought during their last trip to Nigeria. The dog skidded elatedly across the polished oak in the hall, excitement whistling through his teeth.

Bringing up the rear was Pip's dad in his gray Hugo Boss three-piece suit, all six and a half feet of him charging after the dog and the boy, laughing in wild bursts.

"Oh my god, I was trying to do homework," Pip said, restraining a smile as she jumped back to avoid being mowed down. Barney stopped for a moment to headbutt her shin and then scampered off to jump on Victor and Josh as they collapsed together on the sofa.

"Hello, pickle," her dad said, patting the couch beside him.

"Hi, Dad. You were so quiet I didn't even know you were home."

"My Pipsicle, you are too clever to recycle a joke."

She sat down beside them. Josh started excavating his right nostril, and Pip's dad batted his hand away. "How were your days, then?" her dad asked, setting Josh off on a graphic spiel about the soccer games he'd played earlier.

Pip zoned out; she'd already heard it all in the car when she picked Josh up from practice. She'd only been half listening, distracted by the way the replacement coach had stared at her, uncertain, when she'd pointed out which of the nine-year-olds was hers and said: "I'm Josh's sister."

She should have been used to it by now, the lingering looks while people tried to work out the logistics of her family. Victor, the tall Nigerian man, was evidently her stepfather; and Josh, her half brother. But Pip didn't like those words, those cold technicalities. The people you love weren't calculated, subtracted, or held at arm's length across a decimal point. Victor was her dad, who'd raised her since she was four years old, and Josh was her annoying little brother.

Her "real" father, the man who lent the Fitz to her name, died in a car accident when she was ten months old. And though Pip nodded and smiled when her mom would ask whether she remembered the way her father hummed while he brushed his teeth or how he'd laughed when Pip's second spoken word was "poo," she didn't remember him. But sometimes remembering isn't for yourself; sometimes you do it just to make someone else smile.

"And how's the project going, Pip?" Her dad turned to her as he unbuttoned the shirt from the dog.

"It's OK," she said. "I'm just researching at the moment. I did go to see Ravi Singh this morning, though."

"Oh, and . . . ?"

"He was busy, but he said I could go back on Friday."

"I wouldn't," Josh said in a cautionary tone.

"That's because you're a judgmental prepubescent boy who still thinks little people live inside traffic lights." Pip looked at him. "The Singhs haven't done anything wrong."

Victor stepped in. "Josh, try to imagine if everyone judged you because of something your sister had done."

"All Pip ever does is homework."

She swung a cushion into Josh's face, and her dad held the boy's arms down as he squirmed to retaliate, tickling his ribs.

As Pip watched them play-fighting, she couldn't help but wonder whether the Singhs ever laughed like that anymore. Or the Bells.

Maybe laughter was one of the very first things you lost after something like that.

PIPPA FITZ-AMOBI
7/31/19
CAPSTONE PROJECT LOG—ENTRY 2

What happened next in the Andie Bell case is hard to piece together from the newspaper reports, so I have to fill in the gaps with guesswork and rumors until the picture becomes clearer. Hopefully, interviews with Ravi and Naomi—who was one of Sal's best friends—will help.

According to what Angela said, the police would have asked for details about Andie's friends early on, presumably after taking statements from the Bell family.

After some serious social media stalking, it looks like Andie's best friends were two girls named Chloe Burch and Emma Hutton.

Emma Hutton, Sal Singh and 97 others
View 6 more comments

Emma Hutton Oh my god Andie, stop being so gorge.
Like · Reply · 5y

Chloe Burch I wish I didn't have to be in pics with you. Give me your face
Like · Reply · 5y

Andie Bell No ;)
Like · Reply · 5y

Emma Hutton Andie, let's take a nice one at the next calamity? Need new prof pic :)
Like · Reply · 5y

Write a comment . . .

This post was from almost two weeks before Andie disappeared. It looks like neither Chloe nor Emma lives in Fairview anymore, but I'll message them to see if they'll do a phone interview.

Chloe and Emma did a lot on that first weekend (April 19 and 20) to help spread the Connecticut State Police's Twitter campaign: #FindAndie. I don't think it's too big of a leap to assume that the police contacted Chloe and Emma either on the Friday night Andie went missing or the next morning. What they said to the police, I don't know. Hopefully, I can find out.

We do know that police spoke to Andie's boyfriend at the time. His name was Sal Singh, and he was attending his senior year at Fairview High along with Andie.

At some point on Saturday, April 19, the police contacted him:

> *"Detective Richard Hawkins confirmed that officers had questioned Salil Singh as to his whereabouts the previous night, particularly the period of time during which it is believed Andie went missing."*[6]

Friday night, Sal had been hanging out at his friend Max Hastings's house. He was with his four best friends: Naomi Ward, Jake Lawrence, Millie Simpson, and Max.

Again, I need to check this with Naomi next week, but I think Sal told the police that he left Max's around 12:15 a.m. He walked home, and his father (Mohan Singh) confirmed that "Sal returned home at approximately 12:50 a.m."[7] [Note: the distance between Max's house (Courtland) and Sal's (Grove Place) takes about thirty minutes to walk.]

The police confirmed Sal's alibi with his four friends over that weekend.

---

6 www.ustn.com/news/2014/05/03/fairview-murder, 5/3/14

7 www.ustn.com/news/2014/05/03/fairview-murder, 5/3/14

Missing posters went up. House-to-house inquiries started on the Sunday.[8]

On the Monday one hundred volunteers helped the police carry out searches in the local woodland. I've seen the news footage; a whole ant line of people in the trees, calling her name. Later in the day forensic teams were spotted going into the Bell residence.[9]

And on the Tuesday everything changed. I think chronologically is the best way to consider the events of that day, and those that followed, even though we, as a town, learned the details out of order and jumbled:

Midmorning: Naomi Ward, Max Hastings, Jake Lawrence, and Millie Simpson contacted the police from school and confessed to providing false information. They said that Sal had asked them to lie and that he actually left Max's house around 10:30 p.m. on the night Andie disappeared, not 12:15 a.m.

I don't know for sure what the correct police procedure would have been, but I'm guessing at that point, Sal became the number one suspect.

But no one could find him: Sal wasn't at school and he wasn't at home. He wasn't answering his phone. It later came out, however, that Sal had sent a text to his father that Tuesday morning, though he was ignoring all other calls. The press would refer to this as a "confession text."[10]

Tuesday evening, one of the police teams searching for Andie found a body in the woods.

It was Sal.

He had killed himself.

The press never reported the method by which Sal committed

---

8 Forbes, Stanley, "Local Girl Still Missing," *Fairview Mail*, 4/21/14, pp. 1–2.

9 www.ustn.com/news/2014/04/21/fairview-missing-girl, 4/21/14

10 www.ustn.com/news/2014/05/03/fairview-murder, 5/3/14

suicide, but by the power of small-town rumor, I knew (as did every other student at Fairview at the time).

Sal walked into the woods near his home, took a huge dose of sleeping pills, and placed a plastic bag over his head, securing it with an elastic band around his neck. He suffocated while unconscious.

At the police press conference that night, there was no mention of Sal. The police only revealed the information about security footage placing Andie driving away from her home at 10:40 p.m.[11]

On Wednesday Andie's car was found parked on a small residential road (Monroe).

It wasn't until the following Monday that a police spokeswoman revealed the following:

> *"As a result of recent intelligence and forensic information, we have strong reason to suspect that a young man named Salil Singh, aged eighteen, was involved in Andie's abduction and murder. The evidence would have been sufficient to arrest and charge the suspect had he not died before proceedings could be initiated. Police are not looking for anyone else in relation to Andie's disappearance at this time, but our search for Andie will continue unabated. Our thoughts go out to the Bell family, and our deepest sympathies for the devastation this update has caused them."*

Their sufficient evidence:

- They found Andie's phone on Sal's body.
- Forensic tests found traces of Andie's blood under the fingernails of his right middle and index fingers.

11 www.ustn.com/news/2014/04/22/fairview-girl-still-missing, 4/22/14

- Andie's blood was discovered in the trunk of her abandoned car.
- Sal's fingerprints were found around the dashboard and steering wheel, alongside prints from Andie and the rest of the Bell family.[12]

The evidence, they said, would have been enough to charge Sal. But he was dead, so there was no trial and no conviction. No defense either.

In the following weeks there were more searches of the woodland areas in and around Fairview. Searches using cadaver dogs. Police divers in the river. Andie's body was never found. The Andie Bell missing persons case was administratively closed in the middle of June 2014.[13]

Eighteen months later a court order was filed and Andie Bell was declared dead in absentia, based on the circumstances surrounding her disappearance. Andie Bell's death certificate was issued.[14] Despite her body never having been located, she has now been legally declared dead.

After the ruling the district attorney said: "The case against Salil Singh would have been based on circumstantial and forensic evidence. It is not for me to state whether or not Salil Singh killed Andie Bell; that would have been a jury's job to decide."[15]

And even though there has never been a trial, no conviction by a jury; even though Sal never had the chance to defend himself, he is guilty. Not in the legal sense, but in all the other ways that truly matter.

---

12 www.ustn.com/news/2014/05/07/fairview-andie-bell-murder, 5/7/14

13 www.ustn.com/news/2014/06/15/andie-bell-case-closed, 6/15/14

14 www.thenewsroom.com/AndieBellInquest/report57743, 1/12/16

15 www.ustn.com/news/2016/01/15/fairview-murder-DA-statement, 1/15/16

When you ask people in town what happened to Andie Bell, they'll tell you without hesitation: "She was murdered by Salil Singh." No "allegedly," no "might have," no "probably," no "most likely."

He did it, they say. Sal Singh killed Andie.

But I'm just not so sure.

three

It was an emergency, the text said. An SOS emergency. Pip knew immediately that that could only mean one thing.

She grabbed her car keys, yelled goodbye to her mom and Josh, and rushed out the front door.

She stopped by the store on her way to buy a king-size chocolate bar to help mend Lauren's king-size broken heart.

When she pulled up outside the Gibsons' house, she saw that Cara had had the exact same idea. Except Cara's post-breakup first-aid kit was more extensive than Pip's; she had also brought a box of tissues, chips and dip, and a rainbow array of face mask packets.

"Ready for this?" Pip asked Cara, hip-bumping her in greeting.

"Yep, well prepared for the tears." She held up the tissues, the corner of the box catching the ends of her curly ash-brown hair.

Pip pressed the doorbell, and both of them winced at the mechanical song.

Lauren's mom answered the door.

"Oh, the cavalry is here." She smiled. "She's upstairs in her room."

They found Lauren fully submerged in a duvet fort on the bed, the only sign of her existence a splay of ginger hair poking out from the bottom. It took a full minute of coaxing and chocolate bait to get her to surface.

"First," Cara said, prying Lauren's phone from her fingers, nails bitten to the quick, "you're banned from looking at this for the next twenty-four hours."

"He did it by text!" Lauren wailed, blowing her nose and shooting an entire swamp into the tissue.

"Boys are dicks," Cara said, putting her arm around Lauren and resting her sharp chin on her shoulder. "You could do so much better than him."

"Yeah." Pip broke Lauren off another line of chocolate. "Besides, Tom always said 'pacifically' when he meant 'specifically.' "

Cara pointed eagerly at Pip in agreement. "Massive red flag."

"I *pacifically* think you're better off without him," said Pip.

"I *atlantically* think so too," added Cara.

Lauren gave a wet snort of laughter, and Cara winked at Pip; an unspoken victory.

"Thanks for coming, guys," Lauren said tearfully, her pale eyes swollen and puffy. "I didn't know if you would. I've probably neglected you for half a year to hang out with Tom. And now I'll be third-wheeling two best friends."

"That's crap," Cara said. "We're all best friends."

"Yeah." Pip nodded. "Us, and those three mediocre boys we allow to bask in our delightful company."

Cara and Lauren laughed. The boys—Ant, Zach, and Connor—were all currently away during the summer break.

But of her friends, Pip had known Cara the longest, and yes, they were closest. An unsaid thing. They'd been inseparable ever since six-year-old Cara had hugged a tiny, friendless Pip and asked, "Do you like bunnies too?"

They were each other's crutch to lean on when life got too much to carry alone. Pip, though only ten at the time, had helped Cara through her mom's diagnosis and death. And Pip had been her constant two years ago when Cara came out, ready with a steady smile and phone calls into the early hours. Cara's wasn't the face of a best friend; it was the face of a sister.

By extension, Cara's family was Pip's second. Mr. Ward, in addition to being her history teacher, was her tertiary father figure, behind her stepdad and the ghost of her first father. Pip was at the Ward house so often she had her own mug with her name on it and pair of slippers to match Cara's and her older sister, Naomi's.

"OK." Cara lunged for the TV remote. "Rom-coms or films where boys get violently murdered?"

It took roughly one and a half terrible films from the Netflix backlog for Lauren to wade through denial and extend a cautionary toe toward acceptance.

"I should get a haircut," she said. "That's what you're supposed to do."

"I've always said you'd look good with short hair," said Cara.

"And do you think I should get my nose pierced?"

"Ooh, yeah." Cara nodded.

"I don't see the logic in putting a nose hole in your nose hole," said Pip.

"Another Pip quote for the books." Cara feigned writing it down in midair. "What was the one that got me the other day?"

"The sausage one." Pip sighed.

"Oh yeah," Cara snorted. "So, Laur, I was asking Pip which pajamas she wanted to wear, and she just casually says, 'It's sausage to me.' And didn't realize why that was a weird response."

"It's not that weird," said Pip. "My grandparents from my first dad are German. 'It's sausage to me' is a German saying; just means 'I don't care.' "

"Or you've got a sausage fixation." Lauren laughed.

"Says the daughter of a porn star," Pip quipped.

"Oh my god, how many times? He only did one nude photoshoot in the eighties, that's it."

"So, on to boys from this decade," Cara said, prodding Pip on the shoulder. "Did you go see Ravi Singh yet?"

"Questionable segue. But yes, and I'm going back to interview him tomorrow."

"I can't believe you've already started your capstone project," Lauren said with a dying-swan dive back onto the bed. "I want to change mine already; famines are depressing."

"I imagine you want to interview Naomi sometime soon." Cara looked pointedly at Pip.

"Yeah. . . . Can you warn her I might be stopping by next week?"

"Sure," Cara said, then hesitated. "She'll agree to it and everything, but can you go easy on her? She still gets really upset about it sometimes. I mean, he was one of her best friends. Actually, probably her *best* friend."

"Yeah, of course," Pip said. "What do you think I'm going to do? Pin her down and beat responses out of her?"

"Is that your tactic for Ravi tomorrow?"

"Ha."

Lauren sat up then, with a snot-sucking sniff so loud it made Cara visibly flinch.

"Are you going to his house, then?" she asked.

"Yeah."

"But . . . what are people going to think if they see you going into Ravi Singh's house?"

"It's sausage to me."

PIPPA FITZ-AMOBI
8/1/19
CAPSTONE PROJECT LOG—ENTRY 3

I'm biased; I know I am. For reasons I don't even know how to explain to myself, I want Sal Singh to be innocent. Reasons carried with me since I was twelve years old, inconsistencies that have nagged at me these past five years.

But if I'm actually going to solve anything, I have to be aware of confirmation bias. So I thought it would be a good idea to interview someone who is utterly convinced of Sal's guilt.

Stanley Forbes, a journalist at the *Fairview Mail*, just responded to my email, saying I could call any time today. He covered a lot of the Andie Bell case in the local press and was even present at the court hearing when she was declared dead a year and a half later. To be honest I think he's a poor journalist, and I'm pretty sure the Singhs could sue him for defamation and libel about a dozen times over. I'll type up the transcript here right after.

TRANSCRIPT OF INTERVIEW WITH STANLEY FORBES FROM THE *FAIRVIEW MAIL* NEWSPAPER

PIP: Hi, Stanley. This is Pippa; we were emailing earlier.

STANLEY: Yep, yeah, I know. You wanted to pick my brain about the Andie Bell/Salil Singh case, right?

PIP: Yes, that's right. Do you mind if I record our conversation?

STANLEY: Sure, shoot.

PIP: OK, thanks. Um, so first, you attended the court hearing that established Andie as legally dead, correct?

STANLEY: Sure did.

PIP: Since the national press didn't elaborate much further than reporting the verdict, I was wondering if you could tell me what kind of evidence was presented?

STANLEY: Uh, so the main investigator on Andie's case outlined the details of her disappearance—the times and so on. And then he moved on to the evidence that linked Salil to her murder. They made a big deal about the blood in the trunk of her car; they said this suggested that she was murdered and her body was put in the trunk to be transported somewhere else. They said something like "It seems clear that Andie was the victim of a sexually motivated murder, and considerable efforts were made to dispose of her body."

PIP: And did Detective Richard Hawkins or any other officer provide a timeline of what they believed were the events of that night and how Sal allegedly killed her?

STANLEY: Yeah, I kinda remember that. Andie left home in her car, and at some point on Salil's walk home, he intercepted her. With either him or her driving, he took her to a secluded place and murdered her. He put her in the trunk and then drove somewhere to hide or dispose of her body. Mind you, well enough that it hasn't been found in five years; must have been a pretty big hole. And then he ditched the car on that road where it was found—Monroe, I think—and he walked home.

PIP: So because of the blood in the trunk, the police believed that Andie was killed somewhere and then hidden in a different location?

STANLEY: Yep.

PIP: OK. In a lot of your articles about the case, you refer to Sal as a "killer," a "murderer," and even a "monster." You are aware that without a conviction, you are supposed to use the word "allegedly" when reporting crime stories.

STANLEY: Not sure I need a child to tell me how to do my job. Anyway, it's obvious that he did it, and everyone knows it. He killed her, and the guilt drove him to suicide.

PIP: And why are you so convinced Sal's guilty?

STANLEY: Almost too many things to list. Evidence aside, he was the boyfriend, right? And it's always the boyfriend or the ex-boyfriend. Not only that, Salil was Indian.

PIP: Well . . . he was actually born and raised in the United States, though it is notable you refer to him as Indian in all of your articles.

STANLEY: Well, same thing. He was of Indian heritage.

PIP: And why is that relevant?

STANLEY: I'm not like an expert or anything, but they have different ways of life from us, don't they? They don't treat women quite like we do. So I'm guessing maybe Andie decided she didn't want to be with him or something, and he killed her in a rage because, in his eyes, she belonged to him.

PIP: Wow . . . I . . . Honestly, Stanley, I'm pretty surprised you still have a job.

STANLEY: That's 'cause everyone knows what I'm saying is true.

PIP: I don't agree. And I think it's irresponsible to publicly call someone a murderer without using "allegedly" when there's been no conviction. Or, even worse, calling Sal a monster. It's interesting to compare your reporting about Sal to your recent articles on the Stratford Strangler. He murdered five people and pleaded guilty, yet in your headline you referred to him as a "lovesick young man." Is that because *he's* white?

STANLEY: That's got nothing to do with Salil's case; I just call it how it is. You need to relax. He's dead. Why does it matter if people call him a murderer? It can't hurt him.

PIP: Because his family isn't dead.

STANLEY: Look, this is a waste of my time. You really think he's innocent? Against the expertise of senior officers?

PIP: I just think there are certain gaps in the case against Sal, that's all.

STANLEY: Yeah, maybe if the kid hadn't offed himself before getting arrested, we would have been able to fill the gaps.

PIP: That was insensitive.

STANLEY: Well, it was insensitive of him to kill his girlfriend.

PIP: Allegedly!

STANLEY: You want more proof that that kid was a killer, fangirl? We weren't allowed to print it, but my source in the police said they found a death-threat note in Andie's school locker. He threatened her, and then he did it. Do you really still think he's innocent?

PIP: Maybe he is. And you're a racist, intolerant hack who—(Stanley hangs up the phone.)

Yeah, so I don't think Stanley and I are going to be best friends. But he's provided two pieces of information I didn't have before. First: police believe Andie was killed somewhere before being put in the trunk of her car and driven to a second location to be disposed of. Second: this "death threat." I haven't seen a death threat mentioned in any articles or police statements. Maybe the police didn't think it was relevant. Or maybe they couldn't prove it was linked to Sal. Or maybe Stanley made it up. In any case, it's worth remembering when I interview Andie's friends later on.

So now that I (sort of) know what the police's version of events are for that night, and what the prosecution's case might have looked like, it's time for a *murder map*.

I had to make a couple of assumptions when creating it. The first is that there are several ways to walk from Max's to Sal's; I picked the one that heads back through Main Street, because Google said it was the quickest and I'm presuming most people prefer to walk on well-lit streets at night.

It also provides a good intercept point somewhere along Weevil Road, where Andie possibly pulled over and Sal got in the car. There are some quiet residential roads and a farm on Weevil Road. These secluded places—circled—could potentially be the site of the murder (according to the police's version of events).

I didn't bother guessing where Andie's body was disposed because, like the rest of the world, I have no clue where that is. But given that it takes about eighteen minutes to walk from where the car was dumped on Monroe back to Sal's house on Grove Place, I have to presume he'd have been back in the vicinity of Weevil Road around 12:20 a.m. If the Andie-and-Sal intercept happened around 10:45 p.m., this would have given Sal one hour and thirty-five minutes to murder her and hide her body. I mean, timewise, that seems perfectly reasonable to me. It's possible.

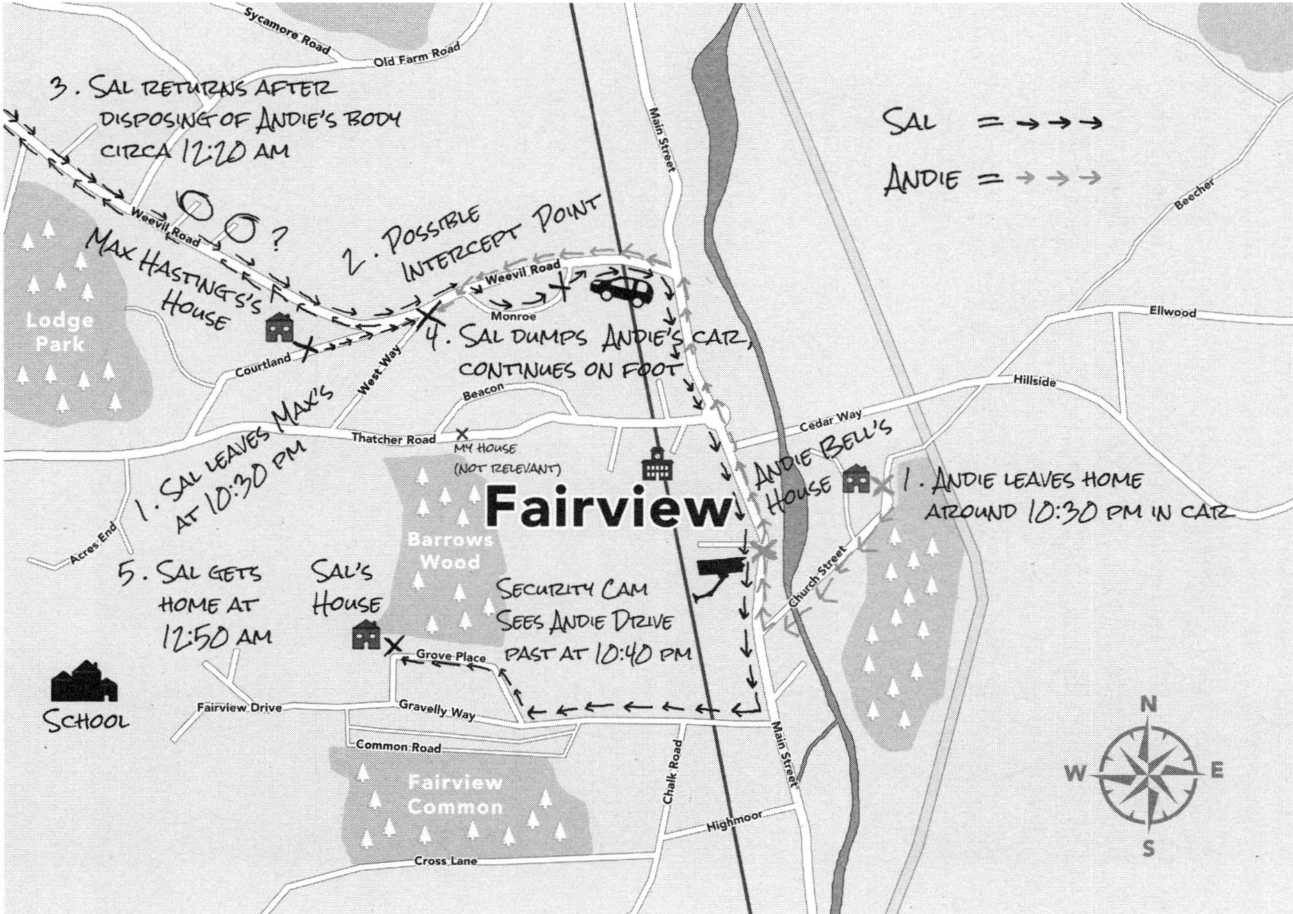
SAL = → → →
ANDIE = → → →
3. SAL RETURNS AFTER DISPOSING OF ANDIE'S BODY CIRCA 12:20 AM
2. POSSIBLE INTERCEPT POINT
MAX HASTINGS'S HOUSE
4. SAL DUMPS ANDIE'S CAR, CONTINUES ON FOOT
1. SAL LEAVES MAX'S AT 10:30 PM
MY HOUSE (NOT RELEVANT)
ANDIE BELL'S HOUSE
1. ANDIE LEAVES HOME AROUND 10:30 PM IN CAR
Fairview
5. SAL GETS HOME AT 12:50 AM
SAL'S HOUSE
SECURITY CAM SEES ANDIE DRIVE PAST AT 10:40 PM
SCHOOL
Sycamore Road
Old Farm Road
Main Street
Weevil Road
Monroe
Courtland
West Way
Beacon
Thatcher Road
Cedar Way
Hillside
Ellwood
Beecher
Lodge Park
Barrows Wood
Acres End
Church Street
Grove Place
Fairview Drive
Gravelly Way
Common Road
Chalk Road
Fairview Common
Highmoor
Cross Lane
N
W
E
S

But here I've spotted one of those inconsistencies. Andie and Sal both leave where they are around 10:30 p.m., so they must have planned to meet up, right? It seems too coincidental for them not to have communicated about meeting. The thing is, the police have never once mentioned a phone call or any texts between Andie and Sal that would equate to a meet-up arrangement. And if they planned this together—at school, for example, where there would be no record of the conversation—why didn't they just agree that Andie would pick Sal up from Max's house? It seems weird to me.

four

Pip stood before the front door and willed it to open. How long had it been since she'd knocked? The seconds grew syrupy and thick as the door stared her down, each minute stretching into forever. When Pip could stand it no longer, she removed the container of muffins from under her arm and turned to walk away. The disappointment burned.

Only a few steps down the path, she heard the sound of scraping and clicking and turned back to see Ravi Singh in the doorway, his hair ruffled and his face drawn tight in confusion.

"Oh," Pip said in a high-pitched voice that wasn't her own. "Sorry; I thought you told me to come back Friday. Today's Friday."

"Um, yeah, I did," Ravi said, scratching the back of his head, with his eyes somewhere around Pip's ankles. "But . . . honestly . . . I thought you were just messing with me. I wasn't expecting you to actually come back."

Pip tried her best to not look hurt. "I'm not messing, I promise. I'm serious."

"Yeah, you seem like the serious type." The back of his head must have been exceptionally itchy. Or maybe Ravi Singh's itchy head was the equivalent of Pip's overexplaining.

"I'm irrationally serious." Pip smiled, holding the Tupperware out to him. "And I made muffins."

"Like bribery muffins?"

"That's what the recipe said, yeah."

Ravi's mouth twitched; not quite a smile. Pip only then appreciated how hard his life must be in this town, the specter of his dead brother reflected in his own face. It's no wonder smiling was hard for him.

"So, can I come in?"

"Fine," he said after an almost devastating pause, stepping back to let her into the house.

"Thank you, thank you," Pip said quickly, and tripped over the front step in her eagerness.

Raising an eyebrow, Ravi shut the door and asked if she'd like a cup of coffee.

"Yes, please." Pip stood awkwardly in the hallway, trying to take up as little space as possible. "Black, please."

"I've never trusted anyone who takes their coffee black." He gestured for her to follow him into the kitchen.

The room was wide and exceptionally bright; the far wall was one giant panel of sliding glass doors that opened onto a long garden exploding with the blush of summer and winding vines.

"How do you have it, then?" Pip asked, resting her backpack on one of the kitchen chairs.

"Milk and three sugars," he said, starting the coffee maker.

"Three sugars? Three?"

"I know. Clearly I'm not sweet enough already."

Pip watched Ravi clatter around the kitchen, the sputtering inferno sounds of the machine excusing the silence between them. He tapped his fingers on the counter as he waited for the coffee. The nervous energy was contagious as he went about pouring and sugaring and milking, and Pip's heart quickened to match his tapping fingers.

He brought the two mugs over, holding Pip's by the scorching base so she could take it by the handle.

"Your parents aren't here?" she asked, setting the mug down on the table.

"Nope." He took a sip, and Pip noted, thankfully, that he wasn't a slurper. "And if they were, you wouldn't be. We try not to talk about Sal too much; it upsets Mom. It upsets everyone, actually."

"I can't even imagine," Pip said quietly. It didn't matter that five years had passed; this was still raw for Ravi—it was written all over his face.

"It's not just that he's gone. It's that . . . well, we're not allowed to grieve for him, because of what happened. And if I say 'I miss my brother,' it makes me some kind of monster."

"I don't think it does."

"Me neither, but I'm guessing you and I are in the minority there."

Pip took a sip of her coffee to fill the silence, but it was far too hot, and her eyes prickled and filled.

"Crying already? We haven't even got to the sad parts." Ravi's right eyebrow peaked up on his forehead.

"Hot," Pip gasped, her tongue scorched and fluffy.

"Let it cool down for a second, or, you know, a few sequential seconds."

Of course. Of course that would be the one thing he remembered from their introduction. *Good one, Pip.* She hoped she wasn't blushing.

"So, what questions did you want to ask me?" he said.

She looked down at the phone in her lap. "Do you mind if I record us, so I can type it up later?"

"Sounds like a fun Friday night."

"I'll take that as you don't mind." Pip opened the zipper on her metallic backpack and pulled out her bundle of notes.

"What are those?" He pointed.

"Prepared questions." She shuffled the papers to straighten the stack.

"Oh wow, you're really into this, aren't you?" He looked at her with an expression that quivered somewhere between quizzical and skeptical.

"Yep."

"Should I be nervous?"

"Not yet," said Pip, fixing him with one last look before pressing the red record button. She caught just the tail end of a smile.

PIPPA FITZ-AMOBI
8/2/19
CAPSTONE PROJECT LOG—ENTRY 4

TRANSCRIPT OF INTERVIEW WITH RAVI SINGH

PIP: So, how old are you?

RAVI: Why?

PIP: Just trying to get all the facts straight.

RAVI: OK, Sergeant, I just turned twenty.

PIP: (laughs) [Oh my god, my laugh is atrocious on audio. I'm never laughing again.] And Sal was three years older than you?

RAVI: Yes.

PIP: Do you remember your brother acting strangely on Friday, April 18, 2014?

RAVI: Wow, straight in there. Um, no, not at all. We had an early dinner at, like, seven, before my dad dropped him at Max's, and he was just chatting along, like normal Sal. If he was secretly planning a murder, it wasn't at all obvious to us. He was . . . upbeat; I'd say that was a good description.

PIP: And what about when he returned from Max's?

RAVI: I had already gone up to bed. But the next morning I remember him being in a really good mood. Sal was always a morning person. He got up and made breakfast for us all, and it wasn't until just after that he got a phone call from one of Andie's friends. That's when we found out she was missing. From that point, obviously, he wasn't upbeat anymore; he was worried.

PIP: So neither Andie's parents nor the police called him on Friday night?

RAVI: Not that I know of. Andie's parents didn't really know Sal. He'd never met them or been to their house. Andie usually came around here, or they hung out at school and parties.

PIP: How long had they been together?

RAVI: Since just before Christmas the year before, so about four months. Sal did have a couple of missed calls from one of Andie's best friends at, like, two a.m. that night. His phone was on silent, though, so he slept through them.

PIP: So what else happened on that Saturday?

RAVI: Well, after finding out Andie was missing, Sal literally sat by his phone, calling her every few minutes. It went to voicemail each time, but he figured if she'd pick up for anyone, it'd be him.

PIP: Wait, so Sal was calling Andie's phone?

RAVI: Yeah, like a million times, throughout that weekend and on the Monday too.

PIP: Doesn't sound like the kind of thing you'd do if you knew you had murdered the person and they would never pick up.

RAVI: Especially if he had her phone hidden somewhere on him or in his room.

PIP: An even better point. So what else happened that day?

RAVI: My parents told him not to go to Andie's house, because the police would be busy searching it. So he just sat at home, trying to call her. I asked him if he had any idea where she'd be, and he was stumped. He said something else I've always remembered. He said that everything Andie did was deliberate, and maybe she'd run off on purpose to punish someone. Obviously, by the end of the weekend, he realized that probably wasn't the case.

PIP: Who would Andie be wanting to punish? Him?

RAVI: I don't know; I didn't push it. I didn't know her well; she only came around a handful of times. I mean, I presumed the "someone" Sal was talking about was Andie's dad.

PIP: Jason Bell? Why?

RAVI: I just overheard some stuff when she was here. I figured she didn't have the best relationship with her dad. I can't remember anything specifically.

PIP: So when did the police contact Sal?

RAVI: It was that Saturday afternoon. They called him and asked if they could come over for a chat. They arrived at, like, three or four-ish. Me and my parents came into the kitchen to give them a bit of space, so we didn't hear any of it really.

PIP: And did Sal tell you what they asked him?

RAVI: A bit. He was a little freaked out that they recorded it and st—

PIP: The police recorded it? Is that normal?

RAVI: I don't know, you're the sergeant. They said it was routine and just asked him questions about where he was that night, who he was with. And about his and Andie's relationship.

PIP: And what was their relationship like?

RAVI: I'm his brother; I didn't see all that much of it. But yeah, Sal liked her a lot. I mean, he seemed pretty pleased he was with the prettiest, most popular girl in the grade. Andie always seemed to bring drama, though.

PIP: What kind of drama?

RAVI: I don't know. I think she was just one of those people that thrives on it.

PIP: Did your parents like her?

RAVI: Yeah, my parents were cool with her. She never gave them a reason not to be.

PIP: And so what else happened after the police interviewed him?

RAVI: Um, his friends came by in the evening, you know, to check if he was OK.

PIP: And is that when he asked his friends to lie to the police and give him an alibi?

RAVI: I guess so.

PIP: Why do you think he did that?

RAVI: I mean, I don't know. Maybe he was panicked after the police interview. Maybe he was scared he would be a suspect, so he tried to cover himself. I don't know.

PIP: Presuming Sal's innocence, do you have any idea where he could have been between leaving Max's at 10:30 and getting home at 12:50?

RAVI: No, because he also told us that he started walking home from Max's at like 12:15. I guess maybe he was alone somewhere, so he knew that if he told the truth, he'd have no alibi. It looks bad, doesn't it?

PIP: It doesn't look great, but it's not absolute proof he had anything to do with Andie's death. What happened on the Sunday?

RAVI: On the Sunday afternoon me, Sal, and his friends volunteered to help put up some Missing posters, hand them out to people in town. On the Monday I didn't see much of him at school, but it must have been pretty hard for him because all anyone was talking about was Andie's disappearance.

PIP: I'm sure.

RAVI: Police were there too. I saw them looking through Andie's locker. Yeah, so that night he was a little off. He was quiet, but he was worried, that's what you'd expect. His girlfriend was missing. And the next day—

PIP: You don't have to talk about the next day if you don't want to.

RAVI: (small pause) It's OK. We walked into school together, and I went off to registration, leaving Sal behind in the parking lot. He wanted to sit outside for a minute. That was the last time I ever saw him. And all I said was "See you later." I . . . I knew the police were at school; rumor was they were talking to Sal's friends. And it wasn't until like two-ish that I saw my mom had been trying to call me, so I went home and my parents told me that the police really needed to speak to Sal and had I seen him. I think officers had been searching his bedroom. I tried calling Sal, too, but it just rang out. My dad showed me this text he got, the last time they'd heard from Sal.

PIP: Do you remember what it said?

RAVI: Yeah, it said: *It was me. I did it. I'm so sorry.* And . . . [small pause] it was later that evening when the police came back. My parents went to answer the door, and I stayed in here listening. When they said they'd found a body in the woods, I was so sure for a second that it was Andie they were talking about.

PIP: And . . . I don't want to be insensitive, but the sleeping pills. . . .

RAVI: Yeah, they were Dad's. He was taking phenobarbitals for his insomnia. He blamed himself afterward. Doesn't take anything anymore. He just doesn't sleep much.

PIP: And had you ever before thought that Sal could be suicidal?

RAVI: Never, not once. Sal was literally the happiest person there was. He was always laughing and messing around. It's cheesy, but he was the kind of person that lit up a room when he walked into it. He was the best at everything he ever did. He was my parents' golden child, their straight-A student. Now they're left with just me.

PIP: And, sorry, but the biggest question then: Do you think Sal killed Andie?

RAVI: I . . . No, no I don't. I can't think that. It just doesn't make sense to me. Sal was one of the nicest people on the planet, you know? He never lost his temper ever, no matter how much I ragged on him. He was never one of those boys that got into fights. He was the greatest big brother anyone could have, and he always came to my rescue when I needed it. He was the best person I ever knew. So I have to say no. But then, I don't know—the police seem so sure, and the evidence . . . Yeah, I know it looks bad for Sal. But I still can't believe he had it in him.

PIP: I understand. I think those are all the questions I need to ask for now.

RAVI: (sits back and lets out a long sigh) So, Pippa—

PIP: You can call me Pip.

RAVI: Pip, then. You said this is for a school project?

PIP: It is.

RAVI: But why? Why did you choose this? Sure, maybe you don't believe Sal did it, but why do you want to prove it? No one else in this town has trouble believing my brother was a monster. They've all moved on.

PIP: My best friend, Cara . . . She's Naomi Ward's sister.

RAVI: Oh, Naomi. She was always nice to me. Always over at our house, following Sal around like a puppy. She was 100 percent in love with him.

PIP: Really?

RAVI: I always thought so. The way she laughed at everything he said, even the unfunny stuff. Don't think he felt the same way back, though.

PIP: Hm.

RAVI: So you're doing this for Naomi? I still don't get it.

PIP: No, it's not that. What I meant was . . . I knew Sal.

RAVI: You did?

PIP: Yeah. He was over at the Wards' house a lot when I was there. One time he let us watch an R-rated movie with them, even though Cara and I were only twelve. It was a comedy, and I can still remember how much I laughed. Even when I didn't quite get the movie, because Sal's laugh was so contagious.

RAVI: Kind of high and giggly?

PIP: Yeah. And when I was ten, he accidentally taught me my first swear word. "Shit," by the way. And another time he taught me how to flip pancakes because I was useless at it but too stubborn to let someone do it for me.

RAVI: He was a good teacher.

PIP: And when I was in my first year at middle school, these two boys were picking on me. I cried about it at the Wards' house, and Sal gave me his KitKat to cheer me up and told me exactly what to say to the bullies. Something like did they really want to get expelled for bullying and start from scratch at a completely new school where they didn't know anyone. It worked—they never picked on me again. Since then, I've . . . Well, never mind.

RAVI: Hey, come on, share. I let you have your interview—even though your bribery muffins taste like cheese.

PIP: Since then, he's always been a hero to me. I just can't believe he did it.

PIPPA FITZ-AMOBI
8/6/19
CAPSTONE PROJECT LOG—ENTRY 5

I've just spent two hours researching this: I think I can send a request to the Connecticut State Police for a copy of Sal's police interview under the Freedom of Information Act.

There are certain exemptions to disclosing information under the FOIA, like if the requested material relates to an ongoing investigation or if it would invade an individual's privacy by divulging personal information. But Sal is dead, so they'd have no reason to withhold his interview, right? I might as well see if I can get access to other police records from the Andie Bell investigation too.

On another note, I can't get these things Ravi said about Jason Bell out of my head. That Sal thought Andie had run away to punish someone and that her relationship with her father was strained.

Jason and Dawn Bell got divorced not long after Andie's death certificate was issued (this is common Fairview knowledge, and I corroborated it with a quick Facebook investigation). Jason moved away and is now living in a town about fifteen minutes from here. It wasn't long after their divorce that he started appearing in pictures with a pretty blond lady who looks a little too young for him. It appears they are married now.

I've been on YouTube watching hours and hours of footage from the early press conferences after Andie went missing. I can't believe I never noticed it before, but there's something a bit off about Jason. The way he squeezes his wife's arm just a little too hard when she starts crying about Andie, the way he shifts his shoulder so he can push her back from the microphone when he decides she's said enough. The voice breaks that sound a little forced when he says: "Andie, we love you so much" and "Please come home; you won't be in trouble." The way Becca, Andie's sister, shrinks under his gaze.

And then during the evening press conference on Monday, April 21, I noticed something HUGE. Jason Bell said, "We just want our girl back. We are completely broken and don't know what to do with ourselves. If you know where she is, please tell her to call home so we know she's safe. Andie *was* such a huge presence in our home; it's too quiet without her."

WAS. PAST TENSE. This was before any of the Sal stuff had happened. Everyone thought Andie was still alive at this point. But Jason Bell said WAS.

Was that just an innocent mistake, or was he using the past tense because he already knew his daughter was dead? Did Jason Bell slip up?

From what I've learned, Jason and Dawn were at a dinner party that night, and Andie was supposed to pick them up. Could he have left the party at some point? And if not, even if he has a solid alibi, that doesn't mean he can't somehow be involved in Andie's disappearance.

If I'm creating a persons of interest list, I think Jason Bell is going to have to be the first name.

PERSONS OF INTEREST

Jason Bell

five

Something in the room felt off, like the air itself was too thick to breathe. In all her years of knowing Naomi, it had never been like this.

Pip gave Naomi a reassuring smile and made a passing joke about the amount of dog hair attached to her own leggings. Naomi smiled weakly, twisting the ends of her tawny hair.

They were sitting in Mr. Ward's study: Pip on the swiveling desk chair, and Naomi across from her in a red leather recliner. Naomi wasn't looking at Pip; she was staring instead at the three paintings on the far wall. Three giant rainbow-colored canvases of the family: her parents walking in the autumn woods; her dad, Elliot, drinking from a steaming mug; and a young Naomi and Cara on a swing. Their mom had painted them when she was dying, her final mark upon the world. Pip knew how important those paintings were to the Wards, how the family looked to them in their happiest and saddest times. Although she remembered there used to be a couple more displayed in here too. Maybe Mr. Ward was keeping them in storage to give to the girls when they grew up and moved out.

Pip knew Naomi had been going to therapy since her mom died seven years ago. And that she had managed to wade through her anxiety, neck just above the water, to graduate from college.

But a few months ago, she'd had a panic attack at her new job in Manhattan and quit to move back in with her dad and sister.

Naomi was fragile, and Pip was trying her hardest not to tread on any cracks. From the corner of her eye she could see the timer scrolling on her voice recorder app.

"So, can you tell me what you were all doing at Max's that night?" she asked gently.

Naomi shifted, eyes moving down to circle her knees.

"Um, we were just, like, drinking, talking, playing some Xbox—nothing too exciting."

"And taking pictures? There's a few on Facebook from that night."

"Yeah, taking silly pictures. Just messing around, really," Naomi said.

"There aren't any pictures of Sal from that night, though."

"No, well, I guess he left before we started taking them."

"And was Sal acting strangely before he left?" said Pip.

"Um, I . . . No, I don't think he was really."

"Did he talk about Andie at all?"

"I, um . . . Yeah, maybe a bit." Naomi shifted in her seat.

"What did he say about her?" Pip asked.

"Um." Naomi paused for a moment, picking at a ripped cuticle by her thumb. "He, um . . . I think maybe they were having a disagreement. Sal said he wasn't going to talk to her for a bit."

"Why?"

"I don't remember specifically. But Andie was . . . She was kind of a nightmare. She was always trying to pick fights with Sal over the smallest things. Sal preferred to give her the silent treatment rather than argue."

"What kind of things were these fights about?"

"Like the stupidest things. Like him not texting her back quick enough. Things like that. I . . . I never said it to him, but I always thought Andie was bad news. If I had said something, I don't know, maybe everything would have turned out differently."

Looking at Naomi's downcast face, at the trembling of her upper lip, Pip knew she needed to bring them out of this particular rabbit hole before Naomi closed up entirely.

"Had Sal said at any point in the evening that he would be leaving early?"

"No, he didn't."

"And what time did he leave Max's?"

"We're pretty sure it was close to ten-thirty."

"Did he say anything before he left?"

Naomi closed her eyes for a moment, the lids pressed so tightly that Pip could see them vibrating, even from across the room. "Yeah," she said. "He just said that he wasn't really feeling it and was going to walk home and call it an early night."

"And what time did you leave Max's?"

"I didn't. I . . . Me and Millie stayed over in the spare room. Dad came and got me in the morning."

"What time did you go up to bed?"

"Um, I think it was a bit before twelve-thirty. Not sure, really."

There was a sudden knock on the study door, and Cara poked her head in, squeaking when her topknot got caught on the frame.

"Sorry, emergency, two secs," she said, lingering as a floating head. "Nai, where the hell did those Butterfingers go?"

"I don't know."

"I literally saw Dad with a full pack yesterday."

"I don't know, ask him."

"He's not back yet."

“Cara,” Pip said, raising her eyebrows.

“Yep, fine, I’ll leave. No one cares that I’m starving,” she said, closing the door behind her again.

“Um, OK,” Pip said, trying to recover their lost tangent. “So, when did you first hear that Andie was missing?”

“I think Sal texted me Saturday, maybe late morning–ish.”

“And what were your initial thoughts about where she might be?”

“I don’t know.” Naomi shrugged. “Andie was the kind of girl that knew lots of people. I guess I thought she was hanging out with some other friends we didn’t know, not wanting to be found.”

Pip took a preparatory deep breath, glancing at her notes; she needed to handle the next question carefully. “Can you tell me about when Sal asked you to lie to the police about what time he left Max’s?”

Naomi tried to speak, but she couldn’t seem to find the words. A strange, underwater silence mushroomed in the small space.

“Um,” Naomi said finally, her voice breaking a little. “We went over on Saturday evening to see how he was doing. And we were talking about what happened, and Sal said he was nervous because the police had already been asking him questions. And because he was her boyfriend, he thought he was going to be a target. So he just said did we mind saying he left Max’s a little later than he did, like twelve-fifteen-ish, so the police would stop looking at him and actually concentrate on finding Andie. It wasn’t, um, it didn’t seem wrong to me at the time. I just thought he was trying to be sensible and help get Andie back quicker.”

“And did he tell you where he was between ten-thirty and twelve-fifty?”

“Um. I can’t remember. No, maybe he didn’t.”

“Didn’t you ask? Didn’t you want to know?”

"I can't really remember, Pip. Sorry." She sniffed.

"That's OK." Pip realized she'd leaned forward with her last question; she shuffled her notes and sat back again. "So the police called you on the Sunday, didn't they? And you told them that Sal left Max's at twelve-fifteen?"

"Yeah."

"So why did you four change your mind and decide to tell the police on Tuesday about Sal's fake alibi?"

"I . . . I think it's because we'd had some time to think about it, and we knew we could get in trouble for lying. None of us thought Sal was involved in what happened to Andie, so we didn't see the problem in telling police the truth."

"Had you discussed with the other three that that's what you were going to do?"

"Yeah, we called each other the night before—that Monday night—and agreed."

"But you didn't tell Sal that you were going to talk to the police?"

"Um," she said, her hands racing through her hair again. "No, we didn't want him to be upset with us."

"OK, last question." Pip watched as Naomi's face ironed out with evident relief. "Do you think Sal killed Andie that night?"

"Not the Sal I knew," she said. "He was the best, the nicest person. Always friendly and making people laugh. And he was so nice to Andie, too, even though she maybe didn't deserve it. So I don't know what happened or if he did it, but I don't want to believe he did."

"OK, done." Pip smiled, pressing the stop button on her phone. "Thanks so much for doing this, Naomi. I know it's not easy."

"That's OK." She nodded and stood up from the chair, the leather squeaking against her legs.

"Wait, one more thing," Pip said. "Are Max, Jake, and Millie around to be interviewed?"

"Oh, Millie's off the grid, traveling around Europe, and Jake's in Detroit now, living with his girlfriend—they just had a baby. Max is still here in Fairview; he just finished his master's and is back home applying for jobs, like me. I see him from time to time."

"Do you think he'd mind giving me a short interview?" Pip said.

"I'll give you his number and you can ask him." Naomi held the study door open for her.

In the kitchen they found Cara trying to fit two pieces of toast into her mouth simultaneously and a just-returned Mr. Ward, in an eyesore of a yellow shirt, wiping down the kitchen surfaces. He turned when he heard them come in, the ceiling lights picking up wisps of gray in his brown hair and flashing across his thick-rimmed glasses.

"You done, girls?" He smiled kindly. "Excellent timing. I just made some coffee."

PIPPA FITZ-AMOBI
8/10/19
CAPSTONE PROJECT LOG—ENTRY 7

Just got back from Max Hastings's house. It felt strange being there, like walking through some kind of crime-scene reconstruction; it looks just the same as it does in those Facebook photos they took on that fateful night five years ago. Max still looks the same too: tall, blond floppy hair, mouth slightly too wide for his angular face, somewhat pretentious. He said he remembered me, which was surprising.

After speaking to him . . . I don't know, I can't help but think something's going on. Either one of Sal's friends is misremembering that night, or one of them is lying. But why?

TRANSCRIPT OF INTERVIEW WITH MAX HASTINGS

PIP: All right, recording. So, Max, you're twenty-three, right?

MAX: Nope, almost twenty-five. I had leukemia when I was little and missed a lot of school, so got held back a year. I'm a miracle boy, didn't you know?

PIP: I had no idea. So, jumping right in, can you describe what Sal and Andie's relationship was like?

MAX: It was fine. I don't think it was like the romance of the century or anything. But it worked.

PIP: And how did their relationship start?

MAX: They just got drunk and hooked up at a party at Christmas. It carried on from there.

PIP: Was that a—what are they called—oh, a calamity party?

MAX: Oh shit, I forgot we used to call house parties "calamities." You know about those?

PIP: Yeah. People at school still throw them—tradition, apparently. Legend is that you started them.

MAX: Man, kids are still throwing messy house parties and calling them "calamities"? That's so cool. I feel like a god. Do they still do the next-host triathlon bit?

PIP: I don't know . . . I've never been. Anyway, did you know Andie before she started a relationship with Sal?

MAX: Yeah, a bit, from school and calamities. We sometimes spoke, yeah. But we weren't ever, like, friend friends. I didn't really know her. Like an acquaintance.

PIP: OK, so on Friday, April 18, when everyone was at your house, do you remember if Sal was acting strangely?

MAX: Not really. Maybe a little quiet.

PIP: Did you wonder why?

MAX: Nope, I was pretty drunk.

PIP: And that night, did Sal talk about Andie at all?

MAX: No, he didn't mention her once.

PIP: He didn't say they were having a disagreement at the time or—

MAX: No, he just didn't bring her up.

PIP: How well do you remember that night?

MAX: I remember all of it. Spent most of it playing Jake and Millie on *Call of Duty*. I remember 'cause Millie was going on about equality and stuff, and then she didn't win once.

PIP: This was after Sal left?

MAX: Yeah, he left really early.

PIP: Where was Naomi when you were playing video games?

MAX: MIA.

PIP: Missing? She wasn't there?

MAX: Um, no . . . She went upstairs for a while.

PIP: By herself? Doing what?

MAX: I don't know. Taking a nap. Taking a dump. Fuck knows.

PIP: For how long?

MAX: I don't remember.

PIP: OK, and when Sal left, what did he say?

MAX: He didn't, really. He just slipped out quietly. I didn't really notice him leave.

PIP: So, the next evening, after you'd all learned that Andie was missing, you went to see Sal?

MAX: Yeah, 'cause we figured he would be pretty bummed out.

PIP: And how did he ask you all to lie and give him an alibi?

MAX: He just came out and said it. Said it was looking bad for him and asked if we could help out and just change the times a bit. It wasn't a big deal. He didn't phrase it like: "Give me an alibi." That's not how it was. It was just a favor for a friend.

PIP: Do you think Sal killed Andie?

MAX: He had to have done it, right? I mean, if you're asking if I thought my friend was capable of murder, the answer would be no way. But then, you know, the blood and stuff. And the only way that Sal would ever kill himself, I think, is if he'd done something really bad. So it all fits.

PIP: OK, thanks, those are all my questions.

There are some inconsistencies between what Naomi and Max said. Naomi thinks that Sal did talk about Andie and told all his friends they were having a disagreement. Max says Sal didn't mention her once. Naomi says Sal told everyone he was heading home early because he wasn't "feeling it." Max says he slipped out quietly.

Of course, I am asking them to remember a night over five years ago. Certain lapses in memory are to be expected.

But then there's this thing Max said, that Naomi was MIA. Though he said he didn't remember how long Naomi was gone, he had just before indicated that he spent "most" of the night with Millie and Jake. Let's just say I can infer that she was "upstairs" for at least an hour. But why? Why would she be upstairs alone at Max's instead of with her friends? Did Max just accidentally let slip that Naomi left the house for a period of time that night?

I can't believe I'm actually going to type this, but maybe Naomi had something to do with Andie. I've known her eleven years. I've spent almost my whole life looking up to her as a big sister. Naomi's kind; the sort of person who'd give you an encouraging smile when you're midstory and everyone else has stopped listening. She's mild tempered; she's delicate, calm. But could she be unstable? Is it in her to be violent?

There's also what Ravi said, that he thought Naomi was in love with his brother. It's pretty clear from her answers, too, that she didn't particularly like Andie. And her interview . . . It was just so awkward, so tense. I know I was asking her to relive some bad memories, but the same goes for Max, and his interview was a breeze. Then again . . . was Max's interview *too* easy?

I don't know what to think, but I can't help picturing a scene: Naomi kills Andie in a jealous rage. Sal stumbles across the scene, confused and distraught. One of his best friends killed his girlfriend. But he still cares about Naomi, so he helps her dispose of Andie's body and they agree to never speak of it. But he can't hide from the terrible guilt of what he helped conceal. The only escape he can think of is death.

Or maybe I'm making something out of nothing.

Either way, I think she has to go on the list.

PERSONS OF INTEREST

Jason Bell

Naomi Ward

six

Pip took the scribbled shopping list out of her mom's hands. "It says 'bread,' not 'thread,' " she said. "Glasses?"

"No," her mom said, pulling a packaged loaf off the shelf. "They make me look old."

"That's OK, you are old," Pip said, for which she received a cold whack on the arm with a bag of frozen peas. As she dramatically feigned her demise from the fatal pea wound, she caught sight of him watching her. Laughing into the back of his hand.

"Ravi," she said, crossing the aisle over to him. "Hi."

"Hi." He smiled, scratching the back of his head, like she thought he might. He looked nice, dressed in a white T-shirt and jeans.

"I've never seen you in here before." "Here" was one of Fairview's only grocery stores, pocket-size and tucked in by the train station.

"Yeah, we usually shop out of town," he said. "But milk emergency." He held up a half gallon of 2 percent.

"Well, if only you had your coffee black."

"I'll never cross to the dark side," he said, looking up as Pip's mom came over with her full basket. He smiled at her.

"Oh, Mom, this is Ravi," Pip said. "Ravi, my mom, Leanne."

"Nice to meet you," Ravi said, hugging the milk to his chest and stretching out his right hand.

"You too," Pip's mom said, shaking his offered palm. "Actually, we've met before. I was the agent that sold your parents' house to them, gosh, must be fifteen years ago. I remember you were about five at the time and always wore a Pikachu onesie with a tutu."

Ravi's chuckled. "Can you believe that trend never caught on?"

"Yeah, well, Van Gogh's work was unappreciated in his own time as well," Pip said as they walked to the registers.

"Go ahead of us," Pip's mom said, gesturing to Ravi.

"Oh, really? Thanks."

Ravi strode up to the cashier and gave the woman working there a small smile. He placed the milk down. "Just that, please."

Pip watched the woman's face as it creased, folding with recognition and disgust. The woman scanned the milk, staring at Ravi with cold, noxious eyes. Fortunate, really, that looks couldn't actually kill. Ravi was looking down at his feet like he hadn't noticed, but Pip knew he had.

Something hot stirred in Pip's stomach. Something like nausea at first, but it kept swelling and boiling until it reached her ears.

"Two forty-eight," the lady spat.

Ravi pulled out a five-dollar bill, but when he tried to give her the money, she shuddered and withdrew her hand sharply. The note fell in a slow glide to the floor, and Pip ignited.

"Hey," she said loudly, marching over to stand beside Ravi. "Do you have a problem?"

"Pip, don't," Ravi said quietly.

"Excuse me, Leslie," Pip read out from the cashier's name tag, "I asked if you had a problem."

"Yeah," the woman said. "I don't want him touching me."

"Why, are you contagious or something?"

"I'm going to call my manager."

"Yeah, you do that. I'll deliver my complaint in person."

Ravi put the money on the counter, picked up his milk, and walked silently toward the exit.

"Ravi?" Pip called, but he ignored her.

"Whoa." Pip's mom stepped forward now, hands up in the surrender position as she came to stand between Pip and the reddening Leslie.

Pip turned on her heels, sneakers screaming against the overpolished floor.

Outside, she could see Ravi thirty feet away, pacing quickly down the hill. Pip, who didn't run for anything, ran to catch him.

"Are you OK?" she said, stepping in front of him.

"No." He carried on around her, the milk carton sloshing at his side.

"Did I do something wrong?"

Ravi turned, dark eyes flashing. He said, "Look, I don't need some kid I hardly know fighting my battles for me. I'm not your problem, Pippa; don't try to make me your problem. You're only going to make things worse."

He kept walking, and Pip watched him go until he passed out of sight. She felt the rage retreat back into her gut, where it slowly simmered out. She was hollow when it left her.

PIPPA FITZ-AMOBI
8/16/19
CAPSTONE PROJECT LOG—ENTRY 8

Let it never be said that Pippa Fitz-Amobi is not an opportunistic interviewer. I was at Cara's house again today with Lauren and the guys. Cara's dad, Elliot, was rambling on about something when I remembered: he knew Sal pretty well, not just as his daughter's friend, but as a teacher. I've already gotten character assessments from Sal's friends and brother, but I thought Cara's dad might have some further, adult insights. Mr. Ward agreed to it; I didn't give him much choice.

TRANSCRIPT OF INTERVIEW WITH ELLIOT WARD

PIP: OK, recording. So, for how many years had you known Sal?

MR. WARD: Um, let's see. I started teaching at Fairview High in 2011. I first taught Salil in his sophomore year for AP US History and then his senior year for AP Gov. so . . . almost three full years, I think. Yeah.

PIP: Did Sal take all APs for history?

MR. WARD: Oh, not only that. Sal was hoping to study history at Yale. I don't know if you remember, but before I started teaching at Fairview, I was a history professor there. I switched jobs so I could be around to take care of Cara and Naomi's mom when she got sick.

PIP: Oh yeah.

MR. WARD: So actually, in the fall semester of that year before everything happened, I spent a lot of time with Sal. I helped him with his essays and his application. When he got his interview for Yale, I helped him prepare for it. He was such a bright kid. Brilliant. He got accepted there too. I was so proud of him.

PIP: So Sal was really smart.

MR. WARD: Yeah, oh, absolutely. Very, very smart young man. It's such a tragedy what happened in the end. Such a waste of two young lives. Sal would have gone on to do great things.

PIP: Did you have a class with Sal on that Monday after Andie disappeared?

MR. WARD: Oh gosh. I think so, actually. Yes, because I remember talking to him after and asking if he was OK about everything. So yes, I must have.

PIP: And did you notice him acting strangely at all?

MR. WARD: Well, it depends on your definition of strange. The whole school was acting strangely that day; one of our students was missing and it was all over the news. I suppose I remember him seeming quiet. Worried.

PIP: Worried for Andie?

MR. WARD: Yes, possibly.

PIP: And what about on the Tuesday, the day he killed himself. Do you remember seeing him at school that morning at any point?

MR. WARD: I . . . No, I didn't because I had to call in sick that day. I had a bug, so I dropped the girls off in the morning and spent the day at home. I didn't know until the school called me in the afternoon about this whole Naomi/Sal alibi thing and that the police had interviewed Naomi and her friends at school. So the last time I saw Sal would have been that Monday during class.

PIP: And do you think Sal killed Andie?

MR. WARD: (sighs) I mean, I can understand how easy it is to convince yourself he didn't; he was such a lovely kid. But, considering the evidence, I don't see how he couldn't have done it. As wrong as it feels, I guess I think he must have. There's no other explanation.

PIP: And what about Andie? Did you teach her too?

MR. WARD: No, well . . . um, yes, she was in the same class as Sal sophomore year, so I had her then. But she didn't take anything with me after that, so I'm afraid I didn't really know her that well.

PIP: OK, thanks. You can go back to peeling potatoes now.

Ravi hadn't mentioned that Sal was going to Yale. There might be more he hasn't told me, but I'm not sure he'll ever speak to me again, not after what happened a couple of days ago.

If Sal was so smart and Yale-bound, then why was the evidence that linked him to Andie's murder so obvious? So what if he didn't have an alibi for the time of Andie's disappearance? He must've been clever enough to get away with it, I'm sure of it.

PS: We all played Monopoly with Naomi tonight, and . . . maybe I overreacted before. She's still on the persons of interest list, but a murderer? There's no way; she's just too nice. Even I have more of a killer instinct than Naomi.

seven

The next day Pip was doing one final read-through of her information request to the Connecticut State Police. Her room was sweltering even with the window open, the sun trapped and sulking in there with her.

She heard distant knocking downstairs as she pressed send on the email. The click that began a wait of at least *twenty working days*. She hated waiting.

"Pips" came her dad's shout from downstairs. "Someone's here for you."

Pip rushed down the stairs, taking the turn as a sock-skid across the oak. She stopped in her tracks when she saw Ravi Singh outside the front door. He was being talked at enthusiastically by her dad. Heat rushed to her face.

"Um, hi," Pip said, walking toward them. Barney barged past with a tapping of claws and got there first, launching his muzzle into Ravi's groin.

"No, Barney, down!" Pip shouted, rushing forward. "Sorry, he's a bit friendly."

"That's no way to talk about your father," her dad said.

Pip raised her eyebrows at him.

"Got it, got it," he said, walking away and into the kitchen.

Ravi bent down to pet Barney, whose tail whipped up a breeze around Pip's ankles.

"How do you know where I live?" Pip asked.

"I asked at the real estate office your mom works at," he said, straightening. Pip noticed him looking down at her, and though his lips twitched trying to contain it, he broke into a smile. That's when she remembered what she was wearing: denim overalls and a white T-shirt with the words TALK NERDY TO ME emblazoned across the chest.

"So, um, what brings you here?" she said. Her stomach lurched, and only then did she realize she was nervous.

"I . . . I'm here because . . . I wanted to say sorry." He looked at her with his big downturned eyes, his brows bunching over them. "I got angry and said some things I shouldn't have. I don't really think you're just some kid. Sorry."

"It's OK," Pip said. "I'm sorry too. I didn't mean to step in and fight your battles for you. I just wanted to help, wanted her to know what she did wasn't OK. But sometimes my mouth starts saying words without checking with my brain first."

"I kind of liked feisty Pip."

"Oh, really? Well, you should see me at a pop quiz. So . . . are we OK?"

"We're OK." He smiled and looked down at the dog again. "Me and your human are OK."

"We were actually just about to head out on a walk; do you want to come with?"

"Yeah, sure," he said, ruffling Barney's ears. "How could I say no to that handsome face?"

Pip almost said, *Oh please, you'll make me blush,* but she bit it back.

"OK, I'll just grab my shoes. Barney, stay."

Pip scooted into the kitchen. The back door was open, and she could see her parents pottering around the flowers, and Josh, of course, playing with his soccer ball.

"I'm taking Barns, see you in a bit," she called outside, and her mom waved a gardening-gloved hand in acknowledgment.

Pip slipped on her not-allowed-to-be-left-in-the-kitchen sneakers, which she'd left in the kitchen, and grabbed the leash.

"Right, let's go," she said, clipping the leash to Barney's collar and shutting the front door behind them.

At the end of the driveway, they crossed the road and headed into the stippled shade of the woods opposite. Pip let Barney off, and he was gone in a golden flash.

"I always wanted a dog." Ravi grinned as Barney circled back to hurry them on. He paused, his jaw moving as he chewed on some silent thought. "Sal was allergic, though, that's why we never . . ."

"Oh." Pip wasn't quite sure what else to say.

"There's this dog at the café I work at, the owner's dog. A slobbery Great Dane called Peanut. I sometimes *accidentally* drop leftovers for her. Don't tell."

"I encourage accidental droppage," she said. "What café do you work at?"

"The Whaler, over in Stamford. It's not what I want to do forever. Especially since I have to take the train. Just saving up so I can get myself as far away from Fairview as I can."

Pip felt an unutterable sadness for him rising up her throat.

"What do you want to do forever?"

He shrugged. "I used to want to be a lawyer."

"That's what my dad does. I think you could be great at that," she said, nudging him.

"Hmm, not when the only grades I got spell 'DUUUDDEE.' "

He'd said it like a joke, but she knew it wasn't. They both knew how awful school had been for Ravi after Andie and Sal died. Pip had heard about the worst of the bullying. His locker painted in red dripping letters: "Like Brother, Like Brother." And that snowy morning when eight older boys had pinned him down and upturned four full trash cans over his head.

That was when, with the clarity of cold slush pooling in her stomach, Pip realized where they were.

"Oh my god," she gasped, covering her face with her hands. "I'm so sorry, I didn't even think. I completely forgot these are the woods where they found Sal—"

"That's OK." He cut her off. "Really. You can't help that these happen to be the woods outside your house. Plus, there's nowhere in Fairview that doesn't remind me of him."

Barney dropped a stick at Ravi's feet, and Ravi raised his arm in mock-throws, sending the dog backward and forward and back, until he finally let go.

They didn't speak for a while. But the silence wasn't uncomfortable; it was charged with the thoughts they were working on alone. And, as it turned out, both their minds had wandered to the same place.

"You really don't think Sal did it, do you?" Ravi asked.

"I just can't believe it." She stepped over an old fallen tree. "My brain hasn't been able to leave it alone. So when this project thing came up for school, I jumped at the excuse to reexamine the case."

"It is the perfect excuse to hide behind," he said, nodding. "I didn't have anything like that."

"What do you mean?" She turned to him, fiddling with the leash that she'd draped around her neck.

"I tried to do what you're doing, three years ago. My parents told me to leave it alone, that I was only going to make things harder for myself, but I just couldn't accept it."

"You tried to investigate?"

"Yes, Sergeant, but I didn't get anywhere," he said, watching his feet. "I couldn't. I called Naomi Ward at college, but she just cried and said she couldn't talk about it with me. Max Hastings and Jake Lawrence never replied to my messages. I tried contacting Andie's best friends, but they hung up as soon as I said who I was. 'Murderer's brother' isn't the best intro. And of course, Andie's family was out of the question. I was too close to the case, I knew. Looked too much like my brother. And I didn't have the excuse of a school project to fall back on."

"I'm sorry," Pip said, embarrassed by the unfairness of it.

"Don't be." He nudged her. "It's good to not be alone in this, for once. Go on, I want to hear your theories." He picked up Barney's stick, now foamy with dribble, and threw it into the trees.

Pip hesitated.

"Go on." He smiled up into his eyes, one eyebrow cocked. Was he testing her?

"OK, I have four working theories," she said, the first time she'd actually given voice to them. "Obviously, the path of least resistance is the accepted story of what happened: Sal killed her, and his guilt or fear of being caught led him to take his own life. But my first theory," she said, holding up one finger, "is that a third party killed Andie, but Sal was somehow involved, like an accessory after the fact, helped bury the body. His guilt leads him to suicide, and the evidence found on him implicates him as the perpetrator, even though he isn't the one who killed her. The actual killer is still at large."

"Yeah, I thought of that too. I still don't like it. Next?"

"Theory number two," she said, "a third party killed Andie, and Sal had no involvement or awareness at all. His suicide days later wasn't motivated by a murderer's guilt, but maybe by a multitude of factors, including the stress of his girlfriend's disappearance. The evidence found on him—the blood and the phone—have an entirely innocent explanation and are unrelated to her murder."

Ravi nodded thoughtfully. "I still don't think Sal would do that. Theory three?"

"Theory three." Pip swallowed, her throat dry. "Andie is murdered by a third party on the Friday. The killer knows that Sal, as Andie's boyfriend, would make the perfect suspect. Especially as Sal seems to have no alibi for over two hours that night. The killer murders Sal and makes it look like a suicide. They plant the blood and the phone on his body to make him look guilty. It works just as they planned it."

Ravi stopped walking for a moment. "You think it's possible that Sal was actually murdered?"

She knew, looking into his sharpened eyes, that this was the answer he'd been looking for.

"I think it's a theoretical possibility." Pip nodded. "Theory four is the most far-fetched of the lot." She took a deep breath and did it in one. "No one killed Andie Bell, because she isn't dead. She faked her disappearance and then lured Sal out into the woods, murdered him, and dressed it up as a suicide. She planted her own phone and blood on him so that everyone believed she was dead. Maybe she needed to disappear for some reason. Maybe she feared for her life and needed to make it look like she was already dead. Maybe she had an accomplice."

They were quiet again, while Pip caught her breath and Ravi considered her answers, his upper lip puffed out in concentration.

They had come to the end of their circuit round the woods; the sunny road was visible through the trees ahead. Pip called Barney over and put him on the leash. They crossed the road and walked to her front door.

There was an awkward moment of silence, and Pip didn't know whether or not to invite him inside. He seemed to be waiting for something.

"So," Ravi said, scratching his head with one hand, the dog's with the other, "the reason I came over is . . . I want to make a deal with you."

"A deal?"

"Yeah, I want in on this," he said, a slight tremor in his voice. "I never had a chance, but you actually might. You're an outsider to the case, you have this school project excuse to open doors. People might actually talk to you. You might be my chance to find out what really happened. I've waited so long for a chance."

Her face felt hot again; the shaking edge in his voice made something tug inside her chest.

"I can agree to that." She smiled, holding out her hand.

"Deal," he said, taking it, though he forgot to shake it. "Which means, I've got something for you." He reached into his back pocket and pulled out an old iPhone cradled in his palm.

"Um, I've actually already got one, thanks," Pip said.

"It's Sal's phone."

eight

"Wait, what?" Pip stared at him, openmouthed. "That's Sal's? How do you have it?"

"The police released it to us a few months after they closed Andie's investigation."

A cautious electricity sparked up the back of Pip's neck. "Can I . . . ," she said, "can I look at it?"

"Of course," he laughed. "That's why I brought it."

Excitement charged through her.

"Holy moly," she said, flustered and hurrying to unlock the door. "Let's go and look at it in my workstation—uh, bedroom."

She and Barney bolted over the threshold, but Ravi didn't follow. She spun back around.

"What's wrong?" she said. "Come on."

"Sorry, you're just very entertaining when you're this intense."

"Come on," she repeated, beckoning him through the hallway and to the stairs. "Don't drop it."

"I'm not going to drop it."

Pip jogged up to her room, Ravi following far too slowly behind. She did a hasty scan of her bedroom for potential embarrassments. Cursing, she dived for a pile of just-laundered bras by her chair, shoving them into a drawer and slamming it shut just as

Ravi walked in. She pointed him into her desk chair, too flustered to sit herself.

"Here you go, then. I charged it last night." He placed the phone into her cupped palms. "Passcode is four fours. He used that for everything."

"Have you ever looked through it?" she asked, sliding to unlock it more carefully than she'd ever unlocked her own phone, even at its newest.

"Yeah, obsessively. But go ahead, Sergeant. Where would *you* look first?"

"Call log," she said, tapping the green phone icon.

She looked through the missed call list first. There were dozens from the April 22, the Tuesday he had died. Calls from "Dad," "Mom," "Ravi," "Naomi," "Jake," and unsaved numbers that must have been the police trying to locate him.

Pip scrolled back further, to the date of Andie's disappearance. Sal had two missed calls that day. One was from "Max-y Boy" at 7:19 p.m., probably to ask when he was coming over. The other one, she read with a skipped heartbeat, was from "Andie<3" at 8:54 p.m.

"Andie rang him that night," Pip said to herself and Ravi. "Just before nine."

Ravi nodded. "Sal didn't pick up, though."

"Pippa!" Her dad's voice sailed up the stairs. "No boys in bedrooms."

Pip's cheeks flooded with heat. She turned so Ravi couldn't see and yelled back, "We're working on my project! My door is open."

"OK, that will do!" came the reply.

She glanced back at Ravi and saw he was chuckling at her again.

"Stop finding my life amusing," she said, looking back at the phone.

She went through Sal's outgoing calls next. Andie's name repeated over and over again. It was broken up in places with the odd call to "home," or "Dad," and one to "Naomi" on Saturday, but from 10:33 a.m. on the Saturday until 7:21 a.m. on the Tuesday, Sal called her 112 times. Each call lasted two or three seconds; straight to voicemail.

"He called her over a hundred times," Ravi said, reading her face.

"Why would he call so many times if he'd supposedly killed her and had her phone hidden somewhere?" said Pip.

"I asked the police that very question years ago," Ravi said. "The officer told me it was clear that Sal was making a conscious effort to look innocent by calling the victim's phone so many times."

"But," Pip countered, "if they thought he was making an effort to act innocent and avoid getting caught, why didn't he get rid of Andie's phone? He could have put it in the same place as her body, and it never would have connected him to her death. If he was trying not to get caught, why would he keep the one biggest bit of evidence? And then feel desperate enough to end his life with this vital evidence still on him?"

Ravi snapped and pointed at her. "The officer couldn't answer that either."

"Did you look at the last texts Andie and Sal sent each other?" she asked.

"Yeah, take a look. Don't worry, they aren't sexty or anything."

Pip opened up the messages app and clicked on Andie's name, feeling like a trespasser.

Sal had sent two texts to Andie after she disappeared. The first on the Sunday morning: *andie just come home everyones worried.* And on Monday afternoon: *please just ring someone so we know youre safe.*

The message preceding them was sent on the Friday she went missing. At 9:01 p.m., Sal texted her: *im not talking to you till youve stopped.*

Pip showed Ravi. "He said that just after ignoring her call that night. Do you know what they could have been fighting about? What did Sal want Andie to stop?"

"No idea."

"Can I just type this up really fast?" she said, reaching over him for her laptop. She parked herself on her bed and transcribed the texts, grammar mistakes and all.

"Now you need to look at the last text he sent my dad," Ravi said. "The one they said is his confession."

Pip moved over to the conversation. At 10:17 a.m., on his final Tuesday morning, Sal said to his father: *it was me. i did it. i'm so sorry.* Pip's eyes ran over it several times, at the pixels of each letter, thinking.

"You see it, too, don't you?" Ravi was watching her.

"The grammar?" Pip asked, looking for the agreement in Ravi's eyes.

"Sal was the cleverest person I knew," he said, "but he texted like an illiterate. Always in a rush—no punctuation, no capital letters."

"He must have had autocorrect turned off," Pip said. "And yet, in this last text, we have three periods and an apostrophe. Even though it's all in lowercase."

"And what does that make you think?" asked Ravi.

"That maybe someone else wrote that text," she said. "Someone who added the punctuation themselves because that's how they were used to writing in texts. Maybe they checked quickly and thought it looked enough like Sal's other messages because it was all lowercase."

"That's what I thought, too, when we first got it back. The police just sent me away. My parents didn't want to hear it either." He sighed. "I think they're terrified of false hope. I am, too, if I'm being honest."

Pip scoured the rest of the phone. Sal hadn't taken any photos on the night in question, and none since Andie disappeared. She checked the deleted folder to be sure. The reminders were all about essays he had to hand in, and one to buy his mom a birthday present.

"There's something interesting in the notes," Ravi said, rolling over on the chair and opening the app for her.

The notes were all old: Sal's home Wi-Fi password, an abs workout, a page of internships he could apply to. But there was one later note, written on Wednesday, April 16, 2014. Pip tapped into it. There was one thing typed on the page: *009 KKJ*.

"License plate number, right?" Ravi said.

"Looks like it. He wrote that down in his notes two days before Andie went missing. Do you recognize it?"

Ravi shook his head. "I tried to Google it, see if I could find the owner, but no luck."

Pip typed it up in her log anyway, and the exact time the note was last edited.

"That's everything," Ravi said. "That's all I could find."

Pip gave the phone one last wistful look before handing it back.

"You seem disappointed," he said.

"I just hoped there'd be something more substantial we could use. Inconsistent grammar and lots of phone calls to Andie sure make him look innocent, but they don't actually open any leads to pursue."

"Not yet," he said, "but I wanted you to see it. Have you gotten anywhere with your interviews?"

Pip paused. Yes, she had, but part of that was Naomi's possible involvement. Her protective instinct flared up, grabbing hold of her tongue. But she knew if they were going to be partners, they had to be all in. She opened her capstone project document, scrolled to the top, and handed the laptop to Ravi. "This is everything so far."

He read through it all quietly and then handed the computer back, a thoughtful look on his face.

"OK, so the Sal alibi route is a dead end," he said. "After he left Max's at ten-thirty, I think he was alone because it explains why he panicked and asked his friends to lie for him. He could have just stopped on a bench on his walk home and played *Angry Birds* or something."

"I agree," said Pip. "He was most likely alone, and therefore has no alibi; it's the only thing that makes sense. So that line of inquiry is lost. I think the next step should be to find out as much as we can about Andie's life and, in the process, identify anyone who might have had motive to kill her."

"Read my mind, Sarge," he said. "Maybe you should start with Andie's best friends, Emma Hutton and Chloe Burch. They might actually speak to you."

"I've messaged them both. Haven't heard back yet, though."

"OK, good," he said, nodding to himself and then to the laptop. "In that interview with the journalist, you talked about gaps in the case. What inconsistencies do you see?"

"Well, if you'd killed someone," she said, "you'd scrub yourself down multiple times, fingernails included, right? Especially if you were lying about alibis and making fake calls to look innocent, wouldn't you think to wash the frickin' blood off your hands so you don't get caught red-handed, literally?"

"Yeah, Sal definitely wasn't that stupid."

"And of course his fingerprints would be found in her car; he was her boyfriend," said Pip. "Fingerprints can't be accurately dated."

"And hiding the body?" Ravi leaned forward. "I've always thought that was a stretch. If she's buried in the woods somewhere, how did Sal have time to dig a hole well enough that she's never been found? OK, so he had time, but was it enough for that?"

"Or any other way of disposing of a body," Pip added.

"And yet this is the path of least resistance, the story everyone believes."

"It is, supposedly," she said. "Until you start asking the right questions."

nine

They probably thought she couldn't hear them. Her parents, bickering in the living room downstairs.

Pip listened through the crack of her bedroom door: Mom wasn't happy that Pip was spending so much time on schoolwork instead of enjoying summer break. She thought that obsessing over Andie Bell was unhealthy, and they should discourage it. Then Dad wasn't happy that Mom wouldn't give Pip the space to make her own mistakes, if that's what they were.

Pip closed her bedroom door; she knew their argument would burn out soon, and she couldn't dwell on it. She had an important phone call to make.

She had messaged both of Andie's best friends last week. Emma Hutton had finally replied a few hours earlier with a phone number, saying she didn't mind answering "just a few" questions in a recorded interview around eight o'clock. When Pip told Ravi this, he'd texted back with a whole page of shocked-face and fist-bump emojis.

She glanced at the clock on her computer task bar. It stood stubbornly at 7:58 p.m.

Pip's knee bounced impatiently against her desk as she waited another whole minute. Then she started her recording app and dialed Emma's number, her skin prickling with nerves. It picked up on the third ring.

"Hello?" said a high voice.

"Hi, Emma, this is Pippa."

"Oh yeah, hi. Hold on, let me just go up to my room."

Pip listened to the sound of Emma's feet skipping up a flight of stairs.

"OK," she said. "You said you're doing a project about Andie?"

"Sort of, yeah. About the investigation into her disappearance and the media's role in it. A kind of case study."

"OK," Emma said, sounding uncertain. "I'm not sure how much help I can be."

"Don't worry, I just have a few basic questions about the investigation as you remember it," Pip said. "When did you find out she was missing?"

"Um . . . it was around one o'clock that night. Her parents called both me and Chloe Burch; we were Andie's best friends. I said how I hadn't seen her or heard from her and told them I would call around a bit. I tried Sal that night, but he didn't pick up until the next morning."

"Did the police contact you at all?" asked Pip.

"Yeah, Saturday morning. They came by to ask questions."

"And what did you tell them?"

"Just the same as I said to Andie's parents. That I had no idea where she was; she hadn't told me she was going anywhere. And they were asking about Andie's boyfriend, so I told them about Sal and that I'd just called to tell him she was missing."

"What did you tell them about Sal?"

"Well, only that at school that week, they were kind of fighting. I definitely saw them arguing on that Thursday and Friday, which was out of the ordinary. He seemed super mad about something."

"What about?" Pip asked. It was suddenly clearer to her why the police might have wanted to interview Sal that afternoon.

"I don't know, honestly. When I asked Andie she just said that Sal was being 'a little bitch' about something."

"Oh," she said, taken aback. "So Andie didn't have plans to see Sal on the Friday?"

"No, she didn't have plans to do anything, actually; she was supposed to stay at home that night."

"How come?" Pip sat up a little straighter.

"Um, I don't know if I should say."

"Don't worry"—Pip tried to hide the desperation in her voice—"if it's not relevant, it won't go in my project. It just might help me better understand the circumstances of her disappearance."

"OK. Well, Andie's little sister, Becca, had been hospitalized for self-harming several weeks before. Her parents had to go out, so they told Andie she had to stay in and take care of Becca."

"Oh" was all Pip could think to say.

"Yeah, I know, that poor girl. And still Andie left her alone that night. Only looking back now can I understand how difficult it must have been having Andie as an older sister."

"What do you mean by that?"

"It's just . . . I don't want to speak ill of the dead, you know, but . . . I've had five years to grow up and reflect on everything, and when I think back to those times, I don't like the person I was at all. The person I was with Andie."

"Was she a bad friend to you?" Pip didn't want to say too much; she needed to keep Emma talking.

"Yes and no. It's really difficult to explain." Emma sighed. "Andie's friendship was very destructive, but at the time, I was addicted to her. I wanted to be her. You're not going to write any of this, are you?"

"No, of course not." Small lie.

"OK. So Andie was beautiful; she was popular; she was fun. Being her friend, being someone she chose to spend her time with . . . it made you feel special. Wanted. And then she would flip and use the things you were most self-conscious about to cut you down and hurt you. And still we both remained by her side, waiting for the next time she would pick us up and make us feel good again. She could be amazing and awful, and you never knew which side of Andie was turning up at your door. I'm surprised my self-esteem even survived."

"Was Andie like that with everyone?"

"Well, yeah, with me and Chloe, anyway. Andie wouldn't let us go over to her house much, but I saw the way she was with Becca too. She could be so cruel." Emma paused. "I'm not saying any of this because I mean that Andie deserved what she got. No, no, that's not what I mean at all; no one deserves to be murdered and put in a hole. I only mean that, appreciating now the kind of person Andie was, I can understand why Sal snapped and killed her. She could make you feel so high and then so low; it was bound to end in tragedy, I think."

Emma's voice shuddered, slipped into a wet sniff, and Pip knew the interview was over.

"OK, I won't keep you; those were all my questions. Thank you so much for your help."

"Sorry," Emma said. "I thought I was over everything. Guess not."

"No, I'm sorry for making you go over it all. Um, actually, I messaged Chloe Burch for an interview, too, but she hasn't got back to me yet. Do you two still talk?"

"No, not really. Like, I'll text on her birthday, but . . . we definitely drifted apart after Andie and then leaving school. I think we both wanted it that way, really: a clean break from the people we were back then."

Pip thanked her again, hung up, and stopped recording. She exhaled and just stared at her phone for a minute. She knew that Andie had been pretty and popular; social media had made that perfectly clear. And she knew that people like that sometimes had their hard edges. But she hadn't expected this. That Emma could still resent herself, after all this time, for loving her tormentor.

Was this the real Andie Bell, hidden behind that perfect smile, behind those sparkling pale blue eyes? Everyone in her orbit so dazzled by her, so blinded, that they hadn't noticed a darkness that might've lurked beneath—not until it was too late.

PIPPA FITZ-AMOBI
8/23/19
CAPSTONE PROJECT LOG—ENTRY 11

Update: I tried to look up the owner of the car with the license plate number 009 KKJ. Ravi was right, you can't look up owner information through the DMV. I guess that particular lead is dead.

So back to the task at hand; I just got off the phone with Chloe.

TRANSCRIPT OF INTERVIEW WITH CHLOE BURCH

[I'm sparing myself from typing the interview intros from here on out; they're all the same and I always sound awkward.]

PIP: My first question is how would you describe Andie and Sal's relationship?

CHLOE: Yeah, good; he was nice to her and she thought he was hot. Sal always seemed calm and chill; I thought he would mellow Andie out a bit.

PIP: Why would Andie have needed mellowing out?

CHLOE: Oh, just because she always had some drama going on.

PIP: And did Sal mellow her?

CHLOE: (laughs) No.

PIP: But they were serious?

CHLOE: I guess so. Define "serious"?

PIP: Well, I . . . Were they sleeping together?

CHLOE: Wow, school projects have changed since I left. Why on earth would you need to know that?

PIP: Did she not tell you?

CHLOE: Of course she told me. And no, they weren't, actually.

PIP: Oh. Was Andie a virgin?

CHLOE: No, she wasn't.

PIP: But she and Sal were exclusive, right?

CHLOE: (small pause) Um, y-yeah, obviously.

PIP: So who had she—

CHLOE: Look, Andie liked her secrets, OK? They made her powerful. She got a thrill out of me and Emma not knowing certain things. But she'd dangle them in front of us because she liked us to ask.

PIP: Like?

CHLOE: Like . . . like where she got all her money from; she would just laugh and wink when we asked.

PIP: Money?

CHLOE: Yeah. That girl was always shopping, always had a load of cash on her. And in our final year, she told me she was saving up to get lip fillers and a nose job. She never told Emma that, just me. But she was generous with her money, too; she'd buy us makeup and stuff and always let us borrow her clothes. Then she'd pick her moment at a party to say something like: "Oh, Chlo, looks like you've stretched that. I'll have to give it to Becca now." Sweet girl.

PIP: Where did her money come from? Did she have a part-time job?

CHLOE: No. I told you, I didn't know. I just assumed her dad was giving it to her.

PIP: Like an allowance?

CHLOE: Yeah, maybe.

PIP: So, when Andie first went missing, was there any part of you that thought she had run away to punish someone? Maybe her father?

CHLOE: Andie had things too good to want to run away.

PIP: But was there tension in Andie's relationship with her dad?

CHLOE: [her tone changes] I don't see how that can be relevant to your project. Look, I know I've been flippant about her—and yeah, she had her flaws—but she was still my best friend who got murdered. I don't think it's right to be talking about her personal relationships and her family, however many years later.

PIP: No, you're right; sorry. I just thought if I knew what Andie was like and what was happening in her life, I could better understand the case.

CHLOE: Yeah, OK, but none of that is relevant. Sal Singh killed her. And you're not going to get to know Andie from a few interviews. It was impossible to know her, even when you were her best friend.

[I apologize and try to bring us back on topic, but Chloe is done. I thank her for her help before she hangs up.]

Well, that ended abruptly. I guess even though Emma and Chloe both think they've moved on, they still haven't quite broken free of Andie's hold. Maybe they're even still keeping some of her secrets; I certainly struck a nerve when I brought up Andie's dad.

And a clue to another possible secret: Chloe's reaction when I asked if Sal and Andie were exclusive. I assumed she'd answer that yes, of course they were. And she did, but she paused first. She stumbled. And then started talking about Andie and her secrets. Is there something there? Is it possible that Andie was secretly seeing someone else behind Sal's back? Did Sal find out and that's why they were arguing? Does this explain Sal's last text to Andie before she disappeared: *im not talking to you till youve stopped.*

I'm not a police officer and this is just a project; I can't make Emma or Chloe tell me anything. And these are the kinds of secrets you only share with your best friends, not some random girl doing her capstone project.

Oh my god. I've just had a horrible but maybe brilliant idea. Horrible and probably stupid. And definitely, definitely wrong. And even so, I think I have to do it.

I'm going to catfish Emma, pretending to be Chloe.

I have that pay-as-you-go SIM card I used on vacation last year. If I put that in my phone, I can text Emma, pretending to be Chloe with a new number. It might work; Emma said they lost contact, so she might not realize. And it might not work. But I have nothing to lose, and maybe secrets to uncover and a killer to find.

Hey Em, it's Chloe, I got a new number recently. So this kid from FV just called me asking questions about Andie for a project. Did she call you too? xx

Omg hi 👋

Yeah she did a couple days ago. It made me get a bit emotional about everything again tbh x

Yeah well Andie had that effect. You didn't tell her anything about Andie's love life, did you?

I'm guessing you mean the secret older guy, not Sal?

Yeah

No I didn't tell her

Yeah, me neither. I always wondered if Andie had told you who it was though?

Nah, you know she didn't. Only thing she said was that she could ruin him if she wanted to, right?

Yeah she liked her secrets.

I'm not even sure he existed tbh. She might have just made it up to seem more mysterious.

Yeah maybe. This girl was asking about Andie's dad as well, do you think she knows?

Maybe. It's not hard to work it out now, he married the whore like right after the divorce.

Yeah, but does she know that Andie knew at the time?

Don't see how she could, we were the only ones that knew. And Andie's dad obviously. Anyway, why does it matter if she knows?

Yeah you're right. I guess I still feel protective of Andie's secrets, you know?

I think it'd be good for you to try to let go more. I def feel better for distancing myself from everything Andie related.

Yeah I'll try. Hey I've gotta go, I've got work early. But we really should catch up soon?

Yeah would love to! Let me know if you're ever in the city. 👍

Will do. Byee xx

Holy moly.

I have never sweated so much in my whole damn life. I almost lost it a couple of times, but I actually pulled it off.

I feel bad, though; Emma is so nice and trusting. But hey, at least that means I haven't quite lost my moral compass.

And just like that, we have two more leads.

Jason Bell was already on the persons of interest list, but now he goes on in *bold* as suspect number one. He was having an affair, and Andie knew about it. More than that, Jason knew that Andie knew. She must have approached him about it, or maybe she's the one who caught him. That explains why their relationship was strained. And all this mysterious money Andie had . . . was it given to her by her dad *because* she knew? Could she have been blackmailing him? No, I shouldn't jump to conclusions.

And the biggest reveal of the night: Andie was secretly seeing an older man during her relationship with Sal. So secret that she never told her friends who he was, only that she could ruin him. My mind goes immediately to that place: a married man. Could *he* have been the source of the secret money? I have a new suspect. One who would certainly have had motive to silence Andie for good.

This is not the Andie I expected to find in my investigation, so far removed from that public image of a beautiful blond victim loved by her family, adored by her friends. A victim taken too soon by her "cruel, murderous" boyfriend. But now that I'm scratching, that image is starting to peel away at the edges.

I need to call Ravi.

PERSONS OF INTEREST

Jason Bell

Naomi Ward

Secret Older Guy (how much older?)

ten

"I hate camping," Lauren grunted, tripping over the crumpled canvas.

"Yeah, well, it's my birthday and I like it," Cara said, reading over the instructions with her tongue tucked between her teeth.

It was the final Friday of summer, and the three of them were in a small clearing in a beech forest on the outskirts of Fairview. Cara's choice for her early eighteenth birthday celebration: to sleep without a roof and squat-pee behind dark trees all night. It wouldn't have been Pip's choice, either, but she knew how to pretend well enough.

"It's technically illegal to camp outside of a registered campsite," Lauren said, kicking the canvas in retaliation.

"Well, let's hope the camping police don't check Instagram, because I've announced it to the world. Now hush," Cara said, "I'm trying to read."

"Um, Cara," Pip said tentatively, "you know this isn't a tent you brought, right? It's a canopy with sides."

"Same difference," she said. "And we have to fit us and the three boys in."

"But it comes with no floor." Pip jabbed her finger at the picture on the instructions.

"*You* come with no floor." Cara butt-shoved her away. "And my dad packed us a separate groundsheet."

"When are the boys getting here?" Lauren asked.

"They texted about two minutes ago they were leaving. And no," Cara snapped, "we're not waiting for them to put it up for us, Lauren."

"I wasn't suggesting that."

Cara cracked her knuckles. "Dismantling the patriarchy, one tent at a time."

"Canopy," Pip corrected her.

"Do you want me to hurt you?"

"Ca-*nope*-y."

Ten minutes later, a full ten-by-twenty-foot white pop-up canopy stood on the forest floor, looking as out of place as anything could. Pip checked her phone. It was seven-thirty already; darkness would be upon them in another hour or so.

"This is going to be so fun." Cara stood back to admire their handiwork, wiping her hands on her jeans. "I love camping. Time for vodka and peach rings until I puke."

"Admirable goal," Pip said. "Do you two want to grab the rest of the food from the car? I'll lay out our sleeping bags and put up the sides."

Cara's car was in the tiny concrete parking lot about two hundred yards from their chosen spot. Lauren and Cara headed off that way through the trees, the woods lit with the final glow of sunset.

"Don't forget the flashlights," Pip called, just as she lost sight of them.

She attached the canvas sides to the canopy, swearing as the Velcro gave out and she had to start from scratch. Wrestling with the groundsheet, she was relieved to hear the tread of Cara and Lauren returning. But when she went to look outside for them, no one was there. Just a bird, mocking her from the darkening treetops with its scratchy laugh.

Pip got back to work, laying the three sleeping bags in a row, trying not to think about the fact that Andie Bell could very well be buried somewhere in these woods, maybe even beneath her right now.

As Pip made the final preparations, the sound of branches breaking underfoot grew louder, and she heard the guffawing that could only mean the boys had arrived. She waved them and the girls over. Ant Lowe, who—as his name suggested—hadn't grown much since they were twelve, although he had bulked out after a summer of playing soccer, his light brown hair gelled away from his forehead. Zach Chen, who'd lived four doors down from the Amobis since Pip was in preschool, his glittering smile stretching across his face, and of course, wearing his favorite green hoodie. And Connor Reynolds, who Pip and Cara had met in middle school, gangly and ever eager to be the class clown. His shaggy blond hair had fallen into his eyes, and his hands were full, carrying a cooler with Zach, so he inadvertently walked into a low-hanging branch.

"You OK?" Lauren laughed.

"Fine," he grunted. "My mom's always telling me to branch out."

"God, your puns get worse every time," Cara said. "How are you ever going to get a girlfriend?"

"Well, how are *you* ever going to get a girlfriend?" he retorted.

"With my hot bod and twinkling personality, obv," she said, donning a silly high voice and flicking her hair.

"Ah, Pip," Ant chimed in, dropping two bags of snacks, "so kind of you to step away from your homework for one second to grace us with your presence."

“Ha,” she said flatly. Shockingly, not the first time she’d heard that joke. “I’m already getting withdrawal.”

“Right.” Lauren clapped her hands. “Ant, can you help me unpack these bags?”

Of course he would; he jumped to it right away. Pip knew that Lauren and Ant had had a failed fling last year that amounted to just four kisses and some drunken fumbling. Lauren swore never again, and she said Ant felt the same way, but Pip could tell he was lying from the way he was always looking at her.

“Shall we open the beer?” asked Zach.

A silver-tinted darkness had taken over the woods, the enclosure glowing like a lantern among the sleeping trees. They were sitting in a circle around the snacks and drinks, the sides of the canopy rolled up for a cross breeze, two battery-powered lamps and three flashlights between them. Lucky they had moved to sit inside, Pip noted as it started to rain.

She didn’t like drinking, didn’t like experiencing that loss of control, though the others always said she was being too sensible. She was much more interested in the chips and sour cream dip, although she had allowed herself to get to the bottom of one beer, sitting with her navy star-patterned sleeping bag up to her waist.

Ant was halfway through his ghost story, the flashlight under his chin making the geography of his face distorted and grotesque. It just happened to be a story about six friends, three boys and three girls, who were camping in a canopy in the woods.

“And the birthday girl,” he said theatrically, “is finishing off a whole bag of peach rings and drinking some nasty red concoction that looks like blood.”

“Shut up,” Cara said, mouth full.

“She tells the handsome guy with the flashlight to shut up. And that's when they hear it: a scraping sound against the side of the canopy. There's something or someone outside. Slowly, fingernails start dragging through the side, ripping a hole in the canvas. 'You guys having a party?' a girl's voice asks. And then she tears through the hole and, with one swipe of her hand, slits the throat of the guy in the green hoodie. 'Miss me?' she shrieks, and the surviving friends can finally see who it is: the rotting zombie corpse of Andie Bell, out for revenge—"

"Shut up, Ant." Pip shoved him. "That isn't funny."

"Why's everyone laughing, then?"

"A murdered girl isn't fair game for your crappy jokes."

"But she's fair game for a school project?" Zach interjected.

"That's different."

"I was just about to get to the part about Andie's secret older-lover-slash-killer," Ant said.

Pip shot him a blistering look.

"Lauren told me," he said quietly.

"Cara told me," Lauren jumped in, slurring the edges of her words.

"Cara?" Pip turned to her.

"I'm sorry," she said, tripping over the words because she was the wrong side of four measures of vodka. "I didn't know it was supposed to be secret. I only told Naomi and Lauren. And I told them not to tell anyone." She swayed, pointing accusatorily at Lauren.

It was true; Pip hadn't specifically told her to keep it secret. She didn't think she had to.

"My project isn't to provide you with gossip." She tried to flatten out her voice when it spiked with annoyance, looking from Cara to Lauren to Ant.

"Doesn't matter," Ant said. "Like, half of our grade knows you're doing a project about Andie Bell. And why are we talking about homework on our last Friday night of freedom anyway? Zach, bring out the board."

"What board?" Cara asked.

"I brought a Ouija board. Cool, huh?" Zach said, dragging his bag over. He pulled out a tacky plastic-looking rectangle and laid it out in the middle of the circle.

"Nope," Lauren said, crossing her arms. "No way. That's way over the scary boundary. Stories are fine, but no communicating with spirits."

Pip snorted at the boys trying to convince Lauren so they could pull whatever prank it was they had planned. She reached over the Ouija board to grab another bag of chips, and that's when she saw it.

A white light flashed from within the trees.

She sat up on her heels and squinted. It happened again. In the distance a small rectangular light turned into view and then disappeared. Like the glow of a phone screen.

She waited, but the light didn't come back. There was only darkness. The sound of rain in the air. The silhouettes of sleeping trees.

Until one of the dark tree-figures shifted on two legs.

"Guys," she said quietly. A small kick to Ant's shin to shut him up. "No one look now, but I think there's someone in the trees. Watching us."

eleven

"Where?" Connor mouthed, his eyes narrowing on hers.

"My ten o'clock," she whispered. Fear like a blistering frost crept into her stomach. Wide eyes spread around the circle.

With an eruption of sound Connor grabbed a flashlight and sprang to his feet.

"Hey, pervert," he yelled with unlikely courage. He bounded out of the canopy and into the darkness, the light swinging wildly as he ran.

"Connor!" Pip called after him, disentangling herself from her sleeping bag. She snatched the flashlight out of Ant's hands and took off after her friend. "Connor, wait!"

Shut in on all sides by spidery black shadows, Pip ran, snatches of lit trees jumping out at her. Drops of rain caught in her light beam.

"Connor!" she screamed again, chasing the only sign of him up ahead, a streak of light in the stifling darkness.

She heard more feet crashing through the forest behind her, someone shouting her name. One of the girls screaming.

A stitch was already starting to split her side as she tore on, the adrenaline swallowing any last dregs of beer that might have dulled her.

"Pip!" someone shouted into her ear.

Ant had caught up, much faster than she was, the flashlight on his phone guiding him through the trees.

"Where's Con?" he panted.

There was no air left in her. She pointed at the flickering light ahead, and Ant took off.

Still, there was the sound of feet behind her. She tried to look around but couldn't see beyond her own circle of light.

She crashed forward, breath sharp and shallow, light swinging at her side. She rounded a large tree and spotted two mismatched hunched figures, swerving before she crashed into them.

"Pip, you OK?" Ant said breathlessly.

"Yeah." She sucked at the humid air, a cramp twisting into her chest. "Connor, what the hell?"

"I lost him," Connor said, his head by his knees. "I think I lost him a while back."

"It was a man? Did you see him?" Pip asked.

Connor shook his head. "No, I didn't see it was a man, but it had to be, right? I only saw that they were wearing a dark hood. Whoever it was ducked out of the way while my flashlight was down, and I stupidly kept following the same path."

"Stupidly chased them in the first place," Pip said angrily. "By yourself."

"Obviously!" Connor said. "Some pervert in the woods at midnight, watching us and probably touching himself. Wanted to beat the crap out of him."

"That was needlessly dangerous," she said. "What were you trying to prove?"

There was a flash of white in Pip's periphery, and Zach emerged, pulling up just before he collided with her and Ant.

"What the hell?" was all he said.

Then they heard the scream.

"Shit," Zach said, turning on his heels and sprinting back the way he'd just come.

"Cara! Lauren!" Pip shouted, gripping her flashlight and following Zach, the other two beside her. Through the dark trees again, their nightmarish fingers catching her hair. Her stitch ripping deeper with each step.

Half a minute later they found Zach using his phone to light up where the two girls stood together, hand in hand, Lauren in tears.

"What happened?" Pip said, wrapping her arms around them both, shivering, even though the night was warm. "Why did you scream?"

"Because we got lost and the flashlight smashed and we're drunk," Cara said, her face pale, pupils so wide that her eyes seemed to glow black

"Why didn't you stay in the canopy?" Connor asked.

"Because you all left us," Lauren cried.

"OK, OK," Pip said. "We overreacted. Everything's fine; we just need to head back to camp. They've run off now, whoever it was, and there are six of us, OK? We're fine." She wiped the tears from Lauren's chin. It took them almost fifteen minutes, even with the flashlights, to find their way back; the woods were an entirely different place at night. Pip spotted the soft yellow glow of the battery lanterns from a distance, and her steps quickened.

No one spoke much as they cleaned up the empty drink cans and food wrappers around the sleeping bags. They dropped the sides of the canopy, safe within its four white canvas walls, their only view of the trees distorted through the plastic-sheet windows.

Pip's chest still ached around her fast-beating heart, but the boys were already starting to joke about their midnight chase through the trees.

"Too soon, guys," Lauren sniffed, drunkenly fumbling with the zipper on her sleeping bag. Pip could no longer bear to watch and helped her into it.

"I'm guessing no Ouija board, then?" Ant said.

"Think we've had enough scares," said Pip. Cara nodded, chugging water and spilling it down her chin. Lauren was already passed out somehow; Zach, too, on the other side of the canopy.

When Cara's eyelids began to wilt, dragged down by exhaustion, Pip crept back to her own sleeping bag. She saw that Ant and Connor were still awake and whispering, but she was ready for sleep, or at least to lie down and hope for sleep. As she slid her legs inside, something crinkled against her right foot. She pulled her knees up to her chest and reached inside, her fingers closing around a piece of paper.

Must have been a food wrapper that got caught. She pulled it out. It wasn't. It was a clean white piece of printer paper folded in half.

She opened it up, eyes skipping across the words.

In a large formal font across the page: *Stop digging, Pippa.*

She dropped it, eyes following as it fell open. Her breath stalled. Disbelief staled to fear. Then the feeling crisped at the edges, burning into anger.

"What the hell?" she said, picking up the note and storming over to the boys.

"Shh," one of them said, "the girls are asleep."

"Do you think this is funny?" Pip said, looking down at them as she brandished the note. "You are unbelievable."

"What are you talking about?" Ant squinted at her, sitting up and leaning back on one arm.

"This note you left me."

"I didn't leave you a note," he said, reaching up for it.

Pip pulled away. "You expect me to believe that? Was this whole stranger-in-the-woods thing a setup too? Part of your joke? Who was it? Your friend George?"

"No, Pip," Ant said, staring up at her. "Honestly, I don't know what you're talking about. What does the note say?"

"Spare me the innocent act," she said. "Connor, anything to add?"

"Pip, you think I would have chased that pervert so hard if it was just a stupid prank? We didn't plan anything, I promise."

"You're saying neither of you left me this note?"

They nodded.

"You're full of shit," she said, turning back to the girls' side of the canopy.

"Honestly, Pip, we didn't," Connor said.

Pip ignored him, clambering into her sleeping bag, using her scrunched-up sweater as a pillow. The note left open on the groundsheet beside her. She turned to stare at it, ignoring Ant and Connor's whispers for her attention.

Pip was the last one awake. She could tell by the breathing.

From the ashes of her anger, something new was born. A feeling between terror and doubt, between chaos and logic.

She said the words in her head so many times that they became rubbery and foreign-sounding.

Stop digging, Pippa.

It couldn't be. It was just a cruel joke. Just a joke.

She couldn't look away, though, her eyes tracing back and forth over the letters.

And the forest in the dead of night came alive around her. Crackling twigs, wingbeats through the trees, and screams. Fox or deer, she couldn't tell, but they shrieked and cried, and it was and wasn't Andie Bell, screaming through time.

Stop digging, Pippa.

part two

twelve

Pip fidgeted nervously under the table, hoping Cara was too busy talking to notice. It was the first time that Pip had ever had to keep things from her, and the nerves kicked around in her stomach.

They'd made it through the third day back at school, when teachers stopped talking about what they were going to teach and actually started teaching. Pip and Cara were in the Wards' kitchen, pretending to do homework, but really, Cara was unspooling into an existential crisis.

"And I told him I still have no clue which college I want to go to, and he's all 'Time's ticking, Cara,' and it's stressing me out. Have you decided yet?"

"Yeah, a few days ago," Pip said.

"You are the worst person to vent to about life plans." Cara snorted. "I bet you already know what you want to do when you're a big girl too. Go on, tell me, where are you applying?"

"Columbia. Going early decision, hopefully."

"Your efficiency offends me."

Pip's phone buzzed on the table.

"Who's that?" Cara asked.

"It's just Ravi Singh," Pip said, scanning the text, "seeing if I have any more updates."

"Oh, we're texting each other now, are we?" Cara said playfully. "Should I be saving a date next week for the wedding?"

Pip threw a pen at her. How ridiculous; they were just working together, that was all.

"Well, *do* you have any Andie Bell updates?" Cara said.

"No," Pip said. "Absolutely nothing new."

The lie made the knot in her gut squeeze tighter.

Ant and Connor were still denying they put the note in her sleeping bag when she'd asked at school. They suggested maybe it was Zach or one of the girls. Of course, their denial wasn't solid proof it hadn't been them. But Pip had to consider the other possibility: What if? What if it was actually someone involved in the Andie Bell case trying to scare her into giving up the project? Someone who had a lot to lose if she kept going.

She told no one about the note: not the girls, not the boys when they asked what it said, not her parents, not even Ravi. Their concern might stop her project dead in its tracks, and she couldn't risk that. She had to keep this secret close to her chest, and she would learn from the master, Miss Andie Bell.

"Where's your dad?" asked Pip.

"Dude, he came in, like, fifteen minutes ago to say he was off tutoring."

"Oh, right," Pip said. Secrets were distracting. Mr. Ward had always tutored three times a week; it was part of the Ward routine, which Pip knew by heart. Her nerves were making her sloppy. Cara would notice she was hiding something; she knew Pip too well. She had to calm down; she was here for a reason. Being skittish would only get her caught.

She could hear the buzz and thud of the television in the other room; Naomi was watching some crime drama that involved a lot of *pew-pew*ing guns.

Now was the perfect moment to act.

"Hey, can I borrow your laptop for two secs?" she asked Cara, relaxing her face so it wouldn't betray her. "Just want to look up this book for English."

"Yep, sure," Cara said, passing it across. "Don't close my tabs."

"Won't," Pip said, turning the laptop so Cara couldn't see the screen.

Pip's heartbeat picked up. There was so much blood behind her face she must be turning red. She leaned down to hide behind the screen and clicked up the control panel.

She'd been up until three last night, the note haunting her when she closed her eyes. So she did some research, trawling through the internet, looking at badly worded instruction manuals for wireless printers.

Anyone could have followed her there into the woods. That was clear. Anyone could have watched her, lured her and her friends out of the canopy so they could leave their message. But there was only one name on her persons of interest list who would have known exactly where Pip and Cara were camping: Naomi.

Pip had been stupid to discount her because of the Naomi she thought she knew. There could well be another Naomi. One who might or might not be lying about leaving Max's for a period of time the night Andie died. One who might or might not have been in love with Sal. One who might or might not have hated Andie enough to kill her.

After hours of reading, Pip had learned there was no way to see the previous documents a wireless printer had printed. And no one in their right mind would save a threatening note like that on their computer, so attempting to look through Naomi's documents would be pointless. But there was something else she could do.

With the steps memorized from a how-to web page, Pip opened up the *Devices and Printers* settings on Cara's laptop and hovered the mouse over the name of the Ward family printer: Freddie Prints Jr. She right-clicked into *Printer Properties* and onto the Advanced tab, checked the box next to *Keep Printed Documents,* clicked apply, and it was done. She closed down the panel and navigated back to Cara's homework.

"Thanks," she said, passing the laptop over, certain that her heart was loud enough to hear.

"No problemo."

Cara's laptop would now keep track of everything that came through their printer. If Pip received another printed message, she could find out for sure if it had come from Naomi or not.

The kitchen door opened with an explosion from the White House, and screaming federal agents. Naomi stood in the doorframe.

"God, Nai," Cara said, "we're working in here; can you turn it down?"

"Sorry," she whispered, as though it compensated for the loud TV. "Just getting a drink. You OK, Pip?" Naomi looked at her with a puzzled expression, and Pip realized she had been staring first.

"Oh . . . yep. Just made me jump," she said, her smile just a little too wide, carving uncomfortably into her cheeks.

PIPPA FITZ-AMOBI
9/6/19
CAPSTONE PROJECT LOG—ENTRY 13

TRANSCRIPT OF SECOND INTERVIEW WITH EMMA HUTTON

PIP: Thanks for agreeing to talk again. This is a really short follow-up, I promise.

EMMA: Yeah, no, that's fine.

PIP: Thanks. OK, so I've been asking around about Andie, and I've heard a rumor I wanted to run by you. That Andie might have been seeing someone at the same time as Sal. An older guy, maybe? Did you ever hear anything like that?

EMMA: Who told you that?

PIP: Sorry, they asked to stay anonymous.

EMMA: Was it Chloe Burch?

PIP: Again, sorry, they asked me not to say.

EMMA: It had to be her. We were the only ones who knew.

PIP: So it's true? Andie was seeing an older man during her relationship with Sal?

EMMA: Well, yeah, that's what she said. She never told us his name or anything, though.

PIP: Did you have any idea how long it'd been going on?

EMMA: Like, not long at all before she went missing. I think she started talking about it in March. That's just a guess.

PIP: And you knew nothing about who it was?

EMMA: No. She liked teasing us that we didn't know.

PIP: And did you mention it to the police?

EMMA: No, because honestly, those are the only details we ever knew. And I thought maybe Andie had made him up for some drama.

PIP: But after the whole Sal thing happened, didn't you think it might be relevant, a possible motive?

EMMA: No, 'cause I wasn't convinced he was real. And Andie wasn't stupid; she wouldn't have told Sal about him.

PIP: But what if Sal found out?

EMMA: I don't think so. Andie was good at keeping secrets.

PIP: OK, final question, I promise. I was wondering if you knew whether Andie ever had a falling-out with Naomi Ward.

EMMA: Naomi Ward, Sal's friend?

PIP: Yeah.

EMMA: Not to my knowledge. But she was Sal's friend, not Andie's.

PIP: I know, but did Andie ever mention any tension with Naomi or say bad things about her?

EMMA: No. But now that you mention it, she definitely was hating on one of the Wards, it just wasn't Naomi.

PIP: What do you mean?

EMMA: You know Mr. Ward, the history teacher? I don't know if he's still at Fairview, but yeah, Andie did not like him. I remember her referring to him as an asshole, among other less delicate words.

PIP: Why? When was this?

EMMA: Um, I couldn't say specifically, but I think it was around that spring break. So not long before everything happened.

PIP: But Andie wasn't taking history with him?

EMMA: No, it must have been something like he'd told her that her skirt was too short for school. She always hated that.

PIP: OK. Thanks again for all your help, Emma.

EMMA: No worries. Bye.

NO. Just no.

First, Naomi, who I can't even look in the eye anymore. And now Mr. Ward? Why are questions about Andie Bell returning answers about the people close to me?

OK, Andie insulting a teacher to her friends in the lead-up to her death could be a coincidence. Entirely innocent.

But—and it's a big "but"—Mr. Ward told me he hardly knew Andie or had anything to do with her in the last two years of her life. So why did she call him an asshole if they had nothing to do with each other? Was he lying, and if so, why?

Even though it physically pains me to think this: Could this innocuous clue indicate that Elliot Ward was the secret older man? I mean, I first thought the "secret older guy" would be in his twenties.

But maybe my instincts were wrong; maybe it refers to someone much older.

Andie told her friends she could "ruin" this man. I thought this meant that the guy—whoever he was—was married. Mr. Ward wasn't married at the time; his wife had died a couple of years before. But he was a teacher, in a position of trust. If there was some inappropriate relationship, Mr. Ward could have faced jail time. That certainly can be classified as "ruining" someone.

Is he the type of person who would do that? No, he isn't. And is he the kind of man a beautiful seventeen-year-old would lust after? I just don't think so.

I should grit my teeth and ask Mr. Ward, that's what I should do. Get some actual answers. Otherwise, I may end up suspecting everybody I know who may have spoken to Andie at some point in their lives.

But how do you casually ask a grown man you've known since you were six why they lied about a murdered girl?

PERSONS OF INTEREST

Jason Bell

Naomi Ward

Secret Older Guy

Elliot Ward

thirteen

Mr. Ward was at the front of the classroom, reading out a passage from their Russian history textbook. He swiped something from the board, and Pip watched as a crack of sunlight climbed up the back of his bright shirt. She waited.

When the bell finally rang for lunch, Mr. Ward called over the scraping chairs, "Read chapter three before next class. And if you want to get ahead, Trotsky on over to chapter four as well." He chuckled at his own joke.

"You coming, Pip?" Connor said, swinging his backpack onto one shoulder.

"Um, yeah, I'll come find you guys in a minute," she said. "I need to ask Mr. Ward something first."

"You need to ask Mr. Ward something, huh?" Mr. Ward had overheard. "That's ominous. I hope you haven't started thinking about the coursework already."

"No . . . Well, yes I have," Pip said, "but that's not what I want to ask you."

She waited until they were the only two left in the classroom.

"What is it?" Mr. Ward glanced down at his watch. "You have ten of my minutes before I start panicking about the panini queue."

"Yeah, sorry," Pip said, grasping inside for her courage. "Um . . ."

"Everything OK?" Mr. Ward asked, sitting back on his desk, arms and legs crossed. "Worrying about your application? I don't think you need to worry. I've already started on your letter of recommendation and—"

"No, thanks, but it's not that." She took a breath and blew out her top lip. "I . . . When I interviewed you before, you said you didn't have anything to do with Andie in the last two years of school."

"Yes, correct." He blinked. "She wasn't in any of my classes after sophomore year."

"OK, but"—her courage returned all at once, and her words raced each other out—"one of Andie's friends said that, excuse the language, Andie referred to you as an asshole and other unsavory words sometime in the weeks before she went missing."

The "why" was hiding there beneath her words; she didn't need to say it.

"Oh," Mr. Ward said, rubbing the dark hair back from his face. He looked at her and sighed. "Well, I was hoping this wouldn't come up. I don't see what good it can do to dwell on it now. But I can see you're being very thorough with your project."

Pip nodded, her silence beckoning an answer.

Mr. Ward shifted. "I don't feel too comfortable about it, saying unpleasant things about a student who has lost her life." He glanced up at the classroom door and scooted over to shut it. "I didn't have much to do with Andie at school, but as Naomi's dad, I knew of her, of course. And . . . it was in that capacity, through Naomi, that I learned some things about Andie."

"Yes?"

"No easy way of saying it but . . . she was a bully. She was bullying another girl in their grade. I can't remember her name now. There was some sort of incident, a video that Andie had posted online."

Pip was both surprised and not really at all. Yet another secret in Andie Bell's life.

"I knew enough to understand that Andie would be in trouble with both the school and the police for what she'd done," Mr. Ward continued. "And I . . . I thought it was a shame because it was the first week back after spring break, and exams were coming up." He sighed again. "What I should have done, when I found out, was tell the principal about the incident. But the school has a no-tolerance policy on bullying, and I knew Andie would be expelled immediately. I . . . well, I just couldn't do it. Even though she was a bully, I couldn't live with myself knowing I'd play a part in ruining a student's future."

"So what did you do?" Pip asked.

"I looked up her father's contact details and I called him, the first day of school after the break."

"You mean the Monday of the week Andie disappeared?"

Mr. Ward nodded. "Yes, I guess it was. I called Jason Bell and I told him everything I'd learned and said that he needed to have a very serious talk with his daughter about bullying and consequences. And I suggested restricting her online access. I said I was trusting him to sort it out, otherwise, I would have no choice but to inform the school and have Andie expelled."

"And what did he say?"

"Well, he was thankful that I was giving his daughter a second chance she possibly didn't deserve. And he promised he would talk to her. I'm guessing now that when Jason did speak to Andie, he mentioned that I was the source of the information. So if I was the target of some choice words from Andie that week, I'm not entirely surprised, I must say. Disappointed is all."

Pip sighed with undisguised relief.

"What's that for?"

"I'm just glad you weren't lying for a worse reason."

"Think you've read too many mystery novels, Pip. Why not some historical biographies instead?" He smiled gently.

"They can be just as disturbing." She paused. "You'd never told anyone before, had you . . . about Andie's bullying?"

"Of course not. It seemed pointless after everything happened. Insensitive too." He scratched his chin. "I try not to think about it because I get lost in butterfly-effect theories. What if I had just told the school and Andie was expelled that week? Would it have changed the outcome? Would the conditions that led to Sal killing her not have been in place? Would those two still be alive?"

"I understand," Pip said. "And you don't remember the girl Andie bullied?"

"No, sorry," he said. "Naomi would remember; you could ask her about it. Not sure what this has to do with the use of media in criminal investigations, though." He raised his eyebrows in a scolding way.

"Well, I haven't decided on my final title yet."

"OK, well, don't go falling down a rabbit hole." He smiled, wagged his finger. "And now I'm running away from you because I'm desperate for a tuna melt."

He dashed into the corridor, and Pip felt lighter, watching him go. That wasn't as hard as she'd thought it would be. And now she had some answers, another real lead to follow. And one less name on her list.

But the lead was taking her back to Naomi. And Pip would have to look her in the eyes again, like she didn't think there was something secret hiding there.

PIPPA FITZ-AMOBI
9/12/19
CAPSTONE PROJECT LOG—ENTRY 15

TRANSCRIPT OF SECOND INTERVIEW WITH NAOMI WARD

PIP: OK, recording. Your dad told me that he found out Andie was bullying another girl in your year. Cyberbullying. He thought there was some online video involved. Do you know anything about this?

NAOMI: Yeah, like I said, I thought Andie was bad news.

PIP: Can you tell me more about it?

NAOMI: There was a girl in our grade, Natalie da Silva, and she was pretty and blond too. They looked quite similar, actually. And I guess Andie felt threatened by her, because at the start of our senior year, Andie started spreading rumors about her and finding ways to humiliate her.

PIP: If Sal and Andie didn't start seeing each other until that December, how did you know all this?

NAOMI: I was friends with Nat. We had biology together.

PIP: Oh. What kind of rumors was Andie starting?

NAOMI: The kind of disgusting things only a teenage girl could think up. Things like her family was incestuous, that Nat watched people undress in the changing rooms and touched herself. Those kinds of things.

PIP: You think Andie did that because Nat was pretty and she felt threatened by her?

NAOMI: I actually think that was the extent of her thought process. Andie wanted to be the girl everyone wanted. Nat was competition, so Andie had to take her down.

PIP: Did you know about this video at the time?

NAOMI: Yeah, it got shared all over social media. It wasn't taken down until a few days later, when someone reported it.

PIP: When was this?

NAOMI: During spring break.

PIP: So what was the video?

NAOMI: As far as I know, Andie had been hanging out with some friends from school, including her two minions.

PIP: Chloe Burch and Emma Hutton?

NAOMI: Yeah, and some other kids. Not Sal or Nat or any of us. And there was this guy, Chris Parks, who everyone knew Nat liked. I don't know all the details, but Andie either used his phone or told him what to do, and they were sending flirty texts to Nat. And Nat was responding 'cause she liked Chris and thought it was him. And then Andie-slash-Chris asked Nat to send a video of her topless, with her face in it, so he'd know it was really her.

PIP: And Nat did it?

NAOMI: Yeah. A little naive, but she thought she was talking to just Chris. The next thing we all knew, the video was online and Andie and loads of other people were sharing it. The comments were so horrible. And practically everyone at school saw it before it got taken down. Nat was inconsolable. She even skipped the first two days back at school after break because she was so humiliated.

PIP: Did Sal know Andie was behind it?

NAOMI: Well, I mentioned it to him. He didn't approve, obviously, but he just said, "It's Andie's drama. I don't want to get involved." Sal was just too laid-back about some things.

PIP: Was there anything else that happened between Nat and Andie?

NAOMI: Yeah, actually. I might have been the only one Nat told, 'cause she was crying in biology right after it happened.

PIP: What?

NAOMI: During that fall semester the school was putting on a play. *The Crucible,* I think. Nat got the main part. Apparently, Andie had wanted it, and she was really pissed off. So after the parts were posted, Andie cornered Nat and she told her . . .

PIP: Yes?

NAOMI: Sorry, I forgot to mention some context. Nat's brother, Daniel, who was like five years older than us . . . He had worked at the school part-time as a janitor when we were like fifteen or sixteen. Only for a year while he was looking for other jobs.

PIP: OK?

NAOMI: OK, so Andie cornered Nat and told her that when Daniel was still working at the school, he had sex with Andie, even though she was only fifteen at the time. Andie told Nat to drop out of the play or she'd go to the police and say she was statutorily raped by Nat's brother. So Nat dropped out because she was scared of what Andie would do.

PIP: Was it true? Did Andie have a relationship with Nat's brother?

NAOMI: I don't know. Nat didn't know for sure, either; that's why she dropped out of the play. But I don't think she ever asked him.

PIP: Do you know where Nat is now? Do you think I could talk to her?

NAOMI: I'm not really in contact with her, but I know she's back at home with her parents. I heard some stuff about her, though.

PIP: What stuff?

NAOMI: Um, I think in college she was involved in some kind of fight. She got arrested and charged with assault, and I think she spent some time in prison.

PIP: Oh god.

NAOMI: I know.

PIP: Can you give me her number?

fourteen

"Did you get all dressed up to come and see me, Sarge?" Ravi said, leaning against his front doorframe in a green plaid flannel shirt and jeans.

Well, Pip *had* put on her nice jacket today; not that she was going to tell him that. "Nope, I came straight from school."

But he was still smiling, eyes glinting like he knew something she didn't. "If anything, I dressed down," Pip added.

"Ah I see," he said, "a plainclothes officer today."

"Exactly," she said. "Speaking of, you're coming with me. Put some shoes on." She clapped her hands.

"Are we going on a mission?" Ravi asked, falling back to slip on some old sneakers discarded in the hallway. "Do I need to bring my night-vision goggles and utility belt?"

"Not this time." She smiled, starting down the garden path as Ravi closed the front door, then followed her.

"Where are we going?"

"To a house where two potential Andie killer suspects grew up," Pip said. "One of them just out of prison for aggravated assault. You're my backup, since we're going to speak to a potentially violent person of interest."

"Backup?" he said, catching up to walk alongside her.

"You know," Pip said casually, "so there's someone there to hear my screams for help."

"Wait, Pip." He closed his fingers around her arm and pulled them both to a stop. "I don't want you doing something that's actually dangerous. Sal wouldn't have wanted that either."

"Oh, come on." She shrugged him off. "Nothing gets between me and my homework, not even a little danger." He looked unconvinced. "I'm kidding. I'm just going to, very calmly, ask her a few questions."

"Oh, it's a her?" Ravi said. "OK, then."

Pip swung her backpack and whacked him on the elbow.

"Hey," she said, "women can be just as dangerous as men."

"Ouch, tell me about it," he said, rubbing his arm. "What have you got in there, bricks?"

"It sounds like Andie was a piece of work," Ravi said in the car when Pip was done catching him up on everything she'd learned since they last spoke. Everything except the dark figure in the forest and the note in her sleeping bag. This investigation meant everything to him, but she knew he would tell her to stop if he thought she was putting herself in danger. She couldn't let that happen.

"And yet," he carried on, "it was so easy for everyone to believe Sal was the monster. Whoa, I'm so deep." He turned to her. "You can quote me on that in your project."

"Of course, footnote and everything," she said.

" 'Ravi Singh,' " he said, drawing his words with his fingers, " 'deep unfiltered thoughts, Pip's bug-faced car, 2019.' "

"Yes." She glanced quickly at him. "Except you didn't use proper referencing style."

"Oh, the shame." He pretended to wince.

The mechanical voice on her phone's GPS interrupted, announcing they'd reached their destination.

"Must be this one," Pip said. "Naomi told me it was the one with the blue door." She pulled over to the curb. "I called Natalie twice yesterday. The first time, she hung up after I said the words 'school project.' The second time, she wouldn't pick up at all. Let's hope she'll actually open the door. You coming?"

"I'm not sure," he said, pointing at his own face. "There's that whole murderer's brother thing. You might get more answers if I'm not there."

"Oh."

"How about I stand on the path there?" He gestured to the slabs of concrete that ran through the yard toward the house, to the point where they turned sharply left to lead to the front door. "She won't see me, but I'll be right there, ready for action."

They stepped out of the car, and Ravi handed over her backpack with an exaggerated grunt.

She nodded at him when he was in position and then strolled up to the front door. She prodded the bell twice, fiddling nervously with the hem of her jacket as a shadowy figure emerged behind the frosted glass.

The door opened slowly and a face appeared in the crack, a young woman with white-blond hair cropped closely to her head and eyeliner ringed thickly around her eyes. Beneath the makeup, she looked eerily like Andie: similar big blue eyes and plump pale lips.

"Hi," Pip said, "are you Nat da Silva?"

"Yes," she said hesitantly.

"My name's Pip." She swallowed. "I was the one who called you yesterday. I'm friends with Naomi Ward; you knew her at school, right?"

"Yeah, Naomi was a friend. Why? Is she OK?" Nat looked concerned.

"Oh, she's fine." Pip smiled. "She's back home at the moment."

"I didn't know she was back." Nat opened the door a little wider. "Yeah, I should catch up with her sometime. So . . ."

"Sorry for showing up like this," Pip said. She looked down at full-length Natalie, noticing the electronic tag buckled around her ankle. "So, as I said when I called, I'm doing a school project, and I was wondering if I could ask you some questions?" She looked quickly back up at Nat's face.

"What about?" Nat shifted the tagged foot behind the door.

"Um, it's about Andie Bell."

"No thanks." Nat stepped back to shut the door, but Pip blocked it with her foot.

"Please. I know the awful things she did to you," she said. "I can understand why you wouldn't want to, but—"

"That bitch ruined my life," Nat spat. "I'm not wasting one more breath on her. Move!"

That's when they both heard the sound of rubber skidding across concrete and a whispered, "Oh crap."

Nat glanced up and her eyes widened. "You," she said quietly. "You're Sal's brother."

It wasn't a question.

Pip turned now, her eyes falling on Ravi behind her, standing sheepishly next to the uneven slab he must have tripped over.

"Hi," he said, ducking his head and raising his hand. "I'm Ravi."

He came to stand beside Pip, and Nat's grip on the door loosened. She let it swing open.

"Sal was always nice to me," she said, "even when he didn't have to be. The last time I spoke to him, he was offering to give up his lunch breaks to tutor me in gov because I was struggling. I'm sorry you don't have your brother anymore."

"Thank you," Ravi said.

"It must be hard for you too," Nat carried on, her eyes still lost in another world, "how much this town worships Andie Bell. Fairview's saint and sweetheart. That bench dedication in the park: 'Taken Too Soon.' Not soon enough, it should say."

"She wasn't a saint," Pip said gently, trying to coax Nat out from behind the door. But Nat wasn't looking at her, only at Ravi.

He stepped up. "She bullied you?"

"Sure did," Nat laughed bitterly, "and she's still ruining my life, even from the grave. You've checked out my hardware." She pointed to her ankle monitor. "Got this because I punched one of my suitemates in college. We were deciding on bedrooms, and this girl started pulling a stunt, exactly like Andie would've, and I just lost it."

"We know about the video she put up of you," Pip said. "She should have faced charges over it; you were still a minor at the time."

Nat shrugged. "At least she was punished in some way that week. Some divine providence. Thanks to Sal."

"Did you want her dead, after what she'd done to you?" Ravi asked.

"Of course I did," Nat said darkly. "Of course I wanted her gone. I skipped two days of school because I was so upset. And when I went back on the Wednesday, everyone was looking at me, laughing at me. I was crying in the corridor, and Andie walked by and called me a slut. I was so angry that I left her a nice little note in her locker. I was too scared to ever say anything to her face, though."

Pip glanced sideways at Ravi, at his tensed jaw and furrowed brows, and she knew he'd picked up on it too.

"A note?" he said. "Was it a . . . Was it a threatening note?"

"No shit," Nat laughed. " 'You stupid bitch, I'm going to kill you,' something like that. Sal got there first, though."

"Maybe he didn't," Pip said.

Nat turned and looked Pip in the face. Then she burst into loud and forced laughter, a mist of spit landing on Pip's cheek.

"Oh, this is too good," she hooted. "Are you asking me whether *I* killed Andie Bell? I had the motive, right, that's what you're thinking? You want my fucking alibi?" She laughed cruelly.

Pip didn't say anything. Her mouth was filling uncomfortably with saliva, but she didn't swallow. She didn't want to move at all. She felt Ravi brushing against her shoulder, his hand skimming just past hers, disturbing the air around it.

Nat leaned toward them. "I didn't have any friends left because of Andie Bell. I had no place to be on that Friday night. I was home playing Scrabble with my parents and sister-in-law, tucked in by eleven. Sorry to disappoint you."

"And where was your brother?" Pip said. "If his wife was home with you?"

"He's a suspect, too, is he?" Her voice darkened. "Naomi must have been talking, then. He was out drinking with his cop friends that night."

"He's a police officer?" Ravi said.

"Just finished his training that year. So yeah, no murderers in this house, I'm afraid. Now fuck off, and tell Naomi to fuck off too."

Nat stepped back and kicked the door shut in their faces.

Pip watched the door vibrating in its frame, her eyes so transfixed that it looked for a moment like the very particles of air were rippling. She shook her head and turned to Ravi.

"Let's go," he said softly.

Back in the car Pip allowed herself to just breathe for a few seconds, to arrange the haze of her thoughts into actual words.

Ravi found his first: "Am I in trouble for, well, literally tripping into the interrogation? I heard raised voices, and—"

"No." Pip looked at him and couldn't help but smile. "We're lucky you did. She only talked because you were there."

He sat up a little straighter in his seat, and his hair brushed against the roof of the car. "So the death threat that journalist told you about . . ."

"Came from Nat," Pip finished, turning the key in the ignition.

She pulled out and drove about twenty feet up the road, out of sight of the da Silva house, before stopping again and reaching for her phone.

"What are you doing?"

"Nat said her brother is a police officer." She thumbed on to the browser app. "Let's look him up."

It came up on the first page of results: Daniel da Silva's LinkedIn profile. It said he was an officer at the Fairview Police Department, had been so since the end of 2013.

"Hey, I know him," Ravi said, leaning over her shoulder.

"You do?"

"Yeah. Back when I started asking questions about Sal, he was the officer that told me to give it up, that my brother was guilty beyond doubt. He does *not* like me." Ravi's hand crept up to the back of his head, losing his fingers in his dark hair. "Last summer I was sitting at a table outside the café by the library. This guy"—he gestured to the photo—"made me move along, said I was 'loitering.' Funny he didn't think anyone else was loitering, just the brown kid with a murderer for a brother."

"What an asshole," she said. "And he shut down all your questions about Sal?"

Ravi nodded.

"He's been a police officer in Fairview since just before Andie disappeared." Pip stared down at her phone into Daniel's smiling face. "Ravi, if someone *did* frame Sal and make his death look like suicide, wouldn't it be easier for someone with knowledge of police procedure?"

"That it would, Sarge," he said. "And there's the rumor Andie slept with him when she was fifteen, which she used to blackmail Nat out of the play."

"Yes, and what if they started up again later, after Daniel was married and Andie was a senior? He could be the secret older guy."

"What about Nat?" he said. "I sort of want to believe her when she says she was home with her parents that night because she'd lost all her friends. But . . . she's also proven to be violent." He weighed up his hands in a conceptual seesaw. "And there's obviously motive. Maybe a brother-and-sister killer tag team?"

"Or a Nat-and-Naomi killer tag team," Pip groaned.

"She did seem pretty angry that Naomi had talked to you," Ravi agreed. "What's the word count on this project, Pip?"

"Not enough, Ravi. Not nearly enough."

"Should we just go and get ice cream and give our brains a rest?" He turned to her with that smile of his. Pip was supposed to go over to Lauren's house later, but she could be a little late. Just a little bit.

"Yes, we probably should."

"As long as you're a cookie dough kinda gal. Quote, Ravi Singh," he said dramatically into an invisible microphone, " 'A thesis on the best ice cream flavor, Pip's car, Septem—' "

"Shut up."

"OK."

PIPPA FITZ-AMOBI
9/14/19
CAPSTONE PROJECT LOG—ENTRY 17

I can't find anything on Daniel da Silva. There's hardly anything to learn from his Facebook profile, other than he got married in September 2013 and he really likes barbecues. There's nothing about his professional life online, either; only an article written by Stanley Forbes three years ago about a car collision on Hillside that Daniel responded to.

But if he was the secret older guy, Andie could have *ruined* him in <u>two different ways</u>: she could have told his new wife he was cheating and destroyed his marriage, *or* she could have filed a police report about statutory rape from two years before. Both circumstances are just rumor at this point, but if true, they certainly would give Daniel a motive for wanting her dead. Andie could have blackmailed him; it's definitely not out of character for her to have been blackmailing a da Silva. If Daniel *is* our killer, he might have disturbed the investigation somehow in his capacity as a police officer. A man on the inside. Perhaps when searching the Bell residence, he could have stolen or tampered with any evidence that would lead back to him (or his sister?).

It's also worth noting the way he reacted to Ravi asking questions about Sal. Did he shut Ravi down to protect himself?

I've looked through all the reports on Andie's disappearance again, staring at pictures of the police searches until it feels like my eyes are about to climb out of their sockets. I found one photo that could be da Silva, taken on the Sunday morning. There's an officer walking through Andie's front door, his back (annoyingly) to the camera, but his hair color and length match da Silva's when I cross-reference social media photos from around that time.

It could be him.

Onto the list he goes.

PERSONS OF INTEREST

Jason Bell

Naomi Ward

Secret Older Guy

Nat da Silva

Daniel da Silva

PIPPA FITZ-AMOBI
9/17/19
CAPSTONE PROJECT LOG—ENTRY 18

It's here!

The Connecticut State Police have responded to my FOI request:

Dear Miss Fitz-Amobi,

FREEDOM OF INFORMATION REQUEST REFERENCE NO: 3142/19

I write in connection with your request for information dated 8/19/19, received by the Connecticut State Police for the following information:

I'm doing a project at school about the Andrea Bell investigation, and I would like to request the following:

1. *a transcript of the interview conducted with Salil Singh on 4/19/14*
2. *a transcript of any interviews conducted with Jason Bell*
3. *records of the findings from the searches of the Bell residence on 4/19/14 and 4/20/14*

I would be very grateful if you could help with any of these requests.

Result
Requests 2 and 3 have been refused citing exemptions under Connecticut General Statutes §1-210(b)(3) (records of law enforcement agencies not in the public interest) and Connecticut General Statutes §1-210(b)(2) (files that constitute an invasion of privacy). This email serves as a partial Refusal Notice under the Connecticut Freedom of Information Act.

Request 1 has been upheld, but the document contains redactions as per §1-210(b)(3) and §1-210(b)(2). The transcript is attached below.

If you are not satisfied with this response, the attached sheet details the appeal procedures available to you under the law.

Sincerely,
Gregory Pannett

Everything else was refused, but I have Sal's interview! However, by refusing, they confirmed that Jason Bell was at least interviewed in the investigation; maybe the police had their suspicions too?

The attached transcript:

SALIL SINGH RECORDED INTERVIEW

Date: 04/19/2014

Duration: 11 minutes

Location: Interviewee's residence

Conducted by officers from the Connecticut State Police

POLICE: This interview is being tape-recorded. It is the nineteenth of April 2014, and the time is now 3:55 p.m. My name is ███████████, and I'm based at ████████████████ with the Connecticut State Police. Also present is my colleague ███████. Could you please state your full name?

SS: Oh, sure, Salil Singh.

POLICE: And can you confirm your date of birth for me?

SS: February 14, 1996.

POLICE: A Valentine's baby, eh?

SS: Yeah.

POLICE: So, Salil, let us get some introductory bits out of the way first. Just so you understand, this is a voluntary interview and you are free to stop it or ask us to leave at any time. We are interviewing you in relation to the missing persons inquiry of Andrea Bell, as someone who has a close relationship with her. Understand?

SS: Yes, sir.

POLICE: As we understand it, you are Andrea's boyfriend, correct?

SS: Yeah. No one calls her Andrea. She's Andie.

POLICE: OK. And how long have you and Andie been together?

SS: Since just before Christmas last year. So around four months. Sorry, do you know anything yet? Do you think she's OK?

POLICE: Well, we cannot rule out that Andie has been the victim of a crime yet. Of course, we hope otherwise. Are you OK?

SS: Um, yeah, I'm just worried.

POLICE: That's understandable, Salil. So, the first question I'd like to ask you is when was the last time you saw Andie?

SS: At school, like I said. We talked in the parking lot at the end of the day, and then I walked home and she was driving home.

POLICE: And at any time up until that Friday afternoon, had Andie ever indicated to you a desire to run away from home?

SS: No, never.

POLICE: Did she ever tell you about any problems she was having at home, with her family?

SS: I mean, yeah, we obviously talked about stuff like that. Never anything major, just normal teenager stuff. I always thought that Andie and ██████████████████████████████ ███████. But there wasn't anything recent that would make her want to run away, if that's what you're asking. No.

POLICE: Can you think of any reason why Andie would want to leave home and not be found?

SS: Um. I don't think so.

POLICE: How would you describe your relationship with Andie?

SS: What do you mean?

POLICE: Is it a sexual relationship?

SS: Um, yeah sort of.

POLICE: Sort of?

SS: I . . . We haven't actually, you know, gone all the way.

POLICE: You and Andie haven't had sex?

SS: No.

POLICE: And would you say your relationship is a healthy one?

SS: I don't know. What do you mean?

POLICE: Do you argue often?

SS: No, we don't argue. I'm not confrontational, which is why I think we're OK together.

POLICE: And were you arguing in the days before Andie went missing?

SS: Um, no. We weren't.

POLICE: So in written statements from ██████████████ ████ taken this morning, they both separately allege that they saw you and Andie arguing at school this week. On the Thursday and the Friday. ████ claims it's the worst she has seen you both argue since the start of your relationship. Do you know anything about this, Salil? Any truth to it?

SS: Um, maybe a bit. Andie can have a temper; sometimes it's hard not to answer back.

POLICE: And can you tell me what you were arguing about in this instance?

SS: Um, I don't—I don't know if— No, it's private.

POLICE: No, you don't want to tell me?

SS: Um, yeah, no. I don't want to tell you.

POLICE: You may not think it's relevant, but even the smallest detail could help us find her.

SS: Um. No, I still can't say.

POLICE: Sure?

SS: Yeah.

POLICE: OK, let's move on, then. Did you have any plans to meet up with Andie last night?

SS: No, none. I had plans with my friends.

POLICE: Because ████████████████, said that when Andie left the house at around 10:30 p.m., she presumed Andie was going to see her boyfriend.

SS: No, Andie knew I was at my friend's house and wasn't meeting her.

POLICE: So where were you last night?

SS: I was at my friend ████████ house. Do you want to know times?

POLICE: Yeah, sure.

SS: I think I got there at around 8:30—my dad dropped me off. And I left at around twelve-fifteen to walk home. My curfew is one a.m. when I'm not staying over somewhere. I think I got in just before one. You can check with my dad; he was up.

POLICE: And who else was with you at ████████ house?

SS: ████████████████████████████

POLICE: And did you have any contact with Andie that evening?

SS: No. I mean, she tried to call me at nine-ish, but I was busy and didn't pick up. I can show you my phone?

POLICE: ██████████████████████████████. And have you had any contact with her at all since she went missing?

SS: Since I found out this morning, I've called her like a million times. It keeps going to voicemail. I think her phone is off.

POLICE: OK, and, ████████, did you want to ask . . .

POLICE: Yeah. So, Salil, I know you've said you don't know, but where do you think Andie could be?

SS: Um, honestly, I think she could just be taking a break somewhere, with her phone off so she can ignore the world for a while. That's what I'm hoping this is.

POLICE: What might Andie need a break from?

SS: I don't know.

POLICE: And where do you think she could be taking this break?

SS: I don't know. Andie keeps a lot to herself; maybe she has some friends we don't know about. I don't know.

POLICE: OK, so is there anything else you might want to add that could help us find Andie?

SS: Um, no. Um, if I can, I'd like to help in any searches, if you're doing them.

POLICE: ██████████████████████████ ██████████████████████████████. All right then, I've asked everything we need to at the moment. I'm going to end the interview there. It's 4:06 p.m., and I am stopping the tape.

OK, deep breath. I've read it over six times, even out loud. And now I have this horrible, sinking feeling.

This does not look great for Sal.

I know it's hard to read nuances from a transcript, but Sal was *very* evasive with the police about what he and Andie were arguing about. I don't think anything is too private that you wouldn't tell the police if it could help find your missing girlfriend.

If it was potentially about Andie seeing another man, why didn't Sal just tell the police? It could have led them to the possible real killer right from the start.

But what if Sal was covering up something worse? Something that would have given him real motive to kill Andie. We know he's lying elsewhere in this interview: when he tells the police what time he left Max's.

It would crush me to have come all this way, just to find out that Sal really is guilty. Ravi would be devastated. Maybe I should never have started this project, should never have spoken to him. I'm going to have to show him the transcript. I told him I was expecting a reply any day now. But this might hurt him. . . . I don't want to hurt him. Maybe I should lie and say it hasn't arrived yet.

Could Sal really have been guilty all along? Sal as the killer has always been the path of least resistance, but was it so easy for everyone to believe because it's also true?

But no: the note.

Somebody warned me to stop digging.

Yes, the note could have been someone's idea of a prank, and if the note was a joke, then Sal could be the real killer. But it doesn't feel right. Someone in this town has something to hide, and they're scared because I'm on the right path to chasing them down.

I just have to keep chasing, even when the path is resisting me.

PERSONS OF INTEREST

Jason Bell

Naomi Ward

Secret Older Guy

Nat da Silva

Daniel da Silva

fifteen

Pip crossed the road, with Josh's wriggling hand in hers and Barney's leash in the other. Outside the café, the one nearest their house, Pip crouched to loop the leash around the leg of a table.

"Sit. Good boy," she said, stroking the dog's head as he gave her a tongue-lolling smile.

She opened the door and ushered Josh inside.

"I'm a good boy too."

"Good boy, Josh," she said, absently patting his head as she scanned the sandwich shelves. She picked out four different flavors, turkey sub for Dad, of course, and cheese and ham "without the gross bits" for Josh.

"Hi, Jackie," Pip said, smiling as she took the bundle to the register.

"Hello, sweetheart. Big Amobi lunch plans?"

"We're assembling patio furniture, and it's getting tense," she said. "Need sandwiches to calm the hangry troops."

"Ah, yes," said Jackie. "Tell your mom I'll swing by next week with that book we were talking about."

"Will do, thanks." Pip took the paper bag from her and turned back to Josh. "Come on, then, bud."

They were almost at the door when Pip spotted her, sitting

at a table alone, her hands wrapped around a take-out coffee. Pip hadn't seen her in town for years; she'd assumed she was still away at college. She must be twenty-one by now, maybe twenty-two. And here she was, just feet away, tracing her fingertips over the lid, looking more like Andie than she ever had before.

Her face was slimmer now, and she'd started dying her hair lighter, just like her sister's had been. But hers was cut short and blunt above her shoulders where Andie's had hung down to her waist. Yet even though the likeness was there, Becca Bell's face did not quite have the composite magic of her sister's, a girl who had looked more like a painting than a real person.

Pip knew she shouldn't; she knew it was wrong and insensitive and all those words Mrs. Morgan had used in her "I'm concerned about the direction of your project" warnings. And even though she could feel the sensible and rational parts of herself rallying in her head, she had already decided. That one flake of recklessness contaminating all other thoughts.

"Josh," she said, handing him the sandwich bag, "can you go and sit outside with Barney for a minute? I'll be two seconds."

He looked pleadingly up at her.

"You can play on my phone," she said, digging it out of her pocket.

"Yes," he said in hissed victory, taking it and bumping into the door on his way out.

Pip's heart kicked up in an agitated protest. She ignored it.

"Hi. Becca, right?" she said, walking over and placing her hands on the back of the empty chair.

"Yeah. Do I know you?" Becca's eyebrows dropped in scrutiny.

"No, you don't." Pip's smile felt tight. "I'm Pippa. I live in town. Just in my last year at Fairview High."

"Oh, wait," Becca said, shuffling in her seat, "don't tell me. You're the girl doing a project about my sister, aren't you?"

Pip stammered, "H-how did you know?"

"I'm, uh . . ." She paused. "I'm kind of seeing Stanley Forbes. Kind of not." She shrugged.

Pip tried to hide her shock with a fake cough. "Oh. Nice guy."

"Yeah." Becca looked down at her coffee. "I just graduated, and I'm doing an internship over at the *Fairview Mail*."

"Oh, cool," Pip said. "I actually want to be a journalist too."

"Is that why you're doing a project about Andie?" She went back to tracing her finger around the lid of the cup.

"Yes." Pip nodded. "And I'm sorry for intruding, and you can absolutely tell me to go away if you want. I just wondered whether you could answer some questions I have about your sister."

Becca sat forward in her chair, her hair swinging about her neck. She coughed. "Um, what kind of questions?"

Far too many; they all rushed in at the same time.

"Oh, like, did you and Andie used to get an allowance from your parents?"

Becca's face wrinkled in surprise. "That's not what I was expecting. And no, not really. They kind of just bought us stuff as and when we needed it. Why?"

"Just . . . filling in some gaps," Pip said. "And was there ever tension between your sister and your dad?"

Becca's eyes dropped to the floor.

"Um." Her voice cracked. She wrapped her hands around the cup and stood, the chair screaming as it scraped against the tiled floor. "Actually, I don't think this is a good idea," she said, rubbing her nose. "Sorry. It's just . . ."

"No, I'm sorry." Pip stepped back. "I shouldn't have come over."

"No, it's OK," Becca said. "It's just that things are finally settled again. Me and my mom, we've found our new normal, and things are getting better. I don't think dwelling on the past—on Andie stuff—is healthy for either of us. Especially not my mom. So, yeah." She shrugged. "You do your project if that's what you want to do, but I'd prefer it if you left us out of it."

"Absolutely," Pip said. "I'm so sorry."

"No worries." Becca's head dipped in a hesitant nod as she walked briskly past and out the café door.

Pip waited several moments for her turbulent heart to slide back down into her chest, and then she followed her out.

"All right," she said, unhooking Barney's leash from the table's leg. "Let's go home."

"Don't think that lady liked you," Josh said, eyes still dancing across her phone screen. "Were you being unfriendly, Hippo Pippo?"

PIPPA FITZ-AMOBI
9/22/19
CAPSTONE PROJECT LOG—ENTRY 19

I know, I pushed my luck trying to question Becca. It was wrong. I just couldn't help myself; she was right there. The last person to see Andie alive. Other than the killer, of course.

Her sister was murdered. I can't expect her to want to talk about it, even if I am trying to find the truth.

It's made me realize I'm lacking a certain insight into Andie's home life, but obviously, it's not even in the realm of possibility to try to speak to her parents.

I've been stalking Becca on Facebook back to five years ago, pre-murder. Other than learning that her hair used to be mousier and her cheeks fuller, it looks like she only had one really close friend in 2014. Jess Walker. Maybe Jess will be detached enough to be less emotional about Andie, yet close enough that I can get some of the answers I desperately need.

Jess Walker's profile is very neat and informative. She's currently in college in New Jersey. I scrolled back to five years ago (it took forever), and back then nearly all her photos were taken with Becca Bell, until they abruptly weren't.

Time to send her a message and see if she'd be willing to do a phone interview.

PIPPA FITZ-AMOBI
9/24/19
CAPSTONE PROJECT LOG—ENTRY 20

TRANSCRIPT OF INTERVIEW WITH JESS WALKER (BECCA BELL'S FRIEND)

[We talk a bit about Fairview, how the school has changed since she left, which teachers are still there, etc. It's a few minutes until I can steer the conversation back to my project.]

PIP: So, I wanted to ask you, really, about the Bells, not just Andie. What kind of family they were, how they got along? Things like that.

JESS: Oh, well, I mean, that's a loaded question right there. [She sniffs.]

PIP: What do you mean?

JESS: Um, I don't know if "dysfunctional" is quite the right word. People use that as a funny kind of tribute. I mean it in the literal sense. Like they weren't quite normal. I mean, they seemed normal unless you spent a lot of time there, like I did.

PIP: What do you mean by not quite normal?

JESS: I don't know if that's a good way of describing it. There were just a couple of things that weren't quite right. It was mainly Jason, Becca's dad.

PIP: What did he do?

JESS: It was just the way he spoke to them, the girls and Dawn. If you only saw it a couple of times, you'd think he was just trying to be funny. But I saw it often, very often, and I think it definitely affected the environment in that house.

PIP: What?

JESS: Sorry, I'm talking in circles, aren't I? It's difficult to explain. Um. He would just say things to them, like little digs about how they looked. The total opposite of how you should talk to your teenage daughters. He'd pick at things he knew they were self-conscious about. He said things to Becca about her weight and would laugh it off as a joke. He'd tell Andie she needed to put on makeup before she left the house, that her face was her moneymaker. Jokes like that all the time. Like how they looked was the most important thing in the world. I remember when I was over for dinner one time, Andie was upset that she didn't get into any of the colleges she'd applied to, only her backup, that crappy local one. And Jason said, "Oh, it doesn't matter; you're only going to college to find a rich husband anyway."

PIP: No way.

JESS: And he did it to his wife too. He'd say really uncomfortable things when I was there. Like how she was looking old, counting the wrinkles on her face. Saying that he'd married her for her looks and she'd married him for his money, and only one of them was upholding their deal. I mean, they would all laugh when he did it, like it was just family teasing. But seeing it happen so many times, it was . . . unsettling. I didn't like being there.

PIP: And do you think it affected the girls?

JESS: Oh, Becca never, ever wanted to talk about her dad. But yes, it was obvious it wreaked havoc on their self-esteem. Andie started caring so much about what she looked like, about what people thought of her. There would be screaming matches when her parents said it was time to go out and Andie wasn't ready, hadn't done her hair or makeup yet. Or when they refused to buy her a new lipstick she said she *needed*. How that girl could ever have thought she was ugly is beyond me. Becca became obsessed with her flaws and started skipping meals. It affected them in different ways: Andie got louder; Becca got quieter.

PIP: And what was the relationship between the sisters like?

JESS: Jason's influence was all over that as well. He made everything in that house a competition. If one of the girls did something good, like got a good grade, he would use it to put the other one down.

PIP: But what were Becca and Andie like together?

JESS: I mean, they were teenage sisters; they fought like hell and then a few minutes later it was forgotten. Becca always looked up to Andie, though. They were really close in age, only fifteen months between them. Andie was in the year just above us at school. And when we turned sixteen, Becca started, I guess, trying to copy Andie. I think because Andie always seemed so confident, so admired. Becca started trying to dress like her. She planned to ask for the exact same car as Andie after she passed her driving test. And she started wanting to go out like Andie, too, to house parties.

PIP: You mean the ones called "calamity parties"?

JESS: Yeah, those. Even though it was people in Andie's year that threw them, and we hardly knew anyone, she convinced me to go one time. I think it was in March, so not too long before Andie's disappearance. Andie hadn't invited her or anything. Becca just found out where the next one was being hosted and we turned up. We walked there.

PIP: How was it?

JESS: Ugh, awful. We just sat in the corner all night, not talking to anyone. Andie completely ignored Becca; I think she was angry she'd turned up. We drank a bit, and then Becca completely disappeared on me. I couldn't find her anywhere in all the drunk people, and I had to walk home, tipsy, all by myself. I was really angry at Becca. Even more angry the next day when she finally answered her phone and I found out what happened.

PIP: What happened?

JESS: She wouldn't tell me, but I mean, it was pretty obvious when she asked me to go and get the morning-after pill with her. I asked and asked, and she just would not tell me who she'd slept with. I think she might have been embarrassed. That upset me at the time. Especially as she had considered it important enough to completely abandon me at a party I never wanted to go to. We had a big fight, and I guess that was the start of the wedge in our friendship. Becca skipped some school, and I didn't see her for a few weekends. And that's when Andie went missing.

PIP: Did you see the Bells much after Andie disappeared?

JESS: I visited a few times, but Becca didn't want to talk much. None of them did. Jason had an even shorter temper than usual, especially the day the police interviewed him. Apparently, on the night Andie disappeared, the alarm had gone off at his business offices during the dinner party. He'd driven there to check it out, but he'd had a lot to drink, so he was nervous talking to the police about it. That's what Becca told me, anyway. But yeah, the house was just so quiet. And even months later, after it was presumed Andie was dead and never coming home, Becca's mom insisted on leaving Andie's room as it was. Just in case. It was all really sad.

PIP: So when you were at that calamity party in March, did you see what Andie was up to, who she was with?

JESS: Yeah. You know, I never actually knew that Sal was Andie's boyfriend until after she went missing; she'd never had him over at the house. I knew she had a boyfriend, though, and, after that calamity party, I had assumed it was this other guy. I saw them alone, whispering and looking pretty close. Several times. Never once saw her with Sal.

PIP: Who? Who was the guy?

JESS: Um, he was this tall blond guy, longish hair, struck me as kind of obnoxious.

PIP: Max? Was his name Max Hastings?

JESS: Yeah, yeah, I think that was him.

PIP: You saw Max and Andie alone at the party?

JESS: Yep, looking pretty friendly.

PIP: Jess, thanks so much for talking with me. You've been a big help.

JESS: Oh, no problem. Hey, Pippa, do you know how Becca's doing now?

PIP: I saw her just the other day, actually. I think she's doing OK. She's interning at the Fairview newspaper. She looks well.

JESS: Good. I'm glad to hear that.

I'm struggling to even process the amount I've learned from that one conversation.

Jason Bell is looking darker and darker the more I investigate. And now I know that he left his dinner party for a while on *that* night. From what Jess said it sounds like he was emotionally abusive to his family. A bully. A chauvinist. An adulterer. It's no wonder Andie turned out the way she did in a toxic environment like that. Jason wrecked his daughters' self-esteem so much that one became a bully like him and the other turned to self-harming. I know from Andie's friend Emma that Becca had been hospitalized in the weeks before Andie's disappearance and that Andie was supposed to be watching her sister the night she went missing. It seems like Jess didn't know about the self-harming; she just thought Becca had skipped school.

So Andie wasn't the perfect girl and the Bells weren't the perfect family. All those smiling family photographs are lies.

Speaking of lies: Max. Max fucking Hastings. Here's a direct quote from his interview when I asked how well he knew Andie: *"We sometimes spoke, yeah. But we weren't ever, like, friend friends. I didn't really know her. Like an acquaintance."*

An acquaintance that you were seen cuddling up to at a party? So much so that a witness presumed *you* were Andie's boyfriend?

And there's this as well: even though they were in the same school year, Andie was young for her grade, and Max had been held back a year *and* has a September birthday. When you look at it like this, there is almost a two-year age gap between them. From Andie's perspective, Max *was* technically an older guy. But was he a *secret older guy?* Right up close and personal behind Sal's back?

I've tried looking Max up on Facebook before; his profile is barren, just vacation and Christmas pictures with his parents and birthday wishes from relatives. I remember thinking before that it seemed way too innocent for him, but I shrugged it off.

Well, not anymore. And I've made a discovery. In some of Naomi's pictures online, Max isn't tagged as *Max Hastings* but as *Nancy Tangotits.* I thought it was some kind of private joke before, but NO, *Nancy Tangotits* is Max's actual Facebook profile. The Max Hastings one must be a tame decoy he kept for colleges and potential employers. The same way some of my friends have started changing their profile names to make them unsearchable when applying to college.

The real Max Hastings—and all his wild, drunken photos and posts from friends—has been hiding as Nancy. This is what I'm guessing, at least. I can't actually get on to see anything: Nancy has his privacy settings on full throttle. I can only see photos or posts that Naomi is also tagged in. It's not giving me much to work with: no secret pictures of Max and Andie kissing in the background, none of his photos from the night she disappeared.

I've already learned my lesson here: when you catch someone lying about a murdered girl, you go ask them why.

PERSONS OF INTEREST

Jason Bell

Naomi Ward

Secret Older Guy

Nat da Silva

Daniel da Silva

Max Hastings (Nancy Tangotits)

sixteen

Pip knocked again, harder this time, hoping she would be heard over the droning of a vacuum cleaner running inside.

It clicked off abruptly, leaving a slightly buzzy silence in its wake. Then sharp footsteps on a hard floor.

The door opened and a well-dressed woman with cherry-red lipstick stood before her.

"Hi," Pip said. "I'm a friend of Max's. Is he in?"

"Oh, hi." The woman smiled, revealing a smear of red on one of her top teeth. She stood back to let Pip through. "He certainly is, come in. . . ."

"Pippa." She smiled back, stepping inside.

"Pippa. Yes, he's in the living room. Shouting at me for vacuuming while he's playing some death match. Can't pause it, apparently."

Max's mom walked Pip down the hall and through the open archway into the living room.

Max was spread out on the sofa, in plaid pajama bottoms and a white T-shirt, his hands gripped around a controller as he furiously thumbed the *X* button.

His mom cleared her throat.

Max looked up.

"Oh, hi, Pippa Funny-Last-Name," he said in his deep voice, his eyes returning to his game. "What are you doing here?"

Pip fought back a grimace with a fake smile. "Oh, nothing much." She shrugged nonchalantly. "Just here to ask you how well you *really* knew Andie Bell."

The game was paused.

Max sat up, stared at Pip, then his mom, then back to Pip.

"Um," his mom said, "would anyone like a drink?"

"No, we don't." Max stood. "Upstairs, Pippa."

He strode past them and up the grand stairs in the hallway, his bare feet thundering on the steps. Pip followed, flashing an apologetic wave back at his mother. At the top Max held open his bedroom door and gestured her inside.

Pip hesitated, one foot suspended above the vacuum-tracked carpet.

Max jerked his head impatiently.

His mom was just downstairs; she should be safe. She planted her foot and strode into his room.

"Thank you for that," he said, closing the door. "My mom didn't need to know I've been talking about Andie and Sal again. The woman is a bloodhound, never lets anything go."

"Pit bull," Pip said. "It's pit bulls that don't let things go."

Max sat back on his maroon bedspread. "Whatever. What do you want?"

"I said. I want to know how well you really knew Andie."

"I already told you," he said, leaning back on his elbows and shooting a glance up past Pip's shoulder. "I didn't know her that well."

"Mmm." Pip leaned back against his door. "Just acquaintances, right? That's what you said?"

"Yeah, I did." He scratched his nose. "I'll be honest. I'm starting to find your tone a little annoying."

"Good," she said, following Max's eyes as they looked over again to a noticeboard on the far wall, littered with posters and pinned-up notes and photographs. "And I'm starting to find your lies a little annoying."

"What lies?" he said. "I didn't know her well."

"Interesting," Pip said. "I spoke to a witness who went to a calamity party that you and Andie attended in March 2014. Interesting because she said she saw you two alone several times that night, looking pretty comfortable with each other."

"Who said that?" Another micro-glance over to the noticeboard.

"I can't reveal my sources."

"Oh my god," he laughed a deep throaty laugh. "You're deluded. You know you're not actually a police officer, right?"

The skin on her neck flashed hot; she didn't like that, him talking down to her.

"You're avoiding the question," she said. "Were you and Andie secretly seeing each other behind Sal's back?"

Max laughed again. "He was my best friend."

"That's not an answer." Pip folded her arms.

"No. No, I wasn't seeing Andie Bell. Like I said, I didn't know her that well."

"So why did this source see you together? In a manner that made her think you were actually Andie's boyfriend?"

While Max rolled his eyes at the question, Pip stole her own glance at the noticeboard. The scribbled notes and bits of paper were several layers deep in places, with hidden corners and curled edges. Glossy photos of Max skiing and surfing were pinned on top. A *Reservoir Dogs* poster took up most of the board.

"I don't know," he said. "Whoever it was, they were mistaken. Probably drunk. An unreliable source, you might say."

"OK." Pip moved away from the door. She took a few steps toward the far wall, then paced back a couple, so Max wouldn't realize as she moved incrementally toward the noticeboard. "So let's get this straight." She paced again, positioning herself closer and closer. "You're saying you never spoke one-on-one with Andie at a calamity party?"

"I don't know if never," Max said, "but it's not like you're implying."

"OK, OK." Pip looked up from the floor, just a couple of feet from the board now. "And why do you keep looking over here?" She twisted on her heels and hurriedly started flipping through the papers pinned to the board.

"Hey, stop."

She heard the bed groan as Max quickly got to his feet.

Pip's eyes and fingers scanned over to-do lists, scribbled names of companies and grad schemes, leaflets and old photos of a young Max in a hospital bed.

Heavy barefooted steps behind her.

"That's my private stuff!"

And then she saw a small white corner of paper, tucked underneath *Reservoir Dogs*. She pulled and ripped the paper out just as Max grabbed her arm. Pip spun toward him, and his fingers dug into her wrist. They both looked down at the piece of paper in her hand.

Pip's mouth fell open.

"Oh for fuck's sake." Max let her arm go and ran his fingers through his untamed hair.

"Just acquaintances?" she said shakily.

"Who do you think you are?" Max said. "Going through my stuff."

"Just acquaintances?" Pip asked again, holding the printed photo up to Max's face. He tried to snatch it, but she pulled back.

It was Andie.

A photo she'd taken of herself in a mirror. Standing on a red-and-white tiled floor, her right hand raised and clutched around the phone. Her mouth was pushed out in a pout, and her eyes looked straight out of the page; she was wearing nothing but a pair of black underwear.

"Care to explain?" Pip said.

"No."

"Oh, so you want to explain it to the police first? I get it." Pip glared at him and took one step toward the door.

"Don't be dramatic," Max said, returning her glare with his glassy blue eyes. "It has nothing to do with what happened to her."

"I'll let them decide that."

"No, Pippa." He blocked her way out. "Look, this is really not how it looks. Andie didn't give me that picture. I found it."

"You found it? Where?"

"It was just lying around at school. I found it and I kept it. Andie never knew about it." There was a hint of pleading in his voice.

"You found a nude picture of Andie just lying around at school?" She didn't even try to hide her skepticism.

"Yes. It was hidden in the back of a classroom. I swear."

"And you didn't tell Andie or anyone that you'd found it?" asked Pip.

"No, I just kept it."

"Why?"

"I don't know." His voice scrambled higher. "Because she's hot and I wanted to. And then it seemed wrong to throw it away after . . . What? Don't judge me. She took the photo; she clearly wanted it to be seen."

"You expect me to believe that you just found this basically naked picture of Andie, a girl you were seen getting close to at parties—"

Max cut her off. "Those are completely unrelated. I wasn't talking to Andie because we were together, and neither do I have that picture because we were together. We weren't together. We never were."

"So you *were* alone talking to Andie at that calamity party?" Pip said triumphantly.

Max held his face in his hands for a moment, his fingertips pressed into his eyes.

"Fine," he said quietly. "If I tell you, will you please just leave me alone? And no police."

"That depends."

"OK, fine. I knew Andie better than I said I did. A lot better. Since before she started with Sal. But I wasn't *seeing* her. I was buying from her."

Pip looked at him in confusion, her mind going back over his last words.

"Buying . . . drugs?" she asked softly.

Max nodded. "Nothing super hard, though. Just weed and a few pills."

"H-holy shit. Hold on." Pip held up her finger to push the world back, give her brain space to think. "Andie Bell was dealing drugs?"

"Well, yeah, but only at calamities and when we went out

and stuff. Just to a few people. A handful at most. She wasn't like a proper dealer." Max paused. "She was working with an actual dealer in town, got him an in with the school crowd. It worked out for both of them."

"That's why she always had so much cash," Pip said, the puzzle piece slotting into place in her head with an almost audible click. "Did she use?"

"Not really. Think she only did it for the money. Money and the power it gave her. I could tell she enjoyed that."

"And did Sal know she was selling drugs?"

Max laughed. "Oh, no," he said. "No, no, no. Sal always hated drugs; that wouldn't have gone down well. Andie hid it from him; she was good at secrets. I think the only people that knew were those who bought from her. But I always thought Sal was a little naive. I'm surprised he never found out."

"How long had she been doing this?" Pip said, feeling a crackle of sinister excitement.

"A while." Max looked up at the ceiling, his eyes circling as though he were turning over his own memories. "Think the first time I bought weed off her was early 2013, when she was still sixteen. That was probably around when it started."

"And who was Andie's dealer? Who did she get the drugs from?"

Max shrugged. "I dunno. I never knew the guy. I only ever bought through Andie, and she never told me."

Pip deflated. "You don't know anything? You never bought drugs in Fairview after Andie was killed?"

"Nope." He shrugged again. "I don't know anything more."

"But were other people at calamities still using drugs? Where did they get them?"

"I don't know, Pippa," Max overenunciated. "I told you what you wanted to hear. Now, I want you to leave."

He stepped forward and whipped the photo out of Pip's hands. His thumb closed over Andie's face, the picture crumpling in his grip. A crease split down the middle of Andie's body as he folded her away.

seventeen

Pip spotted Ant before the others did, waving him over to their table. He crossed the cafeteria, two packaged sandwiches cradled in his arms.

"Hey, guys," he said, sliding onto the bench beside Lauren, of course, already tearing into sandwich number one.

"How was practice?" Pip asked.

Ant looked up at her warily, his mouth open midchew. "Fine," he replied, then swallowed. "Why are you being nice to me? What do you want?"

"Nothing," Pip laughed. "I'm just asking how soccer was."

"No," Zach butted in, "that's far too friendly for you. Something's up."

"Nothing's up." She shrugged. "Only the national debt and global sea levels."

"Probably hormones," Ant said.

Pip wound the invisible crank by her hand, jerkily raising her middle finger up at him.

They were on to her already. Well, at least it was a welcome break from their teasing about never seeing her anymore, even though she saw them every single day at school. "Distracted" was the word Lauren has used last week.

Pip waited a full five minutes for the group to finish their conversation about the latest episode of the zombie show they all watched, as Connor stuffed his ears and hummed loudly because he hadn't seen it yet. Pip hadn't either. How many had she missed? The last three?

"So, Ant," she tried again, "you know your friend George from soccer?"

"Yes, I know my friend George from soccer," he said, glancing to check that Lauren found him as amusing as he found himself.

"He's in the crowd that still does calamity parties, right?"

Ant nodded. "Yeah. Actually, I think the next party is at his house. His parents are out of town for an anniversary or something."

"This Saturday?"

"Yeah."

"Do you . . ." Pip sat forward, resting her elbows on the table. "Do you think you could get us all invited?"

Every single one of her friends turned to stare at her.

"Who are you and what have you done with Pippa Fitz-Amobi?" Cara asked.

"What?" She felt herself getting defensive, words rushing out unchecked. "It's our last year at school, and I thought it would be nice for us all to go. This is the opportune time, before application and homework deadlines creep up."

"That still sounds Pip-ish to me." Connor smiled.

"You want to go to a house party?" Ant said pointedly.

"Yes," she said.

"Everyone will be smashed, people throwing up, passing out. A lot of mess on the floor," Ant said. "It's not really your scene, Pip."

No of course it wasn't—she couldn't think of anything worse—but she stood firm. "Sounds . . . fun. I want to go."

"OK, fine." Ant clapped his hands together with a grin. "Let's do it."

Pip stopped by Ravi's on her way home from school to give him the latest updates. He handed her a black coffee, making another joke about it as she took a sip. Pip choked. Why was she laughing? The joke wasn't even that funny, objectively speaking. She coughed and her cheeks flushed.

"OK," Ravi finally said when she was done talking, his head bouncing in a half nod as he tried to process the image of Andie Bell—cute, button-nosed blonde—as a drug dealer. "OK, so you're thinking the man who supplied her could be a suspect?"

"Yes," she said. "If you have the depravity to peddle drugs to kids, I definitely think you could be the kind of person inclined to murder."

"Yeah, I see the logic," he said, nodding. "How are we going to find this drug dealer, though?"

She set down her mug and focused her eyes on his. "I'm going undercover."

eighteen

"It's just a house party," Pip said, trying to wrestle her face out of Cara's grip.

"Yeah, but you're lucky—you can pull off eyeshadow. Stop wriggling. I'm almost done."

Pip sighed and went limp, submitting to the forced preening. She was still sulking that her friends had made her change out of her overalls and into one of Lauren's dresses that was short enough to be a T-shirt. She thought she'd looked fine before, but Cara and Lauren were both overexcited about their first calamity and wanted to go all out. Lauren was wearing a new sequined dress, and Cara's usual eyeliner wings had grown by an inch. They didn't normally do this kind of thing.

"Girls," Pip's mom called up the stairs, "you'd better hurry up. Victor's started to show Lauren his dance moves down here."

"Oh jeez," Pip said. "Am I done? We need to go and rescue her."

Cara leaned forward and blew on her face. "Yep."

"Awesome," said Pip, grabbing her shoulder bag and phone. "Let's go."

"Hello, pickle!" her dad said loudly as Pip and Cara made their way downstairs. "Lauren and I have decided that I should come to your kilometer party too."

"Calamity, Dad. And over my dead brain cells."

He strolled over, wrapped his arm around her shoulders, and squeezed. "Little Pipsy's going to a house party."

"I know," Pip's mom said, smiling. "With alcohol and boys."

"Yes." Her dad let go and looked down at Pip, a serious expression on his face, and his finger raised. "Pip, I want you to remember to be, at least, a little irresponsible."

"Right," Pip announced, grabbing her car keys and strolling to the front door. "We're going now. Farewell, my strange parents."

"Fare thee well," her dad said dramatically, waving them off.

The three of them strolled up to the front door, and Pip raised her fist to knock. Even the pavement outside was pulsing with the music. The door swung open to reveal a writhing cacophony of slurred chatter and poor lighting.

Pip took a tentative step inside, her first breath already tainted with the acrid smell of vodka, sweat, and the slightest hint of vomit. She caught sight of the host, Ant's friend George, making out aggressively on the stairs with a girl from the grade below, his eyes wide open and staring.

Pip, Cara, and Lauren walked farther down the corridor, Lauren having to step over Paul-from-econ, who was slumped against the wall, loudly snoring.

"Well, this looks . . . like some people's idea of fun," Pip said as they entered the open-plan living room and took in the chaos there: bodies grinding and thrashing to the music, towers of precariously balanced beer bottles, wet carpet patches, and couples pushed up against the condensation-dripping walls.

"You're the one who was so desperate to come," Lauren said, waving to some girls she took drama with.

Pip swallowed. "Yeah. And present Pip is always happy with past Pip's decisions."

Ant, Connor, and Zach spotted them and made their way over, maneuvering through the staggering crowd. "All right?" Connor said, giving Pip and the others clumsy hugs. "You're late."

"Are there cups?" Lauren said, holding up a bottle of vodka and lemonade.

"Yeah, I'll show you," Ant said eagerly, taking her toward the kitchen.

Lauren returned with a drink for Pip, who took frequent imaginary sips as she nodded along with the conversation, laughing at Cara's ridiculous dance moves. How was she so fearless? When the opportunity presented itself, Pip sidled over to the kitchen sink, poured out the cup, and filled it with water.

Later, when Zach offered to refill her cup, she had to pull the stunt again, regretting it immediately when she got cornered by Joe King in the kitchen. He sat behind her in English, and his only form of humor was to say something absurd, wait for his victim to pull a confused face, and then say: "I'm only *Joe* King."

Pip finally excused herself and went to hide in a corner, not quite back in her comfort zone, but close enough. Standing there alone in the shadows, she scrutinized the room, watching the dancers and the overenthusiastic kissers, searching for any signs of shifty hand trades or clenching jaws. Any overwide pupils. Anything that might give her a possible lead to Andie's drug dealer.

Ten minutes passed and Pip didn't notice anything dubious, other than a boy named Stephen smashing a TV remote and hiding the evidence in a flower vase. She watched him wander through the adjacent family room and toward the back door, reaching for a pack of cigarettes from his back pocket.

Of course.

Outside with the smokers should have been the first place on her list to scout out. Pip made her way through the mayhem, protecting herself with her elbows.

There were a handful of people outside. A couple of dark shadows rolling around on the trampoline at the end of the yard. A tearful Stella Chapman wailing into her phone at someone. Two girls on the swing set having a very serious conversation, punctuated by frequent hands-slapped-to-mouths gasps. And Stephen Thompson-or-Timpson, who she used to sit behind in math. He was perched on the garden wall, a cigarette dangling from his mouth as he searched in his various pockets.

Pip wandered over. "Hi," she said, plonking herself down on the wall beside him.

"Hi, Pippa," Stephen said, taking the cigarette from his mouth so he could talk. "What's up?"

"Oh, nothing much," Pip said. "Just came out here, looking for Mary Jane."

"Dunno who she is, sorry," he said, finally pulling out a neon green lighter.

"Not a who." Pip gave him a meaningful look. "You know, I'm looking to blast a roach."

"Excuse me?"

Pip had spent an hour online that morning, researching the current street names on Urban Dictionary.

She tried again, lowering her voice to a whisper. "You know, looking for some herb, the doob, a bit of hippie lettuce, giggle smoke, some skunk, wacky tobaccy. You know what I mean. Ganja."

Stephen burst into laughter. "Oh my god," he cackled, "you are so trashed."

"Certainly am." She tried to feign a drunken giggle. "So, do you have any? Some shwag grass?"

When he stopped hooting to himself, he turned to look her up and down, his eyes very obviously stalling on her chest and pasty legs. Pip squirmed inside; a slurry of disgust and embarrassment. But she had to play along; she was undercover.

"Yeah," Stephen said, biting his bottom lip. "I can roll us a joint." He searched his pockets again and pulled out a small baggy of weed and a packet of rolling papers.

"Yes, please." Pip nodded, feeling anxious and excited and a little sick. "You get rolling; roll it like a . . . rolling pin."

He laughed at her again and licked one edge of the paper, trying to hold eye contact with her while his stubby pink tongue was out. Pip looked away. It crossed her mind that maybe she had gone too far this time for an assignment. Maybe. But this wasn't just a project anymore. This was for Sal, for Ravi. For the truth. She could do this for them.

Stephen lit the joint and took two long sucks on its end before passing it to Pip. She took it awkwardly between her middle and index fingers. She turned her head sharply so her hair flicked over her face and pretended to take a couple of drags.

"Mmm, nice," she said, passing it back.

"You look nice," Stephen said, offering the joint again.

Pip tried to take it without her fingers touching his. Another pretend puff, but the smell was cloying, and she coughed over her next question.

"So," she said, "who do you buy from? You know, so I can get in on that too."

"Just this guy in town." Stephen shuffled on the wall, closer to Pip. "Called Howie."

"And where does Howie live?" Pip said, passing back the

weed and using the movement as an excuse to shift away from him.

"Dunno," Stephen said. "He doesn't deal from his house. I meet him at the station parking lot, down at the end with no cameras."

"In the evening?" Pip asked.

"Usually, yeah. Whatever time he texts me."

"You have his number?" Pip opened her bag and reached for her own phone. "Can I have it?"

Stephen shook his head. "He'd be mad if he knew I was just handing it out. You don't need to go to him; if you want something, you can just pay me and I'll get it for you. I'll even discount." He winked.

"I'd really rather buy direct," Pip said, feeling a prickle of annoyance creeping up her neck.

"No can do." He shook his head again, eyeing her mouth.

Pip looked away quickly, her long dark hair a curtain between them to hide her frustration.

She was just about to give it up when the spark of an idea pushed through.

"Well, how can I buy through you?" she said, taking the joint from him. "You don't even have my number."

"Ah, and what a shame that is," Stephen said, voice so slimy it practically dripped out of his mouth. He pulled his phone from his pocket, jabbed his finger at the screen, and handed her the unlocked phone. "Put your digits in there."

"OK."

Pip opened his contacts and shifted her shoulders, facing Stephen so he couldn't see the screen. She typed the name in the search bar, and it was almost too easy: *Howie Bowers* and his phone number.

She studied the sequence of numbers. Damn, she'd never be able to remember the whole thing. Another idea flickered to life. Maybe she could take a picture of the screen; her own phone was on the wall just beside her. But Stephen was right there, staring at her, chewing his finger. She needed some kind of distraction.

She lurched forward, launching the joint across the lawn. "Sorry," she said, "I thought there was a bug on me."

"Don't worry, I'll get it." Stephen jumped down from the wall.

Pip had just a few seconds. She grabbed her phone, swiped left into the camera app, and positioned it above Stephen's screen.

Her heart was thudding, her chest constricting uncomfortably.

The camera flicked in and out of focus, wasting precious time.

The shot finally cleared and she took the picture, dropping her phone into her lap just as Stephen turned.

"It's still lit," he said, jumping back up on the wall, sitting far too close to her.

Pip held out Stephen's phone to him. "Um, sorry, I've decided that drugs aren't for me. I have to go."

"Don't be a tease," Stephen said, closing his fingers around both his phone and Pip's hand. He leaned into her.

"No thank you," she said, scooting back.

Then Stephen grabbed the back of her head and lunged for her face. Pip twisted out of the way and shoved him so hard that he fell off the garden wall and sprawled on the wet grass.

"You stupid slut," he said, picking himself up and wiping off his pants.

"You degenerate, perverted ape!" Pip shouted back. "I said no."

That was when she realized. She didn't know how or when it had happened, but they were now alone in the backyard.

Fear flushed through her in an instant, her skin bristling.

Stephen climbed back over the wall as Pip turned, hurrying toward the door.

"Hey, it's OK, we can talk for a bit more," he said, grabbing her wrist to pull her back.

"Let me go, Stephen." She spat the words at him.

"But—"

Pip grabbed his wrist with her other hand and squeezed, digging her nails into his skin. Stephen hissed and let go, and Pip did not hesitate. She ran toward the house and slammed the door, flipping the lock behind her. Turning away as Stephen knocked angrily at it.

She wound her way through the crowd on the makeshift dance floor, jostled this way and that. It was too dark and stuffy inside the crush of all these bodies, and Pip couldn't find Cara anywhere. Couldn't find any of her friends. She stood there alone, surrounded by people, an aftershock of fear quaking through her.

PIPPA FITZ-AMOBI
10/1/19
CAPSTONE PROJECT LOG—ENTRY 22

I waited in my car for four hours tonight at the far end of the station parking lot. And I checked, no cameras, so it must have been the right spot. I waited long enough for three separate waves of commuters to get in from Manhattan, Dad among them. Luckily, he didn't spot my car.

And still I didn't see anyone hanging around. No one who looked like they were there to buy or sell drugs. Not that I really know what that looks like; I never would have guessed Andie Bell was the type.

I could just call Howie and see whether he'd be willing to answer some questions about Andie. That's what Ravi thinks we should do. But—let's be real—Howie's not going to give me anything that way. He's a drug dealer. He's not going to admit it to a stranger on the phone like he's casually discussing the weather.

No. The only way he'll talk is if we have the appropriate leverage first.

I'll go to the station again tomorrow evening. Ravi has work, but I can do this alone. I'll just tell my parents I'm doing my English homework over at Cara's house. The lying gets easier the more I have to do it.

I need to find Howie.

I need this leverage.

I need sleep.

PERSONS OF INTEREST

Jason Bell

Naomi Ward

Secret Older Guy

Nat da Silva

Daniel da Silva

Max Hastings

Drug dealer—Howie Bowers?

nineteen

Pip was thirteen chapters in, reading by the harsh flashlight on her phone, when she finally noticed a lone figure crossing under a street lamp. She was in her car, parked down at the far end of the darkened parking lot, every half hour marked with the screech and growl of inbound and outbound trains.

The streetlights had flickered on about an hour ago, that buzzy yellow color giving the area an unsettling industrial glow.

Pip squinted through the window. It was a man in a dark green coat with a furred hood and bright orange lining. His hood was up and his face hidden by shadows, only his downward lit nose visible.

She switched off her phone's flashlight and put down her book. She shifted her seat back so she could crouch on the car floor by the door, hidden from sight, the top of her head and her eyes pressed up against the window.

The man walked over to the very outer boundary of the lot and leaned against the fence there, in a gloomy space just between two lamps. Pip watched him closely, holding her breath because it fogged the window and blocked her view.

The man pulled out a phone. When the screen lit up, Pip could see his face for the first time: a bony face full of sharp lines and edges and neatly kept dark stubble. Pip wasn't the best with ages, but at a guess, the man was in his late twenties or early thirties.

True, this wasn't the first time tonight she thought she'd found Howie Bowers. But those other two men had been dressed in work suits and smart coats, clearly dawdlers of a trainload from the city. This man was different, and there was no doubt he was waiting for something. Or someone.

His thumbs were working away on his phone screen. Probably texting a client. Or she was just getting ahead of herself, in typical Pip fashion. Luckily she had one sure way to confirm that this man was Howie. She pulled out her phone, holding it low to hide its illumination, scrolled down through her contacts to Howie's name, and called him.

Her eyes back to the window, thumb hovering over the end call button, she waited. Her nerves spiking with every half second.

Then she heard it.

Much louder than the outgoing call tone from her own phone. A mechanical quacking sound from the man's hands. Pip watched as he answered and raised his phone to his ear.

"Hello?" came the voice from outside, muffled by her window. Fractionally later the same voice spoke through the speakers of her phone. Howie's voice, confirmed.

Pip pressed hang-up and watched as he lowered his phone and stared at it, his thick brows bunching and eclipsing his eyes in shadows. He tapped the phone and raised it to his ear again.

"Crap," Pip whispered, snatching up her phone and clicking it on to silent. Less than a second later, the screen lit up with an incoming call from Howie Bowers. Pip let the call silently ring out, her heart drumming painfully against her ribs. That was close, too close. Stupid not to withhold her number.

Howie put his phone away and stood, head down, hands back in pockets. Even though she now knew who he was, she didn't have confirmation that he'd been the man who supplied Andie with drugs. The only fact was that Howie Bowers was now currently dealing to kids at school, the same crowd Andie had introduced her dealer to. It could be a coincidence. Though Pip didn't trust coincidences.

Just then, Howie raised his head and nodded pointedly. Sharp clicking footsteps drew closer and louder. Pip didn't dare move. Someone crossed into view: a tall man wearing a long beige coat and polished black shoes, clearly new. His hair was dark and cut close to his head. As he arrived at Howie's side, he spun to lean against the fence beside him. Pip strained her eyes and gasped.

She knew this man. Knew his face from the staff pictures on the *Fairview Mail* website. Knew his voice from their one very fraught phone interview. It was Stanley Forbes.

Stanley Forbes, an outsider to Pip's investigation, who had now cropped up twice. Becca Bell said she was kind of seeing him, and now, here he was, meeting with the man who had possibly supplied Becca's sister with drugs.

Neither of the men had spoken yet. Stanley scratched his nose and then pulled out a thick envelope. He shoved the packet into Howie's chest, and only then did she notice that his face was flushed and his hands shaking. Pip raised her phone and, checking the flash was off, took a few pictures of the meeting.

"This is the last time, do you hear me?" Stanley spat, making no effort to keep his voice down. Pip could just hear the edges of his words through the car window. "You can't keep asking for more; I don't have it."

Howie spoke far too quietly in response, and Pip only heard the mumbled start and end of his sentence: "But . . . tell."

Stanley rounded on him. "I don't think you would dare."

They stared into each other's faces for a tense moment, then Stanley turned on his heels and walked quickly away, his coat fanning out behind him.

When he was gone, Howie looked through the envelope and stuffed it into his coat. But he wasn't going anywhere yet. He resumed standing against the fence, tapping away at his phone. Like he was still waiting for someone.

Minutes later, Pip saw someone else approach. Huddling back in her hiding spot, she watched the boy stride toward Howie, raising his hand in a wave. She recognized him, too: a boy in the grade below her at school, a boy who played soccer with Ant. Robin something.

Their meeting was just as brief. Robin pulled out some cash and handed it over. Howie counted the money and then produced a rolled-up paper bag from his coat pocket. Pip took a few pictures as Howie handed it to Robin and pocketed the cash.

Pip could see their mouths moving, but she couldn't hear the words they exchanged. Howie smiled and clapped the boy on the back. Robin, stuffing the bag into his backpack, wandered up the parking lot, calling a low "See you later" as he passed behind Pip's car, so close it made her jump.

Ducking below the car window frame, Pip scrolled through the pictures she'd taken; Howie's face was clearly visible in at least three of them. And Pip knew the name of the boy she'd caught him selling to. It was textbook leverage, if anyone had ever written a textbook on how to blackmail a drug dealer.

Pip froze. Someone was walking just behind her car, moving with shuffling footsteps, whistling. She waited twenty seconds and looked up. Howie was gone now, heading back toward the station.

And here was the moment of indecision. Howie was on foot;

Pip couldn't follow him in her car. But she really, really did not want to leave it.

Fear started to uncurl in her stomach, driven by one thought: Andie Bell went out in the dark on her own, and she never came back. Pip stifled the voice in her head and climbed out of the car, shutting the door as carefully as she could. She needed to learn as much as she could about this man. He could be the one who supplied Andie, the one who really killed her.

Howie was about forty paces ahead of her. His hood was down now, and its orange lining was easy to spot in the dark. Pip kept the distance between them, her heart getting in four beats between each of her steps.

She drew back and increased the gap as they passed through the well-lit roundabout outside the station. She couldn't get too close. She followed Howie to the right, down the hill, past the grocery store, across the road, and to the left along Main Street.

She trailed behind him all the way up Weevil Road and over the bridge that crossed the rail tracks. Beyond it Howie turned down a small path away from the street, through a yellowing hedge.

Pip waited for Howie to get a little farther ahead before she followed him, emerging on a dimly lit residential road. She kept going, her eyes on the orange-furred hood fifty feet ahead of her. Darkness was the easiest of disguises; it made the familiar unknown and strange. It was only when Pip passed a street sign that she realized what road they were on.

Monroe.

Her heart reacted instantly, now getting in six beats between her footsteps. Monroe, the very road where Andie Bell's car was found abandoned after her disappearance.

Pip saw Howie turning up ahead, and she darted to hide behind a tree, watching as he headed toward a small bungalow, pulled out his keys, and let himself in. As the door clicked shut, Pip emerged from her hiding place and approached Howie's house.

It was a squat semidetached home, with tan brick walls and a mossy slate roof. Both windows at the front were covered by thick blinds, the left one now glowing with streaks of yellow as Howie turned the lights on inside. There was a small gravel plot outside the front door with a faded maroon car.

Pip stared. There was no delay in her recognition this time. Her mouth fell open and her stomach jumped to her throat, filling her mouth with bile.

"Oh my god," she whispered.

She stepped back from the house, pulled out her phone, and dialed Ravi's number.

"Please tell me you're off your shift," she said when he picked up.

"I just got home. Why?"

"I need you to come to Monroe right now."

twenty

Pip knew from her murder map that it would take Ravi about eighteen minutes to walk from his house to Monroe. He was four minutes faster, running when he spotted her.

"What is it?" he said, out of breath and brushing the hair back off his face.

"'It' is a lot of things," Pip said quietly. "I'm not quite sure where to start, so I just will."

"You're freaking me out." His eyes flicked over her face, searching.

"I'm freaking me out too." She paused. "OK, you know how I was looking for the drug dealer, from my lead at the calamity party. Well, he was there tonight, dealing in the parking lot, and I followed him home. He lives here, Ravi. The road where Andie's car was found."

Ravi's eyes wandered up to trace the outline of the dark street. "But how do you even know he's the guy that supplied her?" he asked.

"I didn't for sure," she said. "I do now. But wait, there's another thing I have to tell you first, and I don't want you to be mad."

"Why would I be mad?" He looked down at her, his face hardening around the eyes.

"Um, because I lied to you," she said, her gaze down on her own feet. But she could feel Ravi's stare, and her stomach jumped up, blocking her throat. Why was this so hard? "I told you that Sal's police interview hadn't arrived yet. It did, over two weeks ago."

"What?" he said quietly. A look of unconcealed hurt clouded his face.

"I'm sorry," Pip said. "But when it arrived and I read through it, I thought you'd be better off not seeing it."

"Why?"

She swallowed. "Because it looked really bad for Sal. He was evasive with the police and outright told them he didn't want to say why he and Andie were arguing on that Thursday and Friday. It looked like he was trying to hide his own motive. And I was scared that maybe he'd actually killed her, and I didn't want to upset you." She chanced to look up at his eyes. They were drawn and sad.

"You think Sal is guilty after all this?"

"No, I don't. I just doubted it for a while, and I was scared what it would do to you. I was wrong, I'm sorry. It wasn't my place. But I was also wrong to ever doubt Sal."

Ravi looked at her, scratching the back of his head. "OK," he said. "It's OK, I get why you did it. So what's going on?"

"I just found out exactly why Sal was so weird and evasive in his police interview and why he and Andie were arguing. Come on."

She beckoned him to follow and walked back over to Howie's bungalow. She pointed.

"This is the drug dealer's house," she said. "Look at his car, Ravi."

She watched Ravi's face as his eyes tracked up and down over the car. From windshield to bumper and headlight to headlight. Until they dropped to the license plate.

"Oh," he said.

Pip nodded, staring back at the plate: 009 KKJ.

"Sal wrote that plate number in the notes on his phone," Pip said. "On Wednesday, the sixteenth of April, at about seven-forty-five p.m. He must have been suspicious—maybe he'd heard rumors at school or something. So he followed Andie that evening and must have seen her with Howie and this car. And what she was doing."

"That's why they were arguing in the days before she went missing," Ravi added. "Sal hated drugs. Hated them."

"And when the police asked him about their arguing," Pip continued, "he wasn't being evasive to hide his own motive. He was protecting Andie. He didn't think she was dead. He thought she was alive and coming back, and he didn't want to get her in trouble with the police by telling them she was dealing drugs. And the final text he sent her on that Friday night?"

" 'I'm not talking to you till you've stopped,' " Ravi quoted.

"You know," Pip said, smiling, "your brother has never looked more innocent than right now."

"Thanks." He returned the smile. "You know, I've never said this to a girl before, but . . . I'm glad you came knocking on my door out of the blue to interrogate me."

Blood flushed to her cheeks and she untucked her hair so he wouldn't see. "I distinctly remember you telling me to go away," she said.

"Well, it appears you're hard to get rid of."

"That I am." She bowed her head. "Ready to do some knocking with me?"

"What?" He looked at her, appalled.

"Oh come on," she said, striding toward Howie's front door. "You're finally going to get some action."

"Gah, so hard not to point out all the innuendos. Wait, Pip,"

Ravi said, bounding after her. "What are you doing? He's not going to talk to us."

"He will," Pip said, waving her phone above her head. "I have leverage."

"What leverage?" Ravi caught up with her just before the front door.

She turned and flashed him a scrunched-up, crinkly-eyed smile. And then she took his hand. Before Ravi could take it away, she knocked it three times against the door.

He widened his eyes in a silent rebuke.

They heard shuffling and coughing from inside. A few seconds later the door was roughly pulled open.

Howie stood there, blinking at them. He'd taken off his coat now and was wearing a stained blue T-shirt, his feet bare. He smelled of stale smoke and damp, moldy clothes.

"Hello, Howie Bowers," Pip said. "Please may we buy some drugs?"

"Who the hell are you?" Howie spat.

"I'm the hell person who took these lovely photos earlier tonight," Pip said, scrolling to the pictures of Howie and holding the phone up to face him. She swiped across so he saw the whole range. "Interestingly, I know this boy you sold drugs to. His name's Robin. I wonder what would happen if I called his parents right now and told them to search his backpack. I wonder if they'd find a small paper bag of treats. And then I wonder how long it would take for the police to come knocking around here, especially once I give them a call to help them along."

She let Howie digest it all, his eyes darting between the phone, Ravi, and Pip.

He grunted. "What do you want?"

"I want you to invite us in and answer some of our questions,"

Pip said, glad that Ravi was standing right behind her. She wasn't so scared with him here, his breath warm against her hair. "That's all, and we won't go to the police."

"What about?" he said, picking something from his teeth with his fingernails.

"About Andie Bell."

A look of badly performed confusion spread over Howie's face.

"You know, the girl you supplied with drugs to sell to schoolkids. The same girl who was murdered five years ago. Remember her?" Pip said. "Well, if you don't, I'm sure the police will remember."

"Fine," Howie said, stepping back over a pile of plastic bags, holding the door open. "You can come in."

"Excellent," Pip said, looking back at Ravi over her shoulder. She mouthed, "Leverage" to him, and he rolled his eyes. But as she went to enter the house, Ravi pulled her behind him, crossing the threshold first. He stared Howie down until the man drew back from the door and moved along the tiny corridor.

Pip followed Ravi inside, shutting the door behind her.

"This way," Howie said gruffly, disappearing into the living room.

He fell back into a tattered armchair, an open can of beer waiting for him on the armrest. Ravi stepped over to the sofa and, pushing away a pile of clothes, took the seat opposite Howie, straight-backed and as close to the edge of the couch cushion as it was possible to be. Pip sat beside him, crossing her arms.

Howie pointed his beer can at Ravi. "You're the brother of the guy that murdered her."

"Allegedly," Pip and Ravi said at the same time.

The tension in the room mounted as eye contact shifted between the three of them.

"You understand we'll go to the police with these pictures if you don't answer our questions about Andie?" Pip said, eyeing the beer, which probably wasn't Howie's first since returning home.

"Yes, darling," Howie laughed a teeth-whistle laugh. "You've made that clear enough."

"Good," she said. "I'll keep my questions nice and clear too. When did Andie first start working with you, and how did it come about?"

"I don't remember." He took a large glug of beer. "Maybe early 2013. And she was the one that came to me. All I know is I had this ballsy teenager strolling up to me in the parking lot, telling me she could get me more business if I gave her a cut. Said she wanted to make money, and I told her that I had similar interests. Don't know how she found out where I sold."

"So you agreed when she offered to help you sell?"

"Obviously. She was promising an in with the younger crowd, kids I couldn't really get to. It was win-win."

"And then what happened?" Ravi said.

Howie's eyes alighted on Ravi, and Pip felt him tense where their arms almost touched.

"We met up and I gave her some ground rules, like about keeping the stash and money hidden, about using codes rather than names. I gave her a phone to use for business stuff and that was it, really. I sent her out into the big wide world." Howie smiled, his face and stubble unnervingly symmetrical.

"Andie had a second phone?" Pip asked.

"Yeah, obviously. Couldn't be arranging deals on a phone her parents paid for, could she? I bought her a burner phone, prepaid in cash. Two, actually. I got the second one when the credit on the first ran out. Gave it to her only a few months before she got killed."

"Where did Andie keep the drugs before she sold them?" asked Ravi.

"That was part of the ground rules." Howie sat back, speaking into his can. "I told her this little business venture would go nowhere if she didn't have somewhere to hide the stash and her second phone without her parents finding it. She assured me she had just the place, and no one else knew about it."

"Where was it?" Ravi pressed.

He scratched his chin. "Um, think it was some kind of loose floorboard in her wardrobe. She said her parents had no idea it existed and she was always hiding shit there."

"So the phone's probably still hidden in Andie's bedroom?" Pip said.

"I don't know. Unless she had it on her when she . . ." Howie made a gurgling sound as he crossed his finger sharply across his throat.

Pip looked over at Ravi before her next question, a muscle pulsing in his jaw as he ground his teeth, not dropping his eyes from Howie. Like he thought he could hold him in place with his stare.

"OK," she said, "so which drugs was Andie selling at house parties?"

Howie crushed the empty can and threw it onto the floor. "Started with just weed," he said. "By the end she was selling a load of different things."

"She asked *which* drugs Andie sold," said Ravi. "List them."

"Yeah, OK." Howie looked annoyed, sitting up taller and picking at a textured brown stain on his T-shirt. "She sold weed, sometimes ecstasy, mephedrone, ketamine. She had a couple of regular buyers of Rohypnol."

"Rohypnol?" Pip repeated, unable to hide her shock. "You mean roofies? Andie was dealing roofies at school parties?"

"Yeah. They're for like chilling out though, too, not just what most people think."

"Did you know who was buying Rohypnol from Andie?" she asked.

"Um, there was this rich kid, I think she said. Dunno." Howie shook his head.

"A rich kid?" Pip's mind immediately drew a picture of him: his angular face and sneering smile, floppy yellow hair. "Was this rich kid a blond guy?"

Howie looked blankly at her and shrugged.

"Answer or we go to the police," Ravi said.

"Yeah, it could have been that blond guy."

Pip cleared her throat to give herself some thinking time. "OK," she said. "How often would you and Andie meet?"

"Whenever we needed to, whenever she had orders to collect or cash to give me. I'd say it was probably about once a week—sometimes more, sometimes less."

"Where did you meet?" Ravi asked.

"At the station, or she sometimes came over here."

"Were you . . ." Pip paused. "Were you and Andie involved romantically?"

Howie snorted. He sat up suddenly, swatting something near his ear. "Fuck no, we weren't." His laughter didn't wholly cover the anger creeping up his neck in red patches.

"Are you sure about that?"

"Yes, I'm sure." The cover of amusement was cast aside now.

"Why are you getting defensive, then?" Pip said.

"Course I'm defensive. There's two kids in my house, berating me about stuff that happened years ago and threatening to tell the cops." He kicked out at the crumpled beer can on the floor, and it sailed across the room, clattering into the blinds just behind Pip's head.

Ravi jumped up from the sofa, stepping in front of her.

"What are you going to do about it?" Howie leered at him, staggering to his feet. "You're a fucking joke, man."

"All right, everyone, calm down," Pip said, standing up too. "We're almost finished here; you just have to answer honestly. Did you have a sexual relationship with—"

"No. I already said no, didn't I?" The flush reached his face, peeking out above the line of his beard. "She was just business to me, OK? It wasn't any more complicated than that."

"Where were you the night she was killed?" Ravi demanded.

"I was passed out drunk on *that* sofa."

"Do you know who killed her?" said Pip.

"Yeah, his brother." Howie pointed aggressively at Ravi. "Is that what this is? You want to prove your murdering scum brother was innocent?"

Pip saw Ravi stiffen, folding his hands into fists. Then he caught her eyes and shook the hardness out of his face, tucking his fingers into his pockets.

"OK, we're done here," Pip said, laying her hand on Ravi's arm. "Let's go."

"No, no, I don't think so." In two giant leaps, Howie darted over to the door, blocking their way out.

"Excuse me, Howard," Pip said, her nervousness cooling into fear.

"No, no, no," he laughed, shaking his head. "I can't let you leave."

Ravi stepped up to him. "Move."

"I did what you asked." Howie turned to Pip. "Now you have to delete those pictures of me."

Pip relaxed a little. "OK," she said. "Yes, that's fair." She held up her phone and showed Howie as she deleted every single picture from the parking lot, until she swiped right to a photo of Barney and Josh asleep in the dog bed together. "Done."

Howie stepped aside and let them pass.

Pip pulled open the front door, and she and Ravi stepped outside into the brisk night air, but not before Howie said one last thing: "You go around asking dangerous questions, girl, you're going to find some dangerous answers."

Ravi yanked the door shut. He waited until the house was at least twenty paces behind them before saying, "Well, that was fun. Thanks for the invite to my first blackmailing."

"Welcome," she said. "My first time too. But it worked; we found out that Andie had a second phone, Howie had complicated feelings for her, and Max Hastings had a taste for Rohypnol." She unlocked her phone. "Just recovering those photos, in case we need future Howie leverage."

"Oh, fantastic," he said. "Can't wait. Maybe then I can add blackmail as a special skill to my résumé."

"You know you use humor as a defense mechanism when you're tense?" Pip smirked at him, letting him through the hedge gap ahead of her.

"Yeah, and you turn into a smartass."

He looked back at her for a long moment, and she broke first. They started laughing, slowly at first, still in shock, and then they couldn't seem to stop. Pip's skin hummed with adrenaline as she fell into Ravi, eyes watering. Her stomach felt tight and sore and something else; a warm, fizzing feeling.

The after-laugh sighs only set them off again.

PIPPA FITZ-AMOBI
10/4/19
CAPSTONE PROJECT LOG—ENTRY 23

I should really be concentrating on my application; the deadline for early decision is less than a month away. I've already filled in the Common App, letters of recommendation are sorted out, and the Columbia questions look easy enough. It's the personal essay I'm worried about; I've read through the prompts, but I have no idea what to say. The school counselor says to just be yourself. But how am I supposed to explain exactly who I am when I don't actually know? I'm good at homework, I guess, and I'm motivated. But is that what makes me *me*?

I need to focus on something else before I drive myself crazy.

So, Howie Bowers doesn't have an alibi for the night Andie disappeared. By his own admission he was "passed out drunk" at his house. Without corroboration this could be a total fabrication. He's an older guy, and Andie could have *ruined* him by turning him into the police for dealing. His relationship with Andie had criminal foundations and, judging by his defensiveness, possibly some sexual undertones. And her car—the car that police believe was driven with her body in the trunk—was found on his street.

I know Max *does* have an alibi for the night Andie disappeared, the same alibi Sal asked his friends to give him. But Andie's abduction window was between 10:40 p.m. and 12:45 a.m. There is a possibility that Max could have worked with the later end of that time frame. His parents were away, Jake and Sal had left his house, and Millie and Naomi went to sleep in the spare room "a bit before twelve-thirty." Max could have left the house at that time without anyone knowing. Maybe Naomi could have too. Or together?

Max has a naked picture of a murder victim he claims he was never romantically involved with. He is technically an older guy. He was involved in Andie's drug dealing and regularly bought roofies from her. Rich kid Max Hastings isn't looking so wholesome anymore. Maybe I need to follow this Rohypnol line of intel, see if there is any other evidence of what I'm starting to suspect.

Though they are both looking simultaneously suspicious, there's no Max-Howie team going on here. Max only bought drugs in Fairview through Andie, and Howie only knew vaguely of Max and his buying habits via Andie.

But I think the most important lead is Andie's second burner phone. That's priority number one. That second phone most likely has all the details of the people she was selling drugs to. Maybe confirmation of the nature of her relationship with Howie. And if Howie wasn't the secret older guy, maybe Andie was using her burner phone to contact this man, to keep it secret. The police had Andie's actual phone after they found Sal's body; if there were any evidence of a secret relationship on it, the police would have followed it up.

If we find that phone, maybe we find her secret older guy, maybe we find her killer and this will all be over. As it stands, there are three possible candidates for Secret Older Guy: Max, Howie, or Daniel da Silva. If the burner phone confirms any one of them, I think we'd have enough to go to the police.

Or it could be someone we haven't found yet. Someone like Stanley Forbes, maybe? I know there's no direct link between him and Andie, so he doesn't make the POI list. But doesn't it seem a little suspicious that he's the journalist who wrote scathing articles about Andie's "killer boyfriend," and now he's dating her little sister *and* I saw him giving money to the same drug dealer who'd supplied Andie? Or are these just coincidences?

PERSONS OF INTEREST

Jason Bell

Naomi Ward

Secret Older Guy

Nat da Silva

Daniel da Silva

Max Hastings

Howie Bowers

twenty-one

"Barney-Barney-Barney plops," Pip sang, both the dog's front paws in her hands as they danced around the dining table.

Her mom entered with a dish of roasted potatoes, placing them on a trivet on the table. "Get your brother, Pips?" she said, leaving the room.

"Josh! Dinner's ready," Pip called.

"Well, I could have done that," her mom said, returning with a steaming bowl of broccoli and peas, a small knob of butter melting on top. Pip went to help her dad carry in the plates and the roast chicken, Josh sidling in behind them.

"You finish your homework, sweetie?" Pip's mom asked Josh as they all took their seats at the table. Barney's place was on the floor beside Pip, waiting for her to drop bits of food when her parents weren't looking.

Josh nodded, already loading up his plate, and she turned to Pip next, her fork pointed at her. "And when's the deadline for sending in your application?"

"November first," Pip said. "I'm going to try to send it in early, though; maybe end of next week."

"Have you started your personal essay yet? You want to give yourself plenty of time."

"There's still time. And when am I ever not on top of things, Mom?" Pip said, spearing a piece of overgrown broccoli. "If I ever miss a deadline, it will be because the apocalypse has started."

"OK, sweetie. Just don't spread yourself too thin."

Pip's phone chimed loudly from her pocket, making Barney jump and her mom scowl.

"No phones at the table," she said.

"Sorry. Just putting it on silent."

It could very well be the start of one of Cara's lengthy monologues sent line by line, a chaotic scramble of buzzing and dinging. Or maybe it was Ravi. The thought almost made her smile, but she fought it, knowing her dad would ask, *What's so funny?* She pulled out the phone to flick it to silent, looking down at the screen.

The blood drained from her face.

All the heat rushed down her back, churning in her stomach and pushing her dinner back up.

"Pip?"

"Uh . . . I . . . have to use the bathroom," she said, jumping up from her chair with her phone in hand, almost tripping over the dog.

She darted from the room and across the hall. Her thick woolen socks slipped out under her on the polished oak and she fell, catching her weight on one elbow.

"Pippa?" her dad called.

"I'm OK," she said, picking herself up. "Just slipped."

She shut the bathroom door behind her and locked it. Slamming the toilet lid down, she turned shakily to sit, phone between both hands. She opened the new message.

You stupid bitch. Leave this alone while you still can.

From "Unknown."

PIPPA FITZ-AMOBI
10/7/19
CAPSTONE PROJECT LOG—ENTRY 24

I can't sleep.

School starts in five hours and I can't sleep.

There's no part of me that thinks this can be a joke anymore. The note in my sleeping bag, this text. It's real. I've plugged all the leaks in my research since the camping trip; the only people who know what I've discovered are Ravi and those I've interviewed.

Yet someone knows I'm getting close, and they're starting to panic. Someone who followed me into the woods. Someone who has my phone number.

I tried to message them back, a futile *who is this?* It errored, couldn't go through. I've looked it up: there are websites and apps you can use to anonymize texts, so I can't reply or find out who it is.

Is this Unknown the person who actually murdered Andie Bell? Do they want me to think they can get to me too?

I can't go to the police. I don't have enough evidence. All I have are unsworn statements from people who knew different fragments of Andie's secret lives. I have seven persons of interest, but no one main suspect. There are too many people in Fairview who had motive to kill Andie.

I need tangible proof.

I need that burner phone.

And only then will I leave this alone, Unknown.

twenty-two

"Why are we here?" Ravi asked when he caught sight of her.

"Shhh," Pip hissed, grabbing his coat sleeve to pull him behind the tree. She peeked her head out past the trunk, watching the house across the street.

"Shouldn't you be at school?" he asked.

"I'm ditching, OK?" Pip said. "Don't make me feel guiltier than I already do."

"You've never played hooky before?"

"Only ever missed four days of school. *Ever.* And that was because of chicken pox," she said quietly, her eyes on the large detached house. The bricks speckled from pale yellow to dark russet and were overrun with ivy that climbed up to the roofline. The driveway was empty, and the large white garage door winked the morning sunshine back at them. It was the last house on the street before the road climbed up to the church.

"What are we doing here?" Ravi said, tucking his head around the other side of the tree to look at Pip.

"I've been here since just after eight," she said, hardly pausing to breathe. "Becca's mom left just as I was arriving. My mom says she works part-time at a nonprofit in Norwalk. And Becca left about twenty minutes ago; she's interning at the *Fairview Mail* office. It's only nine-fifteen now, so they should both be out for a while. And there's no alarm on the front of the house."

Her last word slipped into a yawn. She'd hardly slept last night, waking to stare again at the text from Unknown until the words were burned into the underside of her eyelids, haunting her every time she closed her eyes.

"Pip," Ravi said. "Tell me you're not thinking what I think you're thinking." He was looking at her in his telling-off way already.

"We're breaking in," she said. "We have to find that burner phone."

He groaned.

"It's evidence, Ravi. Actual physical evidence. Proof she was dealing drugs with Howie, and maybe the identity of the secret older guy. If we find it, we can phone an anonymous tip in to the police, and they might reopen the investigation and actually find her killer."

"OK, but quick observation," Ravi said, holding up his finger. "You're asking me, the brother of the person everyone thinks murdered Andie Bell, to break into the Bell house? Not to mention the amount of trouble I'd be in anyway as a brown guy breaking into a white family's house."

"Shit, Ravi." Pip stepped back behind the tree, her breath catching in her throat. "I'm so sorry. I wasn't thinking."

She really hadn't been thinking; she was so convinced the truth was waiting for them in this house that she hadn't considered Ravi. Of course he couldn't help her break in. This town already treated him like a criminal—and how much worse would it be for him if they got caught?

"I'm so sorry," she said again, angry at herself, her stomach twisting in uncomfortable knots. "I was being stupid. I know you can't take the same risks I can. I'll go in alone. Maybe you can keep a lookout?"

He paused. "No," he said thoughtfully, fingers burrowing through his hair. "If this is how we're going to clear Sal's name, I have to be there. That's worth the risk. I'll probably regret this, but"—he paused, flashing her a small smile—"we're partners in crime, after all."

"You sure?" Pip shifted, and the strap of her bag fell to the crook of her elbow.

"I'm sure," he said, reaching out and lifting the strap back up to her shoulder.

"OK." Pip turned to survey the empty house. "If it's any consolation, I wasn't planning on us getting caught."

"So what *is* the plan?" he said. "Break a window?"

She gaped at him. "No way. I was planning to use a key. We live in Fairview; everyone has a spare key outside somewhere."

"Oh . . . right. Let's go and scope out the target, Sarge." Ravi looked intently at her, pretending to do a complex sequence of military hand gestures. She flicked him to stop.

Pip went first, walking briskly across the road and over the front lawn. Thank goodness the Bells lived at the very end of a quiet street; there was no one around. She reached the front door, and Ravi darted across, head down, to join her.

They checked under the doormat first, where Pip's family kept their spare key. No luck. Ravi reached up and felt the frame above the front door. He pulled his hand back empty, fingertips covered in dust and grime.

"OK, you check that bush, I'll check this one."

There was no key beneath either, or hidden around the lanterns or behind the thick ivy.

"Oh, no way," Ravi said, pointing at the chrome wind chime mounted beside the front door. He snaked his hand through the metal tubes, gritting his teeth when two knocked together.

"Ravi," she said in an urgent whisper, "what are you—"

He pulled something off the small wooden platform that hung in the middle of the chimes and held it up to her: a key with a little nub of old tape attached.

"Aha," he said. "Student becomes master. I'm coming for your title, Sarge."

"Sure, Singh."

Pip lowered her bag and rustled inside it.

"Wh— I don't even want to ask," Ravi laughed, shaking his head as Pip removed bright yellow rubber gloves and put them on.

"I'm about to commit a crime," she said. "I don't want to leave any fingerprints." She held out her fluorescent yellow palm and Ravi placed the key onto it. "There's a pair in here for you too."

She rummaged through her bag and stood up, handing him a set of purple flower-patterned ones.

"What are these?" he asked.

"My mom's gardening gloves. Look, I didn't have a long time to plan this heist, OK?"

"Clearly," Ravi muttered.

"They're the bigger pair. Just put them on."

"*Real* men wear floral when trespassing," Ravi said, slipping them on and clapping his gloved hands together.

They were ready.

Pip took a breath, shouldered her bag, and stepped up to the door. Holding her wrist steady with her other hand, she guided the key into the lock and twisted.

twenty-three

The sunlight followed them inside, casting a long, glowing strip down the tiled floor. Ravi closed the door and they walked slowly down the hall. Pip couldn't help but tiptoe, even though she knew no one was home. She'd seen this house many times before, photographed at different angles with police swarming outside. But that was the outside. All she'd ever seen of the inside were snatches from when the front door was open and captured by a press photographer.

The border between outside and in felt significant here.

She could tell Ravi felt it, too, by the way he held his breath. There was a heaviness to the air. Secrets captured in the silence, floating around like invisible motes of dust. Pip didn't even want to think too loudly, in case she disturbed it. This quiet place, where Andie Bell was last seen alive, when she was only a few months older than Pip. The house itself part of the mystery.

They moved toward the stairs, glancing into the plush living room on the right and the huge vintage-style kitchen on the left, fitted with robin's-egg blue cabinets and a large wood-top island.

And then they heard it. A small thump upstairs.

Pip froze.

Ravi grabbed her gloved hand with his.

Another thump, closer this time, just above their heads.

Pip looked back at the door; could they make it out in time?

The thumps became a sound of frantic jingling, and a black cat appeared at the top of the stairs.

"Holy crap," Ravi said, dropping his shoulders and Pip's hand, the relief rippling off him.

Pip let out a hollow, anxious laugh, her hands starting to sweat inside the rubber. The cat leaped down the stairs, stopping halfway to meow in their direction.

"Hi, cat," she whispered as it padded down the rest of the stairs and slinked over to her. It rubbed its face on her shins, curling in and out between her legs.

"Pip, I really don't like cats," Ravi said, recoiling as the cat started to press its head into his ankles. Pip patted the cat lightly with her rubber-gloved hand and it started to purr.

"Come on," she said to Ravi.

Leaving the cat behind, Pip headed up the stairs. Ravi followed, and the cat meowed and raced after them, darting between his legs.

"Pip . . ." Ravi trailed off anxiously as he tried not to step on it. Pip shooed the cat, and it trotted back downstairs into the kitchen. "I wasn't scared," he added unconvincingly.

"Sure."

Gloved hand on the banister, she climbed to the top, almost knocking off a notebook and a USB stick that were balanced precariously on the railing. Strange place to leave them.

Upstairs, Pip studied the doors that opened on to the landing. In the back bedroom on the right, the floral bedspread was ruffled and slept in, paired socks on the chair in the corner. The bedroom at the front had a dressing gown strewn on the floor and a glass of water on a bedside table. Neither could be Andie's.

Ravi tapped Pip gently on the arm and pointed. There was only one door up here that was closed. They crossed over to it, and Pip grasped the gold handle to push it open.

It was immediately obvious this was *her* room.

Everything felt staged and stagnant. Though it had all the props of a teenage girl's bedroom—pinned-up photos of Andie with Emma and Chloe at the winter carnival; a small framed picture of her and Sal, his arm round her waist and her eyes glittering; an old brown teddy tucked into the bed; an overflowing makeup case on the desk—the room didn't feel quite real. A place entombed in five years of grief.

Pip stepped onto the plush cream carpet.

Her eyes scanned the room from the lilac walls to the white wooden furniture; everything clean and polished, the carpet showing recent vacuum tracks. Dawn Bell must still clean her dead daughter's room, preserving it as it was when Andie left it for the final time. She didn't have her daughter, but she still had the place where she'd slept, where she'd woken, where she'd dressed, where she'd screamed and shouted and slammed the door, where her mom had whispered good night and turned off the light. Or so Pip imagined, reanimating the empty room with the life that might have been lived here.

Pip looked back at Ravi, and by the expression on his face, she knew there was a room just like this in the Singhs' house.

And though Pip had come to feel like she knew Andie, the one buried under all those secrets, this bedroom made Andie a real person to her for the first time. As she and Ravi approached the wardrobe, Pip silently promised the room that she would find the truth. Not just for Sal, but for Andie too.

The truth that could very well be hidden right here.

"Ready?" Ravi whispered.

She nodded, and he opened the wardrobe.

Inside was a rack bulging with dresses and tops, no room to part even an inch of space between the clothes. Struggling with the rubber gloves, Pip pulled her phone out of her jeans pocket and turned on the flashlight. She got down on her knees, with Ravi beside her, and they crawled under the garments, lighting up the old floorboards inside. They started prodding the slats, tracing their fingers around the shape of them, trying to pry up their corners.

Ravi pushed down one corner at the back, and the other side of the floorboard kicked up. Pip shuffled forward to pull it out of the way, and then they leaned over to look inside the dark gap below.

"No."

She moved the light down inside the small space to be absolutely sure, pivoting the light into each corner. It revealed only layers of dust, disturbed now by their breath.

No phone. No cash. No drug stash. Nothing.

"It's not here," Ravi said.

The disappointment was a physical sensation tearing through Pip's stomach.

"I really thought it would be here," he said.

Pip had too. The burner phone was supposed to be here, supposed to reveal the killer's name, and then the police would do the rest. Pip was supposed to be safe from Unknown. But it wasn't here.

She slid the floorboard back in place and inched backward out of the wardrobe after Ravi, her hair getting tangled in the zipper of a long dress.

"Where could the burner phone be, then?" Ravi asked.

“Maybe Andie had it on her when she died,” Pip said, “and now it’s buried with her or otherwise destroyed by the killer.”

“Or,” Ravi said, studying the items on Andie’s desk, “someone knew where it was hidden and they took it after she went missing, knowing it would lead the police to them if it was found.”

“Or that,” Pip agreed. “But that doesn’t help us now.”

She joined Ravi at the desk. On top of the makeup case was a paddle hairbrush with long blond hairs still wound around the bristles. Beside it a Fairview High School academic planner for the year 2013/2014, almost identical to the one Pip had for this year. Andie had decorated the title page with doodled hearts and stars and small printouts of supermodels.

She flipped through some of the pages. The days were filled with scribbled homework assignments and test dates. November and December had various college open-house days listed. The week before Christmas, Andie had a note to herself: *maybe get Sal a Christmas present.* Dates and locations of calamity parties, people’s birthdays, and strangely, random letters with times scribbled in next to them.

“Hey.” She held it up to show Ravi. “Look at these weird initials all over the place. What do you think they mean?”

Ravi stared for a moment, resting his jaw in his gardening-gloved hand. “Do you remember that thing Howie Bowers said to us? That he’d told Andie to use codes instead of names.”

“Maybe these are her codes,” Pip said, tracing her rubber finger over the random letters. “We should document these.”

She laid the planner down and pulled out her phone again. Ravi helped her tug one of her gloves off, and she opened the camera. Ravi skipped the pages back to February 2014, and Pip took pictures of each page spread until that week in April, just after spring break. The last thing Andie had written on that Friday was: *Start French revision notes soon.*

"OK," Pip said, pocketing her phone and slipping the glove back on. "We—"

The front door slammed below them.

Ravi's head snapped around, terror pooling in the pupils of his eyes.

Pip dropped the planner back in its place and nodded toward the wardrobe. "Get back in," she whispered.

She opened the doors and crawled inside, looking back for Ravi.

He was on his knees just outside. Pip shuffled aside to give him space to crawl in. But Ravi wasn't moving. Why wasn't he moving?

Pip reached forward and grabbed him, pulling him into her against the back wall, and Ravi snapped back to life. He grasped the wardrobe doors and shut them inside.

Sharp-heeled steps in the hallway. Was it Andie's mom, back from work already?

"Hello, Monty." A voice carried through the house. It was Becca.

Ravi was shaking beside her. She moved closer and took his hand, the rubber gloves squeaking as she held on.

They heard Becca on the stairs then, louder with each step, the jingling collar of the cat behind her.

"Ah, that's where I left them," she said, footsteps pausing on the landing.

Pip squeezed Ravi's hand, his face just a few inches away. She hoped he knew she would take the fall if she could.

"Monty, have you been in here?" Becca's voice drew nearer.

Ravi closed his eyes.

"You know you're not supposed to go in this room."

Pip buried her face into his shoulder.

Becca was in the room with them now. They could hear her breathing, hear the clicking of her bones as she moved. More steps stifled by the thick carpet. And then the sound of Andie's bedroom door closing.

"Bye, Monty." Becca's words were muffled now on the other side of the door.

Ravi opened his eyes slowly, squeezing Pip's hand back, his panicked breaths rippling through her hair.

The front door slammed again.

PIPPA FITZ-AMOBI
10/7/19
CAPSTONE PROJECT LOG—ENTRY 25

I guess that's what they mean by "a close call." Ravi still wasn't quite himself by the time he had to leave for work. And the burner phone wasn't even there . . . but the break-in might not have been for nothing.

I emailed the photos of Andie's planner to myself so I could see them bigger on my laptop screen. I've gone through each one dozens of times, and I think there are some things to pick up on here.

This is the week after spring break, the week Andie disappeared. There's a lot to look at on this page alone, starting with the *Fat da Silva 0–3 Andie* scorecard comment. This was just after Andie posted the nude video of Nat online. And I know from Nat that she only returned to school on Wednesday, April 16, and Andie called her a slut in the corridor, prompting the death threat stuffed in Andie's locker.

But judging this comment at face value, it seems Andie was gloating over three victories she'd had over Nat in her twisted games. If the topless video was one of these goals, was blackmailing Nat to drop out of *The Crucible* another? Then what was the third thing Andie did to Nat da Silva? Could that have been what made Nat snap and turned her into a killer?

Another significant entry on that page is on Wednesday, April 16: TS @ 7:30.

If Ravi is right, and Andie was writing things down in code, I think I've cracked this one. It's so simple.

"TS"="train station." As in the train station parking lot. I think

2014

JAN FEB MAR APR MAY JUN JUL AUG SEPT OCT NOV DEC

MONDAY 14

French-passage translation for Friday

Drama-blocking notes on Act 1 Scene 4

[illegible]

Shopping with Chlo Chlo after school

TUESDAY 15

do translation today!!!

↑ Or get Sal's hw

Rehearsal with Jamie and Lex @ Lunch

WEDNESDAY 16

[Fat da Silva 0-3 Andie]

- Geog-read and notes on river chapter

→TS @ 7:30

THURSDAY 17

- get translation from Chris Parks
- get Lex to get fake cigar props
- P 5+6 go back to Em's

FRIDAY 18

Start French revision notes soon

SATURDAY/SUNDAY 19/20

CALENDAR

CONTACTS

TASKS

NOTES

MISC

Andie was reminding herself that she had a meeting with Howie at the station that evening. I know that she *did,* in fact, meet Howie that evening, because Sal wrote Howie's license plate number in his phone at 7:42 p.m. on the very same Wednesday.

There are many more instances of TS with an accompanying time in the photos we took. I think I can confidently say that these refer to Andie's drug trades with Howie and that she was following Howie's instructions to use codes, to keep her activities secret from prying eyes. Having them in her planner was the perfect memory prompt.

There are other initialized entries with times written in the planner.

During this mid-March week, Andie wrote on Thursday the 13: IV @ 8.

This one I'm stumped on. If it follows the same code pattern, then "IV"="I . . . V . . ."

If, like TS, IV refers to a place, I have no idea what it is. There's nowhere in Fairview I can think of with those initials. Or could IV refer to somebody's name? It appears only three times in the pages we photographed.

There's a similar entry that appears much more frequently: HH @ 6. On this March 15 entry, "Calam" presumably means "calamity party." So maybe HH actually just means "Howie's House" and Andie was picking up drugs to take to the party.

An earlier spread in March caught my eye too. The numbers scrawled in and scribbled out above Thursday, March 6, are a phone number: ten digits starting with 475, an area code for Connecticut, it has to be. But why would Andie write a cell phone number in her planner; why not enter it straight into her phone? Unless this number wasn't meant for her *actual* phone; maybe she wrote it down because her burner phone wasn't on her at the

2014

JAN FEB (MAR) APR MAY JUN JUL AUG SEPT OCT NOV DEC

MONDAY 10

Read Chap 9 in encore tricolore
Drama—read Revenger's tragedy
→TS @ 6

TUESDAY 11

Read Revenger's Tragedy

WEDNESDAY 12

Read frickin Revenger's
- order presents for EH
+ CB

THURSDAY 13

- wiki plot of Revenger's
- french questions
→IV @ 8

FRIDAY 14

!!! Geography Exam!!!

SATURDAY/SUNDAY 15/16

Sat: HH @ 6
^before Calam

CALENDAR
CONTACTS
TASKS
NOTES
MISC

time, and that's where she wanted this number to go. Could this be Secret Older Guy's number? Or maybe a new phone number for Howie? Or a new client wanting to buy from her? After she entered it into her second phone, she must have scribbled over it to hide her tracks.

I've been staring at the scribble for a good half hour. It looks to me like the first eight digits are: 475-555-01. It's possible that last number is a 7 instead, but I'm fairly certain it's a 1. For the final two digits, it gets tricky because they're scribbled out so thoroughly. The second final digit looks like a 7 or a 9 or a 1, the way it seems to have a leg and a hooked line at the top. And the final number looks like it has a curve, so either a 6, a 0, or an 8.

This leaves us with nine possible combinations:

475-555-0196 475-555-0190 475-555-0198
475-555-0176 475-555-0170 475-555-0178
475-555-0116 475-555-0110 475-555-0118

I've tried calling the first column. I got the same robotic response to each call: *I'm sorry, the number you have dialed has not been recognized. Please hang up and try again.* In the second column I got a *No longer in service*, a generic phone provider voicemail, and an elderly woman up in New Haven. The last column racked up one *Not recognized*, one *No longer in service*, and another generic voicemail. Chasing this phone number is another dud. I can hardly make out those last two digits, and the number is over five years old now and probably out of use.

I'll keep trying the ones that went to generic voicemails, just in case anything comes of it. But I really need to get going with my application. Should I write about that time I got lost at the zoo? Was that a formative experience? My father dying when I was too young

2014

JAN FEB MAR APR MAY JUN JUL AUG SEPT OCT NOV DEC

MONDAY 3

pick either Revenger's Tragedy or Macbeth
for drama exam
go to Sal's later

TUESDAY 4

watch Macbeth on youtube
Chap 6 of french textbook

WEDNESDAY 5

Geography—Essay plan for Friday ✓
→TS @ 6:30

THURSDAY 6

Start reading the Revenger's Tragedy for drama

FRIDAY 7

period 3—out for lunch with galssss
- French questions

SATURDAY/SUNDAY 8/9

car in the shop

CALENDAR CONTACTS TASKS NOTES MISC

to remember him? Gah, 650 words is far too many for someone who doesn't know who they are.

PERSONS OF INTEREST

Jason Bell

Naomi Ward

Secret Older Guy

Nat da Silva

Daniel da Silva

Max Hastings

Howie Bowers

PIPPA FITZ-AMOBI
10/9/19
CAPSTONE PROJECT LOG—ENTRY 26

No, I haven't got any further with my personal essay. I wrote three hundred crappy words yesterday and deleted them right after. And now I'm finding myself dragged back into the world of Andie Bell, clicking on my capstone project document when I should be opening a blank page. But thinking about a dead girl is so much easier than thinking about myself.

I've read over Andie's planner so many times that I can almost recite her February-to-April schedule by heart. One thing is abundantly clear: Andie Bell was a homework procrastinator. Two other things are quite clear, leaning on assumption: TS refers to Andie's drug deal meetings with Howie at the station parking lot, and HH refers to those at his house.

I still haven't managed to work out IV at all. It appears only three times in total: on Thursday, March 13, at eight; Friday, March 21, at nine; and Thursday, March 27, at nine.

Unlike TSs or HHs, which jump around at all different times, IV is once at eight and twice at nine.

Ravi's been working on this too. He just sent me an email with a list of possible people/places IV could refer to. He's spread the search outside Fairview, looking into neighboring towns as well. I should've thought of that.

HIS LIST:

Imperial Vault Nightclub in Stamford
Ivy House Inn in Westport

Ida Vaughan, aged ninety, lives in Wilton

The Four Café in New Canaan (IV = four in Roman numerals)

Imperial Vault's website says that the club was opened in 2012. From its location on the map, it looks like it's just in the middle of nowhere, a concrete-slab nightclub and parking lot amid a mass of green grass pixels. It holds regular events like "Ladies' Night," and the club is owned by a man named Rob Hewitt. I guess it's possible Andie was going there to sell drugs. We could go look into it, ask to speak to the owner.

The Ivy House Inn doesn't have its own website, but it has a page on TripAdvisor, with only two and a half stars. It's a small family-run B and B with four available rooms, right by Westport station. From the few pictures on the site, it looks quaint and cozy, but it's "near a loud, busy road," according to Carmel672's review. And Trevor59 wasn't happy with them at all; they'd double-booked his room. T9Jones said "the host was lovely" but that the bathroom was "tired and filthy—with dirt tracked all around the tub." She's posted some pictures to bolster her point.

Oh my god, oh my god, oh my god. I've been saying that out loud for at least thirty seconds, but it's not enough. Oh My God.

And why won't Ravi pick up his damn phone?!

That last review includes two close-up pictures of the tub at different angles. And then a long shot of the entire bathroom. Beside the bath is a huge full-length mirror on the wall; we can see the reviewer and the flash of her phone reflected in it. We can see the rest of the bathroom, too, from its cream ceiling with circle spotlights down to its tiled floor. *A red-and-white tiled floor.*

I'm almost certain it's the very same tiled floor from the printed photo that was pinned up behind the *Reservoir Dogs* poster in Max Hastings's bedroom. Andie naked except for a pair of black underwear, pouting at a mirror, this mirror . . . in the Ivy House Inn, Westport.

If I'm right, then Andie went to that bed-and-breakfast at least three times in the span of three weeks. Who was she there to meet? Max? Secret Older Guy?

Looks like I'm going to Westport after school tomorrow.

twenty-four

A few moments of muffled shrieking as the train pulled off again and started to gain speed. It jerked Pip's pen, making her scribble a line down the page through her essay introduction. She sighed, ripped the piece of paper from the pad, and screwed it into a ball. It was no good, anyway.

She was on the train to Westport. Ravi was coming straight from work to meet her at the station. Pip looked away from the blank expectant page and out the window instead; they had to be nearly there. She'd taken the train to fit in some application time but had nothing to show for it.

"Next stop, Westport," the conductor announced, like Pip had summoned him with her thoughts. She packed her notepad into her backpack and stood while the train slackened and came to a stop with a mechanical sigh. She skipped onto the platform and down the stairs.

Ravi was waiting for her outside the station.

"Sarge," he said, flicking his dark hair out of his eyes. "I was just coming up with our crime-fighting theme tune. So far, I've got chilled strings and a pan flute when it's me, and then you come on with some heavy, Darth Vader–ish trumpets."

"Why am I the trumpets?" she said.

"Because you're the scary one and you stomp when you walk; sorry to be the one to tell you."

For some reason Pip didn't mind when it was him teasing her. Maybe she even liked it. She pulled a face at him, then reached for her phone, typing in the Ivy House Inn for directions. The line appeared onscreen, and they followed the five-minute-long walking directions, Pip's blue circle avatar sliding along the route in her hands.

They reached their destination and looked up. There was a small wooden sign just before the drive that read "Ivy House Inn" in faded letters. The driveway was sloped and pebbled, leading to a redbrick house almost wholly covered in creeping ivy. It was so thick with the green leaves that the house itself seemed to shiver in the wind.

Pip and Ravi crunched up the drive to the front door, and Pip jabbed the metal doorbell, letting it ring out for one long note.

They heard a small voice inside, and shuffling steps, then the door swung inward, sending a tremor through the ivy around the frame. An old woman with fluffy gray hair, thick glasses, and a very premature Christmas sweater stood before them and smiled.

"Hello, dears," she said. "I didn't realize we were expecting anyone. What name did you make the reservation under?" She ushered Pip and Ravi inside and closed the door.

They stepped into a dimly lit lobby, with a sofa and coffee table on the left and a white staircase running along the far wall.

"Oh, sorry," Pip said, turning back to face the woman. "We don't actually have a reservation."

"I see, well, lucky for you two we aren't booked up, so—"

"Sorry," Pip cut in, looking awkwardly at Ravi. "I mean, we're not looking to stay here. We're looking for . . . We have some questions for the owners of the inn. Are you . . . ?"

"Yes, I'm the owner." The woman smiled, looking unnervingly at a point just left of Pip's face. "Ran it for twenty years with my David; he was in charge of most things, though. It's been hard since my David passed a couple years ago. But my grandsons are always here, helping me get by, driving me around. My grandson Henry is just upstairs, cleaning the rooms."

"So five years ago, you and your husband were running this place?" Ravi asked.

The woman nodded, and her eyes swayed over to him. "Very handsome," she said quietly, and then to Pip, "Lucky girl."

"No, we're not . . . ," Pip said, glancing at Ravi. She wished she hadn't. Out of the old lady's eyeline, he shimmied his shoulders and pointed to his face, mouthing "very handsome." Pip rolled her eyes and hoped he couldn't read anything else on her face.

"Would you like to sit down?" The woman gestured to a green-velvet sofa beneath a window. "I know I would." She shuffled over to a leather armchair facing the couch.

Pip walked over, intentionally treading on Ravi's foot as she passed. She sat down, knees pointed toward the woman, and Ravi squeezed in beside her, still with that smug grin on his face.

"Where's my . . . ," the woman said, patting her sweater and her pants pockets, a blank look falling over her face.

"Um, so," Pip said, drawing the woman's attention back to her. "Do you keep records of people that have stayed here?"

"It's all done on the, um . . . the computer now, isn't it?" the woman said. "Sometimes by the telephone. David always handled the bookings; now, Henry does it for me."

"So how did you keep track of the reservations you had?" Pip said.

"My David did it. Had a spreadsheet printed out for the week." The woman shrugged, staring out the window.

"Would you still have your reservation spreadsheets from five years ago?" asked Ravi.

"No, no. The whole place would be flooded in paper."

"But do you have the documents saved on a computer?" Pip pressed.

"Oh, no. We threw David's computer out after he passed. It was a very slow little thing," she said. "My Henry does all the bookings for me now."

"Can I ask you something?" Pip said, unzipping her backpack and pulling out a folded printout. She straightened out the page and handed it to the woman. "Do you recognize this girl? Has she ever stayed here?"

The woman stared down at the photo of Andie, the one that had been used in most newspaper reports. She lifted the paper to her face, then held it at arm's length, then brought it close again.

"Yes." She nodded, looking from Pip to Ravi to Andie. "I know her. She's been here."

Pip's skin prickled with nervous excitement.

"You remember this girl staying with you five years ago?" she said. "Do you remember the man she was with? What he looked like?"

The woman's face muddied, and she stared at Pip, her eyes darting right and left, a blink with each change in direction.

"No," she said. "No, it wasn't five years ago. I saw this girl. She's been here."

"In 2014?" Pip said.

"No, no." The woman's eyes settled past Pip's ear. "It was just a few weeks ago. She was here, I remember."

Pip's heart sank a few hundred feet.

"That's not possible," she said. "This girl has been dead for five years."

"But I—" The woman shook her head, the wrinkled skin around her eyes folding together. "But I remember. She was here. She's been here."

"Five years ago?" Ravi prompted.

"No," the woman said, anger creeping into her voice. "I remember, don't I? I don't—"

"Grandma?" A man's voice called from upstairs.

A set of heavy boots thundered down the stairs, and an auburn-haired man came into view.

"Hello?" he said, looking at Pip and Ravi. He walked over and held out his hand. "I'm Henry Hill," he said.

Ravi stood and shook his hand. "I'm Ravi; this is Pip."

"Can we help you with something?" he asked, shooting a concerned look over at his grandmother.

"We were just asking your grandma a couple questions about someone who stayed here five years ago," said Ravi.

Pip looked back to the old woman and noticed that she was crying. Tears snaked down her tissue-paper skin, dropping onto the printout of Andie.

The grandson must have noticed as well. He walked over and squeezed his grandma's shoulder, taking the piece of paper out of her shaking grip.

"Grandma," he said, "why don't you put the kettle on and make us some tea? I'll help out these people here, don't worry."

He eased her up off the chair and steered her toward a door to the left of the hall, handing the photo of Andie to Pip as they passed. Ravi and Pip looked at each other, questions in their eyes, until Henry returned a few seconds later, closing the kitchen door to muffle the sound of the boiling kettle.

"Sorry," he said with a sad smile. "She gets upset when she gets confused. The Alzheimer's . . . It's starting to get bad. I'm actually just cleaning up to put the place on the market. She keeps forgetting that."

"I'm sorry," Pip said. "We should have realized. We didn't mean to upset her."

"No, I know, of course you didn't," he said. "Can I help with whatever it is?"

"We were asking about this girl." Pip held up the paper. "Whether she stayed here five years ago."

"And what did my grandma say?"

"She thought she'd seen her recently, just weeks ago." She swallowed. "But this girl died in 2014."

"She does that quite often now," he said, looking between the two of them. "Gets confused about times and when things happened. Sometimes still thinks my grandad is alive. She's probably just recognizing your girl from five years ago, if that's when you think she was here."

"Yeah," Pip said, "I guess."

"Sorry I can't be of more help. I can't tell you who stayed here five years ago; we haven't kept the old records. But if she recognized her, I guess that gives you your answer?"

Pip nodded. "It does. Sorry for upsetting her."

"Will she be OK?" said Ravi.

"She'll be fine," Henry said gently. "Tea will do the trick."

They stepped out of Fairview station, the town dimming as it turned six o'clock and the sun slumped off to the west. She'd gotten a text from Zach on the train: *Where are you? Did you forget about debate team?* She had; she'd forgotten all about it. She tried to ignore the guilt; she'd make it up to him somehow.

Pip's mind whirled, spinning over the many shifting pieces of Andie's life, separating them and putting them back together in different combinations.

"So," she said, "I think we can confirm that Andie stayed at the Ivy House Inn." The bathroom tiles and the woman's time-confused recognition were proof enough of that.

They turned right, into the parking lot, heading for Pip's car down the far end.

"And if Andie was going to that inn," Ravi said, "must be because that's where she met Secret Older Guy, and they were both trying to avoid getting caught."

Pip nodded in agreement. "So that means that whoever Secret Older Guy was, he couldn't have Andie over at his house. And the most likely reason for that would be that he lived with his family or a wife."

This changed things.

Pip carried on. "Daniel da Silva lived with his new wife in 2014, and Max Hastings was living with his parents, who knew Sal well. Both of them would have needed to be away from home to carry on a secret relationship with Andie. And, let's not forget, Max has a naked photo of Andie taken inside the Ivy House Inn, a photo he supposedly 'found,' " she said, using air quotes around the word.

"Yeah," Ravi said, "but Howie Bowers lived alone. If it was him Andie was secretly seeing, they wouldn't have needed to stay in a hotel."

"That's what I'm thinking," Pip said. "Which means I think we can rule out Howie as a candidate for Secret Older Guy. Although that doesn't necessarily mean he isn't the killer."

"True," Ravi agreed, "but at least it clears the picture a little. It wasn't Howie that Andie was seeing behind Sal's back in March, and it wasn't him she spoke of ruining."

They had deduced all the way over to her car. Pip fiddled in her pocket and blipped the keys. She opened the driver's-side door and shoved her backpack inside, Ravi taking it on his lap in the passenger seat. As she started to climb in, she looked up and noticed a man leaning against the far fence, about sixty feet away, in a green parka coat with bright orange lining. Howie Bowers, furred hood up, nodding at the man beside him.

A man gesticulating wildly as he mouthed silent and angry-looking words. A man in a smart wool coat with floppy blond hair.

Max Hastings.

Pip's face drained. She dropped into her seat.

"What's wrong, Sarge?"

She pointed out his window.

Max Hastings, who had lied to her yet again, saying he never bought drugs in Fairview after Andie disappeared, that he had no clue who her dealer was. And here he was, shouting at that very drug dealer, the words lost to the distance between them.

"Oh," Ravi said.

Pip started the engine and pulled out, driving away before either Max or Howie could spot them, before her hands started to shake too much.

Max and Howie knew each other.

Yet another tectonic shift in the world of Andie Bell.

PIPPA FITZ-AMOBI
10/10/19
CAPSTONE PROJECT LOG—ENTRY 27

Max Hastings. If anyone should go on the persons of interest list in bold, it's him. He's lied twice now in Andie-related matters, and you don't lie unless you have something to hide.

Let's recap: He's an older guy, he has a naked picture of Andie taken in a hotel where he could very well have been meeting her in March 2014, he was close to both Sal and Andie, he regularly bought Rohypnol from Andie, and he evidently knows Howie Bowers pretty well.

This also opens up the possibility of another pair who could have colluded in Andie's murder: Max and Howie.

I think it's time to follow this Rohypnol trail. No normal nineteen-year-old buys roofies for school parties, right? And it's the thing that links this messy Max-Howie-Andie triangle.

I'll message some 2014 Fairview High alumni and see if I can figure out what was going on at calamity parties. If what I'm suspecting is true, could Max and Rohypnol be key players in what happened to Andie that night? I just asked Naomi if she knew whether drinks would get spiked at calamities. She says she never saw or heard anything of the sort. If it *was* happening, Max must have kept it well hidden. Maybe his friends hadn't really known him at all, not the real him.

PERSONS OF INTEREST

Jason Bell
Naomi Ward

Secret Older Guy

Nat da Silva

Daniel da Silva

Max Hastings

Howie Bowers

PIPPA FITZ-AMOBI
10/11/19
CAPSTONE PROJECT LOG—ENTRY 28

Emma Hutton replied to my text while I was at school:

> Yeah, maybe. I do remember girls saying they thought their drinks had been spiked. But tbh everyone used to get really really drunk at those parties, so they were probably just saying it because they didn't know their limits or for attention. I never had mine spiked.

Chloe Burch also replied, forty minutes ago when I was watching a movie with Josh:

> No, I don't think so. I never heard any rumors like that. But girls sometimes say that when they've drunk too much, don't they?

I also emailed a few people who were tagged in photos with Naomi at calamities in 2014. I lied slightly, told them I was a reporter for CNN named Penny because I thought it would encourage them to talk. If they had anything to say, that is. One of them just responded.

> Thu, Oct. 10, 8:43 p.m. (1 day ago)
> From: pfa20@gmail.com
> To: handslauraj116@yahoo.com
> Subject: Information request for an independent CNN news story
>
> Dear Laura Hands,
>
> I'm a reporter working on an independent news story for CNN about underage house parties and drug use. From my research I can see

that you used to attend certain house parties that were nicknamed "Calamities" in the Fairview area in 2014. I wonder if you can offer any comment as to whether you ever heard any rumors or saw any instances of girls having their drinks spiked at these events?

I would be extremely grateful if you can provide any information regarding this matter, and please know that any comments you offer will be anonymized and treated with the utmost discretion.

Thank you for your time.

Yours sincerely,
Penny Firth-Adams

9:22 p.m. (2 minutes ago)
From: handslauraj116@yahoo.com
To: me
Subject: Re: Information request for an independent CNN news story

Hi, Penny,

No worries at all, I'm happy to help.

Actually, I do remember there being talk of drinks being spiked. Of course everyone used to drink to excess at these parties, so the issue was a little confused.

But I did have a friend, Natalie da Silva, who thought she'd had her drink spiked at one of those parties. She said she couldn't remember anything of the night, and she'd only had one drink. I think that was in early 2014, if I remember correctly.

I might still have her phone number if you wanted to get in contact with her?

Good luck with your report. Could you let me know when it airs? I'd be interested to see it.

Best wishes,
Laura

PIPPA FITZ-AMOBI
10/12/19
CAPSTONE PROJECT LOG—ENTRY 29

Two more responses this morning while I was out at Josh's soccer game. The first one said she didn't want to offer any comment. The second one said this:

> 12:44 p.m. (57 minutes ago)
> From: JoannaRiddell95@gmail.com
> To: me
> Subject: Re: Information request for an independent CNN news story
>
> Dear Penny Firth-Adams,
>
> Thank you for your email. I agree that it is a really important topic that needs more attention in mainstream media.
>
> I actually do know of instances of drink spiking happening at those house parties. Around February 2014, one of my friends (who I won't name) got completely messed up. She couldn't speak and could barely move at all. I had to get some guys to help me carry her out to her dad's car. And the next morning she couldn't even remember being at the party.
>
> A few days later she asked me to go with her to the Fairview police station to report the incident. She went and spoke to this young officer; can't remember his name. Then I'm not sure anything ever came of it. But I was always careful to watch my drinks after that.
>
> I hope this is helpful for your report and feel free to come back to me if you have more questions.
>
> All best,
> Jo Riddell

* * *

The plot keeps thickening.

I think I can safely assume that drinks *were* being spiked at calamity parties in 2014, though the fact wasn't widely known to partygoers. So Max was buying Rohypnol from Andie, and girls were getting their drinks spiked at the parties he started. It doesn't take a genius to put the two together.

Not only that, Nat da Silva may very well have been one of the girls whose drink he spiked. Could that be relevant to Andie's murder? And did anything happen to Nat the night she thought she'd been drugged? I can't ask her: she's what I would call an exceptionally hostile witness.

To top it all off, Joanna Riddell said that her friend thought she was drugged and reported it to the Fairview police. To a "young" male officer. Well, I've done my research, and the only young and male officer in 2014 was (yep, you guessed it!) Daniel da Silva. It's a tiny police force for a tiny town. The next-youngest male officer was forty-one in 2014. Joanna said nothing came of the report. Was that just because the unnamed girl reported it after any drug would have been out of her system? Or was Daniel involved somehow . . . trying to cover something up?

I think I just stumbled on another connection between names on the persons of interest list, between Max Hastings and the two da Silvas. I'll call Ravi later, and we can brainstorm what this possible triangle could mean. But my focus needs to be on Max right now. He's lied enough times, and now I have real reason to believe he was spiking girls' drinks at parties and secretly seeing Andie behind Sal's back at the Ivy House Inn.

If I had to stop the project right now, Max would be suspect number one.

But I can't just go and talk to him about this; he's another hostile witness, and now possibly one with a history of assault. He won't talk without leverage. So I have to find some, by way of serious cyberstalking.

If I can get on to his Facebook profile (Nancy Tangotits), I can go through every post and picture, looking for something that connects him to Andie or the Ivy House Inn or drugging girls. Something I can use to make him talk or, even better, go straight to the police with.

twenty-five

Pip placed her knife and fork across her plate with exaggerated precision.

"*Now* may I leave the table?" She looked at her mom, who was scowling.

"I don't see what the rush is," she said.

"I'm just right in the middle of my capstone project and I want to hit my targets before bed."

"Sure, off you go, pickle." Her dad reached over to scrape Pip's leftovers onto his own plate.

"Vic!" Her mom now turned the scowl on him as Pip stood and tucked in her chair.

"Oh, honey, some people have to worry about their kids rushing off from dinner to inject heroin into their eyeballs. Be thankful it's homework."

"What's heroin?" Josh said as Pip left the room.

She took the steps two at a time, leaving her shadow, Barney, at the foot of the stairs, his head tilting in confusion as he tried to follow her to that dog-forbidden place. She'd had the chance to think over all things Nancy Tangotits at dinner, and she had an idea.

Pip closed her bedroom door, pulled out her phone, and dialed.

"Hello, muchacha," Cara chimed down the line.

"Hey," Pip said, "are you busy bingeing *The Crown* or do you have a few minutes to help me be sneaky?"

"I'm always available for sneakiness. What d'you need?"

"Is Naomi in?"

"No, in Manhattan this weekend. Why?" Suspicion crept into Cara's voice.

"OK, sworn to secrecy?"

"Always. What's up?"

Pip said, "I've heard rumors about old calamity parties that might give me a lead for my capstone project. But I need to find proof, which is where the sneakiness comes in."

She hoped she'd played it just right, omitting Max's name and downplaying it enough that Cara wouldn't worry about her sister, leaving just enough gaps to intrigue her.

"Oooh, what rumors?" she said.

Pip knew her too well, and she hated that she was doing this, manipulating her. When did she become this person?

"Nothing substantial yet. But I need to look through old calamity photos. That's where I need your help."

"Hit me."

"Max Hastings's Facebook profile is a decoy—you know, for employers and colleges. His actual one is under a fake name and has really strict privacy settings. I can only see things that Naomi is tagged in."

"And you want to log in as Naomi so you can look through Max's old photos?"

"Bingo," Pip said, sitting down on her bed and dragging the laptop over.

"Can do," Cara's voice trilled. "*Technically,* we're not snooping on Naomi, so this doesn't *technically* break any rules, *Dad.* Plus,

Nai should learn to change her password sometime; she has the same one for everything."

"Can you get on to her laptop?" Pip said.

"Just opening it now."

Pip heard the tapping of keys over the phone. She could picture Cara now, that giant topknot she always wore when she was dressed in pajamas. Which was, in Cara's case, as often as physically possible.

"OK, she's still signed in here. I'm on."

"Can you click on security settings?" asked Pip.

"Yep."

"Uncheck the box next to Log-in Alerts so she won't know I'm logging in from a new machine."

"Done."

"OK," Pip said, "that's all the hacking I need from you."

Cara read out Naomi's email address, and Pip entered it into the Facebook log-in page.

"Her password is Isobel0612," Cara said.

Pip typed it in. "Thanks, comrade. Stand down."

"Loud and clear. Although if Naomi finds out, I'm throwing you under the bus."

"Understood," said Pip.

"Hey, so I texted that girl I met at the movie theater," Cara said tentatively.

"Shit, sorry." Pip exhaled. "I should have asked. Has she replied?"

"Not yet, you know, because I'm destined to be forever alone."

"Well, you can be forever alone with me," Pip said. "And she will reply. Tell me as soon as she does."

"All right, Plops, Dad's yelling. Gotta go."

"OK, bye." Pip dropped the phone and clicked to log in.

Naomi's newsfeed was filled with cats, recipe videos, and motivational quotes over pictures of sunsets.

Pip typed "Nancy Tangotits" into the search bar and clicked on to Max's page.

It didn't take long for Pip to realize why Max had two profiles. There's no way he would have wanted his parents to see what he got up to away from home. Photos of him in clubs, his blond hair stuck to his sweaty forehead, jaw tensed and his eyes reeling and unfocused. Posing with his arms around girls, sticking his tongue out at the camera, shirt splattered with spilled drinks. And those were just the recent ones.

Pip clicked to Max's photos and began the long scroll down toward 2014. It was all much of the same: clubs, bars, bleary eyes. There was a brief respite from Max's nocturnal activities with a series of photos from a ski trip; Max standing in the snow wearing just a Speedo.

She finally reached 2014 and took herself back to January before looking through the photos properly, studying each one.

Most were of Max smiling in the foreground, usually accompanied by Naomi, Jake, Millie, or Sal. Pip lingered for a long time on a photo of Sal flashing his brilliant smile while Max licked his cheek. Her gaze switched between the two drunk and happy boys, looking for any trace of the secrets that existed between them.

Pip searched through photos of Max in crowds, looking for Andie's face in the background, for anything suspicious in Max's hand, for him lurking too close to any girl's drink. She clicked forward and back through so many photos of calamity parties that her tired eyes saw them as flip-book moving pictures. Until she found the photos from *that* night and everything became sharp and static again.

Pip leaned forward.

Max had taken and uploaded ten photos from the night Andie disappeared. Pip immediately recognized Max's house and everyone's clothes from that day. Added to Naomi's three and Millie's six, that made a total of nineteen photos from that night, nineteen shots that existed alongside Andie Bell's last hours of life.

Pip shivered and pulled the duvet over her feet. The photos were similar to the ones Millie and Naomi had taken: Max and Jake gripping controllers and staring out of frame; Millie and Max posing with filters superimposed over their faces; Naomi in the background, staring down at her phone, unaware of the posed photo going on behind her. Four best friends without their fifth.

That's when Pip noticed the time stamp. When it had been just Millie's and Naomi's uploads, it was simply a coincidence, but now that she was looking at Max's too, there was a pattern. All three of them had uploaded their photos from *that* night on Monday the twenty-first, between nine-thirty and ten p.m. Wasn't it a little strange that, in the midst of all the craziness of Andie's disappearance, they all decided to post these photos at almost the exact same time? And why upload these photos anyway? Naomi said she and the others had decided on that Monday night to tell the police the truth about Sal's alibi. Was uploading these photos the first step in that decision? To stop hiding Sal's absence?

Pip typed up some notes about this upload coincidence, then she clicked save and closed the laptop. She got ready for bed, wandering back from the bathroom with her toothbrush in her mouth, humming as she scribbled her to-do list for tomorrow. *Write personal essay* underlined three times.

With a sniff and a jerk Pip sat bolt upright in bed. She leaned against the headboard and rubbed her eyes as her mind stirred awake. She pressed the home button on her phone: 4:47 a.m.

What had woken her?

Something stirred on the edge of her brain. A vague thought, beyond the span of just-awake comprehension. But she knew where it was drawing her.

Pip slid quickly out of bed, the cold room stinging her exposed skin. She grabbed her laptop and took it back to bed, wrapping the duvet around her. Blinded by the backlight of her computer, she opened up Facebook, still signed in as Naomi, and navigated her way back to Nancy Tangotits and the photos from *that* night.

She looked through them all once and then back again a little slower. She stopped on the second-to-last picture. All four friends were in the frame. Naomi was sitting with her back to the camera, looking down. Though she was in the background, you could just make out the lock screen on the phone in her hands. The main focus of the photo was on Max, Millie, and Jake, the three of them standing by the near side of the sofa and smiling as Millie rested her arms over both the boys' shoulders. Max was still holding a controller in his outside hand, and Jake's disappeared out of shot on the right.

Pip shivered.

The camera must have been at least five feet in front of them to get that much in the frame.

And in the dead silence of the night, Pip whispered, "Who's taking the picture?"

twenty-six

It was Sal.

It had to be.

Despite the cold Pip's blood raced, warm and fast, hammering through her heart.

She moved mechanically, a thousand thoughts shouting over each other, but she listened to only one. She downloaded the trial version of Photoshop, saved Max's photo, and opened the image in the program. She enlarged the photo and then sharpened it.

Her skin flashed cold, then hot again.

There was no doubt about it. The numbers projected on Naomi's phone read 12:09.

The friends said Sal left at ten-thirty, but here they were, all four of them at nine minutes past midnight, and not one of them could have taken the photo themselves.

Max's parents were away that night, and no one else had been there—that's what they've always said. It was just the five of them until Sal left at ten-thirty to go and kill his girlfriend.

And here was proof that was a lie. There was a fifth person there after midnight. And who could it have been but Sal?

Pip scrolled to the topmost section of the enlarged photo. There was a window behind the sofa on the far wall. And in the center pane was the flash of the phone camera. You couldn't distinguish the figure holding the phone from the darkness of outside. But just beyond the streaks of white from the flash, there was a faint halo of blue in the reflection. The very same blue as the shirt Sal was wearing that night, the one Ravi still wore sometimes. Pip's stomach flipped at the thought of his name, imagining the look in his eyes when he saw this photo.

She copied and pasted the enlarged image to a blank document and cropped it to show only Naomi with her phone on one page and the flash in the window on another. Along with the original saved photo, she sent each page to the wireless printer on her desk. She watched from her bed as it sputtered out each sheet, closing her eyes for just a moment, listening to it rattle.

"Pips, can I come in and vacuum?"

Pip's eyes snapped open. She pulled herself up from her slumped position, the right side of her body aching from hip to neck.

"You're still in bed?" her mom said, opening the door. "It's after one, lazy. I thought you were already up."

"No . . . I," Pip said, her throat dry and scratchy. "Was just tired, not feeling so well. Could you do Josh's room first?"

Her mom paused and looked at her, her warm eyes strained with worry.

"You're not overworking yourself, are you, Pip?" she said. "We've talked about this."

"No, I promise."

Her mom closed the door, and Pip climbed out of bed. She got ready, pulling her jeans on with a dark-green shirt, fighting to get the brush through her hair. She picked up the three photo printouts, placed them in a plastic folder, and slid them inside her backpack. Then she scrolled to the recent calls list in her phone and dialed.

"Ravi!"

"What's up, Sarge?"

"Meet me outside your house in ten minutes. I'll be in the car."

"OK. What's on the menu today, more blackmail? Side order of breaking and enter—"

"It's serious. Be there in ten."

Sitting in her passenger seat, his head almost touching the roof of the car, Ravi stared down openmouthed at the photo in his hands.

It was a long while before he said anything. They sat in silence. Pip watched as Ravi traced his finger over the fuzzy blue reflection in the far window.

"Sal never lied to the police," he said eventually.

"No, he didn't," Pip said. "I think he left Max's at twelve-fifteen, just like he originally said. It was his friends who lied. I don't know why, but on that Tuesday they lied, and they took away his alibi."

"This means he's innocent, Pip." His big round eyes fixed on hers.

"That's what we're here to test—come on."

She opened her door and stepped out. She'd picked Ravi up and driven him straight to this grassy patch off Weevil Road, leaving her hazard lights flashing. Ravi closed the car door and followed as Pip started up the road.

"How are we testing that?"

"The only way to be sure Sal didn't do it is an Andie Bell murder reenactment." Her steps fell in time with his. "To see, with Sal's new time of departure from Max's, whether he still would have had enough time to kill her."

They turned left down Courtland and traipsed all the way to

Max Hastings's sprawling house, where this had all begun five and a half years ago.

Pip pulled out her phone. "We should give the pretend prosecution the benefit of the doubt," she said. "Let's say that Sal left Max's just after that photo was taken, at ten minutes past midnight. What time did your dad say Sal got home?"

"Around twelve-fifty," he replied.

"OK. Let's allow for some misremembering and say it was more like twelve-fifty-five. Which means that Sal had forty-five minutes, door to door. We have to move fast, Ravi; use the minimum possible time it might have taken to kill her and dispose of her body."

"Normal teenagers sit at home and watch TV on a Sunday," he said.

"Right, I'm starting the stopwatch . . . now."

Pip turned on her heels and marched back up the road the way they'd come, Ravi at her side. Her steps fell somewhere between a fast walk and a slow jog. Eight minutes and forty-seven seconds later, they reached her car, and her heart was already pounding. This was the intercept point.

"OK." She turned the key in the ignition and pulled back onto the road. "So this is Andie's car, and she has intercepted Sal. Let's say that she was driving for a faster pick-up time. Now we go to the first quiet spot where the murder theoretically could have taken place."

She hadn't been driving long before Ravi pointed.

"There," he said. "That's quiet and secluded. Turn off here."

Pip pulled off onto the small dirt road, packed in by tall hedges. A sign told them that the winding single-lane road led down to a farm. Pip stopped the car where a widened passing place was cut into the bushes and said, "Now we get out. They didn't find any blood in the front of the car, just the trunk."

Pip glanced at the ticking stopwatch app as Ravi was crossing around the front to meet on her side of the car: 15:29, 15:30 . . .

"OK," she said. "Let's say that right now they're arguing. It's starting to get heated. Could have been about Andie selling drugs or about this secret older guy. Sal is upset; Andie's shouting back." Pip hummed tunelessly, rolling her hands to fill the time of the imaginary scene. "And right about now, maybe Sal finds a rock on the road or something heavy from Andie's car. Maybe no weapon at all. Let's give him at least forty seconds to kill her."

They waited and she watched the muscles in Ravi's jaw clench and release.

"So now Andie's dead." Pip pointed down at the gravel road. "He opens the trunk"—Pip opened her trunk—"and puts her inside where her blood was found." She bent down and lifted the invisible body, struggling to lay it on the carpeted trunk floor. Then she stepped back and shut it.

"Now back in the car," Ravi said.

Pip checked the timer: 20:02, 20:03 . . . She put the car in reverse and swung out onto the main road.

"Sal's driving now," she said. "His fingerprints get on the steering wheel and around the dashboard. He'd be thinking of how to dispose of her body. The closest possible forest-y area is Lodge Park. So maybe he'd come off Weevil Road here," she said, swerving, the woods appearing on their left.

"But he'd have needed to find a place to get the car up close to the woods," said Ravi.

They chased the woods for several minutes, searching for such a place, until the road grew dark under a tunnel of trees pressing in on either side.

"There." They spotted one together. Pip signaled and pulled off onto the grassy patch bordering the forest.

"I'm sure the police searched here a hundred times, as these are the closest woods to Max's house," she said. "But let's just say Sal managed to hide the body here."

Pip and Ravi got out of the car once more: 26:18.

"So he opens the trunk and drags her out." Pip re-created the action, noticing Ravi avert his eyes. He'd probably had nightmares about this very scene, his older brother dragging a dead and bloodied body through the trees. But maybe, after today, he'd never have to picture it again.

"Sal would've had to take her pretty far in, away from the road," she said.

Pip mimicked dragging the body, her back bent, staggering slowly backward.

"Up here's fairly hidden," Ravi said once Pip had dragged her about two hundred feet through the trees.

"Yep." She let go of Andie: 29:48.

"OK," she said, "so the hole has always been a problem; how he could have had time to dig one deep enough, anyway. But now that we're here"—she glanced around the dappled woods—"there are quite a few downed trees. Maybe he didn't need to dig much at all. Maybe he found a shallow ditch ready-made for him. Like there." She pointed to a large mossy dip in the ground, a tangle of old roots creeping through it, still attached to a long-fallen tree.

"He would've needed to make it deeper," Ravi said. "She's never been found. Let's allow three or four minutes for digging."

"Agreed."

When the time came she dragged Andie's body into the hole. "Then he would've needed to fill it again, cover her with dirt and debris."

"Let's do it, then," Ravi said, his face determined now. He

stabbed his boot into the dirt and kicked a spray of soil into the hole.

Pip followed suit, pushing mud, leaves, and twigs in to fill the small ditch. Ravi was on his knees, sweeping whole armfuls of earth over and on top of Andie.

"OK," Pip said when they were done, eyes on the hole now invisible against the forest floor. "So now she's buried, Sal heads back."

37:59.

They jogged back to Pip's car and climbed inside, kicking mud all over the floor. Pip did a three-point turn, swearing when a four-by-four barreled by.

When they were back on Weevil Road, she said, "Right, now Sal drives to Monroe, where Howie Bowers lives. And he ditches Andie's car."

They pulled into the road a few minutes later, and Pip parked out of sight of Howie's bungalow. She locked the car behind them.

"And now we walk to my house," Ravi said, trying to keep up with Pip, her steps breaking into an almost-run. They were both concentrating too hard for words, their eyes down on their pounding feet, treading in *allegedly Sal's* years-old footsteps.

They arrived outside the Singhs' house, breathless. A sheen of sweat had broken out on Pip's upper lip. She wiped it on her sleeve and pulled out her phone.

She stopped the timer and stared at the numbers, hairs rising all over her body. She looked at Ravi.

"What?" His eyes were wide and searching.

"So we gave Sal an upper-limit time window of forty-five minutes between locations. And our reenactment worked with the closest possible locations and was almost inconceivably efficient."

"Yes, it was the speediest of murders. And?"

Pip held her phone out to him and showed him the timer.

"Fifty-eight minutes, nineteen seconds," Ravi read aloud.

"Ravi." His name fizzed on her lips and she broke into a smile. "Sal couldn't possibly have done it. He's innocent; the photo proves it."

"Shit." He stepped back and covered his mouth, shaking his head. "He didn't do it. Sal's innocent."

He made a sound, gravelly at first. Then a quick bark of laughter, laced with disbelief. A smile unfolded slowly across his face, and he laughed again, the sound pure and warm. Pip's cheeks flushed with the heat of it.

And then Ravi looked up at the sky, the sun on his face, and the laugh became a yell. He roared up into the sky, neck strained, eyes screwed shut.

People stared at him from across the street, and curtains twitched in houses. But Pip knew he didn't care. And neither did she. Her eyes prickled with tears as she watched him in this raw, confusing moment of happiness and grief.

Ravi looked down at her, and the roar cracked into laughter again. Before Pip knew what was happening, he'd wrapped his arms around her and lifted her from her feet. Something bright whirred through her; a feeling with wings. Ravi's breath was in her ear, laughing and crying as he spun her round and round.

"We did it!" he said, putting her down so clumsily that she tripped over his feet. He stepped back and wiped his eyes, looking suddenly embarrassed. "We actually did it. Is it enough? Can we go to the police with that photo?"

"I don't know," Pip said. She didn't want to take this away from him, but she really wasn't sure. "Maybe it's enough to convince them to reopen the case; maybe it isn't. But we need answers first.

We need to know why Sal's friends lied. Why they took his alibi away from him. Come on."

Ravi took one step and hesitated. "You mean, ask Naomi?"

She nodded and he drew back.

"You should go alone," he said. "Naomi won't talk if I'm there. She physically can't talk. I bumped into her last year, and she burst into tears just looking at me."

"Are you sure?" Pip said. "You, out of everyone, deserve to know why they did it."

"It's the way it has to be, trust me. Be careful, Sarge."

"OK. I'll call you right after."

Pip wasn't quite sure how to leave him. She didn't want to leave him. She touched his arm and walked away, carrying that look on Ravi's face with her.

twenty-seven

Pip walked back toward her car on Monroe, her tread much lighter on this return journey. Lighter because now they knew for sure. Sal Singh did not kill Andie Bell.

She called Cara.

"Well, hello, sister," Cara answered.

"What are you doing now?" Pip asked.

"Homework club with Naomi and Max. They're doing job apps, and I'm working on my capstone project. You know I can't focus alone."

Pip's chest tightened. "Both Max and Naomi are there now?"

"Yep."

"Is your dad in?"

"Nah, he's over at my aunt Lila's for the afternoon."

"OK, I'm coming over," Pip said. "Be there in ten."

"Fab. I can steal some of your focus."

Pip said goodbye and hung up. She felt an ache of guilt for Cara, that she was there and would now be involved in whatever was about to come out. Because Pip wasn't bringing focus to the homework club. She was bringing an ambush.

* * *

Cara opened the front door, wearing her penguin pajamas and bear-claw slippers.

"Hey, chica," she said, rubbing Pip's already messy hair. "Happy Sunday. Mi club de homeworko es su club de homeworko."

Pip closed the front door and followed Cara into the kitchen.

"We've banned talking," Cara said, holding the door open for her. "And no typing too loudly, like Max does."

Pip stepped into the kitchen. Max and Naomi were sitting next to each other at the table, laptops and papers splayed out in front of them. Steaming mugs of coffee in their hands. Cara's place was on the other side: a mess of paper and pens strewn across her keyboard.

"Hey, Pip." Naomi smiled. "How're you doing?"

"Fine, thanks," Pip said, her voice suddenly raw.

When Pip looked at Max, he turned his gaze away immediately, staring down at the surface of his taupe-colored coffee.

"*Hi,* Max," she said pointedly, forcing him to look back at her.

He raised a small closed-mouth smile, which might have looked like a greeting to Cara and Naomi, but Pip knew better. It was meant as a grimace.

Pip walked over to the table and dropped her backpack onto it, just across from Max. It thumped against the surface, making the lids of all three laptops judder on their hinges.

"Pip loves homework," Cara explained to Max. "Aggressively so."

Cara slid back into her chair and wiggled the mouse to bring her computer back to life. "Well, sit," she said, using her foot to pull a chair out from under the table. Its feet shrieked against the floor.

"What's up, Pip?" Naomi said. "Do you want some caffeine?"

"And what are you looking at?" Max cut in.

"Max!" Naomi hit him roughly on the arm with a pad of paper.

Pip could see Cara's confused face in her periphery. But she didn't take her eyes away from Naomi and Max, anger pulsing through her. She hadn't known until she saw their faces that this was how she would feel. She thought she would be relieved it was all over, that she and Ravi had done what they set out to do. But their faces made her seethe. These weren't just small deceits and innocent gaps in memory anymore. This was a calculated, life-changing lie. And she would not look away or sit until she knew why.

"I came here first, just as a courtesy," she said, her voice shaking. "Because, Naomi, you've been like a sister to me nearly my whole life. Max, I owe you nothing."

"Pip, what are you talking about?" Cara said, her voice strained with the beginnings of worry.

Pip unzipped her bag and pulled out the plastic folder. She leaned across the table and laid the three printed pages out in the space between Max and Naomi.

"This is your chance to explain before I go to the police. What do you have to say, Nancy Tangotits?" She glared at Max.

"What are you talking about?" he scoffed.

"That's your photo, Nancy. It's from the night Andie Bell disappeared, isn't it?"

"Yes," Naomi said quietly. "But why—"

"The night Sal left Max's house at ten-thirty to go and kill Andie?"

"Yes, it is," Max spat. "What point are you trying to make?"

"If you stop blustering for one second and look at the photo, you'll see my point," Pip snapped back. "Obviously, if you paid any attention to detail, you wouldn't have uploaded it in the first place. So I'll explain. Both you and Naomi, Millie and Jake are in this picture."

"Yeah, so?" he said.

"So, Nancy, who took that picture of the four of you?"

Naomi's eyes widened, her mouth hanging open as she stared down at the photo.

"Yeah, OK," Max said, "so maybe Sal took the photo. It's not like we said he wasn't there at all. He must have taken this earlier on in the night."

"Nice try," Pip said, "but—"

"My phone." Naomi's face fell, and she reached up to hold it in her hands. "The time is on my phone."

Max went quiet, looking down at the printouts, a muscle tensing in his jaw.

"Well, you can hardly see those numbers. You must have doctored this photo," he said.

"No, Max. I got it from your Facebook as it is. Don't worry, I've researched this: the police can access it, even if you delete it now. I'm sure they'd be very interested to see."

Naomi turned to Max, her cheeks reddening. "Why didn't you check properly?"

"Shut up," he said quietly but firmly.

"We're going to have to tell her," Naomi said, pushing back her chair with a scrape that cut right through Pip.

"Shut up, Naomi," Max said again.

"Oh my god." Naomi stood and started pacing the length of the table. "We have to tell her—"

"Stop talking!" Max said, getting to his feet and grabbing Naomi by the shoulders. "Don't say anything else."

"She'll go to the police, Max," Naomi said, tears pooling in the grooves around her nose. "We have to tell her."

Max took a deep, juddering breath, eyes darting between Naomi and Pip.

"Fuck!" he shouted, letting go of Naomi and kicking out at the table leg.

"What the hell is going on?" Cara pulled at Pip's sleeve.

"Tell me, Naomi," Pip said.

Max fell back into his chair, his blond hair in wilting clumps across his face. "Why did you do this?" He looked up at Pip. "Why couldn't you just leave everything alone?"

Pip ignored him. "Naomi, tell me," she said. "Sal didn't leave Max's at ten-thirty that night, did he? He left at twelve-fifteen, just like he told the police. He never asked you all to lie to give him an alibi; he actually had one. He was with you. Sal never once lied to the police; you all did on that Tuesday. You lied to take away his alibi."

Naomi squinted as tears glazed her eyes. She looked at Cara and then slowly over to Pip. And she nodded.

Pip blinked. "Why?"

twenty-eight

"Why?" Pip asked again when Naomi had stared wordlessly down at her feet long enough.

"Someone made us," she sniffed. "Someone made us do it."

"What do you mean?"

"We—me, Max, Jake, and Millie—we all got a text on that Monday night. From an anonymous number. It told us we had to delete every picture of Sal taken on the night Andie disappeared and to upload the rest as normal. It told us that at school on Tuesday, we had to ask the principal to call in the police so we could make a statement. And we had to tell them that Sal actually left Max's at ten-thirty and that he'd asked us to lie before."

"But why would you do that?" asked Pip.

"Because"—Naomi's face cracked—"whoever it was knew something about us. About something bad we'd done."

She slapped her hands to her face and bawled into them, the cries strangled against her fingers. Cara jumped up from her seat and ran over, wrapping her arms around her sister's waist. She looked over at Pip as she held the quaking Naomi, her face pale with fear.

"Max?" Pip said.

Max cleared his throat, his eyes down on his fiddling hands. "We, um . . . Something bad happened on New Year's Eve 2013. Something we did."

"W-we?" Naomi spluttered. "We, Max? It happened because of you. You got us into it, and you're the one that made us leave him there."

"You're lying. We all agreed at the time," he said.

"I was scared."

"Naomi?" Pip said.

"We . . . um, we went out to this party out in Stamford," she said. "And we all had a lot to drink. When the party got shut down, it was impossible to find a ride; we couldn't get a taxi, and it was freezing outside. So Max, who'd driven us there, said that actually he hadn't drunk that much and was OK to drive. And he convinced me, Millie, and Jake to get in the car with him. It was so stupid. Oh god, if I could go back and change one thing in my life, it would be that moment. . . ." She trailed off.

"Sal wasn't there?" Pip asked.

"No," she said. "I wish he had been because he'd never let us be that stupid. He was with his brother that night. So Max, who was just as drunk as the rest of us, was driving too fast up the highway. It was like four a.m. and there were no other cars on the road. And then"—the tears came again—"and then . . ."

"This man comes out of nowhere," Max said.

"No, he didn't. He was standing well back on the shoulder, Max. You lost control of the car."

"Well, then, we remember very differently," Max snapped. "We hit him and spun. When we came to a stop, I pulled off the road and we went to see what had happened."

"Oh god, there was so much blood," Naomi cried. "And his legs were bent all wrong."

"He looked dead, OK?" Max said. "We checked to see if he was breathing, and we thought he wasn't. We decided it was too late for him, too late to call an ambulance. And we'd all been drinking, so we knew how much trouble we'd be in. Criminal charges, prison. So we all agreed and we left."

"You made us," Naomi said. "You got inside our heads and scared us into agreeing, because you knew you were the one really in trouble."

"We *all* agreed, Naomi!" Max shouted, a red flush creeping to the surface of his face. "We drove back to my house 'cause my parents were in Dubai. We cleaned off the car and then crashed it again into the tree just before my driveway. My parents never suspected a thing and got me a new one a few weeks later."

Cara was now crying too. Wiping the tears before Naomi could see them.

"Did the man die?" Pip said.

Naomi shook her head. "He was in a coma for a few weeks; he pulled through. But . . . but . . ." Her face creased in agony. "He's paraplegic. He's in a wheelchair. We did that to him. We should never have left him."

They all listened as Naomi cried, struggling to suck in air between the tears.

"Somehow," Max eventually said, "someone knew what we'd done. They said that if we didn't do everything they asked, they would tell the police. So we did it. We deleted the pictures and we lied to the police."

"But how did someone find out about the hit-and-run?" asked Pip.

"We don't know," Naomi said. "We all swore to never tell anyone, ever. And I never did."

"Me neither," Max said.

Naomi looked over at him with a weepy scoff.

"What?" He stared back at her.

"Me, Jake, and Millie always thought you were the one that let it slip."

"Oh, really?" he spat.

"Well, you're the one that got completely plastered like every night."

"I never told anyone," he said, turning back to Pip now. "I have no idea how someone found out."

"You have a pattern of letting things slip," said Pip. "Naomi, Max accidentally told me you were MIA for a while the night Andie disappeared. Where were you? The truth."

"I was with Sal," she said. "He wanted to talk to me upstairs, alone. About Andie. He was angry at her about something she'd done; he wouldn't say what. He told me she was a different person when it was just the two of them, but he could no longer ignore the way she treated other people. He decided that night he was going to end things with her. And he seemed . . . almost relieved when he came to that decision."

"So just to be clear," Pip said. "Sal was with you all at Max's until twelve-fifteen the night Andie disappeared. On the Monday someone threatens you; makes you go to the police, say he left at ten-thirty, and to delete all trace of him from that night. The next day Sal disappears and is found dead in the woods. You know what this means, don't you?"

Max looked down, picking at the skin around his thumbs. Naomi covered her face again.

"Sal was innocent."

"We don't know that for sure," Max said.

"Sal was innocent. Someone killed Andie, and then they killed Sal, after making sure he'd look guilty beyond reasonable doubt. Your best friend was innocent, and you've all known it for over five years."

"I'm sorry." Naomi wept. "I'm so, so sorry. We didn't know what else to do. We were in too deep. I never thought that Sal would end up dead. I thought if we just played along, the police would catch whoever had hurt Andie, Sal would be cleared, and we'd all be OK. We told ourselves it was just a small lie at the time."

"Sal died because of your *small* lie." Pip's stomach twisted with a rage tempered by sadness.

"What are you going to do with the photo?" Max asked quietly.

Pip looked over at Naomi, whose red puffy face was etched with pain. Cara was holding her hand, staring at Pip with silent tears.

"Max," Pip said. "Did you kill Andie?"

"What?" He stood up, scraping the messy hair out of his face. "No, I was at my house the whole night."

"You could have left when Naomi and Millie went to bed."

"Well, I didn't, OK?"

"Do you know what happened to Andie?"

"No, I don't."

"Pip," Cara spoke up now. "Please don't go to the police with that photo. Please. I can't have my sister taken away as well as Mom." Her bottom lip trembled, and she scrunched her face to fight back the sobs. Naomi wrapped her arms around her.

Pip ached with a helpless feeling, watching them both like this. What should she do? What could she do? She didn't know whether the police would take this photo seriously anyway. But if they did, Cara would be left all alone, and it would be Pip's fault. She couldn't do that to her best friend. But what about Ravi? Sal was innocent, and there was no question of her abandoning him now. Her heart fell away to her stomach; there was only one way through this, she realized.

"I won't go to the police," she said.

Max heaved a sigh and Pip eyed him, disgusted, as he tried to hide a faint smile crossing his mouth.

"Not for you, Max," she said. "For Naomi. For what your mistakes have done to her."

"They're my mistakes too," Naomi said quietly. "I did this too."

Cara walked over to Pip and hugged her from the side, tears soaking into her shirt.

Max left then, without another word. He packed up his laptop and notes, swung his bag on his shoulder, and took off toward the front door.

Cara went to splash her face in the sink and filled up a glass of water for her sister. Naomi was the first to break the silence.

"I'm so sorry," she said.

"I know," Pip said, still grappling with the decision. "I won't go to the police with the photo." She paused. "Because I don't need Sal's alibi to prove his innocence. There's another way."

"What do you mean?" Naomi sniffed.

"You're asking me to cover for you, and I will. But I can't cover up the truth about Sal." She swallowed and it grated all the way down her throat. "I'm going to find who really did this, who killed Andie and Sal. That's the only way to clear Sal's name and protect you at the same time."

Naomi hugged her, burying her face into Pip's shoulder. "Please do," she said quietly. "He's innocent, and it's killed me every day since."

Pip stroked Naomi's hair and looked over at Cara—her best friend, her sister—as a weight settled onto her shoulders. The world heavier than it had ever been before.

part three

PIPPA FITZ-AMOBI
10/14/19
CAPSTONE PROJECT LOG—ENTRY 31

He's innocent.

This project is no longer the hopeful conjecture it started as. No longer me indulging my gut instinct because Sal was kind to me when I was small and hurting. No longer Ravi hoping against hope that his brother wasn't a monster. It's real. No shred of "maybe"/"possibly"/"allegedly" left. Sal Singh did not kill Andie Bell. And he did not kill himself.

If a villain can be made, then he can be unmade. Two teenagers were murdered in Fairview five and a half years ago, and Ravi and I hold the clues to finding the real killer.

I went to meet Ravi in the park after school, and we talked for more than three hours, well past dusk. He was angry when I told him why Sal's friends took his alibi away. A quiet kind of angry. It's not fair, nothing about any of this is fair. But Naomi never meant to hurt Sal—it's clear from her face, clear from the way she's tiptoed through life since. She acted out of fear and I can understand that. Ravi does, too, though he's not sure he can forgive her.

His face fell when I said I didn't know whether the photo was enough for the police to reopen the case; I'd bluffed to get Max and Naomi to talk. The police might think I doctored the image and refuse to apply for a warrant to check Max's profile. Max deleted the photo already, of course. Ravi thinks I'd have more credibility with the police than him, but I'm not so sure; a teenage girl going on about photo angles and tiny white numbers on a phone screen, especially when the evidence against Sal is so solid. Not to mention Daniel da Silva on the force, shutting me down.

The hardest part was when I told him I wanted to protect Naomi. I explained that they are my family, Cara and Naomi both sisters to me, and Cara is innocent. It would kill me to do this to her, to make her lose her sister after her mom too. I promised Ravi we didn't need Sal to have an alibi to prove his innocence; we just have to find the real killer. He pushed back a little, as I would have expected, so we came to a deal: three weeks. Three more weeks to find the killer or solid evidence against a suspect. If we have nothing after that deadline, Ravi and I will go to the police with the photo and see if they'll take it seriously.

So I have just three weeks to find the killer, or Naomi's and Cara's lives get blown apart. Was it wrong of me to ask Ravi to do this, to wait when he's waited so long already? I'm torn, between the Wards and the Singhs and what's right. I don't even know what's right anymore—everything is so muddled. I'm not sure I'm the good girl I once thought I was. I've lost her along the way.

And from the persons of interest list, we have now narrowed it down to five suspects. I've taken Naomi off the list. My reasons for suspecting her—the MIA thing and her being so awkward when answering questions about Sal—have been explained away.

I made a diagram to recap all the suspects:

LIED ABOUT KNOWING HIM; STILL BUYING?

HOWIE BOWERS

- Supplied Andie with drugs to sell
- Possible sexual relationship?
- Lived alone = no alibi that night
- Andie's car was abandoned on his road (Monroe) and her blood found in the trunk.
- Knew exact location of Andie's hiding spot for burner phone and stash, and they are now gone

MAX HASTINGS

- Secret older guy candidate: Andie could have **ruined** his friendships with Sal & co.
- Has a nude photo of Andie taken at the Ivy House Inn
- Bought drugs from Andie and regularly bought Rohypnol
- Girls were getting drinks spiked at calamity parties.
- Knew about the hit-and-run

JASON BELL

- Was having an affair. Andie knew and Jason knew she found out.
- Emotionally abusive to his family?
- Questioned by the police in a formal interview
- Left dinner party for a period of time the night she went missing
- Used past tense when talking about Andie in an early press conference

ANDIE BELL

MAY HAVE DRUGGED HER AT PARTY

NAT DA SILVA

BROTHER & SISTER

DANIEL DA SILVA

Nat da Silva

- Bullied by Andie: *The Crucible* blackmail, topless video, and a mysterious third victory Andie had over her
- Proven to be violent (punched a girl in college and served time for assault)
- Left Andie a death threat in her school locker
- Claims she has an alibi and was in bed by eleven, but could have snuck out later

DRINK SPIKING?

Daniel da Silva

- Secret older guy candidate (Ivy House Inn)
- Andie said they had sex when she was fifteen, and used statutory rape claim to blackmail Nat.
- Andie could have **ruined** him by reporting statutory rape or destroying his new marriage.
- Report of drink spiking (by Max?) made to him and not followed up
- Police officer; may have had access to Andie's house in searches and could have removed evidence that led to him (burner phone)
- Shut down all of Ravi's questions about Sal

Along with the note and text I got, I now have another lead to the killer: the fact that they knew about the hit-and-run. First up, and most obviously, Max knew about it because he was the one who did it. He could have pretended to threaten himself along with his friends so he could pin Andie's murder on Sal.

But, as Naomi said, Max has always partied a lot. Drinking and taking drugs. He could have let it slip about the hit-and-run to someone he knew, like Nat da Silva or Howie Bowers. Or maybe even Andie Bell, who then, in turn, could have told any of the names above. Daniel da Silva was a working police officer who responded to traffic accidents; maybe he put two and two together? Or could one of them have been on the same road that night and seen it happen? It's feasible, then, that any of the five could have learned about the accident and used it to their advantage. But Max remains the strongest option in that respect.

I know Max has an alibi for the majority of the Andie disappearance window, but I do not trust him. As long as he intercepted Andie before 12:45, when she was expected to pick her parents up, it's still possible. Or maybe he went to help finish something that Howie started? He said he didn't leave his house, but he didn't really have to be honest with me. I'm in a bit of a catch-22 here: I can't protect Naomi without simultaneously protecting Max, and I think he knows that. Naomi said she hasn't considered him a friend since the accident and the alibi thing, but she was scared and felt like she had to pretend because of this terrible secret they shared. Well, at least she'll be staying away from him now, which is good because I'm almost certain he's dangerous.

Another new lead I have is that the killer somehow had access to the phone numbers of Max, Naomi, Millie, and Jake (as well as mine). But this doesn't really narrow it down. Max obviously had them, and Howie could have had access that way. Nat da Silva probably had all their numbers, especially as she was good friends with Naomi; Daniel could have gotten them through her. Jason Bell may seem like the outlier in this matter, *BUT* if he did kill Andie and had her phone, she probably had each of their numbers saved on it.

I'm running out of time and I haven't narrowed anything down. I need to try harder, because the clock is against me now. *AND* I still need to write my essay.

twenty-nine

Pip unlocked the front door and Barney bounded down the hall to escort her to the living room.

"Hello, pickle," her dad said as she popped her head in. "We only just beat you back. I'm about to sort out some dinner for Mom and me; Josh ate at Sam's house. Did you eat at Cara's?"

"Yeah," she said. They'd eaten, but they hadn't talked much. Cara had been quiet all week at school. Pip understood; she didn't really know what to say either. *Sorry?* or *I promise I'll fix this?* After Max left on Sunday, Cara and Naomi had asked her who she thought the killer was. She didn't tell them anything, just warned Naomi to stay away from Max. She couldn't risk sharing Andie's secrets with them in case that came hand in hand with threats from the killer.

"How was parents' night?" Pip asked.

"Pretty good," her mom said, patting Josh's head. "Getting better in science and math, aren't you, Josh?"

Josh nodded, assembling Lego bricks on the coffee table.

"Although Miss Speller did say you have a proclivity for being the class clown." Her dad threw a mock-serious face in Josh's direction.

"I wonder where he gets that from," Pip said, throwing the same face right back at him.

He chuckled. "The sass."

"OK, I'm going to get a few hours' work done before bed." She stepped back into the hallway and toward the stairs.

"Oh, sweetie," her mom sighed, "you work too hard."

"There's no such thing," Pip said, waving from the stairs.

On the landing she stopped just outside her bedroom. The door was open slightly, which jarred with Pip's memory of this morning; Josh sprinting down the upstairs hall, squirting two bottles of their dad's aftershave, yelling "Chemical attack!" Pip had made sure to close her door behind her so her room wouldn't forever smell like Pour Homme. Or maybe that had been yesterday morning? She hadn't been sleeping well and the days were sticking to each other.

"Has someone been in my room?" she called downstairs.

"No, we just got in," her mom replied.

Pip went inside and dumped her backpack on the bed. She walked over to her desk and knew with only half a glance that something wasn't right. Her laptop was open, the screen tilted back. Pip always, always closed the lid when she left it for the day. She hit the power button, and as it whirred back to life she noticed that the neat stack of printouts beside her computer had been fanned out. One had been picked out and placed on top of the pile.

It was *the* photograph. The evidence of Sal's alibi. And it wasn't where she'd left it.

Her laptop sang two welcome notes and loaded the home screen. It was just as she'd left it: the Word document with her capstone project in the task bar beside a minimized Chrome tab. She clicked into her log, which opened on the page below her diagram.

Pip gasped.

Below her final words someone had typed: *YOU NEED TO STOP THIS, PIPPA.*

Over and over again. Hundreds of times. Enough to fill four full pages.

Pip's heart drummed beneath her skin. She drew her hands away from the keyboard. The killer had been here, in her room. Touching her things. Looking through her research.

Inside her home.

She pushed away from the desk and bounded downstairs.

"Um, Mom," she said, trying to speak normally over the terror in her voice, "did anyone come over to the house today?"

"I don't know, I've been at work all day and went straight to Josh's parents' night. Why?"

"Oh, nothing," Pip said, improvising. "I ordered a book and thought it would turn up. Um . . . oh, and there was a story going around school today. A couple of people's houses have been broken into; they think they're using people's spare keys to get in. Maybe we shouldn't keep ours out until they're caught?"

"Oh really?" her mom said, looking up at her. "Yeah, I guess we shouldn't, then."

"I'll get it," Pip said, trying not to skid as she hurried for the front door.

She pulled it open and a blast of night air cooled her burning face. She bent down and peeled back the outside doormat. The key was sitting not in, but just next to its original imprint in the dirt. Pip grabbed it, the icy metal stinging her fingers.

She lay under her duvet, arrow-straight. There was a scraping sound somewhere in the house. Was someone trying to get inside? Or was it just the tree that scuffed against her parents' window?

A thud from the front. Pip jumped. A neighbor's car door or someone trying to break in?

She got out of bed for the sixteenth time and went to the

window. Was someone out there watching her? She waited for a sign of movement, for a ripple of darkness to shift and become a person.

Pip let the curtain fall and got back into bed. She shivered, watching the clock turn to three o'clock and on.

The wind howled and rattled her window, and Pip's heart jumped to her throat. She threw the duvet off and tiptoed across the landing to Josh's room. He was sound asleep, his face lit up by his nightlight.

Pip crept over to the foot of his bed and climbed under the covers beside him.

She lay there, listening to his deep breaths, letting his warmth thaw her. Her eyes crossed as she stared ahead, transfixed by the soft blue light.

Josh would be safe, if she was here to watch him.

thirty

"Naomi's been a bit jumpy since . . . you know," Cara said, walking Pip down the hall to her locker. There was still something awkward between them, only just starting to melt around the edges. Though they both pretended it wasn't there.

"Well, she's always been a bit jumpy, but even more now," Cara continued. "Yesterday Dad called her from the other room, and she jumped so hard she threw her phone across the kitchen. Completely smashed the screen. Had to send it off this morning to get fixed."

"Oh," Pip said, opening up her locker and stacking her books inside. "Um, does she need a spare phone? My mom just upgraded and has her old one."

"Nah, it's fine. She found an old one of hers from years ago. Her SIM card didn't fit, but we found an old pay-as-you-go one with some credit left."

"Is she OK?" Pip said.

"Don't know," Cara replied. "Don't think she's been OK for a while. Not since Mom died, really. I always thought there was something more she was struggling with."

Pip closed the locker door and followed her. She hoped Cara hadn't noticed the dark circles under her eyes, barely covered by makeup, or the bloodshot veins running through them. Sleep wasn't really an option anymore. Pip had finished a personal essay, read it twice, and deleted it again. It wasn't right, it wasn't *her.* So now she had to start from scratch with just two weeks to go. Her deadline for keeping Naomi and Cara out of everything was ticking down every second. And when she did sleep, there was a dark figure in her dreams, just out of sight, watching her.

"It'll be OK," Pip said. "I promise."

Cara gave her hand a squeeze as they turned their separate ways down the corridor.

A few doors down from her English classroom, Pip stopped sharply, her shoes squeaking against the floor. Someone was trudging down the hall toward her, someone with pixie-cut white hair and black-winged eyes.

"Nat?" Pip said with a small wave.

Nat da Silva slowed and stopped just in front of her. She didn't smile and she didn't wave. She barely looked at her.

"What are you doing in school?" Pip asked, noticing Nat's electronic ankle monitor as a sock-covered bulge above her shoes.

"I forgot all details of my life were suddenly your business, Piper."

"Pippa."

"Don't care," she spat, top lip arching into a sneer. "If you must know, for your perverted project, I've officially hit rock bottom. My parents are cutting me off, and no one will hire me. I just begged that slug of a principal for my brother's old janitor job. They can't hire violent criminals, apparently."

"I'm sorry," Pip said.

"No you're not." Nat picked up her feet and strode away, the gust of her departure enough to ruffle Pip's hair.

* * *

After lunch Pip returned to her locker to grab her history textbook. She opened the door, and a folded piece of printer paper was sitting on top of her books, pushed through the top slit.

A flash of cold dread. She looked over both shoulders to check that no one was watching and reached in for the note.

This is your final warning, Pippa. Walk away.

She read it only once, folded the page back up, and slipped it under the cover of her textbook. She pulled out the book and walked away down the hall.

It was clear. Someone wanted her to know they could get to her at home and at school. They wanted to scare her. And they were succeeding; terror had chased away sleep the last three nights. But if this person was really prepared to hurt her or her family, wouldn't they have done it by now? Pip couldn't walk away from this, from Sal and Ravi, from Cara and Naomi. She was in too deep.

There was a killer in Fairview. They'd seen her last capstone project entry, and now they were reacting. Which meant that Pip was on the right track somewhere. A warning was all it was—she had to believe that, had to tell herself that when she lay sleepless at night. Even though Unknown might be closing in on her, she was also closing in on them.

Pip pushed the classroom door open with the spine of her textbook, and it swung forward much harder than she'd meant.

"Ouch," Mr. Ward said as it crashed into his elbow.

The door bounded back into Pip and she tripped, dropping her textbook. It landed with a loud thwack.

"Sorry—Mr. Ward," she said. "I didn't know you were right there."

"That's OK." He smiled. "I'll interpret it as your eagerness for learning rather than an assassination attempt."

"Well, we are learning about 1930s Russia."

"Ah, I see," he said, bending to pick up her book. "So it was a practical demonstration?"

The note slipped out from the cover and glided to the floor. It landed on its crease and came to rest, partly open. Pip lunged for the paper, scrunching it up in her hands.

"Pip?"

She could see Mr. Ward trying to make eye contact with her. But she stared straight ahead.

"Pip, are you OK?" he asked.

"Yep." She nodded, flashing a closemouthed smile. "I'm fine."

"Listen," he said gently, "if you're being bullied, the worst thing to do is keep it to yourself."

"I'm not," she said, turning to him. "I'm fine, really."

"Pip?"

"I'm good, Mr. Ward," she said as the first group of chattering students slipped in the door behind them. She took her textbook from his hands and wandered over to her seat, knowing his eyes were following her.

"Pips," Connor said, shoving his bag down on the place beside her. "Lost you after lunch." And then in a whisper, he added, "So why are you and Cara acting all weird? You have a fight or something?"

"No," she said, "we're all fine. Everything's fine."

PIPPA FITZ-AMOBI
10/19/19
CAPSTONE PROJECT LOG—ENTRY 33

Nat da Silva has now climbed to the top of the suspect list. She was at school just a few hours before I found the note, and she has a history of putting death threats in lockers. But it's not definitive, not at all; I didn't actually see her do it with my own two eyes. Could be coincidence, though I hate that word.

Almost everyone on the suspect list has a connection with the high school. Both Max Hastings and Nat da Silva went there, Daniel da Silva used to work there as a janitor, both of Jason Bell's daughters went there. I don't know if Howie Bowers attended; I can't seem to find any information about him. But all these suspects know I go there; any one of them could have followed me, watched me on Friday morning when I was at my locker with Cara.

So maybe it was Nat, or maybe it wasn't. And I've just talked myself back around to square one. Who is the killer? Time is running out.

I still think Andie's burner phone is the most important lead. If we can find it or the person who has it, then our job is done. The phone is physical, tangible evidence. Exactly what we need if we're going to find a way to bring the police in on this. They might sneer at a printed photo with blurry details, but no one could ignore the secret second phone of the victim.

It's possible the burner phone was with Andie when she died and it's lost forever with her body. But let's say it wasn't, that she left it at home before she drove away, got intercepted, and killed. And then the killer thinks to themselves: oh no, the burner phone could lead to me if the police find it when searching the Bell residence.

So they have to go and get it. There are two people on my list who I've confirmed knew about the burner phone: Max and Howie. If Daniel da Silva was Secret Older Guy, then surely he knew about it too. Howie, in particular, knew exactly where it was hidden.

What if one of them went to the Bell house and removed the burner phone after killing Andie, before it could be found? I have some more questions for Becca Bell. I don't know if she'll answer them, and this might be a shot in the dark, but I have to try.

thirty-one

The nerves felt like barbs in her stomach as Pip approached the tiny, glass-fronted building. The words "Fairview Mail" on a small sign beside the door.

Pip pressed the buzzer and a muffled robotic voice came through the speaker.

"Hello?"

"Um, hi," Pip said. "I'm here to see Becca Bell."

"OK," the voice said, "I'll buzz you in. Give the door a good push—it's sticky."

A harsh, whining sound and Pip shoved the door until it unstuck, swinging inward. She closed the door behind her and stood in a small and cold room. There were three sofas and a couple coffee tables but no people.

"Hello?" she called.

Another door opened and a man strolled through, flicking the collar up on his long beige coat. A man with straight dark hair pushed to the side and gray-tinged skin. Stanley Forbes.

"Oh." He stopped when he saw Pip. "I'm just on my way out. I . . . Who are you?"

He stared at her with narrowed eyes, his lower jaw jutted out, and Pip felt goosebumps crawling down her neck. It really was cold in here.

"I'm here to see Becca," she said.

"Oh, right." He smiled without showing his teeth. "Everyone's working in the back room today. Heating's busted at the front. That way." He pointed at the door he'd come through.

"Thank you," she said, but Stanley wasn't listening, already halfway out the front door.

Pip walked to the far door and pushed through. A short corridor opened up into a larger room, with four paper-laden desks pushed against each wall. There were three women, each typing loudly at their computers. None of them had noticed her over the sound.

Pip walked toward Becca Bell, whose short blond hair was scraped back in a stubby ponytail, and cleared her throat.

"Hi, Becca," she said.

Becca spun around in her chair, and the other two women looked up. "Oh," she said, "it's you that's here to see me? Shouldn't you be at school?"

"Yeah, sorry. It's fall break," Pip said, shifting nervously under Becca's gaze, thinking of how close she and Ravi had been to getting caught by her in the Bell house. Pip looked over Becca's shoulder, at the computer screen full of typed words.

Becca's eyes followed hers, and she minimized the document.

"Sorry," she said. "It's the first piece I'm writing for the newspaper, and my first draft is absolutely awful. My eyes only." She smiled.

"What's it about?" Pip asked.

"Oh, um, just about this old farmhouse that's been uninhabited for eleven years now, just off the Fairview end of Sycamore

Road. They can't seem to sell it." She looked up at Pip. "A few of the neighbors are thinking about pitching in to buy it, trying to apply for change of use and doing it up as a café-bar combo. I'm writing about why that's a terrible idea."

One of the women across the room cut in. "My brother lives near there and he doesn't think it's such a terrible idea. Beer on tap just down the road. He's ecstatic." She gave a hacking laugh.

Becca shrugged, glancing down at her hands as she picked at the sleeve of her cardigan. "I just think the place deserves to be a home for a family again one day," she said. "My dad almost bought it and restored it years ago, before everything happened. He changed his mind, in the end, but I've always wondered what things would be like if he hadn't."

The other two keyboards fell silent.

"Oh, Becca, sweetheart," the woman said. "I had no idea that was the reason. Well, I feel awful now." She slapped her forehead. "I'll do the coffee run today."

"No, don't worry."

The other two women turned back to their computers.

"Pippa, isn't it?" Becca spoke quietly, angling to face her. "What can I help you with? If it's about what we discussed before, you know I don't want to be involved."

"This is important," Pip said, her voice dipping into a whisper. "Really important. Please."

Becca's blue eyes locked on hers for a long moment.

"Fine." She stood up. "Let's go out to the front room."

The room felt colder the second time around. Becca took a seat on the nearest sofa and crossed her legs. Pip sat at the other end and faced her.

"Um . . . so . . ." Her voice tapered off. She wasn't quite sure how to phrase it or how much she should tell her. She stalled, staring into Becca's Andie-like face.

"What is it?" Becca asked.

Pip found her voice. "So, while researching, I found out Andie was dealing drugs and selling at calamity parties."

Becca's neat brows drew down to her eyes. "No," she said, "there's no way."

"I'm sorry; I've confirmed it with multiple sources," Pip said.

"She couldn't have."

"The man who supplied her gave her a secret second phone, a burner phone, to use." Pip carried on over Becca's protests. "He said that Andie hid the phone in her wardrobe along with her stash."

"I'm sorry, but I think someone's played a trick on you," Becca said, shaking her head. "There's no way my sister was selling drugs."

"I understand it must be hard to hear, I'm sorry," Pip said. "The police didn't find the burner phone in her room, and I'm trying to find out who might have had access to her room after she went missing."

"Wh . . . but . . . ," Becca sputtered, still shaking her head. "No one did; the house was taped off."

"I mean *before* the police arrived. After Andie left the house and before your parents discovered she was missing. Was there any way someone could have broken into your house without you knowing? Had you gone to sleep?"

"I . . . I—" Her voice cracked. "No, I don't know. I wasn't asleep. I was downstairs watching TV. But you—"

"Do you know Max Hastings?" Pip said quickly before Becca could object again.

Becca stared at her, confusion clouding her eyes. "Um," she said, "yeah, he was Sal's friend, wasn't he? The blond guy."

"Did you ever notice him hanging around your house after Andie disappeared?"

"No," she said. "No, but why—"

"What about Daniel da Silva? Do you know him?" Pip said, hoping this quick-fire questioning was working, that Becca would answer before she thought not to answer.

"Daniel," she said, "yeah, I know him. He was close with my dad."

Pip's eyes narrowed. "How did they know each other?"

"He worked for my dad for a while, after he quit his janitor's job at school," Becca sniffed. "My dad owns a cleaning company. But he took a shine to Daniel and promoted him to a job in the office. He was the one that convinced Daniel to apply to be a police officer, supported him through the training. Yeah. I don't know if they're still close; I don't speak to my dad."

"So did you see a lot of Daniel?" asked Pip.

"Quite a bit. He often stopped by, stayed for dinner sometimes. What has this got to do with my sister?"

"Daniel was a police officer when your sister went missing. Was he involved in the case at all?"

"Well, yeah," Becca replied, "he was one of the first responding officers when my dad reported it."

Pip felt herself tilting forward, her hands against the sofa cushion, leaning into Becca's words. "Did he do a search of the house?"

"Yeah," Becca said. "He and this other policewoman took our statements and then did their primary search."

"Could Daniel have been the one that searched Andie's room?"

"Yeah, maybe." Becca shrugged. "I don't see where you're going with this. I think you've been misled by someone, really. Andie was not involved in drugs."

“Daniel da Silva was the first to access Andie’s room,” Pip said, more to herself than to Becca.

“Why does that matter?” Annoyance started to stir in Becca’s voice. “We know what happened that night. We know Sal killed her, regardless of what Andie or anyone else was up to.”

“I’m not sure he did,” Pip said, widening her eyes in what she hoped was a meaningful way. “I’m not so sure Sal did it. And I think I’m close to proving it.”

PIPPA FITZ-AMOBI
10/22/19
CAPSTONE LOG—ENTRY 34

Becca Bell asked me to leave. It's not surprising. She's had five and a half years of knowing that Sal killed Andie, five and a half years to bury the grief for her sister. And here I come, kicking up the dirt and telling her she's wrong.

And after my conversation with her, I think the frontrunner has changed again. Daniel da Silva and Jason Bell know each other well—another possible murder team? And I've confirmed my suspicions about Daniel; not only did he have access to Andie's room after she went missing, but he could have been the very first person to search it! He had the perfect opportunity to take and hide the burner phone, and remove any trace of himself from Andie's life.

My internet searches bring up nothing useful about Daniel. But I did find this on the Fairview Police Department page. Time to go speak to him in person.

HAVE YOUR SAY MEETINGS

Meet your local neighborhood officers and have a say on policing priorities in your local area.

Upcoming events:

Type: Have Your Say Meeting
Date: Thursday, October 24, 2019
Time: 12:00–1:00 p.m.
Venue: Town Hall, Fairview

thirty-two

"And there are still too many youths loitering in the park in the evenings," an old woman croaked, her arm raised beside her head.

"We spoke about this at a previous meeting, Mrs. Faversham," a female police officer with ringleted hair said. "They aren't engaging in any antisocial behavior. They are just playing soccer after school."

Pip was sitting on a yellow plastic chair in an audience of twenty-two people. The small meeting room in town hall was dark and stuffy, and the air smelled like old books and old people.

The meeting was exceptionally slow and dreary, but Pip was on high alert. Daniel da Silva was one of the seven officers taking the meeting. He was taller than she'd expected, standing there in his uniform, his light brown hair wavy and styled back from his forehead. He was clean-shaven, with a narrow, upturned nose and rounded lips. Pip tried to not watch him for long stretches of time, in case he noticed.

There was another familiar face here, too, sitting just three seats down from Pip. He stood up suddenly, flashing his open palm at the officers.

"Stanley Forbes, *Fairview Mail*," he said. "Several of my readers have complained that people are still driving too fast down Main Street. How do you intend to tackle this issue?"

Daniel stepped forward, nodding for Stanley to retake his seat. "Thanks, Stan," he said. "The street already has several traffic-calming measures. We have discussed performing more speed checks, and if it's still a concern, I am happy to reopen that conversation with my superiors."

Mrs. Faversham had two more complaints to drawl through, and then the meeting was finally over.

"If you have any other policing concerns," another officer said, noticeably avoiding eye contact with old Mrs. Faversham, "please fill out one of the questionnaires behind you. And if you'd prefer to talk to any of us in private, we'll be sticking around for the next ten minutes."

Pip held back for a while, not wanting to appear too eager. She waited as Daniel finished talking to one of the town councilors, and then she pushed up from her chair and approached.

"Hi," she said.

"Hello." He smiled. "You seem a few decades too young for a meeting like this."

She shrugged. "I'm interested in law and crime."

"Nothing too interesting in Fairview," he said. "Just loitering kids and slightly fast cars."

Oh, if only.

"Um, I had a couple of questions I wanted to ask you."

"Shoot," he said. "I'm all ears."

Pip coughed lightly into her fist and looked up. "Do you remember reports being made, about five or six years ago, of drug use and drinks being spiked at house parties thrown by Fairview High students?"

He tensed his chin, and his mouth sank into a thoughtful frown.

"No," he said, "I don't remember that. Do you want to report a crime?"

She shook her head. "Do you know Max Hastings?" she said.

Daniel shrugged. "I know the Hastings family a bit. They were my first call-out after I finished training."

"For what?"

"Oh, nothing big. Their son had crashed his car into a tree in front of the house. Needed to file a police report for the insurance. Why?"

"No reason," she said faux-nonchalantly. She could see Daniel's feet starting to turn away from her. "Just one more thing."

"Yep?"

"You were one of the first responding officers when Andie Bell was reported missing. You conducted the primary search of the Bell residence."

Daniel nodded, lines tightening around his eyes.

"Was that not a conflict of interest, seeing as you were so close to her father?"

"No," he said, "it wasn't. I'm a professional when I have this uniform on. And I have to say, I don't really like where these questions are going. Excuse me."

Daniel began to walk away, but a woman appeared behind him, stepping in beside him and Pip. She had long fair hair and a freckled nose, and a giant belly pushing out the front of her dress. She must have been at least seven months pregnant.

"Well, hi," she said in a forced pleasant tone to Pip. "I'm Dan's wife. How entirely unusual for me to catch him talking to a young girl. Must say you aren't his usual type."

"Kim," Daniel said, placing his hand on her back, "come on."

"Who is she?"

"Just some kid that came to the meeting. I don't know." He led his wife away to the other side of the room. Pip watched them go and headed out the exit, huddling farther into her coat as the cold air closed in on her. Ravi was waiting just up the road, opposite the café.

"You were right not to come in," she said when she arrived at his side. "He was pretty hostile. And Stanley Forbes was there too."

"My favorite person," Ravi said sarcastically, dipping his hands into his pockets to hide them from the bitter wind. "So you didn't learn anything?"

"Oh, I didn't say that," Pip said, stepping in closer to him to shield herself from the cold. "He let one thing slip; don't even know if he realized."

"Stop pausing for dramatic effect."

"Sorry," she said. "He knows the Hastingses, and he was the one who filed the police report when Max crashed his car into the tree by their house."

"Oh." Ravi's lips opened around the sound. "So he . . . maybe he could have known about the hit-and-run?"

"Maybe he could."

Pip's hands were so cold now that they started to curl into claws. She was about to suggest going back to her house when Ravi stiffened, his eyes fixed on a point behind her.

She turned.

Daniel da Silva and Stanley Forbes had just left town hall, the door banging behind them. They were deep in hushed conversation, Daniel explaining something with gestured hands. Stanley turned his head in a wide arc to check around them, and that's when he spotted Pip and Ravi.

Stanley's eyes cooled, his gaze a cold blast in the wind as it flicked between them. Daniel stared, too, but his eyes were just on Pip, sharp and blistering.

Ravi took her hand. "Let's go," he said.

thirty-three

"All right, puppuccino," Pip said to Barney, bending down to unclip the leash from his collar. "Off you go."

He looked up at her with his sloped, smiling eyes. When she straightened up, he was off, bounding up the muddy track and winding between the trees.

Her mom had been right; it was a little too late to be going out for a walk. The woods were darkening already, the sky a churned gray peeking through the gaps in the speckled trees. She wouldn't stay out long, she told herself; she just needed to get away from her desk, get some air.

She'd been working all day on her personal essay, or at least she'd tried to. She had. She just couldn't focus, her eyes wandering away from her whenever she paused, gazing at her list of suspects.

She didn't know what to do next. Maybe try to talk to Daniel da Silva's wife; there was definitely friction between the couple. Or focus on the burner phone, consider breaking into the homes of those suspects who knew about the phone and searching for it there?

No.

She had come on this walk to forget Andie Bell and clear her head. She reached into her pocket and unwound her headphones to continue the true crime podcast she was listening to. She turned the volume up, struggling to hear over the crunch of her boots on the fallen leaves. Listening to the story of another murdered girl so she could forget her own.

She took the short route through the woods as the world darkened around them. When twilight took a turn toward night, Pip veered off the path, dipping into the trees to get to the road faster. She called for Barney when the street was visible, thirty feet ahead.

She stopped at the gate and spooled the headphones around her phone.

"Barney, come on," she called, slipping the phone into her pocket.

A car flew by on the road, its headlights blinding Pip.

"Barney!" she called, louder and higher this time. "Come!"

The trees were dark and still.

Pip wet her lips and whistled.

"Barney! Here, Barney!"

No sound of paws trampling through the fallen leaves. No golden flash among the trees. Nothing.

Fear crept up her toes and down her fingers.

"Bar-ney!" she shouted, and her voice cracked.

She ran back the way she'd come. Back into the dark engulfing trees.

"Barney!" she screamed, crashing along the path, the dog leash swinging empty in her hand.

thirty-four

"Mom, Dad!" She shoved open the front door, tripping over the doormat. The tears stung her cracked lips. "Dad!"

He appeared at the kitchen door.

"Pip?" he said. And then he saw her. "Pippa, what is it? What happened?"

He hurried forward as she picked herself up from the floor.

"Barney's gone," she said. "He didn't come when I called. I went around the whole woods, calling him. He's gone. I don't know what to do. I've lost him, Dad."

Her mom and Josh were in the hallway now, too, watching her silently.

Her dad squeezed her arm. "It's OK, pickle," he said. "We'll find him; don't worry."

He grabbed his padded coat and two flashlights from the hall closet, and made Pip put on a pair of gloves before they headed out.

Night had settled by the time they reached the woods. Pip walked her dad around the path she'd taken, their two beams of light cutting through the heavy darkness.

"Barney!" her dad called in his booming voice, thrown forward and sideways, echoing through the trees.

It was two hours later and two hours colder when her dad said it was time to go home.

“We can’t go home until we find him!” she sniffed.

“Listen.” He turned to her, the flashlight casting shadows across his face. “It’s too dark now. We will find him in the morning. He’s wandered off somewhere, and he’ll be OK for one night.”

Pip went straight to bed after their silent dinner. Her parents both came up to her room and sat on her bedspread. Her mom stroked her hair as she tried not to cry.

“I’m sorry,” Pip said. “I’m so sorry.”

“It’s not your fault, sweetie,” her mom said. “He’ll find his way home. Now try to get some sleep.”

She didn’t. Not much, at least. One thought crept into her head and burrowed there: What if this *was* her fault? What if this was because she’d ignored her final warning? What if Barney wasn’t just lost; what if he’d been taken?

They all sat in the kitchen the next morning, eating an early breakfast none of them were hungry for. Pip’s dad, who looked like he hadn’t slept much either, had already called to take the day off work. He listed their plan of action between bites: He and Pip would go back to the woods and then widen the search and start knocking on doors. Her mom and Josh would stay back and make missing posters to put up along Main Street.

Two hours into the search, they heard barking, and Pip’s heart picked up. But it was just Lauren’s mom walking their beagle and a neighbor’s labradoodle.

Pip’s voice was hoarse by the time they’d circled the woods for the third time. They knocked on their neighbors’ houses up Thatcher Road; no one had seen a lost dog.

* * *

Early afternoon, and Pip's phone blared in the quiet forest.

"Is that mom?" her dad asked.

"No," Pip said, reading the message. It was from Ravi. *Hey, I've just seen missing posters for Barney in town. Are you OK? Do you need help?*

Her fingers were too numb from the cold to type a response.

They stopped briefly for sandwiches and carried on, her mom and Josh joining them now, traipsing through trees and across private farmland, shouts of "Barney" carrying on the wind.

But the world turned on them, and darkness fell again.

Back home, drained, Pip picked through the Thai takeout her dad had collected. Her mom put a Disney film on in the background to lighten the mood, but Pip just stared down at her noodles, wrapping them tighter and tighter around her fork.

Her pocket buzzed and she dropped the fork. She placed her plate on the coffee table and pulled out her phone.

The screen glared up at her.

Pip tried to blink the terror from her eyes as she put the phone facedown on the couch.

"Who's that?" her mom asked.

"Just Cara."

It wasn't. It was Unknown: *Want to see your dog again?*

thirty-five

The next text didn't come until eleven in the morning.

Pip's dad was working from home. He came to Pip's bedroom at around eight and told her that they were going off on another search and would be back at lunchtime.

"You stay here and finish up your essay," he'd said. "Leave Barney to us."

Pip nodded. She was relieved, in a way. She didn't think she could walk alongside her family, calling out his name, knowing that Barney wasn't there to be found. Because he wasn't lost; he was taken. By Andie Bell's killer.

There wasn't time to waste hating herself, asking why she hadn't listened to the threats. Why she'd been stupid enough to think herself invincible. She just had to get Barney back. That was all that mattered.

Her family had been gone for a couple of hours when her phone went off, making her flinch and slosh coffee over her duvet. She read over the text several times.

Take your computer and any USBs or hard drives that your project is saved on. Bring them to the tennis club parking lot with you now and walk 100 paces into the trees on the right side. Do not tell anyone and come alone. If you follow these instructions, you will get your dog back.

Pip jumped up, spattering more coffee onto her bed. She moved fast, before the fear could congeal and paralyze her. She changed into a hoodie and jeans, then grabbed her backpack and upturned it, spilling her schoolbooks and planner onto the floor. She unplugged her laptop and slid it into the bag. The two memory sticks she'd saved her project on were in the middle drawer of her desk. She scooped them out and shoved them in on top of the computer.

She ran down the stairs, stumbling as she swung the heavy bag on her back. She slipped on her boots and coat and grabbed her car keys from the side table in the hall. There was no time to think this through. If she stopped to think, she'd falter and lose him forever.

Outside, the wind was cold against her neck and fingers. She ran to the car and climbed in, her grip shaky on the steering wheel as she peeled out of the drive.

It took her five minutes to get there.

She turned into the parking lot beyond the tennis courts and pulled into the nearest spot. Grabbing her bag from the passenger seat, she got out and headed for the trees that bordered the lot.

Before stepping off the concrete, Pip paused for just a moment to look over her shoulder. There was a kids' club on the tennis courts, shrieking and whacking balls into the fence. A couple of moms with squawking toddlers standing beside a car, chatting. There was no one with their eyes fixed on her. No car she recognized. No person. If she was being watched, she couldn't tell.

She turned to the trees and started to walk, counting each step in her head, panicking that her strides were either too long or too short and she wouldn't end up in the right place.

At thirty paces her heart throbbed so hard that it jolted her breath.

At sixty-seven sweat broke under her arms.

At ninety-four she started muttering under her breath, "Please, please, please."

Then she stopped, one hundred steps into the trees. And she waited.

There was nothing around her, nothing but the shade of half-bare trees and leaves from red to pale yellow covering the mud.

A long high whistling sounded above her. She looked up to watch a bird fly over, a sharp outline against the gray sun. Then she was alone again.

It was almost a full minute later that her phone buzzed from her pocket. Fumbling, she pulled it out and looked down at the screen.

Destroy everything and leave it there. Do not tell anyone what you know. No more questions about Andie. This is finished now.

Pip's eyes flicked over the words. She forced a deep breath and put away the phone. Her skin seared under the gaze of the killer's eyes, watching her from somewhere unseen.

On her knees she slid her backpack to the ground and took out the laptop and the two memory sticks. She laid them out on the autumn leaves and opened the laptop lid.

She got to her feet, and as her eyes filled and the world blurred, she stamped down on the first memory stick with her boot heel. One side of the plastic casing broke and sprang away. She stamped again and turned her left boot onto the other stick, jumping on them both as their parts splintered off.

Then she turned to her laptop, the screen glinting with dim sunlight. She watched her reflection in the glass as she drew up her leg and kicked out. The screen flattened over its hinge, a large crack webbed across it.

The first tear dropped to her chin as she hit it again, at the keyboard this time. Letters came away with her boot, scattering into the mud. She stamped right through the glass on the screen into the metal casing.

She jumped and jumped again, tears chasing each other as they snaked down her cheeks.

The metal around the keyboard was cracked now, showing the motherboard and the cooling fan below. The green circuit board snapped to pieces beneath her heel, and the little fan severed and flew away. She jumped again and stumbled on the mangled machine, falling back in the brittle leaves.

She let herself cry there for a few moments. Then she sat upright and picked up the laptop, its broken screen hanging limply from one hinge, and hurled it against the trunk of the nearest tree. With another thud it came to rest on the ground in pieces, lying dead among the roots.

Pip sat, coughing, waiting for the air to return to her. Her face stinging from the salt.

What was she supposed to do now? She'd done everything they asked; was Barney about to be released to her? She should wait and see, wait for another message. She called his name.

More than half an hour passed. Nothing. No message. No Barney. No sound of anyone but the faint screams of the kids on the tennis court.

Pip pushed up to unsteady feet and picked up her empty backpack. She walked away, one last lingering look back at the destroyed machine.

"Where did you go?" her dad said when she let herself back into the house.

Pip had sat in the car for a while in the parking lot. To let her red eyes settle before she returned home.

"I couldn't concentrate here," she said quietly, "so I went to do my work at the café."

He nodded. "Sometimes a change of scenery is good."

"But, Dad." She hated the lie that was about to come out of her mouth. "Something happened. I don't know how. I went to the bathroom for just a minute, and when I came back, my laptop was gone. No one there saw anything. I think it was stolen." She looked down at her scuffed boots. "I'm sorry. I shouldn't have left it."

Her dad shushed her and folded her into a hug. One she really, really needed. "Don't worry," he said. "Things are not important. They are replaceable. I only care that you're OK."

"I'm OK," she said. "Any sign this morning?"

"None yet, but Josh and Mom are going back out this afternoon, and I'm going to call the local shelters. We'll get him back."

She nodded and stepped back from him. They were going to get him back; she'd done everything she was told to do. That was the deal. She wished she could say something to her family, take some of the worry out of their faces. But she couldn't. It was another of those Andie Bell secrets Pip had found herself trapped inside.

As for giving up on Andie now, could she really do that? Could she walk away, knowing Sal Singh wasn't guilty? Knowing a killer still lived in Fairview? She had to. For Barney, the dog she'd loved since she was a child, and who loved her back even harder. For her family's safety. For Ravi too. How could she convince him to give up on this? He had to, or he could be the next body in the woods.

This wasn't safe anymore. There was no choice. But the decision felt like a shard of glass through her chest. It cracked every time she breathed.

Pip was upstairs at her desk. On it a sheet of paper with *Personal Essay* scribbled at the top and four different beginnings crossed out. The day had grown dark and blustery when someone knocked on the door.

“Yep,” she said, spinning in her desk chair.

Her dad came in and closed the door behind him. “You working hard, pickle?”

She nodded.

He walked over and leaned against her desk, his legs crossed out in front of him.

“Listen, Pip,” he said gently. “Someone just found Barney.”

Pip’s breath stuck halfway down her throat. “Wh-why don’t you look happy?”

“He must have fallen in somehow. They found him in the river.” Her dad reached down and took her hand. “I’m sorry, honey. He drowned.”

Pip wheeled away from him, shaking her head.

“No,” she said. “He couldn’t have. That’s not what . . . No, he can’t be . . .”

“I’m sorry, Pip,” he said, bottom lip trembling. “Barney died. We’re going to bury him tomorrow, in the backyard.”

“No, he can’t be!” Pip jumped to her feet now, pushing her dad away as he stepped forward to hug her. “No, he isn’t dead. That’s not fair,” she cried, the tears rushing down to the dimple in her chin. “He can’t be dead. It’s not fair. It’s not . . . it’s not . . .”

She dropped to her knees and fell back on the floor, hugging her legs into her chest. A black chasm opened up inside her.

“This is all my fault.” Her mouth pressed into her knee, stifling her words. “I’m so sorry. I’m so, so sorry.”

Her dad sat down beside her and tucked her into his arms. “Pip, I don’t want you to blame yourself, not even for a second. It’s not your fault he wandered away from you.”

“It’s not fair, Dad,” she cried into his chest. “Why is this happening? I just want him back. I just want Barney back.”

"Me too," he whispered.

They sat that way for a long time on her bedroom floor, crying together. Pip didn't even hear when her mom and Josh came into the room. She didn't know they were there until they fitted themselves in, Josh sitting on Pip's lap, his little head on her shoulder.

"It's not fair."

thirty-six

They buried him in the afternoon. Pip and Josh would plant sunflowers over his grave in the spring, because they were golden and happy, just like him.

Pip had taken the day off school, crying until she threw up that morning. Cara and Lauren came over at the end of the day, Cara laden with home-baked cookies. Pip couldn't really talk; every word almost stumbled into a cry or a scream of rage. It was an impossible feeling, that she was too sad to be angry but too angry to be sad. Her friends didn't stay for long.

By evening there was a high ringing sound in her ears. The day had hardened her grief, and Pip felt numb and dried out. He wasn't coming back and she couldn't tell anyone why. That secret and the guilt were the heaviest things of all.

Someone knocked lightly at her bedroom door. Pip dropped her pen onto the blank page.

"Yes," she said, her voice hoarse.

The door opened and Ravi stepped in.

"Hi," he said, flicking his dark hair back from his face. "How are you doing?"

"Not good," she said. "What are you doing here?"

"You weren't replying and I got worried. I saw the posters were gone this morning. Your dad just told me what happened." He closed the door and leaned back against it. "I'm so sorry, Pip. I know it doesn't help when people say that; it's just something you say. But I am sorry."

"There's only one person who needs to be sorry," she said, looking down at the empty page.

He sighed. "It's what we do when someone we love dies; blame ourselves. I did it too. And it took me a long time to work out that it wasn't my fault; sometimes bad things just happen. It was easier after that. I hope you get there quicker."

She shrugged.

"I also wanted to say to you"—he cleared his throat—"don't worry about Sal for a bit. This deadline we made for taking the photo to the police, it doesn't matter. I know how important it is to you to protect Naomi and Cara. You can have more time. You already stretch yourself too far, and I think you need a break, you know, after what's happened. And you have to get your app in for Columbia." He scratched his head, and the long hair at the front trailed back into his eyes. "I know now my brother was innocent, even if no one else does yet. I've waited over five years; I can wait a little longer. And in the meantime, I'll keep looking into our open leads."

Pip's heart knotted, voiding itself of everything. She had to hurt him. It was the only way. The only way to make him give up, to keep him safe. Whoever murdered Andie and Sal, they'd shown her they were prepared to kill again. And she couldn't let it be Ravi.

She couldn't look at him. Couldn't look at his kind-without-trying face, or the perfect smile he shared with his brother, or his eyes so brown and deep you could fall right into them. So she didn't look.

"I'm not doing the project anymore," she said. "I'm done."

He straightened up. "What do you mean?"

"I mean I'm done with the project. I've emailed my supervisor telling her I'm changing the topic or dropping out. It's over."

"But . . . I don't understand," he said, the first wounds opening up in his voice. "This isn't just a project, Pip. This is about my brother, about what really happened here. You can't just stop. What about Sal?"

It was Sal she was thinking about. How, above all other things, he wouldn't have wanted his little brother to die in the woods as he had.

"I'm sorry, but I'm done."

"I don't . . . Wh . . . Look at me," he said.

She wouldn't.

He came over to the desk and crouched in front of it, looking up at her in the chair.

"What's wrong?" he said. "Something's wrong here. You wouldn't do this if—"

"I'm just done, Ravi," she said. She looked down at him and knew immediately she shouldn't have. This was so much harder now. "I can't do it. I don't know who killed them. I can't work it out. I'm finished."

"But we will," he said, desperation sculpting his face. "We *will* work it out."

"I can't. I'm just some kid, remember."

"An idiot said that to you," he said. "You're not *just* some anything. You're Pippa fricking Fitz-Amobi." He smiled, and it was the saddest thing she'd ever seen. "And I don't think there's anyone in this world quite like you. I mean, you laugh at my jokes, so there must be something wrong with you. We're so close, Pip. We know Sal's innocent; we know someone framed him for Andie and then killed him. You can't stop. You swore to me. You want this just as much as I do."

"I've changed my mind," she said flatly, "and you won't change it back. I'm done with Andie Bell. I'm done with Sal."

"But he's innocent!"

"It's not my job to prove that."

"You made it your job." He pushed against his knees and stood over her, his voice rising now. "You barged your way into my life, offering me this chance I never had before. You can't take that away from me now; you know I need you. You can't give up. This isn't you."

"I'm sorry."

A twelve-heartbeat silence fell between them, Pip's eyes on the floor.

"Fine," he said coldly. "I don't know why you're doing this, but fine. I'll go to the police with Sal's alibi photo on my own. Send me the file."

"I can't," Pip said. "My laptop got stolen."

Ravi shot a look at the surface of her desk. He charged over to it, spreading her stack of papers and midterm notes, eyes desperate.

"Where's the printout of the photo?" he said, turning to her, notes clutched in his hand.

And now for the lie that would break him.

"I destroyed it. It's gone," she said.

The look in his eyes set her on fire and she withered away.

"Why would you do that? Why are you doing this?" The papers dropped from his hands, gliding like severed wings to the floor, scattering around Pip's feet.

"Because I don't want to be a part of this anymore. I never should have started it."

"This isn't fair!" Tendons stuck out like vines up his neck. "My brother was innocent, and you just got rid of the one small bit of evidence we had. If you stand back now, Pip, you're just as bad as everyone else in Fairview. Everyone who painted the word 'scum' on our house, who smashed our windows. Everyone who tormented me at school. Everyone who looks at me that way they look at me. No, you'll be worse; at least they think he's guilty."

"I'm sorry," she said quietly.

"No, I'm sorry," he said, his voice breaking. He ran his sleeve over his face to catch the angry tears and reached for the door. "I'm sorry for thinking you were someone you're clearly not. You *are* just a kid. A cruel one, like Andie Bell."

He left the room, hands to his eyes as he turned to the stairs.

Pip watched him walk away for the last time.

When she heard the front door open and close, she clenched her hand into a fist and slammed it down on her desk. Her jar of pens shuddered and fell, scattering across the surface.

She screamed herself empty into her cupped hands, trapping it with her fingers.

Ravi hated her, but he would be safe now.

thirty-seven

The next day, after school, Pip was in the living room with Josh, teaching him how to play chess.

Someone knocked on the front door, and the absence of Barney was an immediate punch to the gut. No skittering claws on the polished wood racing to stand and greet.

Her mom pattered down the hall and opened the door.

Her voice floated into the living room, "Oh, hello, Ravi."

Pip's stomach leaped into her throat.

Confused, she put her knight back down and walked toward the front hall, her unease ramping into panic. Why would he come back after yesterday? How could he bear to look at her ever again? Unless he was desperate enough to come and ambush her parents, tell them everything and try to force Pip to go to the police. She wouldn't do it. Who else would die if she did?

She looked toward the front door to see Ravi unzipping a large sports bag and dipping his hands inside.

"My mom sends her condolences," he said, pulling out two large Tupperware boxes. "She made you a chicken curry, you know, in case you didn't feel like cooking."

"Oh," Pip's mom said, taking the boxes from Ravi. "That's very thoughtful. Thank you. Come in, come in. You must give me her number so I can thank her."

"Ravi?" Pip said.

"Hello, trouble," he said softly. "Can I talk to you?"

In Pip's room, Ravi closed the door and dropped his bag onto the carpet.

"Um . . . I—I," Pip stuttered, looking for clues in his face. "I don't understand why you came back."

He took a small step toward her. "I thought about it all night; literally, all night. It was light outside when I finally slept. And there's only one reason I can think of, only one thing that makes sense. Because I do know you; I wasn't wrong about you."

"I don't—"

"Someone took Barney, didn't they?" he said. "Someone threatened you, and they took your dog and killed him so you would stay quiet about Sal and Andie."

The silence in the room was buzzy and thick.

She nodded and her face cracked.

"Don't cry," Ravi said, closing the distance between them in one swift step. He pulled her into him, locking his arms round her. "I'm here," he said, "I'm here."

Pip leaned into him, and everything—all the pain, all the secrets she'd caged inside—came free, radiating out of her like heat. She dug her nails into her palms, trying to hold in the tears.

"Tell me what happened," he said when he finally let her go.

But the words got lost and tangled in her throat. She pulled out her phone and clicked to the messages from Unknown, handing the phone to him. She watched Ravi's eyes darken as he read through.

"Oh, Pip," he said, looking at her wide-eyed. "This is sick."

"They lied," she sniffed. "They said I'd get him back, and then they killed him."

"That wasn't the first time they contacted you," he said, scrolling up. "The first text here is from October eighth."

"That wasn't the first." She pulled open the bottom drawer of her desk and handed Ravi the two sheets of printer paper, pointing at the one on the left. "That one was left in my sleeping bag when I camped in the woods with my friends at the end of August. I saw someone watching us. That one"—she pointed to the other—"was in my locker last Friday. I ignored it and kept going. That's why Barney's dead. Because of my arrogance. Because I thought I was invincible and I'm not. We have to stop. Yesterday . . . I'm sorry, I didn't know how else to get you to stop, other than to make you hate me so you stayed away and dropped this."

"I'm hard to get rid of," he said, looking up from the notes. "And this isn't over."

"Yes, it is." She took them back and dropped them onto the desk. "Barney's dead, Ravi. And who will be next? You? Me? The killer's been here, in my house, in my room. They read my research and typed a warning on my computer. Here, Ravi, in the same house as my nine-year-old brother. We'd be putting too many people in danger. Your parents could lose the only son they have left." She broke off, an image of Ravi dead in the autumn leaves behind her eyes, Josh beside him. "The killer knows everything we know. They've beaten us, and we have too much to lose. I'm sorry that it means I have to abandon Sal. I'm so sorry."

"Why didn't you tell me about the threats?" he said.

"At first I thought it might just be a prank," she said, shrugging. "But I didn't want you to know, in case you made me stop. And then I just got stuck, keeping it a secret. I thought they were just threats. I thought I could beat them. I was so stupid."

"You're not stupid; you were right all along about Sal," he said. "He's innocent. *We* know that, but it's not enough. He deserves for everyone to know that he was good and kind until the end. My parents deserve that. And now we don't even have the photo that proved it."

"I still have the photo," Pip said quietly, taking the printout from the bottom drawer and handing it to him. "Of course I'd never destroy it. But it can't help us now."

"Why?"

"The killer is watching me, Ravi. Watching us. If we take that photo to the police and they don't believe us, if they think we Photoshopped it or something, then it's too late. We would have played our final hand, and it's not strong enough. Then what happens? Josh gets taken? You do? People could die here." She sat on her bed, picking at her socks. "We don't have our smoking gun. The photo isn't enough proof; it relies on massive interpretive leaps, and it's not online anymore. Why would they believe us? Sal's brother and a seventeen-year-old girl. *I* hardly believe us. We just have stories about a murdered girl, and you know what the police here think of Sal, just like the rest of Fairview. We can't risk our lives on that photo alone."

"No," Ravi said, laying the picture on the desk and nodding. "You're right. And one of our main suspects is a police officer. It's not the right move. Even if the police did somehow believe us and reopen the case, it would take them a long time to find the actual killer that way. Time we don't have." He wheeled the desk chair over to face her on the bed and straddled it. "So I guess our only option is to find them ourselves."

"We can't—" Pip started.

"Do you seriously think walking away is the best move here? How would you ever feel safe again in Fairview, knowing the person that killed Andie and Sal and Barney is still out there? Knowing they're watching you? How could you live like that?"

"I have to."

"For such a clever person, you're being a real idiot right now." He leaned his elbows on the back of the chair, chin against his knuckles.

"They murdered my dog," she said.

"They murdered my brother. And what are we going to do about it?" He straightened up, a daring glint in his eyes. "Are we going to forget everything and hide? Live our lives knowing a killer is out there watching us? Or do we fight? Find them and punish them for what they've done to us. Put them away so they can't hurt anyone ever again."

"They'll know we haven't stopped," she said.

"No they won't, not if we're careful. No more talking to the people on your list, no more talking to anyone. The answer must be somewhere in everything we've learned. You'll say you've given up your project. Only you and I will know."

Pip didn't say anything.

"If you need more persuasion," Ravi said, walking over to his backpack, "I brought my laptop for you. It's yours until this is done." He pulled it free and held it out.

"But—"

"It's yours," he said. "You can use it to finish your application and type up what you remember of your log, your interviews. I took some notes myself on there. I know you've lost all your research, but—"

"I haven't lost my research," she said.

"Huh?"

"I always email everything to myself, just in case," she said, watching Ravi's face twitch into a smile. "Who do you think I am, an amateur?"

"Sorry, Sarge, I should've known even your backups would have backups. So are you saying yes, or should I have brought some bribery muffins too?"

Pip reached out for the laptop.

"Come on, then," she said. "We have a double homicide to solve."

They printed everything: every entry from her capstone project log, every page from Andie's planner, a photo of each suspect, the train station leverage photos of Howie with Stanley Forbes, Jason Bell and his new wife, the Ivy House Inn, Max Hastings's house, the newspapers' favorite photo of Andie, a picture of the Bell family dressed up in black tie, Sal smiling and waving at the camera, Pip's catfish texts to Emma Hutton, her emails as a CNN reporter about drink-spiking, a printout of the effects of Rohypnol, a map of Fairview High School, the photo of Daniel da Silva going into the Bell house, Stanley Forbes's articles about Sal, Nat da Silva and information about aggravated assault, a picture of a white Honda Civic beside a map of Monroe and Howie's house, newspaper reports of a hit-and-run on New Year's Eve 2013, screen grabs of the texts from Unknown and scans of the threat notes with their dates and locations.

They looked down together at the reams of paper on the carpet.

"It's not environmentally friendly," Ravi said, "but I've always wanted to make a murder board."

"Me too," Pip said. "And I'm well prepared, supplies-wise." From the drawers in her desk, she pulled out a pot of colored pushpins and a fresh bundle of red string.

"You just happen to have red string ready to go?" Ravi said.

"I have every color of string."

"Of course you do."

Pip took down the corkboard hanging over her desk. The one covered with photos of her and her friends, Josh and Barney and her school schedule. She removed it all, and they started sorting on the floor.

They fastened the pages to the board with flat silver pins, organizing each page around the relevant person in huge colliding orbits. Andie's and Sal's faces in the middle of it all. They had just started making the connection lines with the string and multicolored thumbtacks when Pip's phone rang. A number not saved in her phone.

She pressed the green button. "Hello?"

"Hi, Pip, it's Naomi."

"Hi. That's weird—you're not saved in my phone."

"Oh, it's 'cause I smashed mine," Naomi said. "I'm using a temp until it's fixed."

"Oh yeah, Cara said. What's up?"

"I was at my friend's house this weekend, so Cara only just told me about Barns. I'm really sorry, Pip. I hope you're OK."

"Not yet," Pip said. "I'll get there."

"And I know you may not want to think about this right now," she said, "but I found out my friend's cousin studied English at Columbia. I thought maybe I could see if he'd email you about the school and interview and stuff, if you wanted."

"Actually, yeah, yes, please," Pip said. "That would help. I'm still struggling with my essay a little."

"OK, cool. I'll ask her to reach out. Early decision deadline is soon, right?"

"Yep, in three days."

"You'll get it done, I know you."

"Ok," Ravi said when Pip had hung up the phone, "our open leads right now are the Ivy House Inn, the phone number scribbled out of Andie's planner"—he pointed to its page—"and the burner phone. As well as knowledge of the hit-and-run, and access to Sal's friends' phone numbers and yours. Pip, maybe we are overcomplicating this." He stared up at her. "As I see it these are all pointing to one person."

"Max?"

"Let's just focus on the definites here," he said. "No ifs or maybes. He's the only one with direct knowledge of the hit-and-run."

"True."

"He's the only one here who had access to Naomi's, Millie's, and Jake's phone numbers. And his own."

"Nat and Howie could have."

"Yeah, 'could' have. We're looking at definites." He shuffled over to the Max side of the board. "He says he just found it, but he has a naked picture of Andie from the Ivy House, so he was probably the one meeting her there. He bought Rohypnol from Andie, and girls were getting spiked at calamities; he probably assaulted them. He's clearly messed up, Pip."

Ravi was going through the very same thoughts she'd struggled with, and Pip knew he was about to run into a wall.

"Also," he carried on, "he's the only one here we know definitely has *your* phone number."

"Actually, no," she said. "Nat has it from when I tried to phone-interview her. Howie has it too. I rang him when trying to identify him and forgot to withhold my number. I got Unknown's first text soon after."

"Oh."

"And we know that Max was at school giving a statement to the police at the time when Sal disappeared."

Ravi slumped back. "We must be missing something."

"Let's go back to the connections." Pip shook the pot of pins at him. He took them and cut off a length of red string.

"OK," he said. "The two da Silvas are obviously connected. And Daniel da Silva with Andie's dad. And Daniel also with Max, because he filed the report on Max's crashed car and might have known about the hit-and-run."

"Yes," she said, "and maybe covered up drink-spiking."

Ravi wrapped the string round a pin and then pressed it in, hissing when he stabbed himself in the thumb and a tiny bubble of blood burst through.

"Can you stop bleeding all over the murder board, please," Pip said.

Ravi pretended to throw a pin at her. "So Max also knows Howie, and they were both involved in Andie's drug dealing," he said, circling his finger round their three faces.

"Yep. And Max knew Nat from school," Pip said, pointing, "and there's a rumor she had her drink spiked as well."

Lines of red fraying string covered the board now, webbing and crisscrossing each other.

"So basically"—Ravi looked up at her—"they are all indirectly connected with each other, starting with Howie at one end and Jason Bell at the other. Maybe they all did it together, all five of them."

"Next you'll be saying someone has an evil twin."

thirty-eight

It was her second day back at school after Barney died, and her friends were still looking at her like she would shatter, never once mentioning him, talking around it in wide circles. Lauren let Pip have her last Oreo, and Connor gave up his middle seat at the cafeteria table for her. Cara didn't leave her side, knowing just when to talk to her and when to stay quiet.

Pip spent most of the day working on her personal essay, trying to push everything else out of her head. She'd just have to write about the time she visited her grandparents in Berlin. Did that explain who she was, what made Pip, Pip? Well, no. But she was almost out of time and it would have to do.

Mrs. Morgan cornered her in the hall at the end of the day, her pudgy face stern as she listed the reasons why it wasn't really possible to change a capstone project topic this late. Pip just mumbled "OK" and drifted away, hearing Mrs. Morgan tut "Teenagers" under her breath.

As soon as she got home from school, she went straight to her desk and opened up Ravi's laptop. She would finish writing her essay later, after dinner and well into the night if she had to. Her mom thought she wasn't sleeping because of Barney. But she wasn't sleeping because there wasn't time to.

Pip opened the browser and pulled up the TripAdvisor page for the Ivy House Inn. This was her designated lead; Ravi was working on the phone number scribble from the planner. Pip had already messaged some Ivy House reviewers who'd posted around March and April 2014, asking if they remembered seeing a blond girl there. No responses yet.

She navigated to the website that had actually processed the reservations for Ivy House and found their phone number on the "Contact Us" page. Maybe she could pretend to be a relative of the old woman who owned the place and see if she could access their old booking information. Probably not, but worth a try. Secret Older Guy's identity could be at the end of the line.

She unlocked her cell and clicked on to the phone app. It opened to her recent calls list. She pressed over to the keypad and started to type in the company's number, then her thumbs slackened and stopped. She stared down at the screen, her head whirring as the thought became conscious.

"Wait," she said aloud, going back to her recent calls list.

She looked at the entry right at the top, from when Naomi called her yesterday. Her temporary number. Pip's eyes traced the digits, a feeling of dread curdling in her chest.

She jumped out of her chair so fast that it whirled and crashed into the desk. With her phone in hand, she dropped to her knees and pulled the murder board out from its hiding place under her bed. Her eyes darted straight to the Andie section, to the printed pages around her smiling face.

She found it. The page from Andie's school planner. The scribbled-out phone number and her log entry beside it. She held out her phone, looking from Naomi's temporary number to the scribble.

475-555-0146.

It wasn't one of the nine combinations she had written out. But it very nearly was. She'd thought that the second-to-last digit had to be a 7 or a 1 or a 9. But what if that was just a loopy scribble? What if it was really a 4?

She slumped back. There was no way to be absolutely certain, no way to unscribble the number and see it for what it was. But it would be one unbelievable pigs-flying, hell-freezing-over coincidence if Naomi's old SIM card just happened to have a number *that* similar to the one Andie wrote in her planner. It had to be the same number.

What did that mean, if anything? Was this an irrelevant lead; just Andie copying down the phone number of her boyfriend's best friend? Could Pip discard it as a clue?

But then why did she have a sinking feeling in her gut?

Because if Max was a strong contender, then Naomi was even more so. Naomi knew about the hit-and-run. Naomi had access to the phone numbers of Max, Millie, and Jake. Naomi had Pip's number. Naomi could have left Max's house while Millie slept and intercepted Andie before 12:45. Naomi had been the closest to Sal. Naomi knew where Pip and Cara were camping. Naomi knew which woods Pip walked Barney in—the same ones Sal died in.

Naomi already had a lot to lose because of the truths Pip had uncovered. But what if there was more to it than that? What if she was actually involved in Andie's and Sal's deaths?

Pip was getting ahead of herself, her tired brain running off and tripping her up. It was just a phone number Andie wrote down; it didn't tie Naomi to anything else. But there was something that could, she realized.

Since taking Naomi off the persons of interest list, she'd received another printed note from the killer: the one in her locker. At the start of the semester, Pip had set up Cara's laptop to record everything that came through the Wards' printer.

If Naomi was involved in this, Pip now had a sure way to find out.

thirty-nine

Pip stepped back from Naomi's knife.

"Be careful," she said.

"Oh no!" Naomi shook her head. "The eyes are uneven."

She spun the pumpkin around so Pip and Cara could see its face.

"Looks like a blobfish," Cara cackled.

"It's supposed to be an evil cat." Naomi placed her knife down next to the bowl of pumpkin guts.

"Don't quit your day job," Cara said, wiping pumpkin goo from her hands and sauntering over to the cupboard.

"I don't have a day job."

"Oh for god's sake," Cara grumbled, on tiptoes, looking through the cupboard. "Where did that pack of Butterfingers go? I was literally with Dad two days ago when we bought them."

"I don't know. I haven't eaten them." Naomi came over to admire Pip's pumpkin. "What on earth is yours, Pip?"

"Sauron's eye," she said quietly.

"Or a vagina on fire," Cara said, grabbing a banana instead.

"Now, that is scary," Naomi laughed.

No, this was.

Naomi had had the pumpkins and knives laid out and ready for when Cara and Pip got in from school. Pip hadn't had a chance to sneak off to check the printer yet.

"Naomi," she said, "thanks for calling the other day. I got that email from your friend's cousin about Columbia. It was really helpful."

"Oh good." She smiled. "No problem."

"So when will your phone be fixed?"

"Tomorrow, actually, the shop says. It's taken long enough."

Pip nodded, tensing her chin. "Well, at least you had your old phone with a SIM card that still worked. Lucky you held on to it."

"Well, lucky Dad had a spare pay-as-you-go micro-SIM lying around. And bonus: twenty-five-dollar credit on it. There was just an expired contract one in my phone."

The knife almost fell from Pip's hand. A climbing hum in her ears.

"Your dad's SIM card?"

"Yeah," Naomi said, scoring the knife along her pumpkin's face, her tongue out as she concentrated. "Cara found it in his desk. At the bottom of his junk drawer. It's full of old, useless chargers and foreign currency and stuff."

The hum split into a ringing sound, shrieking and stuffing her head. Pip felt sick, a metallic taste in her mouth.

Mr. Ward's SIM card.

Mr. Ward's old phone number scribbled out in Andie's planner.

Andie calling Mr. Ward an asshole to her friends the week she disappeared.

Mr. Ward.

"You OK, Pip?" Cara asked as she dropped a lit candle into her pumpkin and it glowed into life.

"Yeah." Pip nodded too hard. "I'm just, um . . . just hungry."

"Well, I would offer you a Butterfinger, but they seem to have disappeared, as always. Chips?"

"Uh . . . no thanks."

"I feed you because I love you," Cara said.

Pip's mouth filled, tacky and sickly. No, it might not mean what she was thinking. Maybe Mr. Ward was just offering to tutor Andie and that's why she wrote his number down. It couldn't be him. She needed to calm down, try to breathe. This wasn't proof of anything.

But she had a way to find proof.

"I think we should have spooky Halloween music on while we do this," Pip said. "Cara, can I go get your laptop?"

"Yeah, it's on my bed."

Pip closed the kitchen door behind her.

She raced up the stairs to Cara's room, creeping back down with the laptop, her heart thudding, fighting to be louder than the ringing in her ears.

She slipped into Mr. Ward's study and gently closed the door, staring for a moment at the printer on his desk. Mrs. Ward's rainbow-colored paintings watched her as she opened up Cara's laptop on the leather chair and kneeled on the floor before it.

Once it awoke she clicked to the control panel and into *Devices and Printers.* Hovering the mouse over *Freddie Prints Jr.,* she right-clicked and, holding her breath, selected the top item in the drop-down menu: *See what's printing.*

A small box popped up with six columns: Document Name, Status, Owner, Pages, Size, and Date Submitted.

It was filled with entries. One yesterday from Cara called *Personal Essay rough draft.* One a few days ago from *Elliot Comp: Gluten-free cookies recipe.* Several in a row from *Naomi: Résumé 2019, Charity Job application, Cover letter, Cover letter 2.*

The note was put in Pip's locker on Friday, October 18. She scrolled down.

Her fingers drew up. On October 17, at 11:40 p.m., *Elliot Comp* had printed *Microsoft Word—Document 1.*

An unnamed, unsaved document.

Her fingers left sweaty tracks on the mousepad as she right-clicked on the document. Another small drop-down menu appeared. Her heart in her throat, she bit down on her tongue and clicked the *Restart* option.

The printer clacked behind her and she flinched.

It hissed, sucking in the top piece of paper.

She moved toward it as it started to sputter the page through, a glimpse of fresh black ink, upside down. The printer finished and spat it out.

Pip reached for it.

She turned it around.

This is your final warning, Pippa. Walk away.

forty

Words left her.

It was something primal, the feeling that took over. Numb rage and terror. And a betrayal that seared through every part of her.

She backed away from the printer and looked out of the darkening window.

Elliot Ward was Unknown.

Elliot Ward was the killer. Andie's killer. Sal's. Barney's.

She watched the half-dead trees beckoning in the wind and re-created the scene in her head. Her bumping into Mr. Ward in his classroom, the note gliding to the floor. This note, the one he'd left for her. His deceitful, kind face as he asked whether she was being bullied. Cara dropping off cookies that she and her dad had baked to cheer up the Amobis about their dead dog.

All lies. Mr. Ward, the man she saw as another father figure. The man who'd made elaborate brunch spreads and scavenger hunts for them. The man who bought Pip bear-claw slippers to wear at their house to match the family. The man who told knock-knock jokes with an easy laugh. And he was a murderer.

Cara called her name.

She folded the page and slipped it into her pocket.

"You've been ages," Cara said as Pip returned to the kitchen.

"Bathroom," she said, placing the laptop down in front of Cara. "Listen, I'm not feeling so great. And I should really be editing my college essay; deadline is tomorrow. Think I'm going to head out."

"Oh." Cara frowned. "But Lauren's gonna be here soon, and I wanted us all to watch *Blair Witch.* Dad even agreed, and he's normally such a wimp with scary movies."

"Where is your dad?" Pip asked. "Tutoring?"

"How often are you here? You know tutoring is Mondays, Wednesdays, and Fridays. Think he just had to stay late at school."

"Oh yeah, sorry, the days are blurring." She paused, thinking. "I've always wondered why your dad does tutoring; surely he doesn't need the money."

"Why," Cara said, "because my mom's side of the family is richer than god?"

"Exactly."

"I think he just enjoys it," Naomi said, placing a tea light through the mouth of her pumpkin. "He'd probably be willing to pay his tutees just to let him garble on about history."

"I can't remember when he started," Pip said.

"Um." Naomi looked up to think. "He started just before I was about to leave for college, I think."

"So just over five years ago?"

"Think so," Naomi said. "Why don't you ask him? His car just pulled up."

Pip stiffened. She needed to leave now, get out.

"It's OK, I'm going to head home. Sorry." She grabbed her backpack, watching the headlights flick off to darkness through the window.

"Don't be silly," Cara said, concern lining her eyes. "And hey, we can hang out on Saturday after you've submitted, right? Watch the winter carnival setup?"

"Yeah."

A key scraping. The back door shoved open. Footsteps crossing the family room.

Mr. Ward appeared in the kitchen. The lenses in his glasses steamed up at the edges as he entered the warm room, smiling at the three of them. He placed his briefcase and a grocery bag down on the counter.

"Hello, all," he said. "Gosh, teachers do love the sound of their own voices. Longest meeting of my life."

Pip forced a laugh.

"Wow, look at these pumpkins," he said, eyes wandering between them, a wide grin splitting his face. "Pip, are you here for the movie? I've just picked up some spooky Halloween candy for us."

He held up the bag and waved it with a ghostlike howl.

forty-one

She got home just as her parents were leaving to take a Harry Pottered Josh trick-or-treating.

"Come with us, pickle," her dad said as her mom zipped him into his Ghostbusters costume.

"I should stay in and edit my essay," she said. "And deal with the trick-or-treaters."

"Can't give yourself the night off?" her mom asked.

"Nope. Sorry."

"OK, sweetie. Remember, other sweeties are by the door." Her mom giggled at her own joke.

"Got it. See you later."

Josh stepped outside waving his wand, "Accio candy."

Pip's dad grabbed his marshmallow-shaped head and followed. Her mom paused to kiss the top of Pip's head and then closed the door behind them.

Pip watched through the glass pane in the front door, and when her family reached the end of the drive, she pulled out her phone and texted Ravi: *COME TO MY HOUSE RIGHT NOW!*

He stared down at the mug clasped between his hands.

"Mr. Ward." He shook his head. "It can't be."

"It can, though," Pip said, her knee rattling against the underside of the table. "He doesn't have an alibi for the night Andie disappeared. I know he doesn't. One of his daughters was at Max's house all night, and the other one was sleeping at mine."

Ravi exhaled and it rippled through the surface of his milky coffee. It must have been cold by now, like hers.

"And he has no alibi for the Tuesday when Sal died," she said. "He called in sick to work that day; he told me himself."

"But Sal loved Mr. Ward," Ravi said in the smallest voice she'd ever heard from him.

"I know."

The table suddenly seemed very wide between them.

"So is he the secret older man Andie was seeing?" Ravi said after a while. "The one she met at the Ivy House?"

"Maybe," she said. "Andie spoke of ruining this person; Elliot was a teacher in a position of trust. He would have been in a lot of trouble if she told someone about them. Criminal charges, jail time." She looked down at her own untouched coffee and her warped reflection in it. "Andie called Elliot an asshole to her friends, days before she went missing. Elliot said it was because he found out Andie was a bully and contacted her father about the topless video. Maybe that's not what it was about."

"How did he know about the hit-and-run? Did Naomi tell him?"

"I don't think so. She said she's never told anyone. I don't know how he knew."

"There are still some gaps here," Ravi said.

"I know. But he's the one that threatened me and killed Barney. It's him, Ravi."

"OK." Ravi locked his wide and drained eyes on hers. "So how do we prove it?"

Pip moved her mug away and leaned on the table. "Elliot tutors three times a week," she said. "I'd never really thought it was weird until tonight. The Wards don't need to worry about money; his wife's life insurance paid out a lot, and her parents are still alive and super wealthy. Plus, Mr. Ward used to be a college professor; he probably has a good salary. He only started tutoring just over five years ago, in 2014."

"OK?"

"So what if he's *not* tutoring three times a week?" she said. "What if he . . . I don't know, goes to the place where he buried Andie? Visiting her grave as some kind of penance?"

Ravi pulled a face, lines of doubt crossing his forehead and nose. "Not three times every week."

"Yeah, OK," she conceded. "Well, what if he's visiting . . . *her*?" She only thought it for the first time as the word formed in her throat. "What if Andie is alive and he's keeping her somewhere? And he goes to see her three times a week."

Ravi pulled the same face again.

A handful of near-forgotten memories elbowed their way into her head. "Butterfingers," she muttered.

"Sorry?"

Her eyes darted left and right, grappling with the thought. "Disappearing Butterfingers," she said, louder. "Cara keeps finding food missing from their house. Food she just saw her dad buy. Oh my god. He has Andie and he's feeding her."

"You might be slightly jumping to conclusions here, Sarge."

"We have to find out where he goes," Pip said, sitting up, her legs shaking again. "Tomorrow's Friday, a tutoring day."

"And what if he's actually tutoring?"

"And what if he's not?"

"You think we should tail him?" said Ravi.

"No," she said as an idea dragged itself to the forefront. "I have a better idea. Give me your phone."

Ravi rummaged in his pocket and pulled out his phone, sliding it across the table to her.

"Pass code?" she said.

"One-one-two-two. What are you doing?"

"I'm enabling Find My Friends on our phones." She clicked on the app and sent an invitation to her own phone. She swiped her cell open and accepted it. "Now we are sharing our locations indefinitely. And just like that," she said, shaking her phone in the air, "we have a tracking device."

"You scare me a little bit," he said.

"Tomorrow, at the end of school, I need to find a way to leave my phone in his car."

"How?"

"I'll think of something."

"Don't go anywhere alone with him, Pip." He leaned forward, eyes unwavering. "I mean it."

There was a knock at the front door.

Pip jumped up and Ravi followed her down the hall. She picked up the bowl of candy and opened the door.

"Trick-or-treat!" a chorus of tiny voices screeched.

"Oh, wow," Pip said, recognizing two vampires as the Yardley children from three doors down. "Don't you all look scary!"

She lowered the bowl, and the six kids swarmed toward her, grabby hands first.

Pip smiled up at the group of adults waiting for their kids to cherry-pick the candy. And then she noticed their eyes, dark and glaring, fixed on a point past Pip's shoulder, where Ravi stood.

Two of the women drew together, staring at him as they muttered small, unheard things behind their hands.

forty-two

"What did you do?" Cara said.

"I don't know. I tripped coming down the stairs from econ. I think I sprained it."

Pip fake-limped over to her.

"I walked to school this morning; I don't have my car," she said. "Oh crap, and Mom has a late showing."

"You can get a lift with me and Dad," Cara said, slipping her arm under Pip's to help her to her locker. She took the textbook from Pip's hand and placed it on the pile inside. "Don't know why you'd willingly choose to walk when you have your own car. I never get to use mine now that Naomi's home."

"I just felt like walking," Pip said. "I don't have Barney as an excuse anymore."

Cara gave her a pitying look and closed the locker door. "Come on, then," she said. "Let's hobble out to the parking lot. Lucky for you I'm Muscles McGee; I did nine whole push-ups yesterday."

"Nine whole ones?" Pip smiled.

"I know. Play your cards right and you might win a ticket to the gun show." She flexed and growled.

Pip's heart broke for her then. She hoped that, whatever happened, Cara wouldn't lose this: her happy, silly self.

With Pip propped up against Cara, they staggered up the hall and out of the side door.

The cold wind bit her nose, and she narrowed her eyes against it. They made their way slowly, around the back of the school and toward the teachers' lot, Cara filling the journey with details of the Halloween movie night. Pip tensed every time she mentioned her dad.

Mr. Ward was there already, waiting by his car.

"There you are," he said, spotting Cara. "What happened?"

"Pip sprained her ankle," Cara said, opening the back door. "And her mom's working late. Can we give her a ride?"

"Sure, of course." Mr. Ward darted forward to take Pip's arm and help her into the car.

His skin touched hers.

It took all her strength not to recoil from him.

Backpack settled beside her, Pip watched as he climbed into the driver's seat and started the engine.

"So what happened, Pip?" he asked, waiting for a group of kids to cross the road before pulling out of the parking lot.

"I'm not sure," she said. "I think I just landed on it funny. I'm sure it'll be fine in a couple of days." She pulled out her phone and made sure it was on silent. She'd had it turned off most of the day, and the battery was almost full.

Mr. Ward batted Cara's hand away when she started flicking through the radio stations.

"My car, my music," he said. "Pip?"

She jumped and almost dropped the phone.

"Is your ankle swollen?" he asked.

"Um . . ." She bent forward and reached down to feel it, the phone in her hand. Pretending to knead her ankle, she twisted her wrist and pushed the phone far underneath the back seat. "A little bit," she said, straightening up, her face flushed with blood. "Not too bad."

"OK, that's good," he said, winding through the traffic up Main Street. "You should elevate it tonight."

"Yeah, I will," she said, and caught his eye in the rearview mirror. And then: "I've just realized it's a tutoring day. I'm not going to make you late, am I? Where do you have to get to?"

"Oh, don't worry," he said, indicating left, down Pip's road. "I've only got to get over to Stamford. It's no bother."

"Phew, OK."

Cara was asking what was for dinner as Mr. Ward slowed and swung into Pip's driveway.

"Oh, your mom *is* home," he said, nodding toward her mom's car as he pulled to a stop.

"Is she?" Pip felt her heartbeat doubling, scared he'd hear it in her voice. "Her showing must have been cancelled last minute. I should have checked, sorry."

"Don't be silly." He turned around. "Do you need help to the door?"

"No," she said quickly, grabbing her backpack. "No, thank you, I'll be fine."

She pushed open the car door and started to shuffle out.

"Wait," Cara said suddenly.

Pip froze. *Please say she hasn't seen the phone. Please.*

"Goooooood luuuuuuck with your aaaaaapp," she said, drawing out the words in an off-key tune. "You're going to get in, I just know it."

"Yes, best of luck, Pip." Mr. Ward smiled. "I'd say break a leg, but I think the timing is a little off for that."

Pip laughed, so hollow it almost echoed. "Thanks," she said, "and thanks for the ride." She pushed the car door shut and limped up to the house, her ears pricked, listening to the rumble of their car as it drove away. She opened her front door and dropped the limp.

"Hello," her mom called from the kitchen. "Do you want anything to eat?"

"Um, no thanks," she said, loitering in the entryway. "Ravi's coming over to help me work; read over my essay one last time before I submit."

Her mom gave her a look.

"What?"

"Don't think I don't know my own daughter," she said, washing mushrooms in the colander. "She only works alone and has a reputation for making other kids cry in group projects. Working, sure." She gave her the look again. "Keep your door open. And submit it already! The deadline is at midnight."

"Jeez, I will." She had time. She still had time.

Just as she was starting up the stairs, a Ravi-shaped blur knocked at the front door.

Pip let him in and he called hello to her mom as he followed her upstairs to her room.

"Door open," Pip said awkwardly when Ravi went to close it.

"Got it. All good with the phone?" he said.

She sat cross-legged on her bed, and Ravi pulled the desk chair over to sit in front of her. "Yep, it's under the back seat."

"OK."

He unlocked his phone and opened the Find My Friends app. Pip leaned in closer, and, heads almost touching, they stared down at the map on the screen.

Pip's little orange avatar was parked outside the Wards' house on Hillside. Ravi clicked refresh, but it didn't move.

"He hasn't left yet," Pip said.

Shuffled footsteps moved along the hallway, and Pip looked up to see Josh standing in her doorway.

"Pippo," he said, fiddling with his springy hair, "can Ravi come down and play *FIFA* with me?"

Ravi and Pip looked at each other.

"Um, not now, Josh," she said. "We're a little busy."

"I'll come down and play later, OK, bud?" Ravi said.

"OK." Josh dropped his arm in defeat and padded away.

"He's on the move," Ravi said, refreshing the map.

"Where?"

"Just down Hillside at the moment, before the roundabout."

The avatar didn't move in real time; they had to keep pressing refresh and wait for the orange circle to jump along the route. It stopped just at the roundabout.

"Refresh it," Pip said impatiently. "If he doesn't turn left, then he's not heading to Stamford."

The refresh button spun with fading lines. Loading. Loading. The page refreshed, and the orange avatar had disappeared.

"Where'd it go?" said Pip.

Ravi scrolled around the map to see where Mr. Ward had jumped to.

"Stop." Pip spotted it. "There. He's heading north up Route 124."

They stared at each other.

"He's not going to Stamford," Ravi said.

"No, he is not."

They watched for the next fourteen minutes as Mr. Ward drove up the road, jumping incrementally whenever Ravi hit refresh.

"He's near New Canaan," Ravi said and then, seeing Pip's face, "What?"

"The Wards used to live in New Canaan before they moved to a bigger house in Fairview. Before we met them."

"He turned," Ravi said, and Pip leaned in again. "Down somewhere called Gravesend Road."

Pip stared at the orange dot, motionless on the white pixel road. "Refresh," she said.

"I am," said Ravi, "it's stuck." He pressed refresh again; the loading circle spun for a second and cleared, leaving the orange dot in the same place. He pressed it again, and it still didn't move.

"He stopped," Pip said, clutching Ravi's wrist and turning it to get a better look at the map. She stood up, grabbed Ravi's laptop from her desk, and settled it on her lap. "Let's see where he is."

She opened the browser and pulled up Google Maps. She searched for *Gravesend Road, New Canaan* and clicked to satellite mode.

"How far down the road would you say he is? Here?" She pointed at the screen.

"I think a bit more to the left."

"OK." Pip clicked the spot and opened street view.

The narrow road was enclosed by trees and tall shrubbery that glittered in the sun as Pip clicked and dragged the screen to get a full view of the area. The houses were on only one side, set back from the street.

"You think he's at this house?" She pointed at a small brick house with a white garage door, barely visible behind the trees and a telephone pole.

"Hmm . . ." Ravi looked from his phone to his laptop screen. "It's either that one or the one to the left of it."

Pip looked up the street numbers. "So he's either at number forty-two or forty-four."

"Is that where they used to live?" Ravi asked. Pip shrugged; she didn't know. "Could you find out from Cara?"

"Yeah," she said, "I'm seeing her tomorrow." Her stomach

churned. "She's my best friend, and this is going to destroy her. It's going to destroy everything."

Ravi slipped his hand into hers. It was warm and she felt steadier, holding on to him. "It's nearly over, Pip," he said.

"It's over now," she said. "We need to go there tonight and see what Elliot's hiding. Andie could be alive in there."

"That's just a guess."

"This whole thing has been a guess." She took her hand away so she could hold her aching head. "I need this to be over."

"I know," Ravi said gently. "We are going to end this. But not tonight. Tomorrow. You find out from Cara which address he's going to, if it *is* their old house. And then tomorrow night we can go there, when Elliot's not there, and see what he's up to. Or we call the police with an anonymous tip and send them to that address, OK? But not now, Pip. You can't upend your whole life tonight—I won't let you. I won't let you throw away Columbia for this. Right now, you are going to edit your essay, check it over and submit that application before midnight. OK?"

"But—"

"No buts, Sarge." He stared at her, his eyes suddenly sharp. "Mr. Ward is not ruining your life as well. OK?"

"OK," she said quietly, remembering then that Mr. Ward was an inextricable part of her application, too; he'd written one of her college recommendation letters.

"Good." Ravi pulled her off the bed and into her chair, wheeling her over to the desk and setting the laptop up in front of her. "You are going to forget about Andie Bell and Sal for the next six hours. That's an order." He traced his fingers across her chin for just a second.

Pip looked up at him, at his kind eyes and his serious face, and she didn't know what to say, didn't know what to feel, she was somewhere between laughing and crying and screaming.

When Ravi was gone she opened the Word doc of her essay and read it through. It sounded forced, not like her at all. It sounded like something she thought they wanted to hear, not who she really was.

Be brave, said all the college prep websites. *Be honest.* So she was. She highlighted her entire essay, pressed delete, and started again.

What's wrong with me? she wrote. *I might seem like the ideal student: homework always in early, every extra credit and extracurricular I can get my hands on, the good girl and the high achiever. But I realized something just now: it's not ambition, not entirely. It's fear. Because I don't know who I am when I'm not working, when I'm not focused on or totally consumed by a task. Who am I between the projects and the assignments, when there's nothing to do? I haven't found her yet and it scares me. Maybe that's why, for my senior capstone project this year, I decided to solve a murder.*

forty-three

Someone was watching her; she could feel it. Pip turned and found their eyes: a terrified gaze trapped in a plastic stare. With a mechanical groan the red-and-white carousel slowly started to turn, and the unblinking horse spun away from her midgallop. Replaced by another pair of frightened frozen eyes. Then another.

Pip watched the carousel until a carnival worker whistled to his colleague and the horses creaked to a halt.

Someone shouted for her to move out of the way as another huge truck pulled up onto the grass, people circling it, waving their arms. The vehicle sighed as it slowed to a stop, a folded-up Tilt-a-Whirl ride strapped onto its bed.

Pip walked on, stepping around the wheel-churned tracks in the grass. Her mom would complain about the damage to the park tomorrow night when the carnival opened, just as she did every year.

"Pip!" Cara's voice sailed over to her from just beyond the bumper cars. Pip followed it, remembering only at the last second to put the limp back into her walk. They were all here—her friends. Draped around the bench as they watched the chaos of the emerging winter carnival. It was tradition.

"I tried to text you," Cara said, running up to her and taking her arm. "But then, duh, I remembered you don't have your phone—I do." Cara guided Pip over to the bench, shooing Connor away so Pip could sit. Then she shuffled around in her pocket and pulled out Pip's phone. "You were right, you *had* somehow left it in Dad's car. It was wedged under the back seat."

Pip took it. "Oh, don't know how that happened."

"Did you get your app in, Pip?" Zach asked.

"Yeah, just in time," she sniffed. "Sent it in three minutes before midnight." She had thought she wouldn't make it, barely had time to read over her essay before she pressed submit. And then, of course, spent hours rereading when it was too late to change anything. Then stared at the darkened corners of her room, creating faces out of the shadows, trying to bargain with sleep.

"Yay, you're free," Cara said, waving Pip's arm in celebration for her.

She knew she should feel something; excited or relieved or nervous. But she felt empty, trapped behind a vacant stare, like one of those carousel horses. The bench was hard and cold against her back as she feigned a smile. This bench. *Her* bench. ANDIE BELL, TAKEN TOO SOON. And now Pip knew who by.

They watched the drop-tower ride being set up, its name, Down-Time, wrapped around it in ghoulish font. Then the pirate ship pendulum ride as Connor inserted as many pirate puns into the conversation as possible. Pip felt separated from them all somehow, like she was wrapped in an invisible barrier. Through it she could hardly hear as Ant complained that tickets for the Ferris wheel had gone up to ten dollars or as Lauren admonished him, reminding him it was for charity.

A couple of hours later, a truck pulled up with a new ride they'd never seen before. From a distance it looked like a giant octopus, and her friends stood up to go and get a closer look. Pip didn't move.

"Go ahead," she said to them, pointing down at her ankle as explanation.

"I'll stay," Cara said, taking Zach's place on the bench as the others wandered off across the park. "How are you?" She turned to Pip when they were alone.

"Fine," she lied. "I'm fine. You?"

"Yeah, OK."

"Naomi?"

"A bit less than OK." Cara shrugged. "Spends most of the day upstairs in her room. She didn't shut her door last night when I got in, and I saw she was writing in her diary again. I guess that's good. It's what the therapist tells her to do, you know, the one she's been seeing since Mom . . ."

Pip nodded. It was now—she had to ask now or she might not get another chance.

"Hey, you know my mom's doing a showing of a house on Gravesend Road in New Canaan today," she said. "Isn't that where you used to live?"

"Yeah," Cara said. "How funny."

"Number forty-four."

"Oh, we were forty-two."

"Does your dad still go there?" Pip asked, making her voice flat and disinterested.

"No, he sold it ages ago," Cara said. "They kept it when we moved because Mom had gotten a huge inheritance from her grandma, and they rented it out for extra income while Mom did her painting. But Dad sold it a couple of years after Mom died, I think."

Pip nodded. Clearly Elliot Ward had been telling lies for a very long time.

She looked at Cara then, really looked at her. And the invisible barrier around her closed in, constricting her throat as she tried to push down the tears. The sadness she felt for Cara was black and twisting and hungry. How was any of this fair?

Pip leaned over, wrapped her arms around her friend, and pulled her in.

"What's this for?" Cara's muffled voice in her hair.

"Nothing."

"All right, clingy," Cara said, trying to wriggle free.

Pip didn't want to let her go, didn't think she could. But she had to.

A distant squeal made her look up, draw back. It was Lauren. Ant had just jumped out at her from the other side of the incomplete Waltzer ride.

"You know they got together last night?" Cara said, nodding her head in their direction.

"Really?"

"Yeah. And apparently, they kissed at the calamity party too. Lauren told me last week."

"Oh, I had no idea," Pip said. Yet another thing she'd missed lately. Add it to the list.

Pip's phone was vibrating in her pocket as the others rejoined them at the bench. Messages from Ravi: *Did you get your application in?* She didn't open them, in case Cara saw anything she shouldn't.

It was past five when her mom called to say she was waiting in the parking lot. Pip hugged her friends goodbye, her breath stuttering when Cara said, "See you tomorrow." Because tomorrow might be a different world for them all.

She limped away, past the bumper cars and the swearing carnival worker who'd just cut open his hand. Past a yellow car towing a hot-dog stand in its trailer, and around the corner of the disassembled fun house where she almost ran into someone.

"Oh, sorry," she said, looking up.

It was Mr. Ward.

The sun flashed across his glasses as he smiled down at her.

"Ah, Pip," he said brightly. "Did you get it in?"

"Y-yep." Her breath felt gummy, like it was trying to choke her.

"And your ankle?"

"Not too bad; should be better by tomorrow." Pip could barely hear her own voice over the sound of her heart in her ears. Surely he could hear it too? "Sorry, I've gotta go—my mom's waiting."

"Oh sure," he said, stepping out of the way. "Do you know where Cara is? She's not answering her phone, and I need to drop her home and get over to Target before dinner."

Pip pointed behind her.

"Thanks," Mr. Ward said, nodding to her as he walked away.

Pip limped on, checking over her shoulder. Watching him. When he crossed behind the bumper cars and could no longer see her, she dropped the limp and started to run. She didn't stop until she reached the parking lot and her mom's car, fumbling for the passenger-side handle.

"Hey, sweetie," her mom said, starting the engine. She didn't turn to look at Pip, but it didn't matter; Pip saw, anyway. Her mom's red-rimmed eyes.

She'd been crying.

Pip pretended she hadn't seen and her mom pretended she hadn't either, talking instead about Josh's sleepover tonight. But Pip knew why she'd been crying. Barney, of course. And how much worse would it be when she found out why he really died?

Back home Pip said, "Just going to have a nap. I was up late."

It was another lie. She went to her room to watch the time, pacing from bed to door and back. Waiting. Fear burned to rage, and if she didn't pace, she would scream. Mr. Ward said he was going to Target, the one near New Canaan. And Pip bet she knew where he would be going afterward. She needed him to be there.

When it was after six o'clock, Pip tugged the charger out of her phone and pulled on her coat.

"I'm going to Ravi's for a few hours," she called to her mom.

Outside, she climbed into her car and tied up her dark hair on top of her head. She looked down at her phone, at the lines and lines of messages from Ravi. She replied: *I turned it in, thanks! I'll come to your house after dinner and we'll phone the police then.* Yet another lie, but Pip was fluent in them now. He would only stop her if he knew.

She opened the map app on her phone, typed in the address, and hit *Go*.

The mechanical voice chanted up at her: *Starting route to 42 Gravesend Road.*

forty-four

Gravesend Road was narrow and overgrown, a tunnel of trees pushing in on all sides. Pip pulled onto the curb just after number 40 and flicked off her headlights.

Her heart was a stampede, and every hair, every layer of skin, was alive and electric.

She reached down for her phone, which was propped up in the cupholder, and dialed 911.

"Hello, nine-one-one operator, what's your emergency?"

"My name is Pippa Fitz-Amobi," she said shakily, "and I'm from Fairview. Please listen carefully. You need to send officers to forty-two Gravesend Road in New Canaan. Inside is a man named Elliot Ward. Five years ago Elliot kidnapped a girl named Andie Bell from Fairview, and he's been keeping her in this house. He murdered a boy named Sal Singh. You need to contact Detective Richard Hawkins, who led the Andie Bell case, and let him know: I believe Andie is alive and she's being kept inside. I'm going in now to confront Elliot Ward, and I might be in danger. Please send officers quickly."

"Hold on, Pippa," the voice said, "where are you phoning from now?"

"I'm outside the house and I'm about to go in."

"OK, stay outside. I'm dispatching officers to your location. Pippa, can you—"

"I'm going in now," Pip said. "Please hurry."

"Pippa, do not go inside the house."

"I'm sorry, I have to," she said.

Pip lowered the phone, the operator's voice still calling her name, and hung up.

She got out of the car. Following the street down to number 42, she saw Mr. Ward's car parked in front of the small redbrick house. The two downstairs windows glowed, pushing away the thickening darkness.

As she started toward the house, she triggered a motion sensor floodlight that filled the drive with a blinding white glare. She covered her eyes, a giant shadow stitched to her feet as she walked toward the front door.

She knocked three times.

Something clattered inside. And then nothing.

She knocked again, hitting the door over and over with her fist.

A light flicked on, and through the frosted glass, she saw a blurred figure walking toward her.

A chain scraped from a sliding lock, and the door opened with a damp clacking sound.

Mr. Ward stared at her. Dressed in the same pastel green shirt from earlier, a pair of oven mitts slung over his shoulder.

"Pip?" he said in a voice breathy with fear. "What are you . . . what are you doing here?"

She looked him straight in the eyes.

"I'm just," he said, "I'm just . . ."

Pip shook her head. "The police will be here soon," she said. "You have until then to explain it to me." She stepped one foot up over the threshold. "Explain it to me so I can tell Cara and

Naomi. So the Singhs can finally know the truth about their son."

All the blood left Mr. Ward's face. He staggered back, colliding with the wall. He pressed his fingers into his eyes and blew out all his air. "It's over," he said quietly. "It's finally over."

"Time's running out." Her voice was much braver than she felt.

"OK," he said. "OK, do you want to come in?"

She hesitated, her stomach recoiling inside. But the police were on their way; she could do this. "We'll leave the front door open," she said, then followed him in and down the hall, keeping a three-step distance between them.

He led her right and then into a kitchen. There was no furniture in it, none at all, but the counters were laden with food packets and cooking utensils, even a spice rack. There was a small key glinting on the counter beside a packet of dried pasta. Mr. Ward bent to turn off the stove, and Pip walked to the other side of the room, putting as much space between them as she could.

"Stand away from the knives," she said.

"Pip, I'm not going to—"

"Move away from them."

Mr. Ward stepped away, stopping by the wall opposite her.

"She's here, isn't she?" Pip said. "Andie's here and she's alive?"

"Yes."

She shivered inside her coat.

"You and Andie Bell were seeing each other in March 2014," she said. "Start at the beginning."

"It wasn't like th-th—" he stuttered. "It . . ." He moaned and held his head.

"Elliot!"

He sniffed. "OK," he said. "It was late February. Andie started . . . paying attention to me at school. I wasn't teaching her; she didn't take history with me. But she'd follow me in the halls and ask me about my day. And, I don't know, I guess the attention felt . . . nice. I'd been so lonely since Isobel died. And then Andie started asking to have my phone number. Nothing had happened at this point, nothing at all, but she kept asking. I told her that that would be inappropriate. And yet, soon enough, I found myself in the phone shop, buying another SIM card so I could talk to her without anyone finding out. I don't know why I did it; I suppose it felt like a distraction from missing Isobel. I just wanted someone to talk to. I only put the SIM in at night, so Naomi would never see anything, and we started texting. She was nice to me; let me talk about Isobel and how I worried about Naomi and Cara."

"You're running out of time," Pip said coldly.

"Yes." He straightened up. "And then Andie started suggesting we meet somewhere outside of school. Like a hotel. I told her absolutely not. But in a moment of madness, a moment of weakness, I found myself booking one. She could be very persuasive. We agreed on a time and date, but I had to cancel last minute because Cara had chicken pox. I tried to end things, whatever it was we had at this point, but then she asked again. And I booked somewhere for the next week."

"The Ivy House Inn in Westport," said Pip.

He nodded. "That's when it happened the first time." His voice was quiet with shame. "We didn't stay the night; I couldn't leave the girls for a whole night. We stayed just a couple of hours."

"And you slept with her?"

He didn't say anything.

"She was seventeen!" Pip said. "The same age as your daughter. You were a teacher! Andie was vulnerable and you took advantage of that. You should have known better."

"There's nothing you can say that will make me more disgusted with myself than I already am. I said it couldn't happen again and tried to call it off. Andie wouldn't let me. She started threatening to turn me in. She interrupted one of my lessons, came over, and whispered to me that she'd left a picture of herself, naked, hidden in the classroom somewhere and that I should find it before someone else did. Trying to scare me. So I went back to Ivy House the next week, because I didn't know what she'd do if I didn't. I thought she would tire of whatever this was soon enough."

He stopped to rub the back of his neck.

"That was the last time. It only happened twice, and then it was spring break. The girls and I spent a week at Isobel's parents' house, and with time away from Fairview, I came to my senses. I messaged Andie, and I said it was over and I didn't care if she turned me in. She replied, saying that when school started again she was going to ruin me if I didn't do what she wanted. I didn't know what she wanted. And then, by complete chance, I had an opportunity to stop her. I found out about Andie cyberbullying that girl, and so I called her dad, as I told you, and said that if her behavior didn't improve, I would have to report her and she'd be expelled. Of course Andie knew what it really meant: mutually assured destruction. She could have me arrested and jailed for our relationship, but I could have her expelled and ruin her future. We were at a stalemate, and I thought it was over."

"So why did you kidnap her on Friday, April eighteenth?" Pip said.

"That's not . . . ," he said. "It didn't happen like that at all. I was home alone and Andie turned up—I think around ten-ish. She was irate, just so angry. She screamed at me, telling me I was sad and disgusting, that she'd only touched me because she needed me to get her a place at Yale, like I'd helped Sal. She didn't want him to leave without her. Screaming that she had to get away from home, away from Fairview because it was killing her. I tried to calm her down, but she wouldn't. And she knew exactly how to hurt me."

He blinked slowly.

"Andie ran to my study and started tearing those paintings Isobel made when she was dying, my rainbow ones. She smashed up two of them, and I was shouting for her to stop, and then she went for my favorite one. And I . . . I just pushed her to get her to stop. I wasn't trying to hurt her. But she fell back and hit her head on my desk. Hard. And," he sniffed, "she was on the floor and her head was bleeding. She was conscious but confused. I rushed off to get the first-aid kit, and when I came back, Andie had gone and the front door was open. She hadn't driven to our house—there was no car in the driveway and no sound of one nearby. She walked out and vanished. Her phone was on the floor in the study; she must have dropped it in the scuffle.

"The next day," he continued, "I heard from Naomi that Andie was missing. Andie was bleeding and left my house with a head injury, and now she was missing. And as the weekend passed, I started to panic: I thought I'd killed her. I thought she must have wandered out of my house and then, confused and hurt, got lost somewhere and died from her injuries. That she was lying in a ditch somewhere, and it would only be a matter of time until they found her. And when they did, there might be evidence on her body that would lead back to me: fibers, fingerprints. I knew the only thing I could do was to give them a stronger suspect to protect myself. To protect my girls. If I was taken away for Andie's murder, I didn't think Naomi would survive it. And Cara was only twelve at the time. I was the only parent they had left."

"I don't care about your excuses," Pip said. "So then you framed

Sal Singh. How did you know about the hit-and-run? Did Naomi write about it in her diaries, the ones her therapist told her to keep?"

"Yes."

"And you read them?"

"Of course I read them," he cried. "I had to know my little girl wasn't thinking of hurting herself."

"Then you made her and her friends take Sal's alibi away. And then, on the Tuesday?"

"I called in sick to work and dropped the girls at school. I waited outside, and when I saw Sal alone in the parking lot, I went up to talk to him. He wasn't coping well with her disappearance. So I suggested that we go back to his house and have a chat about it. I'd planned to do it with a knife from the Singhs' house. But then I found some sleeping pills in the bathroom, and I decided to take him to the woods; I thought it would be kinder. I didn't want his family to find him. We had coffee and I gave him the first three pills; said they were for his headache. I convinced him that we should go out in the woods and look for Andie ourselves; that it would help his feeling of helplessness. He trusted me. He didn't wonder why I hadn't taken off my leather gloves. I took a plastic bag from their kitchen, and we walked out into the woods. I had a penknife, and when we were far enough in, I held it up to his neck. Made him swallow more pills."

Mr. Ward's voice broke. His eyes filled and a lone tear snaked down his cheek. "I said I was helping him, that he wouldn't be a suspect if it looked like he'd been attacked too. He swallowed a few more, and then he started to struggle. I pinned him down and forced him to take more. When he started to get sleepy, I held him and I talked to him about Yale, about the amazing libraries, how beautiful the campus looks in spring. Just so he would fall asleep thinking about something good. When he lost consciousness, I put the bag around his head and held his hand as he died."

Pip had no pity for this man before her. Eleven years of memories dissolved, leaving a stranger standing in the room with her.

"Then you sent the confession text from Sal's phone to his dad."

Mr. Ward nodded, staunching his eyes with the heels of his hands.

"And Andie's blood?"

"It had dried under my desk," he said. "I'd missed some when I first cleaned, so I placed some of it under his nails with tweezers. I put Andie's phone in his pocket and I left him there. I didn't want to kill him. I was trying to save my girls; they'd already been through so much pain. He didn't deserve it, I know, but neither did my girls. It was an impossible choice."

Pip looked up to force down her tears. There wasn't time to tell him just how wrong he was.

"And then as more days passed," he cried, "I realized what a huge mistake I'd made. If Andie had died somewhere from her head injury, they would have found her by then. And then her car turns up and they find blood in the trunk; she must have been well enough to drive somewhere after leaving my house. I'd panicked and thought it was fatal when it wasn't. But it was too late. Sal was already dead and I'd made him the killer. They closed the case, and everything calmed down."

"So how do we get from there to you imprisoning Andie in this house?"

He flinched at the anger behind her words.

"It was the end of July. I was driving home and I just saw her. Andie was walking on the side of the main road from Norwalk, heading toward Fairview. I pulled over, and it was obvious she'd got herself messed up in drugs . . . that she'd been sleeping rough. She was so skinny and disheveled. That's how it happened. I couldn't let her return home because if she did, everyone would know Sal had been murdered. Andie was high and disoriented, but I stopped and got her in the car. I explained to her why I couldn't let her go home, but that I would take care of her. I'd just put this place up for sale, so I brought her here and took it off the market."

"Where had she been all those months? What happened to her the night she went missing?" Pip pressed, feeling the minutes escaping from her.

"She doesn't remember all the details; I think she was concussed. She says she just wanted to get away from everything. She went to a friend of hers who was involved in drugs, and he took her to stay with some people he knew. But she didn't feel safe there, so she ran away to come home. She doesn't like talking about it."

"Howie Bowers," Pip thought aloud. "Where is she, Elliot?"

"In the attic." He looked over at the small key on the counter. "We made it nice up there for her. I insulated it, put in plywood walls and proper flooring. She picked out the wallpaper. There aren't any windows, but we put in lots of lamps. I know you must think I'm a monster, Pip, but I've never touched her, not since that last time at Ivy House. It's not like that. And she's not like she was before. She's a different person; she's calm and grateful. She has food up there, but I come to cook for her three times during the week, once at the weekend, and let her down to shower. And then we just sit together in her loft, watching TV for a while. She's never bored."

"She's locked up there and that's the key?" Pip pointed to it.

He nodded.

And then they heard the sound of wheels crunching on the road outside.

"When the police interrogate you," Pip said, hurrying now, "do not tell them about the hit-and-run, about taking Sal's alibi away. He doesn't need one when you've confessed. And Cara does not deserve to lose Naomi as well, to be all alone."

The sound of car doors slamming.

"Maybe I can understand why you did it," she said. "But what you did is unforgivable. You took Sal's life to save your own. You destroyed his family."

A shout of "Hello, police!" came from the open front door.

"The Bells have grieved for five years. You threatened me and my family; you broke into my house."

"I'm sorry."

Heavy footsteps down the hallway.

"You killed Barney."

His face crumpled. "Pip, I don't know what you're talking about. I didn't—"

"Police," the officer said, stepping into the kitchen, hands tensed against his uniform. His partner walked in behind, her eyes darting from Mr. Ward to Pip and back, her tightly scraped ponytail flipping back and forth.

"Right, what's going on here?" she said.

Pip looked over at Mr. Ward and their eyes met. He held out his wrists.

"You're here to arrest me for the abduction and false imprisonment of Andie Bell," he said, not taking his eyes off her.

"And the murder of Sal Singh," said Pip.

The officers looked at each other for a long moment, and one of them nodded. The woman started toward Mr. Ward, and the man pressed something on the radio strapped to his shoulder. He moved back out to the hallway to speak into it.

With both their backs turned, Pip darted forward and snatched the key from the counter. She ran out into the hall and bounded up the stairs.

"Hey!" the male officer shouted after her.

There was a small white hatch in the ceiling at the top. A large padlock was fitted through the catch, attached to a metal ring in the surrounding wooden frame. A small two-step ladder was placed beneath it.

Pip stepped up and slotted the key into the padlock, letting it clatter to the floor. The policeman was coming up the stairs after her. She twisted the catch and ducked to let the reinforced hatch swing down and open.

Yellow light filled the hole above her. And sounds: dramatic music, explosions, and people shouting in tinny, panicked voices. Pip grabbed the loft ladder and pulled it down to the floor, just as the officer thundered up the last few steps.

"Wait!" he shouted.

Pip climbed up, her hands clammy on the metal rungs.

She poked her head up through the hatch and looked around. The room was lit by several floor lamps, and the walls were decorated with a white-and-black floral design. On one side of the loft, there was a mini-fridge with an electric kettle and a microwave on top, and shelves of food and books. There was a fluffy pink rug in the middle of the room, and behind it was a large flat-screen TV that was just being paused.

And there she was.

Sitting cross-legged on a single bed piled high with colored cushions. Wearing a pair of blue penguin-patterned pajamas, the same that both Cara and Naomi had. She stared over at Pip, her eyes wide and wild. She looked a little older, a little heavier. Her hair was mousier than it had been before, and her skin much paler. She gaped at Pip, the TV remote in her hand and a pack of Butterfingers on her lap.

"Hi," Pip said. "I'm Pip."

"H-hi," she said, "I'm Andie."

But she wasn't.

forty-five

Pip stepped closer, into the yellow glow of the lamplight, trying to think over the screeching in her head. She screwed her eyes and studied the face before her.

Now that she was closer, she could see the obvious differences, the slightly different slope to her plump lips, the downturn to her eyes where they should flick up, the swell of her cheekbones lower than they should be. Changes that time couldn't make to a face.

Pip had looked at the photographs so many times these past months, she knew every line and groove of Andie Bell's face.

This wasn't her.

Pip felt detached from the world, floating away, empty of all sense.

"You're not Andie," she said quietly, just as the police officer climbed up the ladder behind her and placed a hand on her shoulder.

The wind was screaming in the trees, and 42 Gravesend Road was lit up with flashes of red and blue, rippling in and out of the night. Four cop cars filled the drive now, and Pip had just seen Detective Richard Hawkins—in the same black coat he'd worn in the press conferences over five years ago—step into the house.

Pip stopped listening to the policewoman taking her statement. She heard her words only as a rockslide of falling syllables, so she concentrated on breathing instead. That's when they brought Mr. Ward out. Two officers on either side, his hands cuffed behind his back. He was weeping, the red and blue lights mirrored on his wet face. The wounded sounds he made woke some instinctive fear inside her; this was a man who knew his life was finished. Had he really believed the girl in his loft was Andie? Had he clung to that belief this whole time? *How?* They ducked his head, put him in a car, and took him away. Pip watched until they were swallowed by the tunnel of trees.

As she finished giving her contact number to the officer, she heard a car door slamming behind her.

"Pip!" The wind carried Ravi's voice to her.

She felt a pull in her chest, and then she was running. She rushed to the top of the driveway and Ravi caught her, his arms tight as they anchored themselves together against the darkness.

"Are you OK?" he said, holding her back to look at her.

"Yes," she said. "What are you doing here?"

"Me?" He tapped his chest. "When you didn't turn up at my house, I looked for you on Find My Friends. Why did you come here alone?" He eyed the police cars and officers behind her.

"I had to," she said. "I had to ask him why. I didn't know how much longer you'd have to wait for the truth if I didn't."

Her mouth opened once, twice, three times before the words found their way, and then she told Ravi everything. She told him how his brother had died, as they stood under shivering trees, lights undulating all around them. When the tears broke down Ravi's face, Pip said she was sorry, because that was all there was to say.

"Don't be sorry," he said with a half cry. "Nothing could have brought him back. But we have, in a way. Sal was murdered, Sal was innocent, and now everyone will know."

They turned to watch as Detective Richard Hawkins walked the girl out of the house, a lilac-colored blanket wrapped around her shoulders.

"It's really not her, is it?" Ravi said.

"She looks a lot like her," said Pip.

The girl's eyes were wide and spinning as she looked around at everything, relearning what outside was. Hawkins led her to a car and climbed in beside her as two uniformed officers got in the front.

Pip didn't know how Mr. Ward had possibly come to believe this girl he found on the side of the road was Andie. Was it delusion? Did he need to believe Andie hadn't died as some kind of atonement for what he did to Sal? Or was it fear that blinded him?

That's what Ravi thought: that Mr. Ward was terrified Andie Bell was alive and would come back home, and then he'd go down for Sal's murder. And in that heightened state of fear, all it took was a blond girl who looked similar enough to convince himself he'd found Andie. And he'd locked her up, so he could lock up that terrible fear of being caught right along with her.

Pip nodded, watching the police car drive away. "I think," she said quietly, "I think she was just a girl with the wrong hair and the wrong face when the wrong man drove past."

And that other itching question that Pip couldn't yet give voice to: What had happened to the real Andie Bell after she'd left the Wards' house that night?

The officer who'd taken her statement approached them with a warm smile. "Do you need someone to take you home?" she asked Pip.

"No, it's OK," she said, "I have my car."

Pip made Ravi get in with her; there was no way she'd let him drive home on his own—he was shaking too hard. And secretly, she didn't want to be alone.

She turned the key in the ignition, catching sight of her face in the rearview mirror before the lights dimmed. She looked gaunt and gray, her eyes glowing inside sunken shadows. She was tired. So unutterably tired.

"I can finally tell my parents," Ravi said when they were back on the main road out of New Canaan. "I don't know how to even start."

Her headlights lit up the "Welcome to Fairview" sign as they crossed into town. Pip drove down Main Street, heading toward Ravi's house, and drew to a stop at the central roundabout. There was a car waiting on the other side of the circle, its headlights bright and piercing white.

"Why aren't they moving? It's their right of way," Pip said, staring at the boxy car ahead, lit up with yellow light from the street lamp above.

"Don't know," Ravi said. "You just go."

She did, pulling forward slowly around the curve. The other car had still not moved. As they drew closer and out of the glare of the oncoming headlights, Pip's foot eased up on the pedal. She looked curiously out of her window.

"Oh shit," Ravi said.

It was the Bell family.

All three of them. Jason was in the driver seat, his face red and striped with tear trails. It looked like he was shouting, smacking his hand against the steering wheel, his mouth moving with angry words. Dawn Bell was beside him, shrinking away. She was crying too, her body heaving as she tried to breathe, her mouth bared in confused agony.

Their cars drew level, and Pip saw Becca in the back seat on their side. Her face was pale, pushed up against the window. Her lips were parted and her brows furrowed, eyes lost in some other place as she stared blankly ahead.

As they passed, Becca's eyes snapped into life and landed on Pip. There was a flicker of recognition. And something heavy and urgent, something like dread.

They drove away down the street, and Ravi let out his breath.

"You think they've been told?" he said.

"Looks like they just have," said Pip. "The girl kept saying her name was Andie Bell. Maybe they have to go and formally identify that she isn't."

She looked into her rearview mirror and watched as the Bells' car finally rolled away across the roundabout, toward the snatched promise of a daughter returned.

forty-six

Pip sat at the end of her parents' bed, well into the night. Her and her story. The telling of it was almost as hard as the living of it.

But the worst part would be telling Cara. By ten p.m. Pip knew she couldn't avoid it anymore. She hovered her thumb over the call button, but she couldn't do it. She couldn't say the words and listen as her best friend's world fell apart. Pip wished she was strong enough, but this would break her too. She opened her messages instead and started to type:

> *I should be calling to tell you this, but I don't think I could get through it, not with your voice at the other end. This is the coward's way out and I'm so sorry. Your dad was the one who killed Sal, Cara. He was keeping a girl he thought was Andie Bell in your old house in New Canaan, and he was just arrested. Naomi will be safe, though, I promise. I know why he did it when you're ready to hear it. I'm so sorry. I wish I could save you from this. I love you.*

She'd read it over, still in her parents' bed, and pressed send, tears falling against the phone as she cradled it in her cupped hands.

* * *

Her mom made breakfast when Pip finally woke up at ten-thirty. They didn't talk about it again; there was nothing more to say, not yet. But still the question of Andie Bell played on Pip's mind; Andie somehow had one last mystery left in her.

Pip tried to call Cara seventeen times, but it rang out each time. Naomi's phone too.

Early afternoon her mom stopped by the Wards' house after picking up Josh. She came back saying that no one was home and their car was gone.

"They've probably gone to their aunt Lila's," Pip said, pressing redial again.

No one quite knew what to do with the afternoon. They sat in the living room, silently watching reruns of quiz shows, exchanging furtive looks over Josh's head, the air bloated with a sad what-now tension.

When someone knocked at the front door, Pip jumped up to escape the strangeness that smothered the room. Still in her tie-dyed pajamas, she pulled open the door.

It was Ravi, standing in front of his parents, the spaces between them perfect, like they'd prearranged the pose.

"Hello, Sarge," Ravi said. "This is my mom, Nisha." He gestured like a game-show host, and his mom smiled at Pip, her black hair in two loose plaits. "And my dad, Mohan." His dad nodded, and his chin brushed the top of the giant bouquet of flowers he held; a box of chocolates was tucked under the other arm. "Parents," Ravi said, "this is *the* Pip."

Pip's polite hello got muddled in with theirs.

"So," Ravi said, "they called us in to the police station earlier.

They sat us down and told us everything, everything we already knew. And they said they'd be holding a press conference once they charge Mr. Ward and will release a statement about Sal's innocence."

Pip heard her mom and heavy-footed dad walking up the hallway to stand behind her. Ravi redid the introductions and continued. "So," he said, "we wanted to come over to thank you, Pip. This wouldn't have happened without you."

"I don't quite know what to say," Nisha said, her Ravi-Sal eyes beaming. "Because of what the two of you did, you and Ravi, we have our boy back. You've given Sal back to us, and there are no words for how much that means."

"These are for you," Mohan said, leaning forward and handing over the flowers and chocolates to Pip. "I'm sorry, we weren't quite sure what you're supposed to get for someone who's helped vindicate your dead son."

"Google had very few suggestions," said Ravi.

"Thank you," Pip said. "Do you want to come in?"

"Yes, do come in," her mom said, "I'll make some coffee."

As Ravi stepped into the house, he took Pip's arm and pulled her back into a lingering hug, crushing the flowers between them, laughing into her hair. When he let her go, Nisha stepped up and folded her into a hug as well; her sweet perfume smelled to Pip like homes and mothers and summer evenings. And then, not sure why or how it happened, they were all embracing, all six of them swapping and hugging again, laughing with tears in their eyes.

And just like that, with crushed flowers and a rotation of hugs, the Singhs took away the suffocating and confused sadness that had taken over the house. They'd opened the door and let out the ghost, for at least a little while. Because there was one happy ending in all of this: Sal was innocent. His family set free from the weight they'd carried all these years. And that was worth hanging on to.

In the living room they sat around a full spread of sandwiches that Pip's mom had improvised, batting Josh's hand away until Ravi's parents had taken their pick.

"So," her dad said, "are you going to the carnival opening tonight?"

"Actually," Nisha said, looking from her husband to her son, "I think we *should* go this year. It'll be the first time since . . . you know. But things are different now. This is the start of things being different."

"Yeah," Ravi said. "I'd like to go. You can never really see the fireworks from our house."

"Awesome," Pip's dad said, clapping his hands. "We could meet you there? Let's say seven-thirty, by the drinks stand?"

Pip wasn't sure she was ready to be around all those people and the questions in their eyes.

"I'll go brew another pot," she said, picking up empty mugs and carrying them into the kitchen.

She stared at her warped reflection in the chrome surface of the coffee maker until a distorted Ravi appeared in it behind her.

"You're being quiet," he said. "What's going on in that big brain of yours? Actually, I don't even need to ask. I already know what you're going to say. It's Andie."

"I can't pretend it's over," she said. "It's not finished."

"Pip, listen to me. You've done what you set out to do. We know Sal was innocent and what happened to him."

"But we don't know what happened to Andie. After she left the Wards' house that night, she still disappeared."

“It’s not your job anymore, Pip,” he said. “The police have reopened Andie’s case. Let them do the rest. You’ve done enough.”

“I know,” she said, and it wasn’t a lie. She was tired. She needed to be free of all this, needed the weight on her shoulders to just be her own. And that last Andie Bell mystery wasn’t hers to chase anymore.

Ravi was right; their part was over.

forty-seven

She had meant to throw it out.

That's what she told herself. The murder board needed to be thrown out because it was finished. It was time to dismantle the Andie Bell scaffolding and see what remained of the Pip beneath. She'd made a good start, unpinning some of the pages and putting them in piles by a garbage bag.

And then, without realizing what she was doing or how it happened, she'd found herself looking through it all again: rereading log entries, tracing her finger across the red string, staring into the suspects' photos.

She'd been so sure she was done. But with half a second and a fleeting glance, Andie had found a way to suck her in again.

Pip was supposed to be getting dressed for the carnival, but instead, she was on her knees, hunched over the murder board. Some of it really did go in the trash bag: all the clues that had pointed to Elliot Ward. Everything about the Ivy House Inn, the phone number in the planner, the hit-and-run, Sal's stolen alibi, Andie's nude photo that Max found at the back of a classroom, and the printed notes and texts from Unknown.

But the board also needed things added, because she knew more about Andie's whereabouts on the night she disappeared now. She grabbed a printout of a map of Fairview and started scribbling.

Andie went to the Wards' house and left not long after with a potentially serious head injury. Pip circled the Wards' house on Hillside. Mr. Ward had said it was around ten-ish, but he must have been slightly off with that guess. His and Becca Bell's estimates of time didn't match, yet Becca's was backed up by security footage: Andie had driven past the camera at 10:40 p.m. That's when she must have headed to the Wards' house. Pip drew a dotted line and scribbled in the time. Mr. Ward had to be mistaken, she realized. Otherwise, it meant that Andie had returned home with an injured head before leaving again. And if that had been the case, Becca would have told the police those details. So Becca Bell was no longer the last person to see Andie alive, Elliot Ward was.

But then . . . Pip chewed the end of the pen, thinking. Mr. Ward said that Andie hadn't driven to his house; he thought she'd walked. And looking at the map, Pip saw why that made sense. The Bells' and the Wards' houses were very close; on foot you just had to cut through the church and over the pedestrian bridge. It was probably a quicker walk than a drive. Pip scratched her head. But that didn't fit: Andie's car was picked up by that surveillance camera, so she must have driven. Maybe she'd parked somewhere near Mr. Ward's but not near enough for him to notice.

So how did Andie go from that point into nonexistence? From Hillside to her blood in the trunk of her car, ditched near Howie's house?

Pip tapped her pen against the map, eyes flitting from Howie to Max to Nat to Daniel to Jason. There had been two different killers in Fairview: one who thought he'd killed Andie and then murdered

Sal to cover it up, and another who'd actually killed Andie Bell. And which of these faces staring up at her could it be?

Two killers, and yet only one of them had tried to get Pip to stop, which meant that . . .

Wait.

Pip held her face as she closed her eyes to think, thoughts firing off and then coming back, altered. And Mr. Ward's face, just as Pip said she'd never forgive him for killing Barney. It had crumpled, his brows tensed. But maybe it hadn't been remorse on his face at all. Maybe it was confusion.

And the words he'd spoken, Pip finished his sentence in her head: *Pip, I don't know what you're talking about. I didn't*—kill Barney.

Pip swore under her breath. She upturned the trash bag, scattering papers all around her, hunting through the mess. She found them; the notes from the camping trip and her locker in one hand, the printed texts from Unknown in the other.

They were from two different people. It was so obvious now, looking at them.

The differences weren't only in form, it was in their tone. In the printed notes, Mr. Ward had called her "Pippa," and the threats were subtle, implied. But Unknown called her a "Stupid bitch," and the threats weren't only implied: they'd made her smash her laptop, and then they'd killed her dog.

She let out her too-full breath.

Two different people. Elliot Ward wasn't Unknown and he hadn't killed Barney. No, that had been Andie's real killer.

"Pip, come on! They'll be lighting the fireworks soon," her dad called upstairs.

She bounded over to her door and opened it a crack. "Um, you guys go on ahead. I'll meet you there."

"What? No. Get down here, Pips."

"I'm just . . . I just want to try to call Cara a few more times, Dad. I really need to talk to her. I won't be long. Please. I'll find you there."

"OK, pickle," he called.

"I'll leave in twenty minutes, I promise," she said.

"OK, call me if you can't find us."

The front door crashed shut, and Pip sat back beside the murder board, the messages from Unknown shaking in her hands. She scanned through her log entries, trying to work out when she had received the texts. The first had come just after she found Howie Bowers, after she and Ravi had spoken to him and learned about Andie's dealing. And then Barney had been taken in the week of fall break. A lot had happened just before that: She'd bumped into Stanley Forbes twice, she'd gone to see Becca, and she'd spoken to Daniel at the police meeting.

Fuck. She scrunched up the pieces of paper and threw them across the room. There were just too many suspects still. And now that Elliot's secrets were out and Sal was to be exonerated, would the killer be looking for revenge? Would they make good on their threats? Should Pip really be in the house on her own?

She scowled down at all their photos. She drew a big *X* through Jason Bell's face with a blue marker. It couldn't be him. She'd seen the look on his face in the car, after the detective must have called them. Both he and Dawn: crying, angry, confused. And something else in their eyes; the smallest glimmer of hope alongside their tears. Maybe, even though they'd been told the girl wasn't Andie, some small part of them had hoped it would still be their daughter. Mr. Bell couldn't have faked that reaction. The truth was in his face.

The truth was in the face. . . .

Pip picked up a photo of the Bell family, and she stared into those eyes.

It didn't come all at once but in little blips, lighting up across her memory.

Then the pieces dropped, falling into place.

She grabbed all the relevant pages from the murder board. Log entry 3: the interview with Stanley Forbes. Entry 10: the first interview with Emma Hutton. Entry 20: the interview with Jess Walker about the Bells; 21 about Max buying drugs from Andie; 23 about Howie and what he supplied her with. Entry 28 and 29 about drink-spiking at calamities. The paper on which Ravi had written: *WHO COULD HAVE TAKEN THE BURNER PHONE???* in large capital letters. And the time Mr. Ward said Andie left his house.

She looked them over and she knew who it was.

The killer had a face and a name.

The last person to see Andie alive.

But there was just one last thing to confirm. Pip pulled out her phone, scrolled down her contacts, and dialed the number.

"Hello?"

"Max?" she said. "I'm going to ask you a question."

"I'm not interested. See, you were wrong about me. I've heard what happened, that it was Mr. Ward."

"Good," Pip said, "then you know that right now I have a lot of credibility with the police. I told Mr. Ward to cover up the hit-and-run, but if you don't answer my question, I'll call the police and tell them everything."

"You wouldn't."

"I would. Naomi's life is already destroyed; don't think that will stop me anymore," she bluffed.

"What do you want?" he spat.

Pip paused. She put the phone on speaker and opened her

recording app. She pressed record and sniffed loudly to hide the beep.

"Max, at a calamity party in March 2014," she said, "did you drug and rape Becca Bell?"

"What? No, I fucking didn't."

"MAX!" Pip roared down the phone. "Do not lie to me or I swear to god I will ruin you! Did you put Rohypnol in Becca's drink and have sex with her?"

He coughed. "Yes, but, like . . . it wasn't rape. She didn't say no."

"Because you drugged her, you vile rapist gargoyle!" Pip shouted. "You have no idea what you've done."

She hung up, stopped the recording, and pressed the lock button. Her sharp eyes stared back at her from the darkened screen.

The last person to see Andie alive? It had been Becca. It had always been Becca.

Pip's reflection blinked back at her, and the decision was made.

forty-eight

The car jerked as Pip pulled roughly onto the curb. She stepped out into the darkened street and up to the front door.

She knocked.

The wind chimes beside it were swaying in the evening breeze, chiming high and insistent.

The front door opened and Becca's face appeared in the crack. She looked at Pip and pulled it fully open.

"Oh, hi, Pippa," she said.

"Hi, Becca. I'm . . . I came to see if you were OK, after last night. I saw you in the car and—"

"Yeah." She nodded. "The detective told us it was you that found out about Mr. Ward, what he'd done."

"Yeah, I'm sorry."

"Do you want to come in?" Becca asked, stepping back to clear the threshold.

"Thanks."

Pip walked past her and into the hallway she and Ravi had broken into weeks ago. Becca smiled and gestured her through into the robin's-egg-blue kitchen.

"Would you like tea?"

"Oh, no thanks."

"Sure? I was just making some for myself."

"OK, then. Black, please. Thanks."

Pip took a seat at the kitchen table, her back straight, knees rigid, and watched as Becca grabbed two flowery mugs from a cupboard, dropped in the tea bags, and poured from the kettle.

"Excuse me," Becca said, "I just need to get a tissue."

As she left the room, Pip's pocket buzzed and chimed. It was a message from Ravi: *Yo, Sarge, where are you?* She flicked her phone to silent and zipped it back into her coat.

Becca reentered the room, tucking a tissue into her sleeve. She brought over the teas and put Pip's down in front of her.

"Thank you," Pip said, taking a sip. She was glad for it now; something to do with her shaking hands.

The black cat came in, strutting over with his tail up, rubbing his head into Pip's ankles until Becca shooed him away.

"How are your parents doing?" Pip asked.

"Not great," Becca said. "After we confirmed she wasn't Andie, my mom booked herself into rehab for emotional trauma. And my dad wants to sue everyone."

"Do they know who the girl is yet?" Pip said into the rim of her mug.

"Yeah, they called my dad this morning. She was on the missing persons register: Isla Jordan, twenty-three, from New Haven. They said she has a learning disability and the mental age of a twelve-year-old. She came from an abusive home and had a history of running away and possession of drugs." Becca fiddled with her short hair. "They said she's very confused; she lived like that for so long—being Andie because it's what pleased Mr. Ward—that she actually believes she's a girl called Andie Bell from Fairview."

Pip took a large gulp. Her mouth felt dry, and there was an

awful tremor in her throat, echoing back her doubled heartbeat. She raised the mug and finished off the tea.

"She did look like her," Pip finally said. "I thought she was Andie for a few seconds. And I saw in your parents' faces the hope that maybe it would be Andie after all. That me and the police could be wrong. But you already knew, didn't you?"

Becca put her own mug down and stared at her.

"Your face wasn't like theirs, Becca. You looked confused. You looked scared. You knew for sure it couldn't be your sister. Because you killed her, didn't you?"

Becca didn't move. The cat jumped up on the table beside her, and still she didn't move.

"In March 2014," Pip said, "you went to a calamity party with your friend, Jess Walker. And while you were there, something happened to you. You don't remember, but you woke up and you knew something felt wrong. You asked Jess to go and get the morning-after pill with you, and when she asked who you'd slept with, you didn't tell her. It wasn't, as Jess presumed, because you were embarrassed—it's because you didn't know. You didn't know what happened or with who. You had anterograde amnesia because someone slipped roofies into your drink and then assaulted you."

Becca just sat there, inhumanly still, like a small fleshed-out mannequin too scared to move. And then she started to cry, the muscles twitching in her chin. Pip's gut congealed as she looked into Becca's eyes and saw the truth there. Because the truth was no victory here; it was just sad and confusing.

"I can't imagine how horrible and lonely it was for you," Pip said, feeling unsteady. "Not being able to remember but just knowing that something bad had happened. You must have felt like no one could help you. You did nothing wrong and you had nothing to be ashamed of. But I don't think you felt that way at first, and you ended up in the hospital. And then what happened? Did you decide to find out what had happened to you? Who was responsible?"

Becca's nod was almost imperceptible.

"I think you realized someone had drugged you, so is that where you started looking? Started asking around about who bought drugs at calamities and who from. And the questions led you back to your own sister. Becca, what happened on Friday, April eighteenth? What happened when Andie walked back from Mr. Ward's house?"

"All I'd found out was someone bought weed and ecstasy off her once," Becca said, looking down and catching her tears in her hands. "So when she went out and left me alone, I looked in her room. I found the place where she hid her other phone and the drugs. I looked through the phone: all the contacts were saved with just one-letter names, but I read through some messages and I found the person who bought Rohypnol from her. She'd used his name in one of the texts."

"Max Hastings," said Pip.

"And I thought . . . ," she cried, "I thought that once I knew, we would be able to fix everything and put it right. And I thought that when Andie got home, I'd tell her and she'd let me cry on her and tell me she was so sorry and that we, me and her, were going to set this right and make him pay. All I wanted was my big sister. And the freedom of finally telling someone."

Pip wiped her eyes, feeling shaky and drained.

"And then Andie came home," Becca said.

"With a head injury?"

"No, I didn't know that at the time," she said. "I didn't see anything. She was just here, in the kitchen, and I couldn't wait any longer. I had to tell her. And"—Becca's voice broke—"when I did she just looked at me and said she didn't care. I tried to explain and she wouldn't listen. She just said I wasn't allowed to tell anyone or I'd get her in trouble. She tried to leave the room, and I blocked her. Then she said I should be grateful that someone had actually wanted me, because I was just the fat, ugly version of her. And she tried to push me out of the way. I just couldn't believe it—I couldn't believe she could be so cruel. I pushed her back and tried to explain again, and we were both shouting and shoving and then . . . it was so fast.

"Andie fell back onto the floor. I didn't think I'd pushed her that hard. Her eyes were closed. And then she was being sick. It was all over her face and in her hair. And," Becca sobbed, "then her mouth was full, and she was coughing and choking on it. And I . . . I just froze. I don't know why. I was just so angry at her. When I look back now, I don't know whether or not I made any decision. I don't remember thinking anything at all; I just didn't move. I must have known she was dying and I stood there and did nothing."

Becca shifted her gaze then, to a place on the kitchen tiles by the door. Where it must have happened.

"And then she went still and I realized what I'd done. I panicked and tried to clear her mouth, but she was already dead. I wanted to take it back so badly. I've wanted to every day since. But it was too late. Only then did I see the blood in her hair and thought I must have hurt her; for five years I've thought that. I didn't know until two days ago that Andie had injured her head before with Mr. Ward. That must be why she lost consciousness, why she was sick. Doesn't matter, though. I was still the one who let her choke to death. I watched her die and did nothing. And because I'd thought it was me that hurt her head, and there were scratches on her arms from me, signs of a struggle, I knew everyone—even my parents—would think I'd meant to kill her. Because Andie was always so much better than me. My parents loved her more."

"You put her body in the trunk of her car?" Pip said, leaning forward to hold her head because it was too heavy.

"The car was in the garage and I dragged her inside. I don't know how I found the strength to do it. It's all a blur now. I cleaned everything up; I'd watched enough documentaries, I knew which type of bleach you have to use."

"Then you left the house just before ten-forty p.m.," said Pip. "It was *you* the security camera picked up, driving Andie's car up Main Street. And you took her . . . I think you took her to that old farmhouse on Sycamore Road, the one you were writing an article about, because you didn't want the neighbors to buy it and restore it. And you buried her there?"

"She's not buried," Becca sniffed. "She's in the septic tank."

Pip nodded, her fuzzy head grappling with Andie's final fate. "Then you dumped her car and you walked home. Why did you leave it on Monroe?"

"When I looked through her second phone, I saw that that was where her dealer lived. I thought if I left the car there, the police would make the connection and he'd be the main suspect."

"What must you have thought when suddenly Sal was the guilty one and it was all over?"

Becca shrugged. "I don't know. I thought maybe it was some kind of sign, that I'd been forgiven. Though I've never forgiven myself."

"And then," Pip said, "five years later I start investigating. You got my number from Stanley's phone, from when I interviewed him."

"He told me some kid was doing a project, thinking Sal was innocent. I panicked. I thought that if you proved his innocence, I'd need to find another suspect. I'd kept Andie's burner phone, and I knew she was having a secret relationship; there were texts to a contact named *E* about meeting up at this place, the Ivy House Inn. So I went there to see if I could find out who this man was. I didn't get anywhere; the old woman who owned it was very confused. Then weeks later I saw you hanging around the station parking lot, and I knew that's where Andie's dealer worked. I watched you, and as you followed him, I followed you. I saw you go to his house with Sal's brother. I just wanted to make you stop."

"That's when you first texted me," Pip said. "But I didn't stop. And when I came to talk to you at your office, you must have thought I was so close to figuring out it was you, talking about the burner phone and Max Hastings. So you killed my dog and made me destroy all my research."

"I'm sorry." She looked down. "I didn't mean for your dog to die. I let him go, I really did. But it was dark; he must have gotten confused and fallen in the river."

Pip's breath caught. But accident or not, it wouldn't bring Barney back.

"I loved him so much," Pip said, feeling dizzy, unjoining from herself. "But I want to forgive you. That's why I came here, Becca. If I've worked all this out, the police won't be far behind me, not now they've reopened the case. And Mr. Ward's story starts to poke holes in yours." She spoke fast, slurring, her tongue tripping over the words. "It's not right what you did, Becca, letting her die, but I know you know that. It's not fair what happened to you. You didn't ask for any of this, but the law lacks compassion. I came to warn you. You need to leave, get out of the country and find a life for yourself somewhere. Because they will be coming for you soon."

Pip looked at her. Becca must have been talking, but suddenly, all the sound in the world disappeared, just the buzz of a beetle's wings trapped inside her head. The table was rippling between them, and Pip's eyelids felt unnaturally heavy, dragging down and down and . . .

"I—I . . . ," she stuttered. The world dimmed, the only bright thing was the empty mug in front of her, wavering, its colors dripping up into the air. "You put somethi— my drink?"

"There were a few of Max's pills left in Andie's hiding place. I kept them."

Becca's voice came to Pip, loud and garish, a shrieking echo, switching from ear to ear.

Pip pushed up from her chair, but her left leg was too weak. It gave out under her, and she crashed into the kitchen island. Something smashed and the pieces were flying around like jagged clouds and up and up as the world spun around her.

The room lurched, and Pip stumbled over to the sink, leaned into it, and rammed her fingers down her throat. She vomited, and it was dark brown and stinging, and she vomited again. A voice came to her from somewhere near and somewhere far.

"I'll work something out, I have to. There's no evidence. There's just you and what you know. I'm sorry. I don't want to do this. Why couldn't you just leave it alone?"

Pip staggered back and wiped her mouth. The room reeled again, and Becca was in front of her.

"No." Pip tried to scream, but her voice got lost somewhere inside. She hurtled back and sidestepped around the island. Her fingers bit into one of the stools to keep her on her feet. She grabbed it and launched it behind her. There was a head-splitting clatter as it took out Becca's legs.

Pip ran into the wall in the hallway. Ears ringing and shoulder throbbing, she leaned into it so it wouldn't mutate away from her, and scaled her way to the front door. It wouldn't open, but then she blinked and it vanished and she was outside somehow.

It was dark and spinning and there was something in the sky. Bright and colorful mushrooms and doom clouds and sprinkles.

The fireworks with a ripping-the-earth sound from the park. Pip picked up her feet and ran toward the bright colors, into the woods.

The trees were walking in a wooden two-step, and Pip's feet went numb. Missing. Another sparkling sky-roar, and it made her blind.

Her hands out in front to be her eyes. Another crack and Becca was in her face.

She pushed and Pip fell onto her back in the leaves and mud. And Becca was standing over her, hands splayed and reaching down and . . . a rush of energy came back to Pip. She kicked out hard, and now Becca was on the ground, too, lost in the leaves.

"I was tr-trying to h-help you," Pip stammered.

She turned and crawled, and her arms wanted to be legs, and her legs, arms. She scrabbled up to her missing feet and ran away from Becca.

More bombs were bursting, and it was the end of the world behind her. She grasped at the trees to help push her on as they danced and twirled at the falling sky. She grabbed a branch and it felt like skin.

It lunged out and gripped her with two hands. They fell onto the ground and they rolled. Pip's head smashed against a tangled set of roots, a snaking trail of wet down her face, the iron-bite of blood in her mouth. The world went dark again as the redness pooled by her eyes. And then Becca was sitting on her, and there was something cold around Pip's neck. She reached up to feel, and it was fingers, but her own wouldn't work. She couldn't pry them off.

"Please." The word squeezed out of her and the air wouldn't come back.

Her arms were stuck in the leaves, and they wouldn't listen to her. They wouldn't move.

She looked up into Becca's eyes. *She knows where to put you where they'll never find you. In a dark place with the bones of Andie Bell.*

Her arms and legs were gone, and she was following.

"I wish someone like you had been there for me," Becca cried. "All I had was Andie. She was my only escape from my dad. She was my only hope after Max. And she didn't care. Maybe she never had. Now I'm stuck in this thing and there's no way out except this. I don't want to do this. I'm sorry."

Pip couldn't remember now what it felt like to breathe.

Her eyes were splitting and there was fire in the cracks.

Fairview was being swallowed by darkness, but those rainbow sparks in the night were nice to look at. One last nice thing to send you on before it all goes black.

And as it did she felt the cold fingers loosen and come away.

The first breath ripped and snagged as she sucked it down. The blackness pulled back, and sounds grew out of the earth.

"I can't do it," Becca said, moving her hands back to hug herself. "I can't."

Then a crash of rustling footsteps and a shadow leaped over them, and Becca was dragged off. More sounds. Shouting and screaming and . . .

"You're OK, pickle."

Pip turned her head, and her dad was here, pinning Becca down on the ground while she struggled and cried.

And there was another person behind Pip, sitting her up, but she was a river and couldn't be held.

"Breathe, Sarge," Ravi said, stroking her hair. "We're here. We're here now."

"Ravi, what's wrong with her?"

"Hypnol," Pip whispered, looking up at him. "Rohypnol in . . . tea."

"Ravi, call an ambulance now. Call the police."

The sounds went away again. It was just the colors and Ravi's voice vibrating in his chest and through her back to the outer edge of all sense.

"She let Andie die," Pip said, or she thought she said. "But we have to let her go. It's not fair. Not fair."

Fairview blinked.

"I might not remember. I might get mm . . . nesia. She's in septic tank. Farmhouse . . . Sycamore. That's where . . ."

"It's OK, Pip," Ravi said, holding her so she didn't fall off the world. "It's over. It's all over now. I've got you."

"How didddu find me?"

"Your tracking device is still on," Ravi said, showing her a fuzzy, jumping screen with an orange blip on the Find My Friends map. "As soon as I saw you here, I knew."

Fairview blinked.

"It's OK, I've got you, Pip. You're going to be OK."

Blink.

They were talking again, Ravi and her dad. But not in words she could hear, in the scratching of ants. She couldn't see them anymore. Pip's eyes were the sky, and fireworks were rupturing inside. Flower sprays of Armageddon.

And then she was a person again, on the cold damp ground, Ravi's breath in her ear. And through the trees were flashing red and blue lights spewing black uniforms.

Pip watched them both, the flashes and the fireworks.

No sound. Just her rattlesnake breath and the sparks and the lights.

Red and blue. Red

and blue. Bled a n

d rue. B e

l l a n

n

d

two months later

"There are a *lot* of people out there, Sarge."

"Really?"

"Yeah, like, two hundred."

She could hear them all; the clattering of chairs as people took their seats in the assembly hall.

She was waiting in the wings behind, her presentation notes clutched in her hands, the sweat from her fingers smudging the ink.

Everyone else in her grade had done their capstone project presentations earlier in the week, to small classrooms of people. But the school thought it would be a good idea to turn Pip's presentation into "a bit of an event," as the principal had put it. Pip had been given no choice in the matter. The school had advertised it online and in the *Fairview Mail.* They'd invited members of the press to attend; Pip had seen a CNN van pull up earlier and the equipment and cameras unpacked.

"Are you nervous?" Ravi said.

"Are you asking obvious questions?"

When the Andie Bell story broke, it had been in the national newspapers and on TV stations for weeks. It was in the height of all that craziness that Pip had had her interview for Columbia. The two interviewers had recognized her from the news, swiping aside their notes of formal questions, asking her instead about the case. Her acceptance letter was one of the very first to come in.

Fairview's secrets and mysteries had followed Pip so closely in those weeks she'd had to wear them like a new skin. Except the one that was buried deep down, the one she'd keep forever to save Cara. Her best friend who'd never once left Pip's side in the hospital.

"Can I come over later?" Ravi asked her.

"Sure. Cara and Naomi are coming for dinner too."

They heard a sharp patter of heels, and Mrs. Morgan appeared, fighting through the curtain.

"I think we're just about ready when you are, Pippa."

"OK, I'll be out in a minute."

"Well," Ravi said when they were alone again, "I better go and take my seat."

He smiled, put his hands on the back of her neck, fingers in her hair, and leaned in to press his forehead against hers. He'd told her before that he did it to take away half her sadness, half her headache, half her nerves before her Columbia interview. Because half less of a bad thing meant there was room for half good.

He kissed her, and she glowed with that feeling. The one with wings.

"You bring the rain down on them, Pip."

"I will."

"Oh," he said, turning one last time before the door, "and don't tell them the only reason you started this project was because you fancied me. You know, think of a more noble reason."

"Get out of here."

"Don't feel bad. You couldn't help yourself, I'm ravishing." He grinned. "Get it? Ravi-shing. Ravi Singh."

"Sign of a great joke, having to explain it," she said. "Now go."

She waited another minute, muttering the first lines of her speech under her breath. And then she walked out onstage.

People weren't quite sure what to do. About half the audience started clapping politely, the news cameras panning to them, and the other half sat deadly still, a sea of eyes stalking her as she moved.

From the front row her dad stood up and whistled with his fingers, shouting: "Get 'em, Pips." Her mom swiftly pulled him back down and exchanged a look with Nisha Singh, sitting beside her. Pip strode over to the principal's lectern and flattened her speech down on top.

"Hi," she said, and the microphone screeched, cutting through the silent room. Cameras clicked. "My name is Pip. And for my senior capstone project, I decided to solve a murder. I did not know that this project would put myself, my friends, and my family in danger, and would end up changing many lives. But what I *do* know"—she paused—"is that this town and the national media still don't really understand what happened here at all. I am not the 'prodigy student' who found the truth for Andie Bell, keeping Sal Singh and his brother, Ravi, relegated to small sidenotes. This project began with Sal. To find the truth for him."

Pip's eyes found Stanley Forbes in the third row, scribbling away in an open notebook. She still wondered about him, him and the other names on her persons of interest list, the other lives and secrets that had crisscrossed this case. Fairview still had its mysteries, unturned stones, and unanswered questions. This town had too many dark corners; Pip had learned to accept she couldn't shine a light into each and every one.

Stanley was sitting just behind her friends, Cara's face absent among them. As brave as she had been through everything, she'd decided today would have been too hard for her.

"I couldn't have fathomed," Pip continued, "that when this project was over, it would end with four people in handcuffs and one being set free after five years in a makeshift prison cell. Elliot Ward has pleaded guilty to the first-degree murder of Sal Singh and to kidnapping in the first degree of Isla Jordan. His sentencing hearing is next week. Becca Bell will face trial later this year for the charge of criminally negligent homicide, illegal disposal of a dead body, and tampering with evidence. Max Hastings has been charged with four counts of sexual assault and two counts of rape, and will also be tried later this year. And Howard Bowers has pleaded guilty to the charge of possession with intent to sell."

She shuffled her notes and cleared her throat.

"So, why did the events of Friday, April 18, 2014, happen? The way I see it, there are a handful of people who carry the blame for what happened that night and the days following, morally if not all criminally. These are: Elliot Ward, Howard Bowers, Max Hastings, Becca Bell, Jason Bell, and do not forget, Andie herself. You have cast her as your beautiful victim and willfully overlook the other layers of her character, because they don't comfortably fit your narrative. But this is the truth: Andie Bell was a bully who used emotional blackmail to get what she wanted. She sold drugs without care or regard for how they might be used. We will never know if she knew she was facilitating drug-assisted sexual assault, but when confronted with this truth by her own sister, she could not find it in herself to show compassion.

"And yet, when we look closer, behind this true Andie, we find a girl who was vulnerable and self-conscious. Andie grew up being taught by her father that the only value she had was in the way she looked and how strongly she was desired. Home for her was a place where she was criticized and belittled. Andie never got the chance to become the young woman she might have been away from that house, to decide for herself what made her valuable and what future she wanted.

"And though this story does have its monsters, I've found that it is not one that can be so easily divided into the good and the bad. In the end this was a story about people and their different shades of desperation, crashing up against each other. But there was one person who was good until the very end. And his name was Sal Singh."

Pip looked up then, her eyes going straight to Ravi, sitting between his parents.

"The thing is," she said, "I didn't do this project alone, as the guidelines require. I couldn't have done it on my own. So I guess you're going to have to disqualify me."

A few people gasped in the audience, Mrs. Morgan loudly among them. A few titters of laughter.

"I couldn't have solved this case without Ravi Singh. In fact, I wouldn't have survived it. So if anyone should speak about how kind Sal Singh was now that you're all finally listening, it's his brother."

Ravi stared at her from his seat, his eyes wide in that telling-off way that she loved. But she knew he needed this. And he knew it too.

She beckoned with a tilt of her head, and Ravi got to his feet. Her dad stood up too, whistling with his fingers again and smacking his big hands loudly together. Some of the students in the audience joined in, clapping as Ravi jogged up the steps to the stage and walked over to the lectern.

Pip moved back from the microphone as Ravi joined her. He winked at her, and Pip felt a flash of pride as she watched him step up to the lectern, scratching the back of his head. He'd told her just yesterday that he was going to retake his school exams so he could go on to study law.

"Um . . . hi," Ravi said, and the microphone screeched for him too. "I wasn't expecting this, but it's not every day a girl throws away a guaranteed A for you." There was a quiet ripple of laughter. "But I guess I don't need preparation to talk about Sal. I've been preparing for that nearly six years now. My brother wasn't just a good person. He was one of the best. He was kind, exceptionally kind, always helping people, and nothing was ever too much trouble. He was selfless. I remember this one time when we were kids, I spilled chocolate milk all over the carpet, and Sal took the fall for me so I wouldn't get in trouble. Sorry, Mom, guess you had to find out sometime."

More chuckles from the audience.

"Sal was cheeky. And he had the most ridiculous laugh; you couldn't help but join in. And, oh yeah, he used to spend hours drawing these comics for me to read in bed because I wasn't a great sleeper. I still have them all. And damn was Sal clever. I know he would have done incredible things with his life, if it hadn't been taken away from him. The world will never be as bright without him in it." Ravi's voice cracked. "And I wish I'd been able to tell him all this when he was alive. Tell him he was the best big brother anyone could ever wish for. But at least I can say it now on this stage and know that this time everyone will believe me."

He looked back at Pip, his eyes shining, reaching out to her. She drew forward to stand with him, leaning into the microphone to say her final lines.

"But there was one final player in this story, Fairview, and it's us. Collectively, we turned a beautiful life into the myth of a monster.

We turned a family home into a ghost house. And from now on we must do better."

Pip reached down behind the lectern for Ravi's hand, sliding her fingers between his. Their entwined hands became a new living thing, her fingertips perfect against the dips in his knuckles, like they'd grown just that way to fit together.

"Any questions?"

Acknowledgments

This book would have remained an abandoned Word document or an unexplored idea in my head if it weren't for a whole list of amazing humans. Firstly, to my super-agent, Sam Copeland, it is incredibly annoying that you're always right. Thank you for being so cool and calm. You're the best person anyone could have on their team, and I will be forever grateful that you took a chance on me.

To the editorial team at Egmont UK—Ali Dougal, Soraya Bouazzaoui, Sarah Levison, and especially Lindsey Heaven—thank you for seeing the heart of this story and for helping me to find it. And to Tracy Phillips and the rights team for their incredible job bringing this book to other parts of the world.

To everyone at Delacorte Press and Random House Children's Books, thank you so much for all your hard work on this book. The biggest thanks must, of course, go to my incredible editor Audrey Ingerson. Thank you so much for believing in me and this book; it means the world and sometimes I still can't believe it. Thank you for being brave enough to take on a super-British book and somehow help me turn it into something that feels like it truly belongs over there. I'm so grateful for your tireless enthusiasm; you've been the best guide I could ever ask for. And enormous thanks to Beverly Horowitz for the amazing opportunity. To Casey Moses, Christine Blackburne, and Alison Impey, thank you so much for the beautiful cover design; I couldn't have dreamed up one more perfect and I'm so happy that your incredible work is the very first thing people will see of the book. Thank you to Trish Parcell, Heather Kelly, and Stephanie Moss for the genius interior designs (Pip's homework has never looked so good). Thank you to Tamar Schwartz and Tracy Heydweiller for all of your amazing hard work, and to Colleen Fellingham and Alison Kolani for your incredible attention to detail. And a massive thank-you to Marketing and Publicity stars Janine Perez, Elizabeth Ward, and Emma Benshoff.

To my debut group for all their support, with special mentions to Savannah, Yasmin, Katya, Lucy, Sarah, Joseph, and Aisha. This whole publishing thing is far less scary when you go through it with friends.

To my Flower Huns (what a useless WhatsApp group name, and now it's in a published book, so we can't ever get rid of it), thank you for being my friends for more than a decade and for understanding when I disappear into my writer's hole. Thanks to Elspeth, Lucy, and Alice for being early readers.

To Peter and Gaye, thank you for your unwavering support, for reading the earliest version of this book and for letting me live somewhere so nice while I write the next one. And to Katie for championing this book from the start and for giving me the first spark of Pip.

To my big sister, Amy, thanks for letting me sneak into your room to watch *Lost* when I was too young—my love of mysteries has grown from there. To my little sister, Olivia, thank you for reading every single thing I've ever written, from that red notebook of scribbled stories to Elizabeth Crowe. You were my very first reader, and I'm so grateful. To Danielle and George—oh, hey, look, you've made it into the acknowledgments just for being cute. You better not read this book until you are an appropriate age.

To Mum and Dad, thank you for giving me a childhood filled with stories, for raising me alongside books and films and games. I wouldn't be here without all those years of *Tomb Raider* and *Harry Potter*. But thank you mostly for always saying I could when others said I couldn't. We did it.

And to Ben. You are my constant through every tear, tantrum, failure, worry, and victory. Without you, I couldn't have done it at all.

Finally, thank *you* for picking up this book and reading to the end. You'll never know how much it means to me.

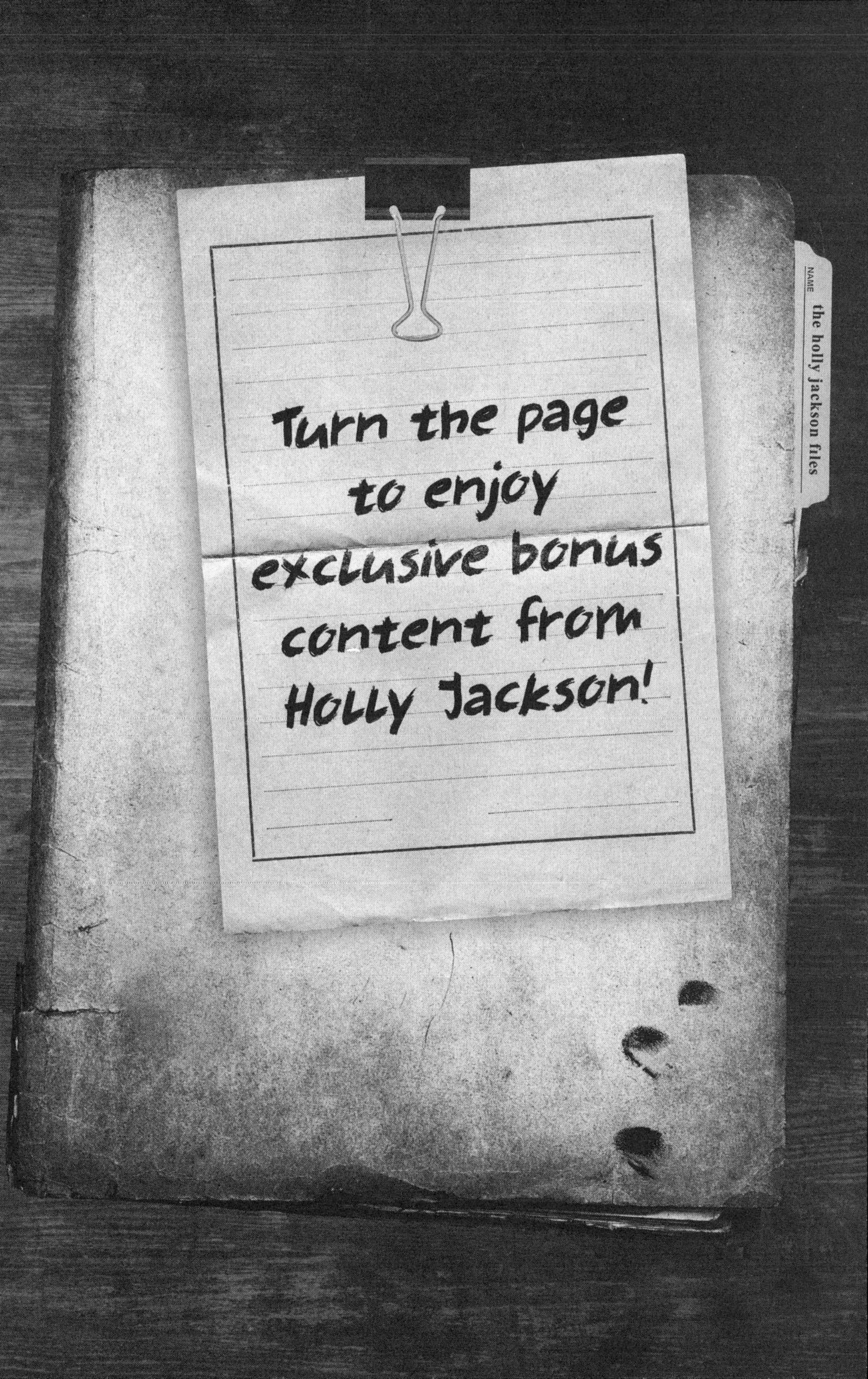
Turn the page to enjoy exclusive bonus content from Holly Jackson!
NAME
the holly jackson files

This is a photo of me from
September 10, 2016,
the day I came up with
the majority of the plot of
A Good Girl's Guide
to Murder whilst on
a long, rainy walk on
vacation in Croatia.

Finding the right title for a book is hard work. Every entry in this list was once a working title or a suggested title for the book, before I came up with the perfect fit:

~~Missender~~

~~Twofold Town~~

~~That Night~~

~~After Kill~~

~~He Said, She Dead~~

~~End Project~~

~~A Study in Killing~~

~~To Catch a Killer~~

~~Little Kill Town~~

~~Read Between the Lies~~

~~Project Murder and Me~~

~~How to Solve a Small Town Murder~~

A Good Girl's Guide to Murder

Published by Delacorte Press, an imprint of Random House Children's Books,
a division of Penguin Random House LLC, New York.

AFTER AND BEFORE

You think you'd know what a killer sounds like.

That their lies would have a different texture, some barely perceptible shift. A voice that thickens, grows sharp and uneven as the truth slips beneath the jagged edges. You'd think that, wouldn't you? Everyone thinks they'd know, if it came down to it. But Pip hadn't.

"It's such a tragedy what happened in the end."

Sitting across from him, looking into his kind, crinkled eyes, her phone between them recording every sound and sniff and throat-clearing huff. She'd believed it all, every word.

Pip traced her fingers across the trackpad, skipping the audio file back again.

"It's such a tragedy what happened in the end."

Elliot Ward's voice rang out from the speakers once more, filling her darkened bedroom. Filling her head.

Stop. Click. Repeat.

"It's such a tragedy what happened in the end."

She'd listened to it maybe a hundred times. Maybe even a thousand. And there was nothing, no giveaway, no change as he slipped between lies and half-truths. The man she'd once looked to as an almost father. But then, Pip had lied too, hadn't she? And she could tell herself she'd done it to protect the people she loved, but wasn't that the exact same reason Elliot gave? Pip ignored that voice in her head; the truth was out, most of it, and that's the thing she clung to.

She kept going, on to the other part that made her hairs stand on end.

"And do you think Sal killed Andie?" asked Pip's voice from the past.

". . . he was such a lovely kid. But, considering the evidence, I don't see how he couldn't have done it. As wrong as it feels, I guess I think he must have. There's no other explanation—"

Pip's door pushed inward with a smack.

"What are you doing?" interrupted a voice from right now, one that lifted with a smirk because he knew damn well what she was doing.

"You scared me, Ravi," she said, annoyed, darting forward to pause the audio. Ravi didn't need to hear Elliot Ward's voice, not ever again.

"You're sitting here in the dark listening to that, but *I'm* the scary one?" Ravi said, flicking on the light, the yellow glow reflecting off the dark hair swept across his forehead. He pulled that face, the one that always got her, and Pip smiled because it was impossible not to.

She wheeled back from her desk. "How did you get in, anyway?"

"Your parents and Josh were on their way out, with a giant Tupperware full of fresh-baked cookies."

"Oh yes," she said. "They're from Costco, don't let my dad fool you. They're on neighborly welcome duties. A young couple just moved into the Chens' house down the street. Mom did the deal. The Greens . . . or maybe the Browns, can't remember."

It was strange, thinking of another family living in that house, new lives reshaping to fill its old spaces. Pip's friend Zach Chen had always lived there, four doors down, ever since Pip had moved here at age five. It wasn't a real goodbye; she still saw Zach at school every day, but his parents had decided they could no longer live in this town, not after *all that trouble.* Pip was certain they considered her a large part of *all that trouble.*

"Dinner's seven-thirty, by the way," Ravi said, his voice suddenly skipping clumsily over the words. Pip looked at him; he was wearing his nicest shirt, and . . . were those new shoes? She could smell after-shave too, as he stepped toward her, but he stopped short, didn't kiss her on the forehead nor run a hand through her hair. Instead he sat on her bed, fiddling with his hands.

"Meaning you're almost two hours early." Pip smiled.

"Y-yeah." He coughed.

Why was he being awkward? It was their first Valentine's Day, and Ravi had booked them a table at The Siren, out of town. Pip's best friend, Cara, was convinced Ravi was going to ask Pip to be his girlfriend tonight. She said she'd put money on it. The thought made something in Pip's stomach swell, spilling its heat up into her chest. But it might not be that: Valentine's Day was also Sal's birthday. Ravi's older brother would have turned twenty-four today, if he'd made it past eighteen.

"How far have you got?" Ravi asked, nodding at Pip's laptop, the audio-editing software Audacity filling the screen with spiky blue lines. The whole story was there, contained within those blue lines. From the start of Pip's project to the very end: every lie, every secret. Even some of her own.

"It's done," Pip said, dropping her eyes to the new USB microphone plugged into her computer. "I've finished. Six episodes. I had to use a noise-reduction effect on some of the phone interviews for quality, but it's done."

And in a green plastic file, beside the microphone, were the release forms she'd sent to everyone. Signed and returned, granting her permission to publish their interviews in a podcast. Even Elliot Ward had signed one from his prison cell. Two people had refused: Stanley Forbes from the town newspaper and, of course, Max Hastings. But Pip didn't need their voices to tell the story; she'd filled in the gaps with her production log entries, now recorded as monologues.

"You're finished already?" Ravi said, though he couldn't really be surprised. He knew her, maybe better than anyone else did.

It had been six weeks since Pip had stood at the front of the school assembly hall and told everyone what really happened. But the media still weren't telling the story right; even now they clung to their own angles because those were cleaner, neater. Yet the Andie Bell case had been anything but neat.

"If you want something done right, you have to do it yourself," Pip said, her gaze climbing the spiking audio clips. Right then, she couldn't decide whether this felt like something beginning or something ending. But she knew which she wanted it to be.

"So what's next?" asked Ravi.

"I export the episode files, upload them to SoundCloud on schedule, once a week, and then copy the RSS feed to podcast directories like iTunes and Stitcher. But I'm not quite finished," she said. "I need to record the intro over this theme song I found on AudioJungle. But to record an intro, you need a title."

"Ah," Ravi said, stretching out his back, "we're still titleless, are we, Lady Fitz-Amobi?"

"We are," she said. "I've narrowed it down to three options."

"Hit me," he said.

"No, you'll be mean about them."

"No, I won't," he said earnestly, with the smallest of smiles.

"OK." She looked down at her notes. "Option A is *An Examination into a Miscarriage of Justice.* Wha— Ravi, I can see you laughing."

"That was a yawn, I swear."

"Well, you won't like option B either, because that's *A Study of a Closed Case: The Andie Bell*— Ravi, stop!"

"Wha— I'm sorry, I can't help it," he said, laughing until his eyes were lined with tears. "It's just . . . of all your many qualities, Pip, there's one thing you lack—"

"Lack?" She spun her chair to face him. "I *lack* something?"

"Yes," he said, meeting her stony eyes. "Pizzazz. You are almost entirely pizzazz-less, Pip."

"I am not pizzazz-less."

"You need to draw people in, intrigue them. Have a word like 'kill' or 'dead' in there."

"But that's sensationalism."

"And that's exactly what you want, for people to actually listen," Ravi said.

"But all of my options are accurate and—"

"Boring?"

Pip threw a yellow highlighter at him.

"You need something that rhymes, or alliteration. Something with—"

"Pizzazz?" she said in her Ravi voice. "You think of one, then."

"Crime Time," he said. "No, oh, Fairview . . . maybe *Un-Fairview.*"

"Ew, no," said Pip.

"You're right." Ravi got up and started to pace. "Your unique selling point is, really, you. A seventeen-year-old who solved a case the police had long considered closed. And what are you?" he looked at her, squinting.

"Lacking, clearly," she said with mock irritation.

"A student," Ravi thought aloud. "A girl. Project. Oh, how about *Project Murder and Me*?"

"Nah."

"OK . . ." He chewed his lip and it made Pip's stomach tighten. "So something murder, or kill, or dead. And you are Pip, who's a student and a girl who's good at . . . Oh shit," he said suddenly, eyes widening. "I've got it!"

"What?" she said.

"I've literally got it," he said, far too pleased with himself.

"What is it?"

"A Good Girl's Guide to Murder."

"Noooo." Pip shook her head. "That's bad, way too try-hard."

"What are you talking about? It's perfect."

"Good girl?" she said dubiously. "I turn eighteen in two weeks; I won't contribute to my own infantilization."

"A Good Girl's Guide to Murder," Ravi said in his deep, movie-trailer voice, pulling Pip up from her chair and spinning her toward him.

"No," she said.

"Yes," he retorted, placing one hand on her waist, his warm fingers dancing up her ribs, making her glow.

"Absolutely not."

NEWSDAY

US > Culture > TV & Radio > Reviews

A Good Girl's Guide to Murder Review: The latest true-crime podcast obsession ends with a chilling finale

BENJAMIN COLLIS | MARCH 27

If you haven't yet listened to episode 6 of *A Good Girl's Guide to Murder,* look away now. Serious **spoilers** below.

Of course, many of us know how this mystery ended from when it exploded on the news last November, but the whodunit isn't the whole story here. The real story of *A Good Girl's Guide to Murder* has been the journey, from a seventeen-year-old sleuth's hunch about a closed case—the murder of teenager Andie Bell, allegedly by her boyfriend, Sal Singh—to the spiraling web of dark secrets she uncovers in her small town. The ever-shifting suspects, the lies, and the twists.

The final episode certainly isn't lacking in twists as it brings us the truth, starting with Pip's shocking revelation that Elliot Ward, her best friend's father, wrote the threatening notes Pip received during her investigation. Irrefutable proof of his involvement and truly a loss-of-innocence moment for Pip. She and Ravi Singh—Sal's younger brother and co-detective on this case—believed that Andie Bell might still be alive and Elliot had been keeping her the whole time. Pip confronted Elliot Ward alone and, in Ward's own words, the whole story unravels. An illicit relationship between student and teacher, allegedly initiated by Andie. "If true," Pip theorizes, "I think Andie wanted an escape from Fairview, particularly from her father, who allegedly, according to a source, was controlling and emotionally abusive. Perhaps Andie believed Mr. Ward could get her into Yale, like Sal, so she could get far away from home."

The night of her disappearance, Andie went to Elliot Ward's house. An argument ensued. Andie tripped, hitting her head against Ward's desk. But as Ward rushed to get a first-aid kit, Andie disappeared into the night. In the following days, as Andie was officially declared missing, Ward panicked, believing Andie must have died from her head injury and when police eventually found her body, there might be evidence that would lead to him. His only chance was to give the police a more convincing suspect. "He cried as he told me," Pip says, "how he killed Sal Singh." Ward made it look like suicide and planted evidence so that police would think Sal had killed his girlfriend and then himself.

But, months later, Ward was shocked to see Andie walking on the side of the road, thin and disheveled. She hadn't died after all. Ward couldn't allow her to return to Fairview, and that's how she ended up his prisoner for five years. However, in a twist truly stranger than fiction: the person in Ward's loft wasn't Andie Bell. "She looked so much like her," Pip claims, "she even told me she *was* Andie." She was actually Isla Jordan, a vulnerable young woman with an intellectual disability. All this time, Elliot had convinced himself—and Isla—that she *was* Andie Bell.

This left the final question of what had happened to the *real* Andie Bell. Our young detective beat the police to that too. "It was Becca Bell, Andie's little sister." Pip figured out that Becca had been sexually assaulted at a local house party (nicknamed calamity parties by attendees), and that Andie had sold drugs at these parties, including Rohypnol, which Becca suspected had played a part in her assault. When Andie was out *that night* with Ward, Becca allegedly found proof in her sister's room that Max Hastings had bought Rohypnol from Andie and was likely Becca's attacker (Hastings will soon face trial for several rape and sexual assault charges). But when Andie returned home, she didn't react the way that Becca had hoped; Andie forbade her sister from going to the police because it would get Andie in trouble. They started arguing and pushing each other, until Andie ended up on the floor, unconscious and vomiting. Andie's postmortem—performed last November when her body was finally recovered—showed that "the brain swelling from a head trauma was not fatal. Though it no doubt caused loss of consciousness and vomiting, Andie Bell died from asphyxiation, choking on her own vomit." Becca froze, allegedly watching Andie die, too shocked and too angry to save her sister's life. She hid Andie's body because she was scared no one would believe that her death had been an accident.

And there it is, our ending. "No angles or filters, just the sad truth of how Andie Bell died, how Sal was murdered and framed as her killer and everyone believed it." In Pip's scathing conclusion, she picks out everyone she finds at fault for the deaths of these two teenagers, naming and blaming: Elliot Ward, Max Hastings, Jason Bell (Andie's father), Becca Bell, Howard Bowers (Andie's drug dealer), and Andie Bell herself.

A Good Girl's Guide to Murder stormed to the top of the iTunes chart with its first episode six weeks ago, and it looks set to stay there for some time. With the final episode released last night, listeners are already clamoring for a season 2 of the hit podcast. But in a statement posted to her website, Pip said: "I'm afraid my detective days are over and there will *not* be a second season of *AGGGTM*. This case almost consumed me; I could only see that once I was out the other side. It became an unhealthy obsession, putting me and those around me in considerable danger. But I will finish *this* story, recording updates on the trials and verdicts of all those involved. I promise I will be here until the very last word."

From the #1 New York Times bestselling author of
a good girl's guide to murder
The Reappearance of Rachel Price
HOLLY JACKSON